WAR OF THE GENERATIONS

I turn for the door and in that instant sense I may have made a fatal mistake.

From under the pillow I catch in my peripheral vision the glint of a submachine gun being whipped out of concealment. I whirl to fire, but discover that Thuc is not holding the weapon.

Hai, my nine-year-old son, is.

He holds it as though he has been taught how to use it.

He holds it on me...

Also by Stirling Silliphant
Published by Ballantine Books:

BRONZE BELL

MARACAIBO

STEEL TIGER

SILVER STAR

Stirling Silliphant

BALLANTINE BOOKS • NEW YORK

Library of Congress Catalog Card Number: 86-90941

ISBN 0-345-32619-9

Manufactured in the United States of America

First Edition: November 1986

For Stir—a star-child . . .
And for Tiana—his mother

═CHAPTER═

1

WHISH!

Artillery?

From where?

By courtesy of whom?

No logic to incoming arty out here fifty miles from the mainland between latitudes two and four in the South China Sea.

Yet what is undeniably a shell crackles like cellophane past *Steel Tiger*'s mizzenmast and dredges up a waterspout two hundred meters off my port quarter.

In these waters, should you foolishly elect as I have to sail a private yacht solo up the east coast of the Malay Peninsula on a northerly slant toward the Gulf of Thailand, you'd better remain supple at all times, keeping a constant watch and a well-lubed weapon handy, for piracy in the China Lake is an historical fact of life. Over the last decade, tens of thousands of Indochinese boat people fled to this very shoreline. During the exodus, pirates battened remorselessly on the refugees. But the heaviest stuff those defenseless victims had to face was .50-caliber machine-gun fire or an occasional rocket assault.

A true devotee of risk, I carry no ordnance aboard *Steel Tiger* beefy enough to fend off seaborne artillery. And who anticipates an attack this far south in Malaysian national waters?

The imminent sunset blurs the sea with strokes of burnt tangerine. For a disconnected moment, I watch the play of colors as the exploding fountain cascades back to the

1

saffron surface. But self-preservation preempts aesthetics and I pull my binos from their molded PVC holder mounted inboard the companionway.

To port and well astern, I identify the silhouette of the Malaysian island Tioman.

To starboard, across an expanding track of darkening sea, I isolate the dreary hump of Jemaja, one of the clustered islands of the Anambas group.

As I'm combing this eastern sector, I observe an occluding pinpoint of light against the black spine of Jemaja.

Muzzle flash of a deck cannon?

I time the round on my stopwatch, using what in Vietnam we called the flash-bang method of range determination.

This second shell prowls forward of my main, but this time to starboard. Again, two hundred meters off.

Bracketing me, are they?

I wait for the dry, sterile clap of the shot to arrive. When it comes, I clock it—twenty-one seconds between flash and bang. Sound travels at three hundred and fifty meters a second in this moist air at this temperature. This puts the unknown hostile a shade over four nautical miles off.

I start the engine, swinging my stern to the distant blot to deny them a broadsided target. At the same time I hold my transom directly into the wind, mild enough at the moment for easy sail-handling.

In a matter of seconds, I drop main and jib to deprive my enemy of the luxury of sighting on my canvas. I jiffy-tie both sails, trot back to the wheel, advance the throttle until I'm off and running.

Already the sun has notched into the Malaysian coastline fifty miles westward, but now in late August, given my present latitude and longitude, I'm confronted by at least another hour of light before I can hope to blend with the darkening sea.

I run my options.

The island of Tioman bears eight miles southwest—an hour's reach at *Steel Tiger*'s top engine speed.

If I can avoid being touched off during the daylight still remaining, I might be able to work my way past the shoals of Tioman and get ashore with the new Israeli M26 Circis sniper rifle I picked up in Singapore from men who understand the need of other men for certain exotic tools. In the hands of the right marksman, the M26 can tag a target out to one thousand meters. From a steady firing platform ashore and with my night scope, I could police up the deck and wheelhouse of whatever it is out there that seems to bear me such singular ill will.

I lack other options.

So be it.

I steer directly toward Tioman.

Through the binos I finally succeed in making out what appears to be a fishing trawler plowing toward me. The wankers aboard her are certainly not your light-beer types. Even at this distance off I can feel their hard-wired decision to terminate me without so much as a word of explanation or apology.

I focus in on them. Could that be a Type 52 recoilless rifle mounted on their foredeck? Type 52 is a Chinese ripoff of the obsolete U.S. M20. I haven't seen one for almost fifteen years, not since my Mamba team took a 52 away from a begrudging gaggle of NVA in Mu Guia Pass near Na Phao in Laos. Lightweight, easily portable, with a range of almost seven thousand meters when firing HE, the 52s were popular set pieces with both the VC and the NVA.

I wild-guess that the trawler is capable of ten knots. My max with *Steel Tiger* is just under eight. This translates out—without benefit of a slide rule—to its closing the gap between us by half a mile every fifteen minutes. But it also puts me inside the reefs of Tioman with enough lead time to set up on the beach and snipe them when they come within range.

Meanwhile, the trawler's got a killing jab of almost four miles to my less-than-a-mile with the M26.

How to rearrange *that* chessboard!

What the hell *is* today?

Twenty-sixth of August?

Definitely not one of my better days.

I dial *Steel Tiger* onto autopilot, go below to unlimber the M26 and the Olympic-grade ammo I'd acquired to round out the ensemble.

I check the seating of the ART scope and advance it to 18X power. With this magnification the human head at half a kilometer will image out in the cross lines plump as a honeydew.

I attach the suppresser to reduce recoil and to eliminate muzzle flash.

I return topside.

A third shell whistles by, again to starboard, but closer now—close enough to shimmer the surface around me like a violated spiderweb.

I listen to the poppling of the displaced water tumbling down, even feel some of the windborne sea spray warm against my cheek.

Through the night scope I manage to isolate the gun crew. Three of them. Strange, I don't read them as pirates. Their movements appear too disciplined. These three are a team, a military team.

Yet I can find no flag streaming from their staff, no identifying marks or numbers on their hull. Whatever numbers might have been there have been painted out. Clearly their intent is anonymity.

They stonk their fourth round directly into my wake.

Fortunately some meters astern.

I release the autopilot and take the helm.

I alter course, instituting an approach to Tioman more zigzag than I wish, yet essential if I'm to frustrate their targeting.

Let the contentious bastards work for their money.

Who knows? Maybe they'll run out of ammo before I run out of luck.

It is precisely as I'm trying to calculate how many shells a trawler of this displacement might reasonably be capable of carrying when something happens that has not happened in all the two years I've cruised *Steel Tiger* in the South Pacific.

A sickening sound zaps me from the engine room, the kind of sound that shoots straight to the scrotum.

Without checking cockpit gauges, I know what's happened.

The geared belt-drive has broken without so much as a warning flutter. One second operative, the next in tatters.

No choice.

I shut down the engine.

Steel Tiger heaves forward gamely with the momentum

of her weight, a few more precious meters, then she breasts down into the soft embrace of the South China Sea and stands dead in the water, a monument to all the world's failed technology.

═══CHAPTER═══

2

Only ten days ago I watched Bali soften behind me as a brisk soldier's wind drove *Steel Tiger* around the skaw of Nusa Dua and westerly toward Bali Strait.

The best course to Singapore, although the longest, would have been to continue west below Java to the Sunda Strait, then to work my way up into the western sector of the Java Sea. This track offers the least exposure to adverse currents and the greatest hope for fair winds.

But full of divine certainty and sensing that the gods of Besakih were still with me for a few more hours, I'd chosen the most direct course, one seldom taken by lone sailors, since along this way the winds play notoriously light and fluky.

I'd reached wide-eyed through Bali Strait, which cleaves Bali from Java, and popped out directly into the inhospitable eastern salient of the Java Sea, an unforgiving mass of water at the best of times.

Yet by nightfall towering Mount Agung on Bali melted off my starboard stern, and by dawn of the next day I'd lost sight of the storied volcano within a belligerent stew of weather churning up to the southeast.

All the while I kept staring back at Bali and blowing mental bubbles of what might have been, fantasies that sank deeper below the horizon with every nautical mile as *Steel Tiger* bore me dutifully toward the destiny I always knew waited for me north of the seventeenth parallel.

Vietnam had never let me go.

I'd zigged and I'd zagged ever since I bugged out of

Saigon in '75, one of the last of the losers. But all of it has only been hemstitching. I always knew that as the logical consequence to my actions in-country, I would have to go back, either to reclaim myself and be done with it for once and all, or go back and die where I should have died. Too many friends and too many enemies, equal conspirators of my past, were eaten by worms in the tortured Indochinese earth, too many to be abandoned without some ultimate rite, God knows which, by those of us who survived.

So now I was going back.

No longer to absolve myself. For that I'm grateful. It's foolish to have to die simply to be able to sleep through the night.

Now at least I had an acceptable excuse.

I was going back to search for the son Doan Thi had borne us after I left. The true phoenix. Out of the ashes of all those yesterdays.

And I was by God going to bring him out!

Clearly, since the intervening ten years hadn't purged me, he was my only hope, my only future, possibly the resolution to what more and more I was perceiving as an ascendant, insistent deathwish.

And if after finding him I were to decide to return to Bali, as I'd promised both Guntur and Dasima, and spend our years with Dasima, letting her teach the boy the grace and gentility of Balinese ways, letting her teach *me* at the same time,—then might I finally put away all my weapons and my need to keep sweeping myself under the horizons across the China Sea?

Hour following hour I thought no thoughts but these— the child, Dasima, and I, together in Bali,—until three days into the Java Sea I let reality steal back in. I started then to lay down the hard foundations for the strategy that might let me infiltrate into Vietnam and get out again with the child.

Alive.

I'd set a course northwest, keeping Madura Island to port and the Kangean group to starboard until I worked my way toward Karimata Strait, Sumatra to one side now, Borneo to the other,—and I managed to lay this course until *Steel Tiger* crossed the equator east of Lingga Archipelago.

Not long after, as night set, the blaze of the Singapore downtown grid fanned up off my bow, brighter than Kipling's dawn-like-thunder.

I stayed in Singapore only long enough to transfer funds from my account at the Oversea-Chinese Banking Corporation into their branch in Bangkok's Chinatown.

And to make the deal for the sniper rifle.

Now, two sunsets north of Singapore, my mind preoccupied with Vietnam, *Steel Tiger* stands dead in the water off Malaysia while an unidentified trawler for reasons beyond my knowing steams toward me with blazing deck cannon.

Ordinarily, I become machinelike under attack.

This time I am personally offended.

How dare these bastards come out of nowhere and try to deny me the right to get to my son? Clearly they have no respect for priorities. Being jobbed in Vietnam in the effort is acceptable. Those are the odds. But being wasted off the Malaysian coast by seaman I might ordinarily drink with in a waterfront bar is not.

I get so worked up about the rank injustice of it all that I remind myself of Danny Thompson, buddy of mine who used to own a liquor store on South Market Street in San Francisco. Danny's store had been knocked over more times than a Wells-Fargo payroll stagecoach. We staked men out for a year and never got lucky. The bad guys just kept falling through the cracks and emptying poor Danny's cash register. One night Danny closed up early and went home to get gooned. He discovered he was out of vodka, so he went back to the store and picked up a quart of Finlandia. When he was locking up again, two dudes fronted him and told him he'd better walk them back into the shop or they'd spread his ass like peanut butter all over the sidewalk. Danny told me later that something inside his skull went white. He described it as a thermonuclear flash. He saw the mushroom, Danny did. He became ten thousand feet tall, invulnerable to such waspish little nothings as. 44 Mags. He swung the quart of vodka from the sidewalk up to the jaw of the nearest dude at the speed of light. The snap, crackle, and pop of the fracturing jaw must have been so horrible that the second dude split without looking back or even wasting a second to blow Danny away.

Let's hear it for Danny!

Can I do less?

I run forward and hoist the main.

Seconds later I have the jib working.

Steel Tiger begins to claw forward, slowly at first, then with gaining momentum, but the wind has shifted and is turning kinkier by the moment. In order to mark even five knots I have to bear off fourteen degrees north of my intended landfall.

Morosely, I contemplate the vast yardage of white bellied above me, a luminous beacon across the oncoming night.

I turn the binos back to the onrushing trawler, everything about the boat and the dauntless life forms aboard her alien yet familiar. It comes to me that they are merely phantoms of myself, fellow celebrants of the mystery, bearing me now toward the pinnacle of aliveness by bearing me the death I have miraculously avoided until this twenty-sixth evening of August.

No longer do I belong to myself or to my dreams of finding a son in Vietnam.

Now I belong only to them—and they to me.

I go below to the nav station, prepare to transmit on Continuous Distress Frequency. Not that I expect anybody out there to be able to do much about my kind of distress.

In all of Malaysia, the nearest navy base is at Johore Strait, hours to the south, with another base at Labuan, six hundred miles east in distant Sabah.

"This is *Steel Tiger*, Bravo, Victor six three zero six . . ."

The first Mayday I've ever sent, come to think about it.

It occurs to me I'm suffering from bunker mentality, getting whipped around and not striking back.

If I'm to emulate Danny, what's needed at this point is an act of mythic heroism.

How do I take the fight to them?

Deep-attack guerrilla methods call for no firm battle lines, but rather for a number of circular fights occurring throughout an extensive and unlimited battlefield.

I return topside.

The sea around me—extensive and unlimited.

Circular fights.... My eyes roam the deck, fix on my half-inflated Zodiac lashed beneath the main boom.

That's it!

The outer edge of the envelope!

If I can't outrun them aboard *Steel Tiger*, I can break free of *Steel Tiger* aboard the zippy little Zodiac and bring the fight to them!

It's so fucking insane, so wonderfully comic, that as I plug the bellows into the pontoon and start foot-pumping, I find I'm congratulating myself so loudly, I don't even hear the next shell exploding close enough to rattle *Steel Tiger* from keel to masthead.

And to drench me with a torrent of seawater.

═══CHAPTER═══

3

Now the Zodiac is plump as a partridge.

I use the main halyard to lower the dinghy over the side of *Steel Tiger*.

By bow and stern I secure her alongside so that she's skimming just above the catskin surface.

Into the Zodiac I lower those items which seem called for under the circumstances: my night binos ... first aid kit—Band Aids for cannon wounds! ... life jacket ... survival knife ... my Browning Hi-Power and four loaded clips simply because I feel culturally deprived without the Belgian steel below my left armpit ... the M26 Circis sniper rifle and its ammo, both nestled within a zippered, unsinkable oilskin ... flare pistol and a dozen flares ... extra fuel for the outboard motor ... flashlight and compass and a chart of the sea sector where these gunsey bastards have put me to all this trouble.

Again I use the halyard to lower most carefully and precisely the heavy Johnson 40-horse that will drive the Zodiac across water as flat as tonight's at a gut-shaking thirty knots. I lock and chain the engine into place on the sturdy teak backboard.

The Zodiac now ready for launch, I prepare myself.

I slip into nightstalkers, then cammy up face and hands, topping it all off with a black wool cap.

Now comes the most delicate work of all, setting *Steel Tiger* on a course that will keep her out of harm's way for the time I have to leave her untended at sea.

Our present slant will keep her well offshore of Malaysia and its westerly rounding coastline past the protruding point of Kuala Dungun, well to port. After that, seven hundred miles of open water lie ahead before she would beach herself at Rayong in southern Thailand. But soon enough, once I bring smoke in on these suckers, the probing shells will cease and desist, and *Steel Tiger* can sail blithely on until, hopefully, mission accomplished, I reboard her.

The key to all this optimism is the autopilot.

I set the heading sensor to allow for less deadband, since the sea condition looks to remain flat for at least another sixty minutes. I adjust the gain to correct the degrees the rudder will be turned for every degree of course error, then I adjust for trim to give the rudder bias to port and to counteract the slight weather helm *Steel Tiger* is showing on her present reach with her present sail trim.

Finally I hook the autopilot to the sat-nav, so that the system will compare *Steel Tiger*'s true position and destination with the course the autopilot is set to follow and will feed the pilot continually updated steering orders.

As I ease myself over the toe railing and into the dinghy, I ask myself, can this caper really fly?

Or am I being guilty, as I have been on occasions in the past, of existential machismo, the flip, who-gives-a-fuck, let's-go-for-it kind of maniacal audacity which inevitably brings hellfire and karma home to roost.

I jazz up the Johnson, cast off lines, and streak across the rustling sea, even as another shell drills overhead and splashes alongside *Steel Tiger*.

Good girl! She bobbles, but sails on.

With mosquito speed, I skim the surface, bisecting the angle between the trawler and *Steel Tiger* so that I'll come darting in on them from their dark side to the east.

I pin the time. I'll be within firing range six minutes from—mark it—NOW!

I begin to psych myself up for another twenty-goose-bump event.

I must be a trauma junkie, for I hear myself contentedly humming a song we used to hear in Vietnam during the late unpleasantness—"A Bridge Over Troubled Waters."

No question about it. The central question of our time is simply how high an adrenaline level you should permit yourself. Nothing else but this question needs to be resolved for a man to find his place in the world today. Fight or flight? Should you stand and hit back or should you run? The most difficult issue any human being —man, woman, or child,—faces in this twentieth century is to try to evolve some sort of workable personal guideline through the shitstorm of endemic violence and its unremitting clutch on the innocents of the world.

Most people recoil from this constant overhang of violence. Their solution is to withdraw or to surrender.

Others, like myself, have made the commitment to deal head on, without apology, with the horror that forever waits out there. This horror wears many masks—the city nightstalkers who smash lives in parking lots or steal through unlocked windows in quiet residential neighborhoods to kill and rape the helpless in their sleep; the more organized, less personal killers who wear uniforms and insignias and who come by land, sea, and air in the name of national interest; the terrorists who wear handmade suits and who sit in government offices and delineate what national interest should be imposed upon whom this month of the year for raison d'état.

An immediate advantage of the commitment to meet violence with superior violence is that you are never taken by surprise. Your reaction is preprogrammed, instantaneous, and inexorable, as befits the provocation. Since you've already acknowledged that to be human is to possess the potential either for good or for bad, you're never shocked by either manifestation. No time is wasted wringing your hands over the whys and wherefors. Your energies go into the punishing counterattack. It is an easy and comforting way to walk through the minefields.

While I'm running these thoughts, making sure I'll suffer no residual guilt for the killings I'm now intent upon performing, I've been carefully unwrapping the M26 as mechanically as a priest unwraps the devices of holy Sacrament. I slip my opening round into the chamber, a jacketed benediction.

Throttle easing, I glide in toward the trawler, flooding toward my enemy along with the lengthening shadows.

I slip forward along one of the Zodiac's pontoons and survey the trawler with my night glasses.

Forward I see three forms crouching in semidarkness and waiting to reload the gun. Definitely a Type 52.

Aft I spot two other silhouettes. They appear to be unpacking additional shells from stowage below and hurrying them forward to the gun crew.

Two other men can be seen inside the main cabin.

I focus on one of these, on the helmsman.

Vietnamese?

A swift re-scan of the others. All Vietnamese!

This far south?

All of them are so intent upon blowing *Steel Tiger* out of the water that none of them troubles to look back my way.

I cut the engine to a silent idle, take up the M26, and stretch out on the starboard pontoon. I bring the scope up to the broad cheekbone of the unsuspecting helmsman.

The pitching of the Zodiac in the sea, though slight, is enough to cause the scope to sweep up and down from the man's waist to the ceiling of the cabin, but midway on each swing his head appears for a split second within the cross-hairs.

Hardly benchrest shooting.

I time the first shot to catch him as I bob up.

When I bob back down, he is no longer standing behind the wheel, but I catch sight of a discoloration on the bulkhead next to which he'd been standing.

My second shot waxes the chief gunner. He makes a foolish turn to determine where the first gunshot has come from. The bullet takes him in the neck.

The five survivors demonstrate a remarkable cool under fire. They don't mill about like refugees from the human-potential movement in Berkeley, but instead drop to cover, depriving me of a third splash.

*Some*one over there is in firm command.

I can feel night scopes sweeping the sea around me. I can sense that I've been discovered. The cold focus of ten calculating eyes literally probes across the water and tattoos my skin.

I rev the engine, make a neat, twisty getaway.

Just in time.

A machine-gun I had failed to notice on the aft deck rips up the water where I'd been lurking. Even as I churn a sweeping wake around the trawler, I comb the aft deck with the glasses.

Ah, so there it is!

A 7.62 mike-mike RPD light machine-gun. One of the Degtyarev models with a one-hundred-round belt.

Can't afford to duel with a Degtyarev at this close range.

I speed east into the enveloping night and batten down to consider step two.

Steel Tiger, I see through the binos, is well away by now and on course, the trawler no longer concerned with her.

Only with me.

I watch my enemies through the glasses.

All five of them cling to cover. They've doused all lights aboard.

Darkly, the boat turns toward me.

Now some of the five aboard must be creeping along the deck, trying to drag the machine-gun onto the bow and intending to keep me under fire until the artillery can be brought into play again and blow me out of the sea.

I try for the thin-faced one snaking the machine-gun forward.

I miss, but the shock of the near hit anchors him in place.

Only yards away the sea lifts under me.

The Zodiac rocks crazily in the explosion.

Jesus, guys!

They're using a rocket launcher! What the hell *don't* they have aboard that bloody boat? Must be the newer version of the RPG-7—the Model 16—because I'm at least six hundred meters off and the Model 7 was never worth shit beyond five hundred meters.

I decide to put more distance between us. The calculations of range have now become critical. If that's a Model 16, it's effective out to eight hundred meters. But I'm still lethal at a thousand yards with the sniper rifle.

Let's fight it out at nine hundred!

In that instant of decision their second warhead sears the water around me with such a stream of explosive force that one of the Zodiac's two pontoons is ripped off and I'm heaved clear of the dinghy and dropped sprawling into the China Sea.

A searchlight blazes across the water, pinning me in its glare.

The Degtyarev opens up again as though someone is chattering at me in Russian.

An opening trench boils toward me across the water. I surface-dive.

Six feet under, hanging down there as long as I can, I experience an astonishingly clear recall of words I'd learned at college, something of Montaigne's: "If you know not how to die, never trouble yourself. Nature will in a moment fully and sufficiently instruct you. She will exactly do that business for you. Take you no care for it."

I thank Montaigne for making the passage brief, for I am out of air.

I slip back up to refill my lungs and I breathe in the hot metallic smell of the searching rounds of the 7.62.

It occurs to me I may have run out of affordable mistakes.

═══CHAPTER═══

4

I surface into the center of their searchlight. I become their performing seal.

The wind off Malaysia precedes them, washing over me with the stink of the trawler's diesel, with the smell of burned gunpowder and scorched iron from their stubborn machine-gun.

Here am I, born of methane and lightning, about to die, my personal ectosystem torn apart by fragments of steel, nickel, and carbon, and not one fucking thing to be done about it except to tread water, keep surface-diving, and wait until they've reached point-blank range.

An ironic coda, outclassed and shellacked by unknown goonies in the South China Sea.

How remarkable that this shutdown I've sought so diligently to postpone all these years turns out to be so trivial.

Yet I always knew that dying was hard only on the survivors. I pity Dasima, waiting in vain in Bali for my return. I pity my father in San Diego, my mother in Paris, who will wonder why I so thoughtlessly fail to communicate. I pity *Steel Tiger* when she beaches herself in the north and is picked to her strakes by fishermen.

Time has ceased now to exist.

Yet my perception of the split seconds remaining to me feels eternal. I measure everything now in nanoseconds as the whips of gunfire lash the sea around me. I search among ragged shadows of earlier times, through the museum of past images and memories. I find little self-pity, merely the regret that I shall never again run under the sun or drink the falling rain. Nor can I discover that splendid last-minute illumination, the bursting, all-revealing final answer. How would I do it again, given the chance? No answer, of course. Only one thought burns through—clear now and pure: How beautifully, how magnificently illogical life is and how much time I have wasted trying to make it logical.

Somehow through the blinding light from the trawler's bow I can see the stars above me.

Angering for death now, I reach out for them, standing high in the water, inviting the bullets.

Looking up only to other suns.

Ignoring the onrushing bow of my killers' boat.

A tunnel opens beside me in the sea and something as elemental as the stars I reach for rushes past me and strikes the trawler.

It heaves up in a flowering of wood and steel and flames and flesh, the heat of its parting seams and torn machinery fanning over me.

I am back into my body, back from the stars, and once more diving deep.

I hang under, claw even deeper, for the sea is boiling with debris. Dark shapes plummet past, sinking away from me.

Wracked for air, I kick back to the surface, gulp in the night.

The trawler is gone. Obscene remnants of it burn here and there for yards about me in a guttering blossom of fire and smoke.

I feel through the water the powerful throbbing of a mighty engine below the surface. I turn in time to see a wide mantle of breaking water curving off the rounded top of a submarine as her hull parts the sea. A trench of dark water opens to port and starboard of her bow, then churns white aft of the con.

She comes to a stop not more than a hundred meters off. In the scattered darkness of early night I tread water and watch her forward deck hatch open and figures materialize.

A voice I recognize instantly cuts across the water.

"John, are you able to swim to us or shall we send a boat?"

Guntur! Colonel Guntur Katrini, commander of Counter Insurgency Operations for the Indonesian security forces.

Less than ten days ago I'd left him with Dasima on the wharf at Benoa in Bali. Now look at him! Reappearing north of the equator aboard an ex-Soviet W-class submarine, one of four submersibles in the Indonesian Navy.

Talk about turnarounds. Not too distantly in the past, I'd fished him out of the Halmahera Sea. My turn now.

I swim toward him, stopping en route to grab hold of the painter on the single Zodiac pontoon still afloat with the portside half of the floorboards and such of my combat inventory that has not yet drifted to the bottom. Miraculously, I find the Circis sniper rifle nestled inboard next to the surviving rubber pontoon.

August 26th is rapidly improving.

The life jacket I brought from *Steel Tiger* floats near the wreckage of the Zodiac. I slip into it, roll onto my back, and kick off toward the sub, towing the pontoon and floorboard behind me.

Something in the water bumps into me.

I flip over. The thin-faced gunner from the trawler lurches out of the sea, arms clawing at me, his mouth round as a cipher. The grab, I sense, is out of desperation, not out of malice. I twist away from his frantic thrashing and drive an elbow into his jawline. He starts to sink. I grasp his hair and pull him up and over the pontoon like wet Kleenex. I make sure the Circis is unloaded and I pocket the box of ammo so he can't blow me away while I'm busy saving his ass. I debate what to do about the flare pistol. It's unloaded and the flares look soggy. I decide the poor bastard's in no condition to reload and burn me away before I can stop him.

Guntur and the submarine's skipper wait for me in a doming of light from the con tower. They seem to be standing on the surface of the sea, so low in the water does the sub lie.

In the light from the con tower, Guntur's brown face radiates, his smile more warming than cognac.

With my best Anglo cool I paddle toward him, as though putzing around in the South China Sea fifty miles from shore is something I do for kicks every evening along about this time.

I try to think of something clever to lay on Guntur when I swim within conversational range.

The best I can do is a single word, a concept.

"Epiphany!" I call across the water to Guntur. "You're a collector of words. I give you 'epiphany.'"

"I accept it," he shouts back, "as the finest compliment of my life. You have a rare gift, John—the right word at the right time. For I must indeed seem like an apparition to you—a supernatural figure out of the pantheon."

It strikes me that this particular conversation would never occur in the movie version of my rescue. When men hoist you aboard a sub at sea in the final seconds of your life and give you back the possibility of more tomorrows, the dialogue seldom runs to such words as "epiphany," "apparition," and "pantheon." But then, it's not every day you're scooped out of the drink by a warrior as literate as this Hindu colonel, Guntur Katrini, the uncle of the girl who waits for me back in Bali.

I file it under small world and reach for his sinewy forearm. He pulls me straight out of the water and into his arms.

After a moment I say, "You cut it close."

"You were doing fine"—he grins with that same cookie-jar grin I recall from other times—"until they got your Zodiac. We could hardly torpedo them while you were circling. I didn't come all this distance to blow *you* out of the sea."

"Speaking of that, why did you come?"

"Let's ask *them*," he says softly.

Puzzled, I glance around.

Crewmen have lifted not only the thin-faced Vietnamese from my pontoon, but are now hoisting a second survivor over the bow of the sub.

"It will take a few minutes to prepare for their interrogation," Guntur says. "Meanwhile, let me take you below. You need warm clothes and liquids."

He sees me looking down at my gear awash in the broken Zodiac.

"It shall all be brought aboard. I'll have the gunner's mate clean the rifle at once."

"I'd rather clean it myself, Guntur, if that won't offend anyone." I ease the wet and glistening Browning from my shoulder holster. "This needs attention, too, before the salt water does its nasty little number."

Guntur introduces me to the sub's commander, a young officer wearing his braided visor to the back of his head, where he'd turned it while keeping his eye to the scope.

"That first shot was in the pinpoint category, Captain. My compliments."

His English is better than my Indonesian.

"Our country owes you a great debt, Captain Locke," he says. "Allah guided the torpedo to its mark."

They take me below.

In the officers' wardroom as I drink hot tea and wash the metal parts of both guns in soap and water, Guntur updates me.

"When we could no longer see you past the point of Nusa Dua," he says, "I took Dasima home. While she was occupied making appropriate gifts to the gods, I hurried into Denpasar—to the hospital—to speak with the Vietnamese girl who tried to kill you. She had, of course, vanished. But, surprisingly, she left this."

He holds out a note to me, in spite of the fact he can see I'm rinsing both guns in clear water.

"Shall I read it to you?" he asks.

"Please."

"It's addressed to me. Obviously, you gave her my name."

"I told you I did. In case she needed anything after I'd left."

"Ah, yes," he admits. He reads, "'Colonel Katrini, my one regret is that I leave without having succeeded. That John Locke remains alive and unpunished is a knife in my heart. Yet I do not want him killed by others. According to my horoscope, I must take revenge for my sister. For this reason be warned that a second strike force stands ready to attack him the moment I have returned home and reported that my mission has failed. He is to be ambushed at sea north of Singapore before he enters the Gulf of Thailand. The single favor I ask of you is that you help him to reach Bangkok and from Bangkok try to enter Vietnam in search of his son. I know that if he does this, somehow I will find him. And I will kill him. And watch him die on the ground at my feet as he watched my sister die after he shot her in the back.'"

"Please hand me the rust deterrent," I ask Guntur.

He hands me an LPS–3 spray, which I lay like perfume over both guns. Then I field-strip the Browning so that I can dry it piece by piece and spray each element properly.

Guntur waits patiently for my response.

I have none. The matter is too painful.

"So," he continues, "I suggested to higher authority in Jakarta that a training cruise for one of our subs might be in order. Because of your recent services in our behalf, the suggestion was immediately approved. We have been tracking you ever since you entered the Java Sea."

The young captain appears in the doorway of the ward-room.

"Ready on deck, sir," he announces to Guntur.

"Come," Guntur says to me. "You may finish cleaning the guns later while we're catching up with *Steel Tiger*. I presume she's in no immediate danger."

"None," I agree.

Back on deck, I find the two prisoners standing stripped and naked, feet awash, hands lashed behind them, a semi-circle of Indonesian crewmen covering them with Model 12 Beretta SMGs.

"You may wish to ask them certain questions," Guntur says.

"Indeed I do."

I join the two in the penumbra of the light from the con tower.

The second man I recognize from the trawler's gun crew. He'd been the loader. For a Vietnamese he's over-weight, pudgy above the hips, a Buddha belly.

"Why weren't you flying your national colors?" I ask the two Vietnamese in their language.

Their faces become even more impassive. Their lips put me in mind of jammed zippers.

"What were you doing in these waters?"

Except for the drumming of water against the sub's steel hull, total silence.

"Why did you deliberately attack an unarmed American private yacht?"

I begin to get bored with the monotonous sound of my own voice.

"What were your orders?"

I've moved so close to them now I can smell their last meal on the fat one's breath. Rice and dried shrimp.

"Who issued the orders?"

I can almost feel the sputtering behind me of Guntur's short fuse. I try to explain this to the two prisoners. "Please understand," I tell them in Vietnamese, "I bear you no bad feelings for your attack. You were simply following orders. Since I am still alive and very grateful to be alive, I am filled with charity and forgiveness toward both of you. But my friend, the colonel, is a warrior and lacks mercy. I assure you, you are better off dead than alive in his hands. You must give me the answers to these questions, or I will be powerless to save you."

Still no response. Does Christianity only work in certain latitudes and longitudes?

"What base did you sail from?"

Guntur moves so swiftly I am not aware he's in motion until I discover the thin-faced Vietnamese hurtling away from me and tumbling into the sea. Guntur has come up behind me and shoved him overboard.

The man's screams tear at my eardrums. He appears to be dangling on an invisible pulley, surging up and down in the water, violating all the rules of gravity, and with each rise and fall he appears hideously different, malformed, discolored, missing vital parts. Then finally he is tugged under forever and the dark water off the sub's port quarter pools darker around the point into which he's shrunk. Only now do I see the fins roiling the surface as the sharks swash about the blood pool, then hunger deeper in pursuit of their sinking prey.

So this is what Guntur meant when he told me earlier it would take a few minutes to prepare for the interrogation. He has had crewmen chum the water to attract every predator in the neighboring sea lanes.

The fat Vietnamese vomits on the deck. I was right—rice and dried shrimp.

Guntur approaches him almost blandly.

"Tell him," Guntur says, "that I expect him to answer your questions."

"I know you!" I accuse Guntur. "Even if he does, you'll still push him in. I can't be a party to that!"

"Astonishing!" Guntur marvels. "Despite all your time in Asia, you still retain this curious tenderness toward

23

your enemies—providing they're not shooting at you. Surely you're aware that torture in order to obtain a confession has been legally acceptable to every nation on earth since ancient times, except, of course, for a temporary disavowment during the eighteenth century, the so-called Age of Englightenment. But in our time, Lenin and his police-butcher Dzerzhinsky made it legitimate again because it fit their need to put the interest of the party above individual rights. Since most governments at the totalitarian end of the spectrum deal in torture—and since this man comes from a repressive and totalitarian state— I intend to judge him by the rules of his own political system, not by yours!"

"Simply promise me you won't kill him—*if* he talks," I insist.

"Very well," Guntur says, "although I can find no reason whatsoever to delay him from seeking his next reincarnation."

"I'm curious, Guntur. Why'd you push the thin man to the sharks, not this one?"

"The thin one looked abstemious, this fat one indulgent. The thin one was accustomed to self-denial. He would not have spoken. This pig will speak."

I turn back to the Vietnamese. He trembles from some deep epicenter, his eyes still flexing in horror at the sight of the murky water just beyond.

"I shall repeat the questions," I say to him in Vietnamese. "Why did you attack me?"

Guntur is right. Guntur, it seems, is always right. The pudgy one is eager to talk.

He embarked, he tells me, from the port at Rach Gia, on South Vietnam's western coast. There had been seven of them assigned to intercept and to kill the American John Locke north of Singapore. To thwart identification, the trawler proceeded to sea without her national ensign and with her hull numbers and port of hail painted out. *Steel Tiger* was to be blown out of the water and care taken to ensure that no single piece of flotsam remained on the surface afterward. These orders were issued by an officer of the Mât Vu, Hanoi's secret police force, more commonly known as the Công An. No, he had never seen this officer before. Nor were any of the seven told his name, but it was understood that the orders came down from higher authority in the Mât Vu.

To protect the man, now that I have the information I need, I link my arm in his.

"He goes below, right?" I ask Guntur. "Into the sub and is put ashore tonight, okay?"

Somewhat reluctantly, Guntur agrees. He speaks in Indonesian to the skipper, who issues the appropriate orders. I release my hold on the prisoner. Two crewmen lead him to the forward hatch, let him scamper gratefully below.

"Fascinating," Guntur says, "that Hanoi's secret-police apparat is so dedicated to your demise."

"Isn't it?" I agree. "I could understand it if I'd fucked over the Libyans or the Bulgarians, but why would any group of men as sophisticated as Hanoi's Politboro authorize a personal vendetta? It simply doesn't fit their needs or their political behavior."

The wind has backed. It stiffens out of the southeast and begins to push the sea into dark foothills against the night horizon.

I am seized by the need to be back aboard *Steel Tiger*, to be alone, to run blank discs through my mind at a speed of one hundred megaflops and see what, if anything, prints out.

CHAPTER

5

In a matter of twenty-six minutes the Indonesian submarine has overtaken *Steel Tiger*.

We glide along the windlopped surface until we come up five hundred meters off *Steel Tiger*'s port quarter. Speed is reduced until we are running abeam of my untended ketch.

From the con tower I share with Guntur and the sub's skipper, I peer across the corbeau sea at my self-contained movable nest, dwarfed now by her steel escort, but sailing as truly as if she had a Fastnet race crew aboard her manning every winch.

I marvel at the beauty of her sheer. In the night her white freeboard ghosts along so magnificently I feel my emotive sense choking up my throat. I long to shout "I love you!" across the space between us. Guntur might not understand. Surely the skipper will.

I cup my hands and cry at the top of my voice, "I love you!"

Gunter *does* understand.

"She's still twenty hours south of the Erawan Oil platforms and well clear of Redang and the rocks of Ko Kra," he says. "Plenty of time to enjoy supper with us—and please note I did not say *last* supper. The chef has prepared a Thai feast in celebration of your miraculous survival and to mark your imminent arrival in Thailand. I also need to share certain data with you before we send you on your way."

"We'll maintain a deck watch, Captain Locke," the skipper assures me.

Much as I want to be aboard *Steel Tiger*, how can I refuse the people who've put me back in business? Besides, I can smell *pla duk* being grilled in the galley below. Seldom are you able to get this fresh-water fish except in August and September, when the rivers are swollen by monsoon rains and the rice fields dazzle the eye with their layered greens. I am easily seduced by the scent of shallots, ginger, *ma-dun* and coriander leaves.

After an incredible desert, *san-ka-ya*, coconut-cream custard served with chopped jackfruit stone, the skipper leaves Guntur and me alone in the officers' wardroom.

"I give you two names," Guntur says. "Remember them both. Either might save your life. First, Colonel Chutai Bunnag. He commands the Second Cavalry Division in Thailand, with headquarters in Bangkok. The Second Cav is Thailand's single most important armored force. Traditionally it is the key factor in any military power play. The colonel is closely allied with the prime minister and the supreme commander. He and other fellow Class Five officers now hold nine out of the army's seventeen divisional commands. The colonel and I have much in common, just as you and I do, John. I have already spoken to him about you. He has arranged for the navy to send a patrol craft to meet you near Ko Phangan and escort you in. You will be automatically cleared through customs and immigration and be permitted to keep your firearms, though they will have to be kept aboard, under guard, until you leave for Vietnam, when you will be authorized to take with you whatever ordnance you need for the task you've set yourself. You have been authorized to carry your Browning pistol. The colonel will issue you a special army covert-operations permit for the weapon."

"I'm impressed, Guntur. And grateful. *Very* grateful."

"Remember I told you that in this part of the world loyalties run deep, especially within the military. How can I do any less for the man who helped us save Bali from a bloodbath—a man who one day soon may return to Bali and become my nephew-in-law?"

Guntur expects no comment.

I do not disappoint him, for all that lies somewhere

down the yellow brick road. I dare not let myself think that far ahead for fear of failing in the earlier stages.

"The second name," he says, "is Pham Van Ky. He is the single most important agent we have in Vietnam. When you reach Hanoi, you must contact him."

"How?"

"You will visit the quarter lying northeast of the Restored-Sword Lake with its thirty-six streets. He lives with a family of artisans on Hàng Bac. The houses are like matchboxes, the ground floor jutting out, the upper floor receding, with a single window facing the street. In Pham Van Ky's window you will observe potted dwarf plants."

"Guntur," I remind him, "I happen to know—and only because Doan Thi wrote a poem about it—that almost *all* the houses in that ancient section of Hanoi have small rock gardens and potted dwarf plants in their windows."

"But *his* grows from a silver vase, which he keeps polished to reflect the moonlight."

"My apologies," I say. "And again, my thanks. I shall not forget those names—Colonel Chutai Bunnag and Pham Van Ky. Nor yours either, Guntur."

I grasp his shoulder for a sentimental moment.

He brings an object from his pocket.

An amulet.

"Dasima asked me to give you this," Guntur says. "It is a charm to protect you against danger and to ensure your power. She debated whether to give you an amulet of the type the Thais call *phra khreuang*, a Buddha pendant, but decided against it because you are not a practicing Buddhist. She decided instead on the *khreuang-rang* category. This charm is designed to protect within a specified area of influence."

He hands me the amulet—a molded phallus.

"This is not to be worn around the neck," Guntur informs me.

"Around the . . . ?" I ask, my eyes widening at the thought of Dasima's enterprise.

"Quite," he says. "Dasima is wearing the mate of this. No man, she asked me to tell you, will ever remove it— no man but you, John."

"God damn, Guntur," I laugh, "how the hell am I supposed to keep the thing from falling off? Unless I go around with a permanent erection."

Guntur joins me in the laughter. "Frankly, if I had to wear it," he suggests, "I'd hang it from my waist."

And so we settle the matter.

Later, crossing the black water between the submarine and *Steel Tiger*, Guntur with me and three crewmen in the sub's rubber dinghy, the laughter is gone. The impossibility of the mission ahead of me lies like a knot in the forefront of our minds. How appropriate that the night looks scavanged by low black corvine clouds!

With my salvaged gear and the Circis rifle, I climb from the dinghy speeding alongside *Steel Tiger* onto the deck of my ketch. Guntur, seated on the rubber thwart of the dinghy, turns his eyes to me while the little boat races him back to the submarine.

We do not wave to each other.

I go below and turn on the cabin lights.

The sub commander has given me our precise fix as of five minutes earlier. I study the chart on my nav table and decide to alter my northing to three-forty, which should carry me past both the Erawan Oil field and the Plathong platforms to starboard with Ko Samui and Ko Phangan to port.

I return topside.

I set the autopilot on three-four-zero, adjust the traveler, and trim the sails to accommodate the wind shift out of the southeast, slotting jib and main into a marriage that should give me optimum reach on the new heading. I'm simply too damned zonked to bother setting the mizzen staysail, even though with it up I could add another knot or two.

I go below and activate the radar alarm box, setting my warning perimeter four miles out and turning up the alarm volume to sound through the external speaker in my aft stateroom. Then I drop onto my bunk, shoes and all, and let myself sink swiftly into sleep.

═══CHAPTER═══

6

In the gay of dawn I come topside for the private ritual that in all my time at sea has never been the same.

To drink in the look and the smell of the new day.

It is a birthing process.

A wordless communion.

An unflagging renewal, whispered to me in the earth's first and most enduring language, a language all blue-water sailors understand.

Even the delirium of last night's assault becomes a misty eidolon as I watch first daylight escaping through the ridges of the Kapuas Mountains on distant Borneo and creeping toward me across the long reach of ashen water.

A textbook wind fans in from the east. This is the "good" monsoon of August, which blows classically from the east and southeast, drier than the west or "bad" monsoon, which can torture winter months in Asia. In general, the monsoon is stronger during the daylight hours along windward coastlines, weaker at night. This morning I feel something like thirteen knots steady on my face.

I can smell the bottom of *Aowthai*, the Gulf of Thailand. She's an often sloppy, mostly unpretty pot of shallow water, hardly more than two hundred and fifty feet at her deepest point. I often had the fantasy during the worst of the pirate attacks against the Indochinese boat people that the neatest way to put these marauders out of business would be to drain the goddamned Gulf. Had

I been God at the time, I'd have pulled the plug on the sucker.

Thailand, not Malaysia, now lies off my port beam, the coastal town of Songkhla sixty miles to the west. Even this far out I can feel the impact of a different culture. You first sense this in the shifting rhythm of your heartbeat. Your eyes change focus to accommodate the new light, the different colors. The distant shoreline sends out a tonality different from those of Malaysia, Singapore, and Indonesia, all left in my wake. Everything this morning seems changed, even the air enveloping me as *Steel Tiger* drives north toward Bangkok.

Why am I so light-hearted this morning?

Must be the joy of finding myself still alive, burdensome as that can be at times.

Yeah, must be.

Although I'm still ripped at myself for not listening to the warning flutter of the loose V-belt. There had to be a warning flutter. V-belts, along with everything else on a boat, always talk to you. They tell you in advance. But you have to be tuned in. I wasn't when the belt broke. I was all zoomed in on that fucking Chinese cannon. I guess you can't have it both ways.

I decide to replace the belt before I stir up breakfast.

I heave *Steel Tiger* to, dampening her motion. Helm down, set to windward, jib aback, main trimmed and idling to leeward, the ketch settles in. But before ducking below I check her drift. It's almost okay, across the wind and slightly to leeward as she works her way sideways in her stalled state, but I want her to forereach slightly—say by a knot, knot and a half—so I ease the weather jib sheet and set up the main to balance it. Now she moves ahead slightly as she drifts. This forward motion will keep her from luffing to any unexpected wave and from falling back on her steering gear.

I go below.

Steel Tiger has a fair beam carried well aft to increase belowdecks volume, so I have good access to the engine room and open working space. I break out one of the spare V-belts and go bite the bullet.

I have seldom been seasick, but working on your back belowdecks in a cramped area can sooner or later reach the vomiting center in the brainstem of even the staunchest seaman. Don't let anyone tell you motion sickness is primarily psychological. On the contrary, it is primarily physiological, a completely normal response to abnormal sensory stimuli, the kind you start receiving in the engine room of a sailing yacht where your inner-ear organs are picking up not only the movements you can see but also those you cannot—the motion of the boat, the shifting of the sea under you.

Knowing this hastens the work. Soon enough, before imbalance sets in, I have the new V-belt tautly in place.

Topside again, I purge my lungs with air and my gaze with the long horizon of the Gulf. I take the diesel through her prefiring stages, then press her off. The engine purrs instantly. I leave her idling while I release *Steel Tiger* from her irons. Soon I have her back on course, jib and main sheeted out to cup the southeast wind. I set the mizzen staysail flying, and *Steel Tiger* bounds ahead like a greyhound free of constraints.

After breakfast, I decide to invest the remaining time on two projects—in getting the Browning Hi-Power up to maximum readiness, since it is the only weapon I'll be permitted to bear in Bangkok against the Mât Vu's agents in Thailand; and in digging out of the boat's library Joseph Conrad's autobiographical novel *The Shadow Line*, for Conrad sailed these same waters almost a century ago, and I'm curious to reread his descriptions of what I'm about to see.

I duck into the compact machine shop in the forepeak sail bin and start work on the single weapon that has sustained me through more confrontations than I care to count.

When John Browning died in 1926, he was hard at work on creating still another autopistol. Completion of his unfinished work was taken over by Dieudonné Saïve at Fabrique Nationale in Herstal, Belgium, who designed the new weapon around the 9 mike-mike Parabellum cartridge—producing the internationally renowned Model 1935 Grande Puissance, or, as it's known in English, the Browning Hi-Power, able to accept a double-row magazine nesting thirteen cartridges.

The hours fall by as I make the long-delayed conversions I've been planning ever since I sailed from Australia to New Caledonia earlier this summer.

I checker the gun's forestrap, then square and check the trigger guard. Squaring the trigger guard will facilitate firing in the two-handed position. I bevel the magazine to permit smoother reloading, then, using a conversion kit I've been carrying aboard since I left Sydney, I emplace the Seecamp mechanism, converting the gun into true double-action combat mode. I install a screw-in barrel bushing to improve pointability, then finally I lay down finger grooves in the pistol grip. Previously I had installed thumb-safety lever and Commander-type hammer, so that now, hefting the gun's compact thirty-two ounces, I feel that even John Browning himself would have approved of this ultimate handgun.

From cartridge inventory, I unstow a box of the round-nose projectiles I use for target practice when I'm at sea, a regular fifteen minutes a day, as vital to longevity as my daily yoga and aerobics. I note that I'm still adequately stocked with target rounds, but that I'm down to three boxes of the 9mm Parabellum Super Vel 90-grain JHPs I depend on for less recreational usage. Over the years I've learned that when you need to transfer all four hundred and thirty-five foot-pounds of kinetic energy packed into each Super Vel to human tissue, you need a flat-nose cylinder, not sharp-nosed target rounds. I make a mental note to order more Super Vel the first chance I get in Bangkok.

With the Browning and some target rounds in hand I return topside. I string a paper target at eye level between backstay and the aft lifelines, then I take up a firing position on deck some twenty-five feet forward.

I plant the loaded Browning within a new shoulder rig created by the good people at Special Weapons Products in Mira Loma, California, something they call their Twenty-Four Hour holster, designed for types who have to wear a concealed firearm for extended periods. It's made of ballistic nylon with an adjustable Velcro, metal-reinforced, thumb-break retention system. It also comes with a belt tie-down, so you don't have to hold the holster anchored with one hand as your other pulls the gun, the way you have to do with a lot of holsters that simply dangle from the shoulder.

For a few minutes I practice only my draw, getting a shooting grip on the gun while it's still in the holster, then lifting it up and punching it across in a straight line toward the target. The trick to these fast shoulder draws is to bring your free hand up to meet your weapon hand as you're zapping the gun across your chest, so that you end up in the Weaver stance. At the same time all this is happening, your index finger should be going into the trigger guard and starting your pull. The very instant you have sight alignment, your trigger pull must be completed, so that target acquisition and firing occur simultaneously.

When the draw begins to feel instinctive from the new holster, I place a stopwatch where I can read it and allow myself the next twenty seconds to fire all thirteen rounds. At nineteen seconds the magazine has been emptied.

I go aft for target check. The black center has been eaten out. Only two of my thirteen rounds have broken out of the bull's-eye.

Two too many.

So much for John Browning's gift to the world.

Now time for Joseph Conrad's.

I stretch out on the cabin top and begin to reread *The Shadow Line* for the tenth time. This writer of an earlier time captured the sea and its infinite meaning to the human soul more than any other writer since Homer.

On Conrad's third and last voyage to Asia almost a hundred years ago, he took ill in Singapore and was unable to sail with the ship that had brought him to the Far East. When he recovered, he skippered trade boats around the Dutch East Indies for a while. Eventually the marine superintendent in Singapore requested him to report to the British Consul in Bangkok, where he was to be signed on as master of the *Otago*.

In his novel I can feel his excitement literally pumping out of the pages upon being given the news. "A ship, my ship. She was mine, more absolutely mine for possession and care than anything in the world, an object of responsibility and devotion. I didn't know how she looked. I had barely heard her name, and yet we were indissolubly united for a certain period of our future, to sink or swim together."

As I read I discover that the palm of my left hand, as though with a life of its own, like the planchette on a Ouija board, is moving back and forth across the teak decking of *Steel Tiger*'s cabin top, caressing it, reassuring it—and me.

It is in this affective state that two days later Mr. Conrad delivers me to the rise of Ko Samui, one of Thailand's largest Gulfside islands. Violet and white clouds streak the sky above the Thai coastline. The meteorologist within me interprets the lenticular formation as having been created by swift winds blowing at high altitude perpendicular to the Bilauktaung Range. The Conrad in me reads the heavens as a royal Siamese mantle. I think of King Chulalongkorn, Rama V, sitting on his throne as Conrad sailed into Siam. Rama V's father, the previous king, Mongkut, had been the first Siamese ruler to permit his children to learn English. He engaged the services of Anna Leonowens to come from England to teach the nine-year-old Prince Chulalongkorn. I find myself wondering if Yul Brynner ever bothered to learn the Thai language for the thousands of nights he so memorably played King Mongkut.

As *Steel Tiger* bears me closer to Samui I am able to smell the seaborne aroma of roasting coconut flesh and to watch the three-tiered ferryboat arriving from the port town of Ban Don, thirty-two kilometers to the west.

Off its bow, I spot an oncoming PGM71 patrol craft flying the Thai flag and heading on a no-nonsense course directly toward a rendezvous point off my bow.

I hoist the Thai flag to fly to starboard just below the spreader on the mainmast. Against the velvet sunset its red, white, and blue horizontal stripes snap handsomely.

Moments later the patrol boat swings smartly about and powers within hailing distance alongside *Steel Tiger*.

"Captain John Locke," the young CO calls from the bridge of the PGM71, his voice crackling through the bullhorn. "I am Lieutenant Thongsook. At your service, sir."

"Thank you, Lieutenant," I call back. "You and your boat are a welcome sight. If you can, I'd be honored to have you come aboard for dinner. I've been saving a very fine bottle of French champagne for some special occasion. And this is it!"

"Thank you, sir," he calls. "Do you have everything you need? Can I bring you anything?

"I'm okay, thanks. Twenty hundred hours all right with you?"

"I shall come aboard at twenty hundred hours. And welcome to Thailand, sir."

He salutes me.

In return, I snap off one of my best highballs.

I feel almost euphoric, given the spectacular sunset and the knowledge that Bangkok lies only fifty-five cruising hours to the north. With the Thai patrol boat riding shotgun, I can now bank on the fact that only three days from today I'll be ashore and plotting how to get into Vietnam to find my son.

For one self-indulgent moment I imagine how sweet life could be if, as I cross the border into Vietnam, a young NVA lieutenant would step from behind cover and instead of machine-gunning me would salute me and cry out, "Welcome to Vietnam, Captain Locke. We forgive you for everything you did here. That was another time, another lifetime. We embrace you."

I go below to prepare dinner.

CHAPTER

7

Two nights later we arrive at the head of the Gulf of Thailand.

The sky crackles with thunder. Clusters of cumulonimbus overhang the entire northern sector, the heavy, dark formations towering into vast high-level plumes of water and ice. At lower altitudes, ragged scuds deliver a steady beat of rain onto *Steel Tiger*'s deck.

In the flare of lightning I can barely make out the bar at the mouth of Mae Nam Chao Phraya, the river that leads inland past Bangkok, some twenty miles upriver— a distance, according to ancient Siamese seafarers, measured by the sound of four trumpetings of an elephant, plus nine beatings of a gong.

Lieutenant Thongsook and I handle our farewells via VHF, he to return to base at Ban Sattahip, I to anchor out for the night. I have no intention of chancing an upriver passage in darkness without more personal navigational knowledge of this crowded waterway, the lifeline into one of Asia's most teeming cities.

Because of Guntur's intervention with high authority in Bangkok, the young lieutenant has been able to handle all the paperwork in clearing me and *Steel Tiger* into the country. Over our first night's dinner together, he's granted me pratique and issued me a tourist visa good for sixty days. Permission has been given for me to tie *Steel Tiger* up at a navy base on the Thonburi side of the river.

I awaken before dawn, eager to get upriver.

In the first of the westering light I see what Conrad

saw a century ago—the straight line of the flat Thai shore joined to the stable sea, edge to edge, with a perfect and unmarked closeness, in one leveled floor, half-brown, half-blue, under the enormous dome of the clearing sky. Off to both sides of the bar, lines of fishing stakes bristle in random disorder, half-submerged bamboo fences "crazy of aspect," Conrad wrote, "as if abandoned forever by some nomad tribe of fishermen now gone to the other end of the ocean," for there is no sign of human habitation as far as my eyes can reach, only barren islets set in an unmoving block of slate-gray sea. So many times I've marveled as I've approached a major port from the sea to find the way into the harbor virtually invisible. The head of this Gulf is the same: other than an almost imperceptible opening in the monotonous sweep of shoreline, there is no clue that this is the mighty Mae Nam Chao Phraya.

The wind, though still delicate at this early hour, is steady out of the southeast, allowing me to enter the river under sail on a broad reach. With the tide at slack, I glide silently upriver in the palm of the wind. The river is congested with water hyacinths, giving me the uneasy feeling that I'm sailing through somebody's garden. Along the banks other piers rotting in the water are exposed by the low tide to be fish traps. The fish swim in when the tide is at flood and are trapped inside the staked areas at ebb. Family shipyards line the banks, trawlers being fashioned by hand out of wood.

I sail past innumerable bends and confront at last the "great gilt" pagoda Conrad saw, still a landmark duly noted by every vessel passing up and down the river.

But something more than the intoxication of sight-seeing begins to hit me right in the numbers.

Why do I feel I've been here before? Is it the evocative magic of Conrad's words recalled, reinforced, and reincarnated? Or have I in some previous life sailed up the Chao Phraya? Not in this lifetime, that's a fact. I spent a few weeks—but only a few—in Bangkok after I bailed out of Saigon in '75 and began looking for a way to heal. But on that first and only visit to Thailand, I never set foot beyond the city limits except for the long ride out to Don Muang International Airport.

I stare down at the dun water, with its islands of

hyacinth, and begin to feel what the salmon must feel when he fights his way back to his spawning pool. How does he manage to do that? I've never been able to go through a day without trying to comprehend things as elemental as why *do* salmon return to their birthplace or why do lemmings rush to the sea or homing pigeons home or elephants lie down to die in remote burial grounds, although some smartass told me one time that it's the fucking trip that kills them. So I carry a full inventory of reference books stowed along one bulkhead in the master cabin.

Okay, the reason the salmon knows what river he's supposed to turn into is because he was programmed in the egg sac with electrodes in his olfactory bulb. The second he's exposed to water from his spawning grounds, bingo, his receptors start firing, like a starter's gun, and he takes off.

Now, staring down into this water, receptors in my own brain start pinging.

The river runs alongside me, its ripples and shadows an endless obelisk of hieroglyphs I can almost translate—almost, yet their meaning, hidden beneath the surface, continues to elude me.

One image emerges—the face of the only woman I have ever truly loved, Doan Thi, smiling up at me from the river, her lustrous Vietnamese eyes alive with fire-light, her lips moving, just below the surface.

If only I could hear what she's trying to tell me! About our son? *Where* I can find him? *How* I can find him? Goddamn it, Doan Thi, none of this would have happened, none of it would be happening now, if only you'd listened to me in those final weeks, escaped from Saigon with me, not tied up your hair and gone out to welcome the invaders!

For a moment a passing cloud obscures the reflection of her face on the water. Desperately, I seek the image again. Now I remember! She and I are together in a sampan on the Perfume River, just outside of Hué—in Central Vietnam, I a Category 1, statistically expected to be killed in combat, she the leading poetess of Asia, daring openly to have an affair with a barbarian almost fifteen years younger than she. The reflection I imagine now is the reflection I saw then, in another river, her face trembling on the water. We had made love for the first time only a few hours earlier, during the time known as hát qiã qao, the rice-flailing. Doan Thi had planned it that way. Everything she did always had a hidden resonance. Afterward, the song of the farmers pounding rice still beating in my ears, she had taken me to the gate of the Emperor Ngo Mon, from where we could see the walls of the citadel and the winding, lotus-covered moat, even the Throne Room, with its wide courtyard balanced by two ponds partly hedged in by frangipani. From the citadel we had floated along the Perfume River to Linh Mu pagoda, with its seven-tiered tower, and in broad daylight, on the river grass, had unashamedly fused like naked cells. Only later, when I came to appreciate Hué—this was before its destruction during the '68 Tet offensive—did I comprehend the full delicacy of Doan Thi's stage-framing the start of our love affair in so serene a setting. I remember, of course, the lacquered sunsets, the sampans graven on the river, the echoing gongs of the pagodas, but most of all I remember Doan Thi whispering, "After you, let there never again be anybody. Change me so that I am no longer as I was before you touched me."

It translates affectedly into English, but in Vietnamese it came out like music, and when I hear music, I dance.

Later, she asked me, "Is happiness so terrible a crime?" I thought it a strange question, but I was young then. I had all the answers.

Ask me now, Doan Thi. Ask me now.

The outskirts of Bangkok rush me back into present time.

Directly ahead in midstream a rusty freighter with a crimson hull and a bile-green superstructure slightly askew to port thumps up a muddy turbulence. I read her port of hail on the transom—Bangkok. Her name is *Harinpanich #50*, another meaningless detail to clutter my mind.

Along the banks houses of sticks and grass cling like matted nests. Yet here and there in the distance, great mounds of gold-leafed spires reach dewdrop peaks to the sky, their lotus clusters descending to the *baling*, the sturdy supporting platforms.

Beyond the tin-roofed riverside warehouses, Bangkok rises in a contention of centuries,—Japanese-financed skyscrapers, towers of glass and aluminum growing out of a matrix of palaces and temples, holy wats next to VD clinics, all the banal ironies that Asians take for granted and Europeans and Americans find disconcerting.

The river broadens as though to accommodate the rush of water traffic coming from upstream, downstream, and both sides—river buses with numbers on their roofs racing at flank speed from one express dock to another, cross-river ferries skittering from bank to bank, then long-tailed taxis, the *rua hang yao*, with their props extended and roostertails flying behind them as they stitch in and out on collision courses that seldom are. Long, slow wooden rice barges trail each other downriver, so low in the water their gunwales are almost submerged. Tugboats tow other barges upriver; empty now, they ride high in the water, exposing their graceful parchment-colored hulls.

I become so fascinated with the ballet around me and the palpable impact of the city just upriver of my bow that I fail to see the fragile sampan cutting toward me from the mouth of one of the many *klongs* that weave through the city like the canals of Venice.

Not until the sampan is almost alongside me do I react.

The boat is little more than a scooped-out log with only enough space for the walnut-faced old woman who propels it with a long oar she swishes back and forth over the stern. Spread at her feet is an array of fruit.

She bumps alongside me, yet taking care not to damage *Steel Tiger*'s gel-coat. With surprising vigor, she stands, balancing herself remarkably on the shallow shell of her little boat, and with one hand she grasps one of the stanchions, letting *Steel Tiger* pull her and her dugout along.

She lifts a luscious-looking sample toward me with her free hand, holding it by its stem, for the skin itself is covered with spikes. The fruit looks somehow strange, as though the back of it has been hacked away.

But more curious, the jackfruit is making a sound. A sound I've heard before. Once you've heard it, you never forget it. That is, if you live.

It's the sound of an armed Soviet Fl grenade. The Fl fuse comes in time delays of from zero to thirteen seconds. I've already heard three clicks. God knows how many I failed to hear before this old witch armed it and hid it in the jackfruit.

The Browning lies in its holster on the cockpit seat near the wheel.

I draw and fire within the span of two more clicks of the Fl, aiming for the woman's hand, so she'll drop the jackfruit, and to avoid detonating the grenade by direct fire.

The round strikes where I've intended.

The old woman spins in pain, grabbing at her hand and letting go of *Steel Tiger*'s stanchion.

The jackfruit drops, not into the river, but into the dugout.

I am less than twenty feet distant when the grenade concealed within the jackfruit explodes, but I have flattened myself onto the sole of the cockpit, encased as it is with Kevlar layered into the fiberglass.

Now I rise cautiously, looking back to where I'd last seen the dugout floundering off my stern.

It has been transformed into a broad sheet of blood clotted with fragments of wood, fruit, and human flesh all guttered together across a passing flotilla of purple hyacinths.

I stand, time-locked, until I realize that despite the pressing river traffic everywhere around me, nobody has taken notice of this minor incident.

Well, there it is.

Clearly, I have arrived in Thailand, a country where the prevailing belief is that you are not punished *for* your sins, but *by* your sins.

CHAPTER

8

Bow, stern, and spring lines secure *Steel Tiger* to a dock at the navy base across river from downtown Bangkok. A Thai LIULOM-class patrol craft looms alongside the ketch, putting me in mind of a mastiff guarding a whippet, yet filling me with a sense of security, at least where *Steel Tiger* is concerned.

I wish I could borrow a little of that same sense for my own situation. I'm feeling really shagged after the Bali-to-Bangkok voyage and the fucksticks who tried to splash me at latitude four north. I'm urgently in need of what we used to call in Nam an E and E program—that's not R and R, that's escape and evasion. I need a pit stop. I need basing flexibility. I need a place to chill out, a place where everything isn't coming at me. Jesus, old ladies with grenades in jackfruit!

The officer of the day, properly stimulated from command on high, has assigned not one, but two trim young naval ratings, each armed with an SMG, to walk the dock to port and starboard of *Steel Tiger*.

I leave her with the feeling that she will still be there when and if I get back.

I've packed a canvas duffel bag with what I think will carry me through the next week or two. I'll need that much time in Bangkok to formulate a plan to guarantee inserting me into Vietnam—and a plan for dusting me back out when I've found and liberated my son.

I know a place of temporary sanctuary.

Outside the base, I cross warily toward a lineup of

taxis. By this time I'm so paranoid that I'm letting wacky scenarios from old spy movies spill through my mind. Irrationally, I conclude that the first taxi in line with that chubby driver, the one with smallpox scars, the one pretending to be dozing behind the wheel, is in fact a Mât Vu assassin planted there to await my daring to set foot outside the walled navy headquarters. Well, fuck that!

I slap fifty baht into the palm of his hand and tell him to take off, drive anywhere he wants to—but not with me. I don't even know if he speaks English, but no matter, you can go anywhere inside central Bangkok for thirty-five baht. I've done right by number one cabbie. Let him report back to his cadres that the fucking American is not as stupid as he looks. Actually, this particular Yank was clever enough to perceive the trap, to slap fifty baht on the line, then speed away in the back of the second cab, having slammed the door and convinced the next cabbie in line to drive him out into the anonymous center of the world's largest traffic gridlock, the streets of a city of six million people where almost a million buses, taxis, motorcycles, private cars, and motorized tricycle-taxis called *tuk-tuk*s are all grinding through one gigantic parking lot.

Away from the base, feeling secure with this driver picked at random, I lean my head back into the shiny, plastic-coated seat and tell him to take me to the T. and A. Club on Patpong Street.

Patpong runs between Silom and Surawong roads, only a brief hustle from the Dusit Thani Hotel, a street of wall-to-wall nightclubs, staid enough in daylight hours, but at night a glitzy, neon-lit frenzy spilling over onto Patpong II, which runs parallel, then onto Patpong III, lined with gay bars and surging with transvestites, the *kra-toeys* of Bangkok, some of whom, I remember now, look more seductive than many of the real girls.

When I bumped out of Saigon in '75 to wait in Bangkok for some word of Doan Thi, I ran into former buddies from combat days in Nam. Several of them, especially some of the sergeants, had already decided way back then to deep-six the U.S.A.—who needed all that heavy shit back home?—and to stay in Asia forever. Patpong Street became the center of their new world, Patpong and the neighborhood out near Soi 21, New Petchburi Road, which, during the frantic days of the R and R crowd was referred to as the Strip, a paradise of soul food, country music, massage parlors with numbered girls—I'll take fourteen and twenty-six, please, and throw in number forty-two—and short-time motels and special restaurants where you could be hand-fed by scantily-clad waitresses.

We come to a stop at a main intersection in the center of the city. *At* is an inaccurate word. We come to a stop a quarter of a mile from a traffic signal. We are a phalanx four lanes wide, at least a hundred cars deep. Most of the cars have already switched off their engines, for gasoline is expensive in Thailand and it appears we may be here awhile.

My driver smiles at me in his rearview mirror and shrugs his narrow shoulders eloquently. There is total acceptance in the gesture. In France the paving blocks would already be torn up and hurled at the police officer who sits indifferently a quarter of a mile away from us, sheltered in his traffic booth with his signal board and all his little blinking lights, and scans the morning paper as he lets the mile-long mass of cars from our left cross our T, giving them their turn, even as, I must assume, he will eventually give us ours.

The cabbie on my driver's side—the steering wheel is to the right in Bangkok—climbs out and brings his checkerboard over to our cab. My driver greets him, the two exchanging *wai*s, hands upraised to each other, palms together, just below the nose. This disposed of, they busily set up the board on the hood of our cab and begin playing, using Coke bottle tops as their checkers.

I sit relaxed, feeling safe at last, a stranger in a new metropolis, shrouded in exhaust fumes, while a small army of vendors pads by outside, smiling in at me and offering food and flowers for sale, newspapers, lottery tickets, and "genuine" Rolex watches. Through a window I survey the vast, hand-painted expanse of movie billboards. One in particular catches my eye—a poster for a movie starring a budding Lolita with the improbable name of Ranee Greenburgh. From the art it would appear that Miss Greenburgh is appearing in a tumultuous flick involving two star-crossed teenage lovers. Who says never the twain shall meet?

Half an hour later, already feeling nostalgic about the

one particular sergeant I'm looking for, I'm finally delivered to the T. and A. Club.

The entrance lies cloistered between the overpowering cleavage of two gigantic rubberized titties that curve down pendulously from the roof to within ten feet of the sidewalk. Red light bulbs ring each nipple, although mercifully now in broad daylight neither nipple is lit.

The club is closed, I find, but the front door is unlocked. I enter.

A black American, big enough to make me wonder how I'd handle him if he chose to come out after me, peers at me from behind the bar where I've interrupted the process of his taking inventory.

"Sorry, friend," he says, with the kind of condescending good humor anybody with his muscles can afford, "we don't open till the sun go down."

"Looking for Gil Hamlin."

This freezes him in the middle of his bottle count.

"Oh." Neither a question nor a statement. More like a drawbridge going up.

"Tell him John Locke."

"What's that gonna do for him?

"Probably make him fart," I say.

"Well, I be *shit*!" he howls delightedly. "You sure know ol' Gil Hamlin. Locke, you say? John Locke?"

I nod. He pushes a button under the counter.

"You two together in Nam?"

"Yes."

"All *right*!" he says. "What can I pour for you? On the house!"

I cross to the bar, set my duffel bag on the floor, and settle onto a stool. Nothing like an empty bar in mid-morning.

"Been a while since I had a Singha beer. Still as good as I remember?"

"If the good Lord makes anything better than Singha beer and Thai girls," he says, "he's keeping it to himself."

He uncaps a Singha, pours it into the frosted mug he brings from the freezer, slides the mug in front of me.

The foam dances for an instant on my lips, the icy beer opens my throat. The man's right. At least about the beer. I've never been with a Thai girl.

"Call me Toang," he says, his huge palm reaching toward

me across the bar, testing me, waiting to see if I lay a
white man's pallid handshake on him or go for the brothers' grip. I don't disappoint him.

"Toang," I repeat. "Sounds Thai. I figured you from
Chicago."

"Close, man. Peoria. I gotta be the only dude in Siam
comes from Peoria. Toang's the nickname they gave me.
In Thai *toang*'s a large cockerel, but when they call me
that, they ain't talkin' about a young rooster—they talkin'
cock! Chicks around here ain't never seen nothin' like
it!"

"Shit Hook!"

I turn at the sound of my nom de guerre to see Gil
Hamlin grizzling toward me. He wraps me in a burly
embrace as powerful as I recall it from the past.

He's let his sparse, straw-yellow hair grow into a long
ponytail, which hangs along his spine like a fuse daring
somebody to light it. He's wearing fancy crocodile boots
and a belt buckle of Burmese jade massive enough to have
come right out of the forehead of some profaned Buddha
in a Rangoon pagoda. He's gone slightly to belly, but
despite the intervening peaceful years since I had him for
a time on my Mamba team as radioman, he still looks as
formidable as he did in those meaner years.

"Been expecting you, Shit Hook!" he says, releasing
me, letting me breathe again. "Tip Bradley called from
Bali, said to keep an eye out for you. He says you're the
numero-uno have-gun-will-travel honcho in the China
Lake. Still mowin' 'em down, huh, Skipper?"

"Now and then," I admit.

"Well," he concedes, "no shortage of assholes out
there."

I am no longer hearing his voice in present time. Instead,
he comes to me as I heard him then, a silhouette against
the jungle line, huddled over the AN/PRC 74 we carried
in those days, the single-sideband radio with extended
range we used for commo between the OP and the PB.
Gil was the best, able to use tactical brevity codes and
to reduce on-air time better than any other radioman I
ever served with. Because of this natural and intuitive
speed he always reduced our exposure to opposing forces
radio directional scanners. I hear him now whispering our
grid coordinates: "Location TR–2 Shackle—Vox—Aro—

over." A language stripped of all humanity, a language of code and coordinates—the language of death when we called in air strikes, the language of life when we called for extraction.

But I also remember why I had to transfer him off my SOG recon team. The poor bastard had a gas problem. He was always and forever farting. Everything he ate or drank turned to gas. If he wasn't passing air, his stomach would be rumbling. You could hear him rumbling and farting from fifty yards off, and his gas smelled like the sewers of Calcutta. I'd never take him on a mission without forcing him to fast for twenty-four hours before we humped off, and I'd starve him till we got back,—otherwise he would have unwittingly betrayed us to the enemy, fucked up some really perfecto ambushes. You can't draw down on an unsuspecting foe and start farting and stinking up the area before you lay fire onto him. I used to look at poor Gil and wonder about the condition of the enzyme-producing colonies in his digestive tract.

"How's your farting problem?" I ask.

From behind the bar Toang lets out a hoot and slaps the counter with his gigantic palms, making my beer mug skitter off a few inches.

"Worse than ever!" Gil scowls. "I take even a sip of water, it's Gas City! Would you believe I haven't had head in the last three years? You ready for that shit? In *Bangkok*! Where they *invented* cock-sucking! I mean, what girl's going to put up with *that*? Get her fucking ears blown off? Jesus, Skipper, why'd you have to ask?"

"I was thinking of asking if I could bunk in for a couple of weeks with you. But I'd rather take my chances in the street than spend the next fourteen nights dodging your farts."

"Hey, don't worry, Shit Hook," he says. "You're all patched in."

"What do you mean?"

"On the phone Tip told me everything—about Doan Thi's death. Sorry, man. I know what she meant to you. And he told me about the kid you got somewhere in-country. Tip really wants to go in with you—he's ready to fly up here from Bali. I'm ready too, John."

I have trouble with the unexpected lump in my throat. Troopies like Tip and Gil and all the others I was thick with are the only reason any of us managed to come out of Nam with any sense of perspective intact. As everybody now knows, it was a war of small units, a war of private relationships—three or four guys, or six or seven, all hanging together. You weren't out there killing the enemy because they were raping your old lady in San Francisco, but because they were managing on a pretty systematic basis to blow your buddies away. Not in all my years in Vietnam did I ever fight for flag or country or for that fucking tower of Babel on the Potomac. You were fighting for the guy on your left flank and the guy behind you with the M-60 covering your ass. And the experts can write ten billion more words on the right and the wrong of it all—and what it meant and why we went in there to juggle French chestnuts and how could we possibly know what the China pawn was back in the late fifties and all that shit—but there was nothing more to it than the guys you were in it with. Just that. Period.

"If you and Tip think I'm going to fuck up your lives, forget it!" I tell Gil. "Toang, could I have another Singha?"

"Coming up, man."

"But I do need a place to set up a think tank," I tell Gil, "where I can let down and not figure I'm going to be diced from behind. Where I can start to plan this thing out. When I do go in, I'll be the only American. I'll take maybe two, three indigs with me—strictly a low-profile operation. In. Zap. Out."

"I'm trying to tell you," Gil says, "that I got you already set up. I'm putting you into the royal suite. My own personal pad, upstairs—in the fucking *pent*house, man. *No*body gets past the kind of manpower that works in this club. Toang here is my security boss. He's got clodos working for him who make him look like a midget, sumo types from Japan, a couple of Sikhs from the Punjab who are so goddamn scary I don't even dare make eye contact with them, even though I hand out the paychecks. Skipper, I guarantee you, won't nobody you're not expecting come knocking on your door!"

"Thank you, Gil." I hoist the second Singha in his direction and let it slide down.

Already I'm feeling less frantic than I felt only an hour ago, when I did that ridiculous hop, skip, and jump into the second cab in line outside the Royal Naval Base.

"Wait'll you see this place in action tonight," Gil says proudly. "Fifty go-go girls onstage at all times. And fifty more waiting their turn while they circulate among the customers and hold the heavy drinkers' cocks. Best-looking pussy in Thailand. Most of 'em from up north around Chieng Mai. All mine, Skipper. Not bad for a kid who majored in switchblades at Central High. You any idea what the take is here on Friday and Saturday nights?"

"In the thousands, I'd guess."

"Any weekend I don't bank twenty-five grand I kill myself. I'd like to know how those rear-echelon motherfuckers we had to put up with in Nam are doing back in the States on their scroungy twenty-two grand a year. Bastards always treating us legs like fuckin' mushrooms—keepin' us in the dark and feedin' us shit! Cocksuckers with size thirty-two boots and size two heads with eagles and stars on their collars, their cocks all shriveled up with heat stroke, shaking their heads at the pure pity of their hard duty behind the lines because their walk-in ice lockers weren't working and all their strawberry ice cream melted or some stupid Charley just blew up their water-purification truck. Fuck 'em all!"

"I'll drink to that," I say.

And I do.

I'm remembering how fervently Gil hated all noncombat officers. I was never able to find out the root cause of his hostility toward this particular echelon. He'd come to me out of the 5th Special Forces Group, a hard-charging sergeant, even then spouting his conviction that each and every desk officer without exception was the pathogen infecting the body of every fighting man in-country—the contagion, the toxemia, the sarcoma, the excrescence, the chancre, the ultimate mongolism. Somewhere he'd heard that it took nine people behind the lines to service every one of us out looking for the enemy, and no matter how many times I tried to point out that we were a highly technological service society, that we had to have communications people, medical people, rescue people, supply people, planning people, he would hit me with the question, "Then how come we're losing?"

"Cocksuckers!" he dumps on Toang, who must have heard this a hundred times before. "You imagine that? Nine to fucking one! The gooks turned it the other way around. They probably had nine *chien si* fighters out in the boonies kickin' ass and only one desk officer, but I betcha that one was carrying his goddamned desk on his back and moving south with the rest of 'em. Hell, they had country girls in black pajamas so young they hadn't had their periods yet who coulda kicked the shit out of most of our fat-ass brass. Tell 'im about the silly bastards paying us for prisoners, skipper!"

"Well, they had their reasons," I say rather lamely, because I could never make a case for paying bounty to soldiers. Who fights a war for money? I should say, what *soldier* fights a war for money?

"Tell 'im!" Gil urges.

"Well," I say to Toang, "we were always short when it came to proper intelligence about our enemy, so snatching prisoners became a priority for the operations group Gil and I were serving with at the time. Word came down offering all three American team leaders on every recon group a reward of five days of R and R for every POW we brought in, plus a cash payment of seven hundred dollars to the indig team with us. So we began to develop special ambush techniques in which we'd wax the forward and rear components of any enemy unit we found and spare a couple of the enemy in the center."

"We even carried handcuffs and concussion grenades," Gil says, "so we could stun the survivors, not scatter 'em around the bushes. Like a bunch of fuckin' cops out to bust the bag guys. Shit, I'd like to have just five minutes alone with the cocksucker who thought that one up!"

"Seems pretty smart to me," Toang says. "How you gonna know what's comin' down, man, unless you bag yourself some of the cats from the other team?"

"What kind of shit is that?" Gil yells. "*Team*? You think Nam was fuckin' Monday night football?"

"What pissed us off," I explain to the silent Toang, "was not the operational orders that we take prisoners, but the goddamned insulting concept that the only way we could be induced to follow the order was to be paid off, rewarded by something other than our personal convictions. It sort of sums up the whole American fuck-up in Vietnam—the dangerous misconception that everything has a pricetag, and if you got the cash, you can buy the world and everybody in it. Not true!"

"Fuckin' A it's not true!" Gil shouts. "Right on, Skipper! Right on!"

I begin to feel somewhat like a pathogen myself, infecting my former sergeant and buddy of another lifetime, Gil Hamlin, riling him up about a time that has passed and a place we can't go back to, yet here I am intending to do just that. Why do I bring all this back to friends who've managed to put it behind them? I did this to Tip in Bali when I showed up there, almost got him killed. Now I've got Gil ready to rip flesh, Gil, who hires a hundred sexy go-go dancers and who banks twenty-five grand every Monday.

Yet in a way I envy Gil for his physical and emotional simplicity. When he has gas, he farts. Most of us hold it in if we're in earshot of someone else. When Gil gets angry, he farts out his anger like so much gas. There is a case, I suppose, to be made for this, yet I'm sure there is an adversarial point of view. There always is.

I find it almost impossible to feel anger. Whether this is because I have been through so much that is outrageous that I have emotional shutdown or because I have always been able to see the ironic and ridiculous side of things, no matter how threatening, so that I never really feel threatened, I still don't know. I do recall one time in San Francisco when I'd chased all over town to put the handcuffs on one particularly nasty sonofabitch who'd walk into banks and fill a sack with some teller's money then blow the teller away. He'd done this six times that first year I was a cop in the City on the Bay, and every man on the force was looking for him, along with three teams of FBI agents, and I got him. Locke the Rookie lucked into the bastard, and I had all I could do, for I wasn't that long out of Vietnam, not to just put him out of his misery right there on the sidewalk on Market Street. But I cuffed him instead and he was stretched out there, down on the sidewalk with its candy wrappers and dried-out gum and tobacco spit, like one more piece of shit on the sidewalk, but shit with glittering eyes. He had crazy red hair and blazing freckles and these glittering eyes. "When I get out," he whispered to me while I was waiting for a patrol car to haul his ass away, "I'm coming after you." Only time in my life I can isolate as my becoming a gout of red fury. It was as though my skull broke open and I spilled everything locked up in there all over this clown. I leaned down close to his ear, so close I could see the wax like an amber plug inside, so close I wondered if he could hear. "Don't *tell* me about it," I whispered back, the way a cobra would talk if it could, "*surprise* me! Now you've really gone and spoiled it, because when you come out of the slammer, you'd fucking better consider you're out there naked, walking around with a target on your ass. This time I shot you just once, but that's only because I ran out of bullets missing you. That's the only reason you're still talking smart. But the next time you see me, you're a dead, decayed motherfucker, because the next time if I don't have enough bullets, I'll send for another box. So don't tell me all this shit about you'll come looking for me. You're not going to have to go to any trouble at all, because as soon as your ass hits the street, just look over your shoulder. I'll be right there. Looking back at you down the barrel of my .44 Magnum! And that's the last fucking thing you're ever going to see on this earth!"

Whether it was the sheer volume of this outpouring or my raw passion which cowed the miserable bastard, I never knew. But no matter. He withered under every word and passed out of my life—just another dwarf.

I hear Gil asking me a question.

"Sorry, Gil," I say. "You were asking?"

"Yeah. How the fuck do you plan to pull it off? Just finding the kid could take months. But getting him out! Jesus!"

"I don't really know. Not yet. But ask me again two weeks from now, when I shove off."

"Two weeks? You gonna lay all this out in two weeks?"

"What else have I got to do with my time?" I ask him.

He picks up my duffel bag, carries it toward the inside door.

"Let me show you *what else*, Skipper."

I toss down the last of my second Singha, nod to Toang, and hurry after Gil.

The door opens into a small foyer leading to an elevator. Gil holds the elevator grill open for me.

We ride up to the third floor.

Another foyer, this one leading nowhere.

We've stepped into a three-sided cul-de-sac. No doors. Only steel panels on the walls.

Gil fishes out an electronic scanner, feeds a code into it. Something buzzes overhead. I look up. Lights in a tiny panel are blinking in sequence. Then silence again. The forward steel panel begins to slide upward.

"Fuckin' A, huh?" he grins.

We walk through the opening, the steel panel closing behind us like a plunging guillotine blade. Strictly spaceship hardware.

We're crossing a small accounting office. Two Chinese men are clicking away on the keyboards of their PCs. Paper currency is stacked everywhere around them—dollars, yen, pound sterling, bahts, rupiahs, and traveler's checks, American Express, Barclay's, Cook's, Visa and MasterCard, all being counted and entered into the graphics on the display terminals of the PCs. I note that both men are carrying M–52 pistols in shoulder holsters and that each has a little Skorpion VZ61 with wire butt attached and 20-round curved magazines notched into place. This is the same type of weapon the Red Brigades used to kill Aldo Moro in Rome.

The two Chinese don't trouble to look up. It's as though the smell and sound of their employer is grooved into their reactive instincts.

Gil leads me through another door into a windowless corridor. Two smaller doors, one to either side, appear on the walls of the corridor, but at the far end toward which he leads me, ornate double doors carved into benevolent and malevolent vietnamese gods dominate the hallway, the *ông thiên* and the *ông ác*.

Gil unlocks the double doorway and ushers me into a sumptuous private apartment.

Six Thai girls. All wearing a *pasin*, the national dress, but each *pasin* is a different shade of pastel.

I am face to face with a rainbow.

All six girls are smiling at me, each with her palms pressed together, tips of fingers at the bridge of the nose, but their dark, mischievous eyes are leveled straight at me.

"You asked," Gil says, dropping my bag on the gleaming tile floor at my feet, "what else you have to do with your time."

He leaves me with the six tittering girls.

For the briefest second I conjure up the concept of

Ulysses and how steadfastly he sailed onward to Pene-
lope, blocking the ears of his crewmen so they would not
be seduced by the calling of the Sirens, leaving his own
ears free to hear—and to be tempted, yet taking the precaution of having himself tied to the mast so he couldn't
jump ship.

For the next second I think of Dasima waiting for me
in Bali, a model of fidelity and rectitude.

But then abruptly I am left here alone in Bangkok,
without any thought but of the two combatants, guilt in
the far corner, lustful curiosity in this corner, and the bell
about to ring.

I can feel Dasima's amulet rising.

She neglected to have Guntur tell me—Is the amulet
to protect me or to give me the stamina I now apparently
may have need for?

"Hi," I say to the smiling group.

It does not rank with my best, but I have never been
alone with six Thai girls before.

"Hi!" they chorus back, still smiling demurely at me.

The tallest of the group, more Chinese-looking than
the other five, probably a Meo girl from the northern
mountains, steps forward gracefully. Her feet, I see, like
the others', are bare.

"I am Chankare," she says in a soft, almost childlike
voice, hardly more than a whisper, yet there is authority
in it. I assume she is what we would call in the States the
spokesperson.

"And this," she continues, "is Mook."

Mook's sleek black hair cascades back from a perfect
and rounded forehead all the way below her tiny waist.
Mook lifts her hands to me, placing them before her lips
like the opposing petals of a lotus blossom. She herself
appears to have risen fresh from a lotus pond.

"Noy."

Noy smiles at me even more radiantly than she has
been ever since I entered the apartment. I notice the saucy
corners of her full lips, the way they turn up, and the
perfect joining of her eyes at each corner.

"Lek"

Lek evaluates me with an artless smile, but I read a
smoldering sensuality in her dark eyes, an intense but
partially concealed passion. Her skin is browner than the

others', but her small body seems to shine with inner strength and muscle tone. Her eyes stay on me more penetratingly than the eyes of the other five. Something about her causes my blood to reverse, to start pumping out of my brain and directly, urgently, to my groin.

"Daeng."

Daeng is the shyest, the most nubile. She reminds me of all the fresh young things who step off the Greyhound buses every day in L.A., looking for the sonic alchemy of life, for the obliterating, solid-gold riffs that might just might turn her willing bones to jelly.

"Wilai..."

Wilai comes closest to the standards any red-blooded long-haul American trucker would stomp grapes to have along in his big International rolling from Salinas to Jersey—long legs, hornet waist, applelike glutes, and breasts that strain at the silk of the *pasin* she's wearing.

"Can you remember all six names?" Chankare challenges playfully.

"Are those your *names* or your *nick*names?" I ask.

The girls chatter among themselves in Thai and titter like sparrows. They appear pleased the American knows there is a difference.

"Our nicknames," Chankare replies. "May we tell you their meaning?"

"Please," I say.

She places a dainty hand on her chest. "Chankare— I—it means 'moonlike.'"

"I believe it," I reply.

She points to Mook, with her waterfall of hair.

"Mook, 'pearl'.... Noy, 'tiny'.... Lek, 'small'.... Daeng, 'red'.... Wilai, 'beautiful'. And *your* nickname?"

"Shit Hook," I say.

They break up. With this kind of an audience, I could make a fortune as a stand-up comic.

"We all think you Numbah One," Chankare says. "You ever make love with Thai girl?"

"I've led an underprivileged life," I say.

Apparently, it doesn't translate. Chankare looks confused, the others still waiting for my answer. I decide to keep communication at a more basic level.

"No," I say. "I have never been this lucky before."

"Ha!" she cries happily. "You lucky man. Now you

have Chankare, Mook, Noy, Lek, Daeng, and Wilai—all same time. And not just for little while. Bossman Gil— he say we stay with you all night."

"God be with me," I whisper.

They surround me, laughing and chattering, undressing me as though they're unpacking a picnic basket to see what's been packed under the red-and-white checkered napkin.

I stand before them in full nudity, my manhood already semierect from finding itself in such erotic circumstances. As we all know, but many refuse to acknowledge, certain parts of our anatomy have a mind of their own.

Chankare, with disarming candor and total innocence, clasps my penis appraisingly, hefts it for the others to marvel at. Somehow I feel I'm at auction, or at least a part of me is. Chankare utters a single syllable. It sounds like a cry of simultaneous alarm and delight.

"*Yy!*" she cries as the others giggle.

"*Yy?*" I ask.

"*Big!*" She sighs, rolling her eyes as though in mortal terror.

"*Mii kanaat lek gwaa nii mai?*" Wilai asks. Once again the circle around me bursts into carnival laughter.

"What did Beautiful say?" I ask.

"She wants to know—do you have have a smaller size for her?"

At that moment, before I can reply, Lek discovers Dasima's amulet.

Animatedly, she chatters about it to Moonlike.

And of course Moonlike asks me what it is.

"A very beautiful girl in Bali gave it to me. To protect me from devils, djinns, lions, and other enemies."

With a delicate little twist of her fingers, Moonlike unties it from around my waist and hangs it around my neck.

"Let it protect your heart. We will protect the rest of you."

She gives a whispered order and Mook pads off to one side of the vast suite, where a marble tub is sending up smoke signals from the hot perfumed water steaming in it. Mook turns on a dozen jets within the pool-size tub.

The girls slip out of their *pasins*, shedding them and leaving them in a heap of color about the floor, then, all naked, with perfect innocence, each one of them Eve before the Apple, they lead me to the tub and to Mook, who has also removed her silk wrapping and has slid like a water nymph into the bubbles, her long hair spreading like an ink blot over the surface as she submerges with a languid sigh to her breasts and arches her head back to let her hair plunge deeper.

I am led to the tub. With an exploratory big toe I test the water temp. It's been warmed by angels. I slide in, the others trooping in after me with little cries and whoopings. I find myself the nuclear center of six glistening young bodies.

Chankare selects a massive bar of French soap and begins to turn the hair on my chest into a mat of suds. Wilai soaps me from behind, taking particular pleasure, it strikes me, in sliding the soap between my glutes. Now Noy and Lek begin to rub me down with gigantic muffs they've slipped over each hand. Lek is standing eye to eye with me. I read Islam in her, rather than Buddha, for there is a singular, warriorlike strength deep inside her she cannot conceal. She is clearly a girl whose faith is still alive, whose customs are still practiced. Almost indolently, sure of herself already where I am concerned, she brushes my groin with her sopping glove. I feel the current between us.

"How about letting me do some work?" I suggest to Chankare. Chankare whispers in Thai to Mook. Mook hands me a bar of soap and I go to work ardently on anything in reach, which, in fact, is everything. For a kid who was taught never to sit on strange toilet seats, I've come a long way. For a man in his mid-thirties who, believe it or not, has never participated in an orgy, or even attended one as a spectator, soaping twelve breasts and nipples and assorted creases and crevices while everyone is laughing cleanly and openly as though we were all winning at church bingo is a fantasy so cosmic I decide not to deal with it rationally, but simply to enjoy it and worry about Vietnam tomorrow.

I am led, pink and humming, in a state of growing tumescence, out of the tub, then toweled to a crimson state by Noy and Chankare. In the process Chankare observes the glistening drop on the tip of my penis where early evidence of my lubricity has already surfaced.

She kneels in front of me and with her tongue rolls the drop around the head of my penis, then rises, chattering to the others something that sounds like "*mawl kaeng.*"

"I tell them," she says to me, "you taste as sweet as egg custard."

They all marvel as my erection grows.

"Big boy!" Noy laughs. I didn't know she spoke English.

Flocking around me, they conduct me to Gil's shamefully decadent bed covered with pillows and satin sheets. The seven of us arrange ourselves in midfield and I begin to feel like Gulliver must have felt to have found himself strung out by Lilliputians.

"I make love to you with my mouth," Chankare says "I don't fuck. Only with mouth."

"Any other rules?" I ask.

"Rules?"

"I mean—who fucks—who sucks?"

"Everyone else do whatever you wish. But I Boss Girl. I don't fuck. Not unless I want to."

"Fair enough," I concede.

"We want you fuck Daeng first."

I glance down at Daeng, who kneels shyly at a position I would estimate as forty-five degrees south of my left knee.

"She still virgin," Chankare says. "Great honor you be her first man."

"How does she feel about it?" I ask.

Chankare laughs, reaches out a palm and places it on the girl's breast. She speaks to the others in Thai and they all laugh.

"Her heart beat like captured bird. She like you. She on pill. Okay you come in her pussy."

Without further ado, Chankare settles between my legs and delicately begins to invest me with her lips. Almost at the same moment Wilai melts her breasts into my chest and seizes my lips with hers, her tongue circling inside my mouth and dueling with my tongue. Someone is sucking my big toe. I suspect that might be Daeng, hanging out there on the sideline before the coach sends her in for the touchdown play. I feel another tongue in my right ear. I *think* it's my right ear. Ah, Mook! Pearl is driving straight into me through the eardrum. I recognize Noy. Her assignment is to nibble on my left knee, a surprisingly erogenous part of the body. Where is Lek? I manage to free an eye from Mook's flood of hair and see Lek sitting only inches away, staring down at me with her dark eyes. Then she reaches for my hand.

Incredible! I feel more from her touch than from all the others.

Chankare is world class. Just as she draws me to climax she bites me playfully, the sharp pain stopping the orgasm, then Daeng takes her place, and standing above me, lowers herself sacrificially onto me, the other girls all stopping now to tend to her, to guide her through it, Lek suddenly gripping me to better direct me into the girl. Daeng is smiling down at me, her small breasts already reddening, nipples hard as the tips of bullets. I reach my palms up and cup her breasts, holding them captive, and tease her nipples between my thumbs and forefingers. I feel her tight labia slowly parting for me, then I am clasped by something warmer and tighter than I have ever known. The girl lowers herself upon me until I have penetrated her fully and our bodies have met, interlocked. Chankare and the others keep whispering to her in Thai, instructing her. Gently she begins to ease herself up and down on me. I feel her clasping me now, tightening and releasing as she moves up, down, around, creating her own rhythm and universe of time. Abruptly, every circuit in my body is switched on. I hook my middle finger around the end of her spine, press her firmly closer, and begin to tilt upward, driving my pelvis into hers. She starts to whimper, but not in pain, rather with small expanding gulps of joy as she gives her body its full freedom, letting go of her thoughts, whatever they may be at this moment. Her rising passion matches mine and we roll together across the bed like tumbleweed driven by desert wind. I make love to her with mindless heat while the other five girls seem airbrushed out, somewhere off in another dimension, although I am vaguely aware that they are kissing and stroking and nibbling at the girl and laughing encouragement to her.

Her young body shakes and bucks. She gasps, then cries out and shudders against me and I empty myself into her, filling her, feeling her surge open deep inside to encase and prolong my spasms. She collapses onto me and kisses my lips, my ears, my eyelids. I clasp and hold her and for a moment let myself be deceived that I've led the temple virgin to the sacred groves and in turn, as divine reward, have been purged of all my doubts and fears.

Yet I know better.

What I truly feel is separation, as though I have left my body and am looking down at six girls and one man on a silken bed, the seven of them romping and laughing like harmless maniacs, seven pitiful creatures with no thought of tomorrow.

I realize that while my tissue, my bones, my blood, my vital organs, the apparition named John Locke, is still here in Bangkok, the part of me which I least understand is already elsewhere, already in Vietnam, searching, searching.

I have never missed Doan Thi more.

═CHAPTER═

9

Uncertainty in the wind, dark clouds whipped by lightning, thunder rumbling across the city, rain drenching Patpong Street—my kind of morning, I remark to Gil as I punch the time clock. Day One in Bangkok.

"So where do you start?" he asks as we wait in the doorway of the T. and A. Club for the cab he's called. He seems intensely interested, the way a kid is fascinated by the prospect of another kid about to sail off the barn roof with homemade wings—envying the solo flight, certain of the impending disaster, and eager not to miss a second of it.

"Believe or not, at the American Embassy."

"The Embassy? What the fuck do *they* know? About *any*thing? Christ, John, if they find out you're planning to hash into Nam, they'll shit a brick."

"Don't sell them short."

"Motherfuckers! Goddamn State Department! They don't give a shit about the *people*! Only their goddamn policy, that's all they tend to. Whatever the hell *that* is! God knows *they* don't know."

"Some good guys here in the Bangkok Embassy."

"Names, please?"

"One I've kept in touch with over the years—the one I'm going to see this morning. Al Wilson."

"*Captain* Al? Not *that* one!"

"Same man. I should say, same name. Hardly the same man. But then, who of us is?"

"I thought he bought the ranch at Ang Kham."

"He lived—came home with one good lung. One's better than none."

"How come I never see him around? I know most of the American crowd here. I didn't even know he was living in Bangkok."

"Low-profile guy, I guess . . . Gil, I don't know how to thank you for letting me operate out of here."

"Shit, man, you're the biggest excitement to hit town since the Young Turks blew their coup back in '81."

My taxi sloshes in. I see that its windshield wipers are out of sync. One is trembling slowly back and forth, about to fail at any moment; the other whanging away at double time.

"About last night," I start.

"Just tell me one thing, John. Did you nail all six?"

"All but Chankare."

"Oh? How'd you miss her?"

"Because I understand the meaning of the word *no*. She was definitely into fellatio, but not into intercourse."

Gil looks immensely happy to hear this.

"Sonofabitch!" he cries. "Bless her hot little twat! Didn't find you attractive, huh, John?"

"I tried. I was going for the full half dozen. I mean, when you're making history, you don't stop five sixths of the way to the mark, right? But she wasn't about to let me make it an even six. Frankly, I was saved by the bell. I'm very grateful to her for holding out. This way I got the credit, but didn't have to pay the piper."

"Well, sonofabitch!" he repeats. "The little cunt is faithful, after all! Maybe I'll take her to Hong Kong some weekend and buy her a string of pearls."

He opens the umbrella he's holding, walks me under it through the downpour to the cab. I climb in, closing the door between us, look back as the taxi eases out and see him dancing in the rain like a gigantic Gene Kelly with a ponytail, kicking his heels together. I can only assume Chankare means something special to him and that he had honored me by sending her to my—I should say his—bedroom to welcome me to Siam.

"American Embassy," I tell the driver. I discover he speaks no English. I bring out the city map of Bangkok, unfold it to the appropriate section, lean over his shoulder, circle the Embassy on Wireless Road with a pen. He smiles at me in his rearview mirror and nods.

The streets flow with rainwater. We stream along bumper to bumper as deep as our hubcaps, hundreds of separate wakes crisscrossing each other, making tiny rivulets and waves rolling over the curbs. Yet I see about me that same awesome patience from the hundreds of drivers on the roads. I begin to fall in love with Thailand. Any society that can smile through such apocalyptic gridlock possesses secrets that should be shared with the rest of the world.

On Wireless Road I suddenly catch sight of a flag I haven't seen for ten years—a field of red with a yellow star—the cloth, though sodden from the rainfall, whipping in the rising wind. It flies from the roof of an estate set back off the avenue behind a gray cinderblock wall, isolating the grounds from Wireless Road.

The flag of the Socialist Republic of Vietnam.

I tap the driver's shoulder and point urgently into an alleyway. He turns in, stops.

I make hand motions I hope will convey I want him to wait. I step out into the rain and walk back along the sidewalk to the beginning of the block-long wall and I come to a driveway and an iron gate. Through openings I am able to look onto the grounds of the Vietnam Embassy and see the residence of their ambassador and his staff.

No one is in sight. In this downpour why should they be? Yet where are the sentries? The guards? Where is the military presence? Vietnam has one of the largest armies in the world. This Embassy could be Liechtenstein's.

I stand owllike in the rain and blink my eyes at the door to one side of the gate. Apparently it leads into the blocky building that must house their visitors' reception area. A plaque inset in the cinderblock near the door states that office hours are from 8:30 to 11:30 and 1 to 4—except Saturdays and Sundays.

Office hours! The enemy I never wanted to have as an enemy keeps office hours?

Another waymark!

I slump back, dripping, into the taxi and motion the driver to continue while I deal with this.

Yet only seconds later he glides up to another gate, this one three times as large as the other. This one bristles with alert Thai troopers wearing special security uniforms.

We're at the American Embassy.

Jesus Christ! Right next door to the Vietnamese Embassy?

Neighbors?

At least, in Bangkok.

I'm grinning at the thought of the fucking irony of it all as I pay the driver twice as much as the fare should be, but ironies merit celebration. He starts to return change. I smile no and enter the grounds of the Embassy of the United States of America through a pedestrian gate dominated by sharp-eyed guards, all Thai, obviously loaned by the government for the protection of American personnel.

Why, I wonder, have no personnel been assigned to protect the Vietnamese?

These grounds are spacious, opening like a Honolulu park around a three-story white stucco building sitting back of a long, circular drive.

At an inside gate I present myself to two more Thai uniformed guards, advise them I'm expected by one of the political officers at the Embassy, a Mr. Al Wilson. One of the two dials Al's office. I hear a woman's voice respond. Yes, she confirms, Mr. Wilson is expecting Mr. John Locke.

The guard hangs up.

"Passport, please, sir."

I hand it to him.

He checks it carefully, looking twice from my passport photo to me, then handing it to his companion to have him look too. Apparently I match, for he drops my passport into a rack where two dozen other passports nestle and hands me a pass.

"Wear this at all times, sir, while you are on the grounds. And before you leave, please have the officer you're visiting sign it. Return it here and we shall return your passport."

"Seems a fair trade," I say.

To the rhythmic slushing of water in my wet socks I move toward the stucco building, pinning the pass to my lapel and taking casual note of the high degree of security everywhere on the grounds, guards in slickers covering their weapons.

Fascinating! It's the same all over. The world's two most powerful nations, Russia and the U.S.A., maintain the most diligent security for their Embassy staffs. Why not?

When you're king of the mountain, everybody wants a piece of your ass.

I run through another security check inside the lobby of the main building. A guard dials Al's office to report that I have arrived. The same woman's voice informs me that she will be right down to collect me. While I wait, I note the trophies on the reception counter—all for winning tennis tournaments.

"Mr. Locke?"

A middle-aged woman with swollen ankles calls me from inside the heavy grillwork surrounding the staircase on which she stands.

"Yes."

She nods to the U.S. Marine guard who sits inside the grilled fortress in front of a wall of TV surveillance screens flickering with a dozen images. He buzzes me past the grillwork.

"Mrs. Mapleton," she says, giving me her hand.

"Morning, Mrs. Mapleton," I say. She turns and hobbles back up the stairs. I follow her, wondering what it is that has made walking so painful for her. She walks in a way, however, that is intended to induce guilt in the visitor responsible for making her leave her office. In my case, the technique is highly unsuccessful. I just keep ignoring her performance and smiling at her as though she's capable of running the mile under four minutes.

She leads me along the hallway of the second floor to a door with a number but not with an identifying name. Al, I happen to know, is a spook, but since we live in such delicate times, he, like others with his job, is known socially as a "political officer."

He's out from behind his desk as Mrs. Mapleton sighs me into his tiny office. He doesn't bother to wait until she's closed me in before he embraces me. He still feels hard, although the massive wounds he suffered and the years of pain have exacted a visible toll, mostly on his face, which has become a delta of wrinkles. Yet his eyes burn with an almost apostolic light. Even when he'd been my first captain-instructor, he was into what Pentagon types would call weird shit, such things as higher levels of consciousness and electromagnetic flow and out-of-the-body experience. It was from him, when I was first transferred to SOG in Vietnam, that I learned many of the techniques which ultimately made me a better officer, better in the sense that I was able to help my men survive.

Take polarity, as one example. I knew nothing about it before Al taught me.

"Let me show you a little secret, Locke," he said to me during one of his early training sessions. He placed both his palms along the outsides of my biceps and ran them down my arms, but without touching me, down the arms and my sides like those hand-held electronic scanners they still use at the smaller airports where the budgets can't hack the walk-through model. Then he flung his hands as though to rid himself of the aura he'd just scooped off me on both sides. He repeated the same downward scraping of the radiance from my body, this time cleaning off the aura around the outside of both legs. Again he tossed the unseen residue away. Finally he kneeled and scooped upward along the inside of my legs, then once more shucked his hands free.

"Now," he commanded, "hold your right arm, fist clenched, out to the side of your body and keep it extended against the pressure I'm going to exert on it to try and push it down. Resist that pressure with all your strength."

I did as commanded and he pushed down on my arm. It took force, but he pushed it down.

"Now," he said, "let's try it again."

He repeated the gestures, scraping away my aura, but this time he reversed direction, scooping upward along both arms, upward along the outside of my legs, then downward on the inside.

"Arm out again," he ordered. "Try even harder this time to keep me from pushing it down."

Determined to show him how strong I was, I held the arm out, fist clenched. He barely touched me, barely used any strength, but I found my arm collapsing under the small leverage he imposed, as though all my muscles, sinews, and determination were so much overcooked pasta.

I couldn't believe it.

"What happened?" I asked.

"Simply reversed your polarity," he said. "In one direction—the first time—you were drawing from the strength of the earth and the sky. All your inner psychic forces were flowing in the proper direction. But the second time I put you into opposition with those same unseen forces. You were neutralized—and powerless—as though I'd switched you off. This is only one of many ancient techniques known to warriors centuries ago. Remember what I teach you, Locke. Teach it to your men, not just as a lesson, but as a way of life, a way to live. Never let any man go into combat unless he is fully switched on, physically, mentally, emotionally—and *mystically*. Lead him in at his max, drawing on everything that's out there. Let it work for and with him against his enemy."

He makes me recall something Pascal wrote: "No two men differ so much as one man differs from his prior self." If I didn't remember these same burning eyes, I would hardly recognize the Al Wilson in this minuscule embassy office with its spartan furniture, its Thai calendar with full-color photos of the royal family, as the same Captain Al Wilson who operated in the heart of enemy country as though he and his team were invisible and immortal. He still has a few of the mannerisms I remember, the trait of never quite looking you in the eye, as though he is perpetually peeking out past you, staring out to the periphery, and hunkered against some approaching trouble the rest of us haven't yet sensed or seen coming.

He settles across from me into a curious-looking chair he must have designed for himself to help him sit in less pain, for the machine-gun fire that raked him from top to bottom had blown away his right hip. I'd heard that he was largely bionic when they put him back together.

"I've been hearing about you, John," he says suddenly.

"I hope you don't believe all of it."

He doesn't respond. Either tact or lack of interest in so banal a response.

"What can I do for you?" he asks.

His desk has nothing on it. So it can't be that he's in a rush to finish some report or other. It's been years since we've seen each other, certainly worth five minutes of bullshit and small talk. But he never dealt in trivia. Always a bull's-eye guy.

After a perplexed pause, I finally say, "I don't know, Al. But I have to start somewhere. I knew you were here in the embassy, although I don't know exactly what you do around here."

"I make suggestions to the ambassador."

"Suggestions?"

"Mostly in the PR arena."

"And he listens?"

"Yes, most intently. Which is crucial in an area as hot as Thailand, surrounded as we are by Marxist countries with a long history of belligerence. I suppose the best description of what I do is 'information-age tactics.' Conflict *illumination* instead of conflict *resolution*. During the time I was in hospitals and staring up at the ceiling, I pretended the ceilings were whiteboards—and I filled them with the scrawlings of my thoughts. That's when I worked all this out—everything I learned in Vietnam. Principally that the mission has to be high. Whether a long-term objective or a short-term mission. Otherwise the participating soldier is turned into a pawn, a political expendable, and your casualties start to mount, and civilian resistance to government policy begins to boil up. *But*— if you can elevate your mission above that of your opponent, you can intimidate your adversary into inaction— precisely what Ho Chi Minh did to our American society. Now it's our turn. Now we have the opportunity of turning the tables and reversing our defeat—but without sacrificing a soldier or firing a shot. The government in Hanoi is torn by contention between emerging factions. It has failed to nationalize the South and in my opinion it never will succeed in doing that. Insurgents operate within the country and Hanoi's once-pure infrastructure is already suffering from corruption and personal aggrandizement. You begin to see the long-range consequences of the area in which I now deal—combat on the idealistic level, combat sans guns, the combat of ideas and principle. Only the purest morality will triumph."

"Impressive," I admit. "I wish we had operated on that level back in the '50s—and never jumped in to begin with."

"It's never too late," he says, "assuming you believe in the value of preserving the human species."

"Al, I'm dealing on a much more basic level. I just found out I have a ten-year-old son in Vietnam—the child Doan Thi had after I left Saigon. And she's dead. So that leaves me."

"I'm sorry, John. I know what she was to you. But I am delighted to hear you have a son."

"That's why I'm in Bangkok. This is my staging area. And that's why I've come to you. To see if you could help me lay out a program—one that might have at least a fifty-fifty chance of working—to find him and bring him out with me."

"Your present concept is simply to go in there and *do* it, right? A quick, covert operation."

"Wouldn't you?"

"Not that way, no."

"Then how?"

"Remember what I just told you—about elevating your mission above that of your adversary. So, okay. Offer the Hanoi propagandists a chance to make points with the world media. Give them bait they can't refuse. Use their need to win the hearts and minds of the world, something they had until '75, something they've let slip away from them."

"I'm trying to follow this, Al."

"We can get word to Hanoi that John Locke, one of America's most decorated war heroes, wants to exorcise his private demons about the war. He wants to return to Vietnam for two purposes—to claim the son he fathered and as an example to the child he wants to walk the battlefields on which he fought—and that Captain Locke has further asked Hanoi to send one of *their* most decorated war heroes to meet with him on those battlefields. With full media coverage, the two of you will embrace, you will walk the killing ground together, and you will put it behind you for all time, the American and the Vietnamese. And not just behind the two of you, but through you behind all the millions of combat veterans you both represent—a symbolic burial of the lingering hatred and suspicion."

I am silent for a long, long time. The concept has wings.

"Incredible," I say at last. "But there are two things wrong with it."

"Oh?"

"First, how would Washington react? They're several years away from any kind of normalization with Vietnam. Or more. I doubt that they'd like any individual taking the play in his own hand. It could only fan the old fires, make the divisions even deeper."

"What the hell do you care what Washington thinks?"

Surprised, I study him. He means it. Clearly, he is nobody's lackey, no State Department puppet worried about the seating arrangements at next week's dinner party. He fucking *means* it!

"Second reason—and the operative pain in the ass . . ."

I tell him about the attack in the South China Sea and the Russian grenade in the jackfruit.

"The other team hardly seems in a mood to bury the hatchet anywhere except in the back of my skull. For some reason or other I've got the Mât Vu on my case."

"Wrong conclusion," he says. "Your facts are correct, your conclusion possibly is not. The Mât Vu is one thing. But the Hanoi Politburo and Central Committee are something else entirely. The people in charge in Hanoi would never authorize the kind of personal terrorism you're being subjected to, not at this stage. I would suspect that some lower-level bureaucrat in the Mât Vu is orchestrating these attacks against you for personal, not national, reasons, and is doing it without the knowledge or the authorization of his superiors. John, let me speak to certain contacts I have with Hanoi. Their embassy is right next door—"

"I know." I smile. "That's really something, isn't it?"

"Let me sound out those responsible elements in their government who believe that Vietnam *must* move more to the West and open the country to an accommodation with Washington. Let me test my concept of you walking old battlefields and walking out with your son so that Hanoi can show the world it is not a repressive society. We'll see what bounces back."

"How long might that take?"

"A month, maybe two, maybe even three. Or maybe I can get a yes or a no in a matter of days."

"Sorry, Al. I can't sweat it that long."

"Why not? You've waited ten years so far."

"I didn't know I had a kid until a couple of weeks ago. Besides, I don't know how smart it is to alert Hanoi I'm coming in."

"You're still thinking *conflict* resolution, not *illumination* resolution. I should think living out here the way I hear you do—and your relationship with Doan Thi— might have caused you to assimilate a more Asian way of looking at things."

He has me there, of course.

"I understand it, Al. I applaud it. I even envy it. But no matter how much I try, I seem to end up every time reacting like a typical American, like a—a fast-food junkie. I want it *now*!"

"Well, you simply can't *have* it now! *Nobody* ever can, John, not really. Until people see that, and back off and let things cool down, we're all going to keep going around in tighter and tighter circles until we blow up the goddamned planet."

"Al," I say, seeing what I have to do, seeing it now clearly for the first time, "it's been illuminating. And I don't mean that cynically. It really has been. I wish I had the insight, the will, to put myself in your hands and go for the cosmic moves. Walk the old killing grounds, embrace my enemy, tell the world how I really feel. I'd like that. I'd do it this very minute if I could. But something tells me that won't get me my son. You know what I'm saying, Al. I have to do it *my* way. I can't gamble on *your* way. And I have to do it right away."

"Then you're going to get yourself killed, son," he says, looking me straight in the eye for the first time. I'm looking through a door into the pure soul of a man who's way past where I am, a place I may never get to. "I'm sorry that's going to happen, John. I hoped that I'd taught you survival is everything."

"But survival with *honor*," I insist. "You taught us that, Al—survival with honor."

"Yes," he admits, "I did teach that in those days, didn't I? I'm not so sure I was right. Honor is too dangerous a principle to trust to everybody. It's one of those pushbutton words that can kill. And, John, in your case we're not talking about honor, are we? We're talking about a higher level of thinking—a way to go—a *new* way to go.

Why don't you at least think about it for a few days? Then come on back and we'll start the wheels turning."

"I'm not at your stage, sir," I tell him. It is an admission that hurts, hurts like hell, but it's the truth as I see it at this instant in my life.

"Very well," he says finally. "There's someone else you might want to talk to. You remember Arty Moore?"

"The crazy chopper pilot?"

"That's the one."

"Yeah, I remember—'74, I think it was—he was transferred to Saigon from a base in Thailand, up near Nakhon Phanom, wasn't it?"

"Mmm," he nods. He scrawls an address and a phone number on the white inside of a matchbook he fishes from his jacket. "I'll call him today," he says, "and tell him to expect you."

"What can *he* do?"

Direct and indelicate. But that's where I am.

"He's a fast-food junkie too—with a lot of fascinating friends in strange places. All yesterday's men, John, like you. Men who still believe the only way to settle disputes is with force."

He stands, hand extended.

"I hope you find your son. I hope you bring him out. I hope you both have long and positive lives. Good-bye John."

"Good-bye, sir."

I walk out, feeling a sharp, even palpable sense of personal loss.

Somehow, powerless to do otherwise, I have managed to leave the best of me behind in Al's office, while the worst of me plunges out along a dark, uncertain way.

═══CHAPTER═══

10

Sunlight, breaking through morning clouds, spangles traffic on Wireless Road as I step outside the gate of the U.S. Embassy and find myself once again back in rustling Bangkok.

Al had called from his office as I arrived at the passport counter. I took the call in an isolated booth. He begged me to reconsider his agenda. I no-thanked him, but assured him our session together had given some shape and coherence to my planning. I was now fully resolved to sneak in on the people who were teaching my son to grow up Marxist. I was going to blindside them before they knew what hit them.

That was it! That was the whole beautiful core of it, the kernel, the Plan, magnificently simple at its heart, like a third-down blitz, complex only in its execution. Now all I needed was certain key information out of Vietnam, certain special personnel I now intended to pick, and some additional equipment, then I'd be over the fence. And thanks to you, Al, for making me capable of doing it— and for caring. For chrissakes, John, I heard his voice shrieking back at me, you can't just go assholing around in Vietnam. You're six feet tall, Caucasian, and blue-eyed. You think you're going into *Sweden*? How in Christ you gonna *blend*, man? I've been thinking about that, I told him, as the impassive guard slapped my passport into my palm and I surrendered the duly signed pass he'd issued me earlier. I can wear brown contact lenses and widen my nose with clay and dye my hair and skin—maybe walk on crutches or something to break up my height. Look what they do in the movies, turning people into monsters and creating all kinds of special effects. Then take a makeup artist in with you, Al said, trying to sign off with a joke. But actually it wasn't a joke, because for the past few hours I'd been toying with exactly that idea— a makeup man as an integral part of my strike team, someone to make sure I kept looking Asian at all times, once we were in-country. Al then told me he'd tried to reach Arty Moore, but instead he got some assistant who told him Arty would be out at his salt farm at Samut Sakhon for the next week or so and if it was important enough, they'd get word to him to expect a visitor by the name of John Locke. It *is* that important, Al had assured them. So drive down and talk to him, Al insisted. It's not even an hour away. And there's a great fish restaurant right at the fork of the river. You might as well enjoy what little time is left to you, John. Once more, Al bids me good-bye and for some inane reason or other the sound of his saying good-bye again makes me think I'm hearing a scream turned inside out, soft, silent, more chilling than the scream.

Outside the embassy, I perch on the curb and survey the lines of approaching traffic for an empty cab. None in sight. I walk over to the food stalls along the Embassy wall. One girl, her hair tied back with what looks like a Khmer headband, is vending dried squid hanging like fly-paper from racks on her pushcart. I select one of the pieces and without making any eye contact with me she uses tongs to snag the chunk and place it on a small grill in which charcoal glows. The squid smokes off a remembered scent which I inhale dreamily, although I will concede that other troopies I served with in Nam often turned green at the first whiff of squid. The thin shreds properly grilled, the vendor presses them through a small, hand-cranked machine, flattening them even more. She prepares a bag from a stack of SOC printouts left over from the Indochinese war—another of those odd inversions, it strikes me, one of the reminders that are everywhere. Well, at least in this instance *someone* has benefited from our snowfall of wartime paperwork.

She trades me the squid in its conical container for a palmful of bahts.

I return to the curb and begin to munch nostalgically as I resume my taxi watch.

Looking back on the next few moments, if I were ever to do that, I would suspect that my alert needle was hovering at somewhere around fifty percent of its usual level, while fifty percent of me was standing down, letting the squid bear me back in memory to the first time I ever tasted it, in Saigon, when Doan Thi introduced me to its deep-sea chewiness—stinky-taffy, I called it that first time and spit it out.

Yet the part of me that never sleeps homes in on a particular motorcycle flashing up with the oncoming traffic. It plummets ahead, abnormally close to the curb, creating a lane of its own, independent of the other traffic.

The driver puts me in mind of the Black Knight—his boots, his leathers, his jacket, his helmet with its lowered visor, all raven black. It is not only the totality of his blackness which compels my full attention, but the locked-in dedication in the way he leans toward me, like a weathervane defying the wind direction.

Another figure huddles on the jumpseat in back of him, this one cloaked in a yellow slicker that trails behind in the bike's slipstream like the twin tail feathers of a bird.

In the split second of my sensing the two young men, I find myself, for no reason whatsoever, concentrating on the wet tennis shoes of the passenger, the fabric alongside the outer edge worn and ragged behind the big toe. This boy wears no helmet and his hair is slicked back by the just-finished rainstorm and all I can think of, seeing him like this, is a yellow embryo being born out of a womb of wet tennis shoes. I think this only for a fraction of a second, because I am now seeing the muzzle of what looks to be a small SMG—either a MAC–10 or a mini-Uzi. It makes little difference which at this range.

As the motorcycle guns straight in toward me and I watch the front sight lifting toward my chest, I make the kind of lightning calculation I've been conditioned to make without warm-up. I decide to dive, not back across the sidewalk, where the rider can sweep my flank as he passes, but out into traffic. For the gun is already pointed at me on the inboard side of the motorcycle; my crossing in front of them and into the street will force him to pull the weapon back in and reverse its lane of fire, unless he wants to cut the driver in half.

I run in front of the bike and jump onto the hood of a passing taxi before the boy in the yellow slicker can make the crossover adjustment.

Browning out, paint-daubed front sight in line with his breastbone, I lay three rounds in before he can hold down on his trigger. He spins off like a flying bottlecap.

A faint voice echoes from somewhere—"Spare the driver"—but during such reactive instants, the voice doesn't register in time to stop my second three-round burst, this discharge into the driver's face mask, flipping his helmet off and exposing a frozen, perplexed look that vanishes as the top of his head slides to one side.

The driver of the cab I've jumped onto apparently has trouble seeing where he's steering, for he smashes into the car in front of us which has had to brake in the long column of traffic.

I am flung off the hood. I land on pavement, but roll onto one shoulder and then back onto my feet before I end up under somebody's wheels. Apparently, during all this, the motorcycle with its dead driver still clutching the handlebars has thumped into another lane and directly under an oncoming truck.

Thai guards pour from the Embassy gate, their weapons searching for gunmen.

I slip the Browning back into the shoulder holster, and keeping low, below the hoods of the stopped cars, work my way to the far side of Wireless Road and dart between the cars moving slowly in the opposite direction in these far lanes.

One of the guards sees me. He shouts to the others. His white-gloved finger trembles at me like the needle of a compass. Seven of them sprint toward me with their assault rifles, surely set for full automatic fire, and I picture myself dying on Wireless Road from friendly fire, a real bummer. But traffic delays them long enough to let me run alongside a taxi carrying two Japanese businessmen in the back, a briefcase open between them.

I pull the door open, slide in, ducking low, but smiling up at the two.

It is a measure of their discipline that they seem neither alarmed nor indignant.

"Sorry," I say. "Someone is trying to kill me."

I ease up, peer back through the rear window.

We have left the guards behind.

But certainly not the questions. By no means, not the questions. They ride on my shoulders, whispering in my ears.

How, in a city this complex, this large, this snarled in traffic, did the assassin on the bike know where and when to pinpoint me?

Gil knew where I was going.

So did the cabbie who dropped me at the embassy.

So did any number of people at the embassy—guards, telephone operators, Miss Swollen Ankles, Al himself.

Forget Gil and Al. I'd lie on the block, staring up at the guillotine blade, knowing either had the controls, and fall asleep like a stuffed boa, not a thought in my head, not a worry.

So then—one of the others?

I lay a banknote on the knee of one of the two Japanese, who to this moment have not uttered a word nor changed their carefully masked expressions. It is as though their neutral reactions have been stapled over their faces.

"My share. And thanks for the ride," I say, and dive out as decorously as it is possible to dive when your cab comes to a stop in Bangkok traffic.

I run through the blockage across wide Rama IV boulevard and into Lumphini Park to walk along the banks of its small, graceful lakes and to simmer down.

11

Entering Lumphini Park under a glassy midmorning sky I pass a sign:

TOURIST OFFICE

Tel. 28115051, 2821143, 28110372

Overseas visitors needing assistance may contact the Tourist Assistance Center on Ratchadamnern Nok Avenue 24 hours a day. Efficient assistance is offered by the Crime Suppression Police and Officers of the Tourist Authority of Thailand. Please contact or phone the above numbers.

"Good morning, sir," I imagine myself saying. "Is this the Tourist Assistance Center?"

"Good morning to you, sir. It is indeed. Are you an overseas visitor needing assistance?"

"Definitely. I just shot and killed two young men. In front of the American Embassy. Does that fall into your department or the Crime Suppression Police or the Officers of the Tourist Authority?"

"Have you seen the Grand Palace yet, sir? All tours of Bangkok should start at the Grand Palace."

"Thank you. That is a very good suggestion. I shall take it under consideration. You have been very helpful."

I watch a circle of boys nimbly kicking a small ball of woven rattan back and forth across the circle, knocking it from one player to the other with any part of their bodies, apparently, except their hands. Adidas tennis shoes slapping upward, side of the foot catching the ball artfully, heels, elbows. Their laughter as they play is more healing than my imaginary call to the Tourist Center. I place my thoughts within their circle of play and go catatonic, my eyes wide open, my thoughts locking into single entrainment, the reptile brain, the mammal brain, and the human brain all combining into a single unit.

No longer can I hear the children's laughter, the thwack-thwack of rubber shoes on woven rattan.

Instead I hear Thanh Hoa's voice from Bali.

"She named him Le Hoan. Hai," she is telling me. I'm staring at the snapshot of an Amerasian boy, a boy with incredible haunted eyes—Doan Thi's marvelous eyes—and my features. A photo of myself as a boy, with dark eyes superimposed over the face of the boy I was.

"When was he born?" I ask Thanh Hoa.

"January fourteen, 1976."

"Where is he now?"

"In Hanoi."

"Who has him?"

"The father is the third-ranking member of the Politburo."

How many times in the past three weeks since I met Thanh Hoa outside the sentry gate at COIN-OPS headquarters in Bali have I run and rerun *that* tape? What could be clearer? It's simply over the wall and into Honoi, a recon of the residence of whomever Number Three turns out to be, making sure I've got the right boy, then a clean, surgical strike, and back over the wall, and out, to a whole new life.

Both for the boy and for me.

At that first moment of contact, will he recognize me? Will he see himself reflected in my face? What dart of emotion will pierce him at that first second? I almost tremble at the mere imaging of that initial meeting. What will I say; the very first words from my lips, what will they be? Vietnamese, obviously, for he will not have been taught English, I'm certain. I shall have to concentrate on this. It will be something to fall asleep on every night between now and the time I hold him in my arms. How perfect Stanley's inquiry, now that I consider it. "Dr. Livingston, I presume?" Did Stanley actually *say* that or did some screenwriter years later sitting in his lonely office on the second floor of the Thalberg Building in Culver City come up with it for the movie?

I hear water lapping softly, without threat, like tiddly-winks landing on a carpet.

I see I'm settled here on the bank of this tiny lake in Lumphini Park, the distant windows of the Dusit Thani Hotel across Rama IV pulsing with reflections of the clouds crabbing northeasterly above me. My butt is cold and wet from the grass and mud still soaked from the morning rainstorm.

I rise, having absolved myself, having forgiven the two assassins who came on a black Yamaha YZ 250-OF to blow me into the Embassy wall. Now let them serve a higher purpose—let them lead me to my enemies.

For that I will need the first of the two names Guntur confided to me—Colonel Chutai Bunnag, commanding the 2nd Cavalry Division.

From the Dusit Thani Hotel to the military headquarters district of Bangkok near the Grand Palace is something like five clicks, I remember from those summer days of '75 when I walked this city south to north from the Krung Trep Bridge to the Rama VI Bridge and east to west from Thonburi across the Chao Phraya River all the way out to Soi 71.

I decide to walk the five clicks.

But first the obligatory call from the lobby of the Dusit Thani. Colonels in charge of tanks are not just sitting around in their offices waiting for you to drop in.

The colonel, regrettably, is not available, his aide advises me after I have carefully and specifically identified myself as being the John Locke about whom the mystic Indonesian warrior Colonel Guntur Katrini had called Colonel Chutai. "It is not," the aide explains, "that the colonel is unaware of your having arrived in Bangkok. He is, in fact, eager to welcome you. But this morning certain events have involved him and he is not free. Possibly by tomorrow. Where may we call you, sir?"

"Tell him," I say on the phone, "that if the events which have involved him occurred in front of the American Embassy an hour or so ago, I might be of some assistance, especially since it was I who shot the two men on the motorcycle."

If you listen carefully, I believe, you can almost hear cardiac arrest as it happens, even through the frequently scratchy Bangkok telephone lines. From the silence which follows my statement I should guess the aide may be in urgent need of defibrillation. But he rallies gamely, although his voice has dropped at least five decibels.

"The colonel will see you the moment you arrive. Do you know where to come?"

"Yes."

"How soon can you be here?"

"I'm walking from the Dusit Thani. Say thirty minutes."

"Walking?"

"Faster than a taxi, especially now, since it's almost noon."

"Sir, we shall send a car—with a *siren*. Would you please expect it within the next ten minutes—in front of the hotel."

"Very well," I agree.

Within three minutes I can hear the siren—assuming it's *my* siren, not that of an ambulance or a CSU police siren. Within seven minutes since I hung up the lobby phone, the military vehicle has slid up in a blur of brown paint and a trim-looking cav noncom has jumped out to open and hold the back door for me.

We rocket east across the city toward the Grand Palace. Neither the driver nor the noncom who's opened the door for me speaks at any time during the zippy crosstown transit. Could be our mutual language problem or could be they've been ordered to maintain stony silence in the presence of this hot potato American they're delivering.

We turn into Rajadamnern, a broad avenue that reminds me of the Champs-Élysées, and whip past Democracy Monument. Abruptly, Wat Phra Keo is shimmering in the noonlight ahead like a magic mist escaping from a sacred urn. The *wat* stands within the compound of Grand Palace surrounded by high, crenellated walls. Rising above the walls are gilded spires, the *chedis*, pointed as the bonnets of Thai dancers, and the *prangs*, immense rounded spires breasting the sky.

My eyes drift in and out of the layered dimensions of these golden structures supplicating the heavens like upraised hands and fingers, some cupped, some rigidly straight, as the staff car wheels around, literally throwing me across the backseat with the change of direction. I look away from Wat Phra Keo to see that we've entered a sentry gate, all systems go, and now race along a line of M–41 tanks.

Guntur had told me that the 2nd Cavalry Division consists of two regiments—the 2nd Regiment in Bangkok and the 4th, with two battalions in Bangkok and one in Saraburi, 108 kilometers north.

As we dust along the military road past the parked M–41s, impressed as I am by their mint appearance—the sign of a crack commander and polished crews—I still have an infantryman's prejudiced reaction. How helpless these machines are without foot soldiers to protect them. I've been taught to look at tanks the way cavemen must have appraised mastadons—seeking out all their vulnerable nooks and crannies under the tangle of fur, learning where the vital areas hide. I know what a properly placed shape charge will do to any tank, turning monster into coffin of fire. Nothing would ever get me to fight from inside the best tank in the world.

We stop in front of a headquarters building.

The noncom escorts me into the building and down a gleaming central hallway to an office complex where a lieutenant waits for us.

"This way, please, sir."

I'm led through a humming outer office where soldiers are tapping computer keyboards, but everything very hushed, like a Christian Science reading room. The Thais are not a noisy people.

The lieutenant knocks on an inside door. A man's voice replies from inside. Again, softly—not the voice of an American colonel, for sure.

The lieutenant opens the door and I enter an office reassuringly left over from the time of Maugham, when ceiling fans were de rigueur. Colonel Chutai is already out from behind his carved teak desk and halfway across the room, hand extended. There will be no ceremonial bowing here, I can see. He has the grip of a blue-ribbon arm wrestler, a grip so strong, in fact, that feeling it, I glance down at his forearm, for he is wearing a short-sleeved khaki uniform shirt and I note that his sinews are firmly modeled. His short-cropped hair gives him the silhouette of a brand-new artillery shell—brassy and deadly, something in the 105mm category, at the very least. In a word, the colonel looks like an officer you don't fuck with.

"Tea?"

"Yes, thank you."

"Thai or Chinese?"

"Thai. Iced, please."

His eyes lift toward the doorway. The waiting lieutenant nods, vanishes with the click of the gently closing door. From somewhere on the ceiling I hear a house lizard snapping up an insect. Or possibly the little *jing-jok* snared its prey along the fourteen-foot-long terrain map of Thailand, Burma, Laos, Kampuchea, and Vietnam that occupies one wall of the colonel's office. I speculate—in which country was the insect caught?

The colonel indicates one of two wicker chairs facing each other like contending chessmen across a cocktail table. I settle into the indicated chair. The colonel occupies the other.

He hands me a document he's been holding since I entered his office.

"Your permit for the Browning. Issued *yesterday*."

I accept the paper. It's impressively stamped and documented.

"Carry it with you at all times until you leave. May I see the weapon, please?"

I slip it from the shoulder holster, release the clip, which still holds six rounds. I unchamber the ready seventh, thumb it back into the mag-box with the others, and hand him the disarmed pistol.

He holds it with professional envy, I can see, and is in fact sighting down it toward the door when the lieutenant returns with an orderly carrying a tray with our tea. I half-expect to see both men duck, possibly even see the orderly flip the tray up in alarm and toss our tea, but the two appear unflappable, as though accustomed to the sight of firearms pointing their way.

The orderly serves us. Then he and the lieutenant leave.

The colonel returns the gun to me.

"Tell me what happened," he says.

I tell him.

He sips his tea and in long silence considers what I've said.

Another insect gets eaten, I hear. This one somewhere in Laos, without question. Ill omen?

The colonel sets his cup down, carefully turning the handle to the west, causing me to wonder what secret ritual this may be. Or is it simply a personal mannerism with no significance and in fact the colonel can't tell west from north? This is one of the things it's taken me years to overcome, this imparting of mysticism to every movement, every gesture of an Asian. We've been so brainwashed over the years by all the reverential travel writers and all the Charlie Chan fortune-cookie one-liners that we Westerners tend to assign oversignificance to the smallest gesture we observe in the Orient rather than relating to what we see and sense on simple human terms. Asians, like people all over the world, pick their noses, scratch their rectums, cup their genitals, break wind, and fornicate. They do not have a special ritual when they release a bedfart. No ancestor is prayed to at the moment of achieving orgasm. Maybe the younger Asians scream "Oh, shit!" like their teenage counterparts in the States when they come, but I am not an expert in such sociological matters—only supposing. The point is, it isn't all tea ceremonies, though the tea ceremonies are there. It isn't all Zen and the Art of Fingernail Maintenance or the Sound of One Hand Clapping. Not anymore it isn't.

"Mr. Locke," the colonel says, interrupting my reverie, "let me tell you the official, army version of the incident at the American Embassy this morning. Shortly after you left, two criminals apparently intending to rob the poor vendors who do business outside the wall of the Embassy approached on motorcycle. The driver was armed with a Chinese machine-pistol, the passenger with a Russian-made submachine gun. As they prepared to accost and to rob the vendors, our security forces on duty at the Embassy gate observed their concealed weapons and immediately ordered the two to surrender the firearms. The two criminals refused and drew their weapons and in self-defense our forces were compelled to open fire. In the exchange, the two criminals were killed. Fortunately, our people suffered no casualties. The incident had no political implications and it was pure coincidence that it happened outside the American Embassy. It could as easily have happened outside the Soviet Embassy or anywhere in the city, for that matter. We have released a full account of the incident to the afternoon papers. How does all this strike you?"

"Like God's own truth, sir." I smile. "Had I been there and seen it, I would have given you an identical account. As we might say in the States, that's a big ten-four."

He smiles back at me, a transient gleam, like a tiger's eye glimpsed in a thicket at midnight.

We sip our tea.

"Who were they?" I ask finally.

"The official version is that they carried no identity papers and every effort is being made to determine who they were. For your personal—and confidential—information, the driver is a Vietnamese who escaped two days ago from a refugee camp on the border near Laos. The one with the machine-gun is a man we've been watching for some time. We think he may have been an agent for the Mât Vu. May I suggest, Mr. Locke, you let me assign two good men to cover your flanks until you leave Thailand. The Vietnamese are causing us enough problems. I shouldn't like to have you shot down on the streets of Bangkok,—not only for your sake, but for ours, as well. We're having enough image problems as it is."

"Thank you, Colonel. But this morning cleared my head. I promise you, from here on I'll be impossible to sight out in the clear. And I won't travel alone. Believe me, when I have to, I can disappear. And it's obvious I have to."

"I must say," he comments after a moment, "I am most impressed by your cool marksmanship under combat conditions. I've just come from the police morgue. I could have laid a coin over the three entry wounds in each assassin. What was the range?"

"Nothing spectacular, sir. Hardly twenty-five feet, if that."

"But you were firing, I'm told, from a moving cab and they were pursuing on a motorcycle."

"The Browning and I go way back, Colonel."

He finishes his tea. He studies me almost vigilantly.

"Why does the Mât Vu want to kill you?"

"If I knew that, Colonel, I'd sleep a lot better. I'm not at all flattered by their singular dedication to my case."

"Since you won't accept bodyguards, I will try to put certain other elements in contact with you, elements who might prove helpful not only to your survival, but to your mission."

"Guntur told you my mission?"

"He did indeed. And asked that I provide you with whatever you might need—within reason, of course, and providing our assistance neither involves nor compromises us. You have to understand, Mr. Locke, that our government's policy is to strive with the other ASEAN nations toward the stabilization of all Indochina, a policy beset with problems such as Pol Pot, Hanoi, Peking, Washington, and Moscow all looking over everybody's shoulders. Hanoi's troops occupy the adjoining puppet states of Laos and Kampuchea and we are compelled to maintain strong defensive forces along our borders, which they persist in breaching from time to time. In addition, we have thousands of refugees camping in Thai territory at considerable expense to our economy. So we do not wish to exacerbate an already delicate situation. But you should have no doubt our sympathies are with you against our old enemies, the Vietnamese."

"You mentioned elements you might put in touch with me."

"I'm not free to divulge their identity—not until I've consulted with them. You see, I have no influence on their decisions. They are acting in total independence of my government. They may not wish to work with an American. In that case..."

He lets his offer stagger to a stop.

"What I can use, sir," I tell him, "is terrain information, long-range weather forecasting from the Royal Thai Air Force, and any ground intelligence you may have about the disposition of military units in Laos."

I get up and cross to the wall map.

"Presently I'm thinking my best method of insertion into Vietnam is to cross the Mekong from Nakhon Phanom at night—hopefully during a heavy rainstorm, some two weeks hence—into Laos, with a small, highly mobile yet heavily armed jungle unit, men I shall call in from my combat times in that same area. We shall cross..."

I trace it for him on the map as he strides over to stand alongside me. I move my finger northeasterly toward Lak Sao in Laos.

". . . in this direction, then enter Vietnam through Keo Neua Pass, straight across to Vinh, then on up to Hanoi using some kind of cover transportation such as an ambulance or military supply truck. Whatever updates on the Laos areas you can let me see would prove very helpful."

"You may count on having our latest intelligence, Mr. Locke. And whatever else you may think you need."

The colonel jots a number on a card, hands me the card.

"Call me anytime at this number."

"Thank you, sir."

For a reason that I understand but couldn't possibly explain, I find myself saluting him.

He returns the salute, but smiling at me.

I feel better than I have all morning.

Outside headquarters again, I see that the rain has returned. Only a few minutes ago, when I arrived, a flat white haze had covered the sky like skimmed milk drying in a kitten's saucer. But now I wait on the splattered veranda until a staff car sloshes in. I jump in back with Colonel Chutai's personal aide. Both the driver and the noncom sitting up front are armed with SMGs at the ready. We splash out past the tanks and into the city overhung with black anvil-tops. Rain sloppy as pigeon shit drenches the avenues and obscures our way.

The staff car delivers me back to Patpong Street, directly beneath the sodden facade of pendulant breasts overhanging the doorway of the T. and A. Club, a skirt of water flapping between the mammoth tits.

It seems a fitting place of refuge, behind the waterfall, nestled between boobs. I look out the car windows before I make the dash to dryness—ingrained procedure—and in the process experience one of these now-and-then phenomena of startling observation, as though some force outside me—or possibly inside, I don't know which, plucks at my eyeballs, extracts them from their sockets and spitballs them into another dimension. There I can see the lurking dragon in close-up.

I'm watching a line of three waiting taxis.

Curiously, the first cab in line is refusing entry to two

women trying to climb in, the two sharing a broken umbrella. The driver motions them back to the second cab in line, while they argue with him much too politely for my taste.

I stare hard at this first taxi, at its one windshield wiper ready to fail, operating weakly at only half the speed of the other. Hadn't I seen that same wacky worn rubber blade this morning? Hadn't I, for chrissake, *ridden* in that same cab? Ridden to the Embassy, where I was bushwacked? Has the same driver been stationed outside the T. and A. Club only to watch for me, to make himself available to me, then to notify the Mât Vu of my whereabouts? Come on, baby, don't be so weird! But in a city with so many thousands of cabs, what are the chances of seeing the *same* cab, in the *same* locale, the *same* morning?

I share my reactions with Colonel Chutai's aide.

He speaks in Thai to the noncom, who instantly whips out a pad and squints through our steamy windshield to jot down the ID number of the taxi.

"We shall ask the Crime Suppression Unit to pick him up at once—and interrogate him," the lieutenant assures me.

"Thank you."

I leap out, splash through the wall of water and into the club.

In one corner of the closed, half-lit club Gil is conducting a meeting with a couple of dozen of the meanest-looking hardcases I've even seen, despite my time on the vice and narcotics squads in San Francisco and my proclivity to hang around some of the Pacific Rim's dicier waterfront dives. I make them as the club's security team, Gil's bouncers, a pack of real Cossacks. I spot Toang standing silently behind Gil, as though watching over him personally. Toang appears to be the only American. I isolate the two long-haired, bearded Sikh guards Gil had mentioned as being on his payroll. These two tarantulas are well over six and a half feet standing flatfooted in the mud, and when you add on their turbans, the effect is brain-melting. Gil has played no favorites,—Chinese, Japanese, Filipino, Thai, Malaysian, and Indonesian all appear to be part of the mix.

"Just talkin' about you, Shit Hook," Gil calls to me

from the far corner of the club. "Come on over and meet my DZ team."

At close range they're even scarier. I count twenty-one of them, including Toang, forty-two eyes fixed on me. Make that forty—two of the group have each lost an eye, ripped out somewhere along the way.

"This is Captain John Locke," Gil announces proudly. "Hardly six feet tall, but in hand-to-hand combat—watch out! He can bounce just about anybody's ass—including any of yours, no matter how tough you figure you are, so take pride in what I'm asking you to do. This is a real man, not some candy-ass, so when *he* needs help, you know things are bad. Some real heavy shit is comin' down, like what happened this morning at the American Embassy."

"How'd you know about that, Gil?" I ask softly, a chill of alarm and suspicion curling over my spine like a snake falling on me from the ceiling.

"When you didn't come right back, like I figured you would, I called that ol' buddy of yours, Al Wilson, at the embassy. You'd think somebody had shit in his coffee. He was ranting and raving about bad kharma and action and reaction. When I finally got him calmed down, he told me a couple of goonies had tried to light you up outside the Embassy, but that you'd blown their asses, then disappeared. Sounded to me like he was more concerned about the fucking diplomatic effect than he was about you."

"That's all been handled," I assure Gil. "It's cool now. The official version is I wasn't even there." I look around at the impassive faces half-surrounding me. "Okay? If anybody asks, that's all it was—a couple of hotshots came by the embassy with guns to knock over the vendors, but the security guards took them out."

"Okay, guys," Gil calls to the group, "everybody got that? The skipper wasn't even there. But that's yesterday's news. From now on," he says to me, "*we're* going to look after your security. As of this second you never leave these premises without me and Toang right next to you. In my car—which only happens to be bulletproof." He adds this somewhat proudly and I suspect that in all Thailand there can't be more than half a dozen bulletproof passenger cars, if that many, and it's comforting to learn that a former sergeant of mine owns one of them.

"I called the team together," he continues, "to lay out the plan of operations. Okay, here's how we've laid it out. Whenever you're upstairs in the penthouse suite, we'll have four men on the roof—two on the roof of the club itself, two across the street on the roof of the Pussy Willow Club, just to make sure nobody with a fucking rocket launcher or a bag of claymores decides to blow his way in from the top. When you're down here in the club during off-hours—like now—four of the boys will form up around you in case some asshole tries to come in uninvited. And as of now we're keeping the front door locked when we're closed, with guards both outside and inside. All other entrances—back, cellar, and windows—will be under guard around the clock. We've set up all our communications so that if a heavy force of gunmen gets in and manages to take some of our people out, we have backups and reserves ready to move into the firing line. And when you feel like coming downstairs and enjoying the club when we're open and swinging at night, we'll have the corner booth reserved for you—with six men stationed around your table. You get up to take a piss, they come along and they take a piss too."

"What if I have visitors?"

"Visitors? What visitors?"

"I have to pick men to come with me where I'm going when I leave. It seems safer to have them come here than for me to go out to where they are."

"Good point. Okay, you invite anybody here you want, Skipper. But we'll body-search the motherfuckers before we let them near you, then we'll watch them through a microscope every second they're with you."

"Gil, I'm impressed," I tell him. "And damned grateful." I look out again and into all forty eyes. "To all of you," I add.

Later, with Gil and Toang at the bar, the three of us savoring the remarkable Singha beer, I ask Gil if he can trust each and every one of his twenty security men.

"With my balls!" he replies. Since I'm confident he has nothing more precious to commit, I decide that if this ex-sergeant of mine, with whom I've been through some mindfucking times, can sum it all up with three such trusting words, then I will lay mine on the block with his.

Already, the decision made, the trust extended, I can feel the weight beginning to lift off my shoulders, all systems opening up for go, protons pumping. Now I can finally devote my time to the Big Picture, not just concentrate on dodging from one minute to the next, from one ambush to another. Believe me, that is a debilitating and erosive way to go. You don't get sharper. You get duller, each time closer to what French paratroopers call *enfants perdus*, the situation they found themselves in at Dien Bien Phu.

Gil has liberated me.

But then, I've always had a soft spot for good sergeants.

CHAPTER

12

His name, it turns out, is Lieutenant Chamnan Pangsapa. In Thailand you call a person by his title, if he happens to have one, linked to his *first*, not to his *last* name. So the colonel's aide becomes Lieutenant Chamnan, not Lieutenant Pangsapa.

Shortly before the club is due to open its doors to horny Australians, Americans, Chinese, Malaysians, and Japanese businessmen, Toang, acting as officer of the day, calls me in the penthouse from his domain at the downstairs bar and tells me they have just now completed body-searching, disarming, and X-raying my first visitor and are satisfied that the ID he's shown them proves beyond doubt that he is in fact what he claims to be, the aide-de-camp to one of Thailand's most powerful commanding officers, Colonel Chutai of the 2nd Cavalry, and that the lieutenant bears documents and information he's been ordered to turn over only to me personally.

The young officer enters what is soon to become my operations center. He appears somewhat shaken by the intensive screening process he's had to undergo in order to reach me. Apparently, it included an anal probe, or so I assume from his flushed, unhappy face and his continuously trying to readjust his rectum whenever I look away from him.

He's brought me a briefcase packed with detailed topographical maps of Laos, listings of troop and militia deployment, dispositions of barracks, locations of checkpoints and communications centers all the way from the

Mekong River on the western edge of Laos to Keo Neua Pass on the eastern border.

"We're still missing long-range weather forecasts," the lieutenant tells me. "They are being prepared and should be ready before this time tomorrow. I hope, sir, there may be a more efficient way of delivering them."

"Tomorrow when you come," I console him, "have them call me. I'll come down."

"Thank you, sir."

I rifle through the trove of information he's brought me.

"Invaluable!" I tell him. "Thank you. And please tell the colonel how much I appreciate this."

"I shall, sir."

"By the way, what happened with that cab driver?"

"Most baffling, sir."

"In what way?"

"The police picked him up moments after we requested that he be interrogated. It turns out that he was not the right driver."

"What do you mean?"

"He did not match up with the driver's ID. The police think he may have killed the driver and stolen his cab."

"What does *he* say?"

"He refuses to speak. Not even to state his name. He had no papers on him. Until this hour the police have been unable to get him to say *any*thing—anything at all."

"Is he Thai?"

"Nobody thinks so."

"Let me guess. Vietnamese?"

"We believe so, sir, but there is such a mixture of races now in Thailand—that it is no longer a simple matter to differentiate. We are only assuming he is Vietnamese because of what happened at the Embassy this morning. But even if he were to speak Thai, what would that prove? I speak English, but I am not an American."

"You speak it well, Lieutenant. Where did you learn?"

"I took my tank training in America, sir." He smiles nostalgically. "I even fell in love with an American girl. But she didn't want to leave the States. And I still love Big Macs. Fortunately, we have several excellent McDonalds right here in Bangkok."

Is it the real turtle soup? Or only the mock? I ask

myself. When I start asking zany questions, it's time to lighten up. I'll get to the maps and the troop dispositions later tonight, I decide abruptly. Suddenly I crave the company of strangers and the throbbing of music.

"Let me buy you a drink, Lieutenant, and please don't tell me you're on duty. Your mission has just been completed."

I take him with me out of the penthouse. Two Japanese sumo-types are stationed outside my door. Both cradle AK–47s lovingly. Gil always preferred the AK–47, even the Chinese-made version, to our M-16, so I'm not surprised he's issued them to the force on patrol.

The moment I step out of the elevator and into the club on the ground floor I'm flanked by six men from Gil's security force. They stream the lieutenant and me through a crowd of men, some with their wives or their dates, already at this early hour lining the bar and occupying most of the booths in the front part of the club.

The T. and A. consists of a vast central space broken into four separate sections like the leaves of a four-leaf clover, each section with its own raised dance platform, but all linked by a circling bar behind which ten barkeepers are now working under Toang's supervision. On each of the four dance floors twelve seminaked girls in the briefest of sequined bikinis gyrate to a disco beat while revolving star-wars glass globes above their heads fire laser streaks of red and blue and silver rays down at them. Strangely, there is nothing sordid about the scene, none of that "where the elite of the fleet greets the meat off the street" Norfolk-San Diego-Honolulu sleaze. Certainly the jocks who've come alone are here to grab ass and cup tits while they buy brinks for the hustling bar girls. Then later, as the men sit alone, working their scotches down, eyes glued on the dancers like hot-nostriled Arabs about to bid on horses, they will make their deals for number 17 or 77,—for all the girls are numbered like lots at an auction, and the men will pay their fee and lead their choice out, arms around tiny, willing waists, off to a nearby short-term hotel. Moments later numbers 17 and 77 will bounce back in, looking as untouched as new green growth in a field, and once more climb back up there onto the stage and prance and kick to the beat until another bidder takes them out again. Astonishing that the girls retain their childlike innocence, even when they're trying to look seductive. I see one of them trying a pouty sexpot number for the effect as she dances, then breaking up as the girls around her laugh above the music and imitate her, puffing out their lips and rolling their eyes, not to put her down but to share her fun. How different from Saigon! You could feel the hatred of Saigon bar girls, knowing they could never go home again, knowing that they had bid good-bye forever to revered ancestors, every Yankee fuck one more irreversible step down the road of no return, yet still doing it anyway, doing it for the money only, working on their backs with surly eyes on dark, patchy ceilings. Of course, in all fairness, those were different nights. I remember when I came to Bangkok ten years ago in the aftermath of the war, it was still R and R time, desperate and subhuman and gelatinous, even here in Bangkok. But a decade has mercifully passed, and most of the despair has blown away with each new monsoon wind. Now as the guards seat the young lieutenant and me in my reserved corner booth, my eyes widen to the semidarkness and I see in recesses here and there about the club groups of girls wheeling jubilantly to the music, dancing even when it's not their turn. I ask the lieutenant why this is—why I don't feel depressed to see a hundred girls for sale in this one club on a street of clubs.

"Because *they're* not," he replies, simply enough.

"We have a popular song in Thailand about one of these 'entertainment' girls. 'I sell my body, but not my heart,' it goes. These girls feel no self-pity. They have what we call *maibenlai*—you would call it a never-mind attitude. And to us, making love is as natural as living and dying."

I discover Lek dancing on the platform nearest me. She's barely covered by a glittering red bikini and she moves in black high-heel shoes to the music the way I remember her moving with me—was it just last night? She bends over, smiling back at the crowd from between her legs, her hair sweeping the floor in time to the music, and I think her eyes find me across the darkness.

Later, the lieutenant gone, I'm alone in the penthouse and spreading maps across the floor. In my mind I begin to walk Laos, dividing the distance to be covered by the twelve days I've allotted to the crossing—ten miles a day made good through enemy territory—one hundred and twenty miles from Nakhon Phanom in Thailand to the Annam Cordi mountain range and the doorway to Vietnam. I hear a gentle knocking on the door. I know it is Lek and that indeed she has seen me while she was dancing.

"Yes?" I say to my side of the door.

"Lek," she says to her side.

I unlock the door. The two Japanese guards have that special light in their eyes, the look one man has for another when he knows the other is about to get laid and he isn't.

"Did they search you?" I laugh to Lek.

"They know better!" she says.

I let her in and chain the door after her.

If she's come to kill me, I wouldn't know where she could have concealed the weapon, so scanty is her bikini. Under her long hair, I suppose, a knife, even a small-caliber pistol held on by Velcro. Oh, shit, Locke! Stop it! Yet playfully, in spite of last night's intimacy and the special fire that had burned between us, I find one of my hands pretending to caress her, lifting her hair playfully and sliding down her shoulder and spine—what terrible artifice is this?—then cupping her backside to complete the deception.

"I ask Boss Gil if okay I stay with you. He say okay. What do you say?"

"I say okay."

"Good. I stay."

She kicks off her high heels, lifts one small arched foot to my chest.

"Please, you rub Lek's foot. Foot hurt. Shoe too tight."

I massage her foot.

"Strong hands."

Her eyes are like black almonds. She seems unable to peer deeply enough into me to suit her. It's as though she's searching for something she hasn't found yet and suspects that it may lie hidden in me. Wrong place to look, love. This is one looking glass no girl should tumble through, not as long as wonderland continues to be wasteland.

"I know you like Lek," she says.

"How do you know?"

"Silly fool," she giggles, and pulls her foot from my

hand, then raises the other foot with awesome flexibility almost to my shoulder.

I massage this foot, feeling her skin softening in my palms like melting butter.

"When you come up here," I point out, "you're not downstairs working. And when you're not working, you're not making money."

"You want to pay me?"

"Yes."

"Okay." She shrugs. "Gil tell everyone you stay for two weeks. I be your girl for two weeks? Or you want other girls?"

"No other girls, Lek. Just you."

"Good!" She smiles. "I be your Thai girl. After two weeks, you never forget Lek."

"What about you?" I ask. "After two weeks, will you ever forget *me*?"

"Oh, first night you go, maybe even two nights, I miss you. Then"—she laughs—"I stop thinking about you—I go back dancing. Be happy."

"We'll make a dynamite duo," I say.

"Always I dream someday I meet one man I like, so I fall asleep with his cock in my mouth. Maybe you that man."

"I'd like to qualify," I reply.

How illuminating are the dreams you dream when a girl as smoldering as Lek envelops you in her mouth as though fate itself has delivered your phallus to her frenzied care. As I fall asleep with Lek's lips fanning gently like the wings of a butterfly, opening and closing over me, I drift off into a Laos I never knew existed. The ominous jungle I know, the foreboding mountain clefts in which I've hidden, begin to flicker like a TV image out of adjustment. Then abruptly they regain their focus and flatten out before me into an infinity of meadowland. And all the old-time B-movie warlords with their designer uniforms and Pierre Cardin sunglasses, their hordes of guerrillas with stringy, shoulder-length hair and pocked cheeks, are transfigured into benevolent shepherds wearing silken chitons and pointing my way to Vietnam, just over the hill, sire, just a little farther now, noble sire, and all your dreams will come true. But even Lek's lips and all my dreams stop at Keo Neua Pass.

I awaken alone, good morning dying on my lips.

Lek is gone, except for her fragrance which clings to my skin like the clean scent of freshly husked rice.

Almost involuntarily, I grope swiftly under my pillow. The Browning is still there, cold as my groin.

Distrustful bastard!

I ask the two guards outside my door what time she left.

They tell me it was shortly before six this morning.

I find the note she's left me, scrawled in a childish handwriting. She's tucked it into the pissing slot of my jockey shorts.

"Lek wrong. When you go, I not cry for two nites. I think maybe I cry for three—maybe four. Have nice day."

Gil personally brings me breakfast on a tray,—fresh mango, poached eggs, and black coffee.

"So what's on the program for today, Skipper?" he asks.

"I've got to get down to Samut Sakhon and see Arty Moore."

"Who the fuck's Arty Moore?"

"You were gone when I met him. Saigon, during exodus. He was flying for Air America, bopping into all kinds of weird places. Al suggested I see him. Apparently he's got connections I may be able to use."

"Okay," Gil agrees.

They pack me into the back of a delivery truck they keep parked inside the loading dock and ship me out with the regular morning run they make to pick up booze.

I rattle around inside the windowless cargo compartment for a measured half hour, the drapes between me and the two security people up front tightly drawn, then abruptly the truck slows and stops.

The curtains sweep back suddenly. Through the windshield of the truck I see the reach of rice fields and wallowing in hock-high brown ditch water the chest, head, and horns of that indispensable, benign creature, a water buffalo, his soulful, patient eyes, it seems, fixed on mine.

"Quick!" the driver says to me. The other guard, riding shotgun, opens his door, steps out, allowing me to climb over the seat and follow him out onto the shoulder of what appears to be a major highway. Just ahead, engine running, I see a waiting BMW, with Toang at the wheel and Gil out on the road, waving me toward him.

I trot over and Gil almost shoves me into the backseat, climbs in beside me, slamming the door as Toang squirts the car out as suddenly as toothpaste popped from a tube.

"Way to go!" Gil exults, looking out the back window and watching his panel truck turn back toward the city. "We slipped you out under cover, when we left, doing everything we could to attract attention except blowing bugles, so any cocksucker watching the club to spot you is still back in town holding his dick. We even sat here on the highway waiting to be sure no car was in sight before we signaled the boys to roust you out of the back of the truck. Let those gook bastards get calluses on their asses squatting outside the club waiting for you to show!"

"Glad you're enjoying this," I comment.

"Fuckin' A we are! Told you we need excitement in our lives. Just too goddamn much money and pussy. Makes a man soft, right Toang?"

"On the one, Gil baby!"

Gil's plan of spiriting me out from under the vigilant eye of possible Mât Vu agents is almost as delicious as Colonel Katrini tracking me all the way from Bali in a submarine. With friends like these, a man can almost afford to take on more than his quota of Indians.

"What kind of firepower did you bring along?" I ask, more out of amusement than any need for a specific inventory of our capability under attack.

"We got a bucket of hand grenades in the trunk, a couple of Lewes rockets, three AK–47s and a brand-new Ithaca Mag–10 Roadblocker. Goddamn, can you imagine the pitiful look on some motherfucker's face if he tries to highjack *us*?"

"Shee-eet!" Toang grins. "Never gonna get that lucky."

Happily, we don't. The drive is blissfully uneventful.

Al has told me I'd find Arty Moore at a salt farm near a cluster of windmill-powered waterwheels and a system of ditches spilling the Gulf waters into retaining basins. Apparently he's a consultant to the Sciences Department, working on a contract to help the Thai salt farmers improve the quality of the salt they bring to market.

Off in the near distance beyond the waterfront town of Samut Sakhon we see rows of turning windmills. They appear higher, more gossamer, than the windmills I've watched with such wonder in the Lowlands, but then, the Dutch are a sturdy people and the Thais more delicate. I would expect grace from a Thai windmill and I am not disappointed.

We bump along into a network of flat white salt basins and follow a road past rows of salt glistening in the noon-time sun, cone after cone, tiny white tents, as far as I can see.

Arty Moore appears just ahead, popping up as unexpectedly as a silhouette target on a police firing range, striding around from behind a warehouse, bridging a decade in one instant. He's deeply involved in a discussion with what must surely be salt farmers.

He stops in the middle of a sentence, peers toward our BMW, which I've asked Toang to stop this side of Arty, so I can check out his response time. For a moment he stands like an alerted crane, balancing on one leg, the other partly lifted, head slightly atilt, blinking our way. Then I see his brain-flash of recognition and he tosses up his skinny arms in a holy-shit gesture and ambles toward us. His clothes still hang from bony shoulders. He's the nearest thing to a walking clothesrack I've ever known. As he comes closer, I try to determine if he's changed. But this is not easy, for Arty always had an instantly forgettable face, like the third lead in a private-eye TV series, the one who never gets to say "Let's go, guys!" at the end of act two. He still looks to be on the larky side, as though scissored capriciously out of a schoolboy's sketch pad and then turned into a paper glider. He must be forty-seven now, forty-eight, for I remember him telling me that he first came to Vietnam in November of '61, landing in Bien Hoa under the code name Operation Farm-gate, one of the young officers in the 4400th Combat Crew Training Squadron from Eglin Air Force Base in Florida send to Indochina to teach the South Vietnamese how to fly T–28 Nomad fighters, designed originally for training, not for the Jungle Jim unconventional stuff they subsequently got involved in. Now here he is, almost a quarter of a century later, still surviving, never having gone back to the States, as far as I know, in all that time. Definitely, one of the rice-bowl crowd who've seen Asia being paved, sanitized, and modernized.

"Locke!" he shouts. And I'm out of the backseat and we're grabbing at each other and slapping shoulders and holding on as though we don't dare let go or we'll lose something we may already have lost but won't admit to, ever.

"Do I hear things about *you*!" he says. "A legend in your own time—that's the word I hear."

"Even way out here in the salt farms?"

"This is just my cover, John. I'm still full-time with the Agency, one of the old whores, so I get the word. Who are your friends?"

"Gil Hamlin—he and I spent time together in the boonies during the late unpleasantness. And this is Toang, from Peoria, who was young enough to miss out. Arty Moore, fellas."

Gil and Toang climb out, shake hands with Arty.

"Bloody historic moment this," Arty says. "Definitely a diary entry. Had a long session on the phone with Al from the embassy just an hour ago. I'd say we need to talk, John. Hard and heavy—and right now. Unless you want to drive back into town. Great fish restaurant on the river—fresh crab that'll melt on your tongue."

I glance over at Gil. "You fellas hungry yet?"

"I know the restaurant," Gil says, shaking his head. "Right there where the ferry docks. Too public. I think you guys should have your chat right here. Nothing out there but the Gulf, and nobody can get down this road without coming through me and Toang first."

Gil unlocks the trunk, hands an AK–47 and two clips to Toang, then takes the other assault rifle for himself.

Arty watches, duly impressed.

"I like your friends' style." He grins. "Okay, let's walk."

I nod to Gil and Toang and move off with Arty, down the road bordered with salt stacks, out toward the nearby Gulf and the complex of drain ditches thrusting inland like spider legs.

CHAPTER

13

Arty rambles as we walk, as though letting a flood of irrelevant words sweep out of his mind while his true center concentrates on my problems.

"Problem out here is to get all these farmers to work together. They need to dig a much larger canal than this one so they can retain the seawater twenty-four hours a day instead of having to wait for high tide. This bloody canal just isn't large enough or deep enough to do the job. But no matter how much we and the Salt Cooperative people lecture them—and try by God to *show* them— they're stubborn. They insist on doing it the way their grandfathers did it. Then on top of that a whole lot of them refuse to dig out the plants that grow in their retaining and drying basins. Goddamn plants rot, make the water even murkier."

"I should have thought that was impossible," I comment, for the canal water has the tone of cold café au lait.

"The Gulf of Thailand contains a great mixture of organic matter. You add that to the plants that just keep growing, getting bigger and bigger roots that make holes in the banks, and you get organic water leaking out and depositing dirty salt all over the place. Then there's the crabs. They keep making holes everywhere. Between the plants and the crabs and the thick-skulled farmers, I go crazy out here."

He stops in front of one of the salt piles.

"See these? We keep telling them to load the salt into the carrier from the top down. But no!—They have to dig it out from the bottom, dirt and all, so the clean salt up here on top falls to the bottom and gets dirty, like the bottom salt. But you didn't come out here to get a lecture on salt-farming, did you, John?"

"I never use the stuff." I grin. "Dries up the blood."

"If it were only salt your blood had to worry about," he says, his face suddenly somber, "you'd be home free."

"Al said you might be able to help me."

"I can help you live, and I can help you die," he says after a long silence during which his forty-seven-forty-eight-year-old hard-to-remember face turns memorable to my sight, for I read genuine compassion in his eyes. "Which will it be, John?"

"Any other options than those?"

He shakes his head. "If you try to go in, you're a dead man. Stay out, let us get the message around that you don't intend to come in and you could still enjoy many happy years of sailing. Think of all the thousands of islands you've never seen."

"Arty, it doesn't wash," I say. "They came after me in Bali. *Before* I ever intended to go back in."

Could be my imagination, but he appears to turn as white as his salt piles.

"Say again, please, John!"

I tell him about Thanh Hoa. About the six guerrillas who tried to light me up in the mountains of Bali. About the incredible set-piece they'd staged.

The information seems to stagger him.

"Okay," he says finally. "We'll have to feed that one into the computers. That places an entirely different face on matters."

"Nothing's changed," I assure him. "From the second I heard that Doan Thi had my child and that he's being raised in Hanoi, there's never been any doubt in my mind about what I have to do. Living or dying's got nothing to do with it. It's a go-mission, Arty, and nothing and nobody's going to stop me as long as I'm still breathing."

He resumes our walk, his eyes sweeping the flat fields.

"I love it here in Indochina," he says. "From that first day I touched down at Bien Hoa I knew I'd found the one place in the world I'd choose to die in. And I will die here, never having gone back. They can toss me into a rice field, lay me out on salt for the crabs, it won't matter which—just as long as whatever's left of me becomes as much a part of the soil as I've become. Life here, as you know as well as I do, John, is different from anywhere else. Are you sure you want to take the chance of ending all this for yourself—*this* year, *this* soon? Why not, instead, *wait*, let the appropriate channels find your son for you? Believe me, Hanoi is going to *have* to make some kind of deal with Washington within the next five years, no matter how much smoke they're blowing up everybody's ass about the long haul and the historical imperatives. The leaders who really believed that are old men now. The new cadres will take over—and like everyone else these days, they're impatient. Hell, I guarantee, John, we'll have Wendy's and Colonel Sanders Chicken franchises in Hanoi by 1990. So wait—*wait*!"

"Fuck waiting!" I shout at him. Who are all these solicitous old buddies of mine who are suddenly warning me and coddling me and holding out bedroom slippers to me? Nobody was doing that back in '68 and '69 when I was humping around in Laos and north of the DMZ. Why now? Has dying suddenly gone out of fashion?

"My son is nine years old," I cry out, "and I've never seen him and he's never seen me. He's being raised by some fucking hardliner who drills Leninist and Stalinist ideology into him with every tick of the clock. Arty, you of all people, being with the Agency, must know that they've banned any reading material in Vietnam that was printed before 1975. They just tossed away all the past, all the old values, and what they're preaching now is regionalism—that to be North Vietnamese—not South or Central, only *North* Vietnamese is the greatest glory a man can be endowed with. They're recycling the same arrogance as the French, and they're pounding it into the kids' heads that they're the world's most exceptional race because they defeated the French and the Japanese and the Chinese and the Americans. What they aren't teaching them is *why*. They don't tell them that thinkers prepared the revolution, but bandits are carrying it out. Do you know what the children are taught to read in school? Books where the word *American* goes along with the picture of a little girl pushing a big-nosed giant of a downed American pilot toward a cage at gunpoint. And you tell me to wait five fucking years until my son is fourteen and will shoot me on sight?"

"All right, John," he says so softly I'm not sure I've heard him. "Al tells me you're going over the wall with maybe six people, right?"

"Right. But not till I have certain basic information in hand. And not till I've got the right six people, and all the gear we're going to need to get the job done."

"So basically we're talking intelligence, recruitment, and supply."

"That's it, Arty."

"Okay, let's take intelligence. What do you need to know?"

"Thanh Hoa told me my son,—incidentally, his name is Le Hoand Hai—is being raised by the third-ranking member of the Politburo. I need to know who that is."

Arty stops in his tracks.

"She lied to you!"

"What do you mean?"

"The third-ranking member of the Politburo is in his seventies. I can tell you what he had for breakfast yesterday, John. He lives alone, I know for a fact. Hell, if I wanted to, I could mail him a postcard. I know his address and even the way his bedroom is furnished."

"*How* do you know?" I ask defensively, shaken by what he's telling me.

"You have to understand, John, that by now—ten years after we cut and ran—we've got plenty of stay-behind assets in Nam."

I haven't heard that Agency phrase for some time.

"It takes five to seven years to train and emplace an agent," he says. "Then they've got to live their cover for a reasonable period of time before they can become productive. Obviously, we have no Americans on site, but we've got some crackerjack Vietnamese operating in there, even some high-ranking cadres who perceive that the revolution has broken all its promises and that the old fascist police have been replaced by communist police. By now, I can get information into and out of Vietnam in a matter of hours. So when I tell you I *know* Number Three isn't raising your son, you simply have to take my word as gospel."

"Okay," I say, "so she could have been wrong. In that

case, I need to know which member of the Politburo *is* bringing him up."

"How about this? How about *none* of them?"

I stare at him.

"That's right, John! I'll get a double-check query in there before tonight, but from everything I know, not one of those men has your son. They're all in their sixties and seventies. They've got enough problems without trying to raise a nine-year-old Amerasian boy. Now, it's possible that the surrogate father could be a member of the Secretariat, maybe that's what this contact of yours meant. I'll check that out right away."

"I'm beginning to think Thanh Hoa's the key to this," I say. "Can you find out for me exactly what her position in the hierarchy is? How much power does she have? And where can I find her? She told me she's in charge of "supervising the building of a library to be named after Doan Thi."

"Can do!" he says reassuringly, and some of the panic I've been feeling since he shot down my image of the Politburo's Number Three raising my son begins to leave me.

"Maybe from her," I say, "I can find out why the Mât Vu is trying to eliminate me. That's something else your people may be able to dig out. What *is* this vendetta? Why *me*?"

"Now that one *is* fascinating," he agrees. "I've already got feelers working on that one. We *all* want to know, John, because that kind of wet work is becoming more and more frowned upon within the career infrastructure of the various intelligence agencies. All I can say now is that's most unusual. Any other items in the information arena?"

"None that I can think of at the moment."

"Okay, let's move to recruitment. Where are you going to find the men you want? I presume you're thinking only of Vietnamese."

"That's right," I say. "I know there must be a lot of Vietnamese here in Thailand I can make deals with. I've got a good-size supply of cash sitting right here in a bank to pay them with. But I want men with more motivation than just big bucks. I'm planning on contacting some of the Vietnamese who fought with me on my Black Mamba recon team. One in particular I'm thinking of for my One-One. Best jungle fighter I ever saw in action."

"Who is that?"

"You wouldn't know him, Arty. But I have an address for him in Bangkok. I plan to look him up as soon as I get the rest of my shit together."

"So you're in good shape in that department?"

"Not yet. But I will be in two more weeks."

"In case you're not, I give you two words to think about—*khang chien*."

"*Khang chien*? What's that mean?"

"We call them the KC—the Vietnamese resistance. They have at least ten thousand members in Vietnam—the United Front of Patriotic Forces for the Liberation of Vietnam. It's a growing force, John, and you and the KC might find that you have coterminous interests."

"I wonder if that's what Colonel Chutai meant when he mentioned 'certain elements' he might put in touch with me?"

"Chutai? Have you been to see *him*?"

"I have."

"John, I'm impressed. Talk about friends in high places! I'm beginning to get a little more optimistic about your chances. You've gone from zero percent to—well, at least you're on the scale now. Close to the bottom, but at least *on*."

"He said they might not want to work with an American."

"And he's right. They didn't do too well working with us before. This time they plan to try it on their own. But you never know. Shall I talk to them?"

"By all means!"

"All right," he says. "Now—supply."

By now we've walked all the way to the Gulf. I stare off to the south toward Bali, but my sight blanks out hundreds and hundreds of miles short of the mark.

"Supply—no problem," I tell him. "I've got the money—and the contacts—to buy whatever we'll need."

"Maybe I can help you, even there," he says. "We've got a few new gadgets that weren't around when you were in combat. Some of them are state-of-the-art, especially in communications. If you put it all together, John, and you do go in, I'll see that a couple of things are made available to you."

"How about a crystal ball?" I ask.

Together, we turn away from the Gulf and begin the long walk back to where the BMW waits with Gil and Toang on guard.

Even at this distance I can read the disappointment in their body language that no ambushers have risen from the salt beds to attack me.

CHAPTER

14

"**H**ow'd it go?" Gil asks as Toang speeds the BMW across the tessellated countryside inlaid with plateaus of salt glistening in the mid-day sun.

I glance back through the rear window at Arty's figure already small, almost obscure now in the distance, and I wonder how my famous mother would paint him at this moment—"Isolated Yankee on Thai Landscape."

I haven't thought of my mother since a few nights ago when I was treading water and reaching up out of the South China Sea toward the accepting stars. It occurs to me I've been neglecting her in my thoughts ever since I docked in New Caledonia as June was ending. What will she say when I arrive unannounced at the threshold of her Paris loft, turn the raspy buzzer on her door, stand waiting with one proudly poised arm around my son's shoulders, greet her in her paint-daubed artist's smock as she impatiently flings the door open, a rebuke on her lips for the tradesman who's dared interrupt her, then her startled face as she adjusts to the sight of me with the grandson she's not even aware she has?

"He got his shit wired or what?" Gil is asking.

"Well," I say, returning instantaneously from Paris to Thailand, "at the moment it's all spores and cuttings. No roots. But I think he'll be able to tell me things I have to know before I go in."

"Real inky guy. He really CIA?"

"Old-guard. One of Langley's monuments."

"What else you got scheduled for Day Two?" Gil asks.

"Where's Pak Nam from here?"

"For me, within farting distance. Just a few minutes from here—over on Route Three. You into crocs?"

"I don't copy."

"The Samut Prakarn crocodile farm in Pak Nam is one of the largest in the world. More than twenty thousand crocs out there, both the fresh and salt-water Thai variety. The trainers put on a helluva show for the tourists. And the crocs really work like hell. I guess they got the word that if they can't cut it onstage, they'll end up as a pair of boots. Ever eat croc, John?"

"I have a deal with sea-going crocs in this part of the world," I say. "I don't eat them, they don't eat me."

"Tastes like frog. So what's in Pak Nam?"

"Well, since the Mât Vu has temporarily lost contact with me—and since I'm in a holding pattern until Arty gets me some answers—I was just thinking I might as well start recruiting. You know anything about a Muay-Thai boxing camp in Pak Nam?"

"Yeah, one of the most famous in Thailand. You got somebody there?"

"Yes," I say. "A man who carried me on his back for hours the first time I got hit. Stayed with me until they dusted me up. This was soon after you finished your tour."

"All *right*!" Gil says. "Toang, you know where to go."

The man I'm remembering is Nguyen Van Hanh. He'll be in his mid-forties now, with a son who would have turned eighteen. I recall that Nguyen told me the boy was born the year before the '68 Tet offensive.

Of all the point men who ever served on my Black Mamba team, Nguyen was far and away the most gifted. He possessed the inborn stillness of the forest itself. He was at home among the rocks and trees and the animal life in the uncharted and frequently untracked wilderness of Laos. Nothing is more sepulchral than the crashing silence that descends upon you when you've been inserted into a denied area and your slick has zipped off and left you standing in hostile country. I see Nguyen often in my memories, fifteen yards ahead, depending on the density of the vegetation through which we were humping—closer, if line of sight was impeded—zigzagging low to the leafy floor, blending, scarcely breathing, giving off no sound, no smell, stopping for frequent, irregularly spaced listening breaks during which we all froze in place, avoiding ridgelines and the crests of ravines leading down to rivers, a green handkerchief daubed with black tied across his nose and mouth to keep out the pollen from the elephant grass which clogged your throat and lungs and crawled across your skin like maddened termites. I never saw him again after the morning I was hit, except to remember him helping them load me into the medi-vac. By the time my wounds had healed and I reported back to CCN, he'd been transferred from covert operations to one of the elite ARVN Ranger groups. I heard later he'd been involved in the September '72 action to retake Quang Tri from the NVA who rolled back the 3rd ARVN Division that Easter with three divisions and a gaggle of unexpected T–54 and PT–76 amphib tanks zonking down Highway 1 from the DMZ. Then I lost track of him until the late seventies, while I was into my macho street-cop number in San Francisco. One day out of nowhere his letter plopped onto my desk while I was working Homicide, and then we wrote back and forth from time to time. This address in Pak Nam is the most recent I have for him.

"What makes you think he'll sign on?" Gil asks, quite properly. "Who the hell ever wants to go back into Nam? Only reason I'd go in with you is because I'm as fucking crazy as you are."

"He'll never go back," I admit.

"Then what the fuck?"

"His wife and son were killed by artillery fire in Dalat during the final NVA drive to Saigon. It took him three years of writing to me and half a dozen letters before he finally admitted they were dead. The ink was smeared on the letter where he'd wept when he wrote me, and I could see where he'd tried to blot it up."

"Jesus!" Gil whispers, shaking his ponytail in a sudden waggle of sympathy which I find is all the more touching coming from such a grizzly bear.

"Anyway," I say, because you can't go on forever weeping for the dead, "through him maybe I can pinpoint a few other good men who need to go back for one reason or another. Or maybe, because he lost a son and I hope to find one, he may decide to come."

"Maybe," Gil agrees. "He's got a long-term vested interest in you. Once you save a guy's ass, you feel like he belongs to you from then on. Who knows, he might even let himself get suckered into saving you again."

"Let's find out," I say.

We arrive at the camp at an auspicious moment.

A new student, still a boy, still pencil-thin, clearly in the junior flyweight category, is undergoing the traditional rite of passage that all students must perform upon their acceptance into camp, the *khuen kruh* ceremony.

By American training standards, the camp is truly primitive, a clearing in the midst of tall betel palms and banana trees, with lean-tos open to weather, yet sheltering punching and kicking bags from the tropical sun and the monsoon rains. Thatched huts for the teachers, Quonset huts salvaged from the Burma campaign for student dormitories, a cooking center, and rough wooden tables and benches spread around the perimeter. Centered is the camp's provincial stadium Muay-Thai ring, open on all four sides, roofed over by a fluted, galvanized-iron peak supported by four palm logs. A white picket fence, as well-maintained as any in Maine, forms a rectangle around the ring itself. Wooden bleachers are built into an L along two sides of the ring, and folding wooden chairs, two rows deep, are set at ringside for the influential and the affluent.

But at this moment the stadium is deserted. The entire training camp attends the *khuen kruh* ceremony.

The boy stands alone, with awesome purpose and dignity, in front of a Buddha shrine. On all sides of him his newly issued Muay-Thai fighting gear has been precisely arranged, anklets, groin gourd, blue trunks, boxing gloves, bandages, armbands, mouth guard, and the sacred *mongkon*, a looped cord thick as a thumb, which all Thai boxers wear as a crown during their prefight ritual in the ring and which the handler lifts from the boxer's head before the combat begins, praying as he blows on the fighter's hair to invite good fortune during the punishing minutes which inevitably follow the gong for the first round.

Gil, Toang, and I come in quietly enough from behind the rows of silent, disciplined young fighters already in training. They stand behind the handlers and teachers. At the front of this phalanx of the faithful I discover Nguyen, clearly head instructor and master of the camp.

I study Nguyen, see his hooded eyes fixed on the boy undergoing the ceremony. Nguyen appears unmarred by the passage of time. He could still be frozen in place in the Laos bush, his ears so open to the sound of existence around him that he once asked me if I could hear the mountain frost melting in the morning sunlight. I listened hard, but heard nothing. Yet I saw that he heard.

The new student makes his offerings to the Buddha, flowers first, then a strip of white cloth, finally three coins and a joss stick.

His pledge is spoken to the Buddha, yet through the Buddha to Nguyen. "I come today," he whispers, "to worship the teacher. I solemnly promise to be your honest disciple. I will treasure all traditions, rules, and everything I will learn from you. I swear that my words are honest and are to be kept forever. Earth, heaven, and the four directions are my witnesses. With my body, my soul, and my words, I surrender to you and obey you as your disciple with the highest respect. I beg you to teach me everything you know, to help me succeed, to protect me from dangers, and bless me with love and happiness, forever."

The boy kneels in meditation. The other fighters and their teachers begin to chant, voices rising.

It is then that Nguyen turns his sharp dark eyes my way and I know that he has seen me from the beginning, seen me without looking at me.

Dear Buddha, give me six such men for the next thirty days and I'll bring you strips of white cloth, joss sticks, candles, votive gold-leaf paper, and flowers until the final moment of my life. More, I'll bring myself, all of me, as earth, heaven, and the four directions are my witnesses.

But certainly, I tell myself, if Nguyen trains young men in Muay-Thai techniques, he should have a few Vietnamese among his students. Or he will know whether or not other camps scattered around Thailand include Vietnamese boxers who might already have hung up their gloves, usually by the time they've reached their mid-twenties, but men who are still looking for action. The training turns out silent fighters, fighters who do not whimper or complain. The first thing a novice is taught is to ignore pain. No matter how much you hurt, you do not reveal your pain. You smile through it, ignore it, discard it, and you keep on fighting. Only the loss of consciousness or death in the ring is accepted as a reason for not staying in there and trying to kick the living shit out of the other guy. This is drilled into you every day and every night of your training for years: Pain does not exist. Say "I feel no pain." Now say it a thousand times a thousand times a thousand times until you no longer know what the word *pain* means and you wonder why you have to keep repeating a word you don't comprehend.

Of all the hand-to-hand combat styles I've studied over the years and had to use against all kinds of unfriendlies, even including the deadly *bando*, the Burmese boxing based on animal moves, I've never known any technique that doesn't run into trouble when it comes up against the Muay-Thai style.

Forget karate moves. While you're trying to decide which form to use out of the too many you've been taught and the few you may have mastered, a Thai boxer will break your ribs or cave in the side of your head, because his mind is uncluttered. He knows only a few moves and he will not reward you with a grimace or a groan if you hit him. He'll simply keep on coming at you. And coming. And coming.

Forget your typical European streetfighter, who charges in, like an asshole, straight at you, moving up and down.

Forget the flailing arms of the Hong Kong dock fighter.

There is simply no way of getting to a Thai boxer without using his own techniques against him. First of all you have to elevate your personal threshold of pain to the vanishing point. Once you've managed to hang up that problem, now spend the next few years concentrating on a few basic moves. Perfect them to the point where they become instinctive, part of your muscle memory. Work on your *dtai tao*, your roundhouse kick, and toughen your instep to the degree where it's more like the ball of a hammer than a human foot. Unhinge your waist and stretch out your lower back through years of exercise and practice so that you can torque your body almost ninety degrees while your ground-supported leg snaps you upward, bringing the thrusting knee of your striking leg up and around and into your opponent's kidney or rib cage or sternum, then leap up and smash him in the jawbone with your other knee. If he hasn't dropped in his tracks by then, he's not human. You work on your shoulders until they're so powerful, yet so flexible, that you can swivel your elbows one hundred and eighty degrees with such force you can drive them through a man's temple.

Nguyen detaches himself from teachers and students as the ceremony concludes. He hurries toward me, his face alight with the past, like a lantern glowing suddenly from within, and three feet from me he stops almost ritualistically, raises his palms, pressing them together, then lowering his head to meet the thumbs of both hands, showing me and all who may be watching the respect due from an inferior to a superior. I'm moved, yet embarrassed at the same instant, since the more appropriate *wai* would have been that which is used between equals, hands close to the body, fingertips reaching to neck level and not above the chin. I long to pull his hard, sinewy body into my arms and grasp him as a comrade I have never, never forgotten, but you do not embrace a Vietnamese. They are a society which does not approve of physical contact in public, particularly between men.

"I never dared hope I would ever see you again," he says.

"We've invested a lot of money in airmail stamps," I say. "The way rates keep going up, I figured it's cheaper to drop in."

I introduce him to Gil and Toang, then I ask if there's somewhere we can talk. Out of earshot of interlopers.

"But someplace Toang and I can keep an eye on things," Gil adds with overly dramatic emphasis.

"Are you in some danger?" Nguyen asks, naturally enough, since Gil has done everything but fall into firing stance.

"Not here," I say. "Not at this moment. But I will admit that lately the Mât Vu is giving me a hard way to go."

His face turns stony.

"The Mât Vu?"

"Afraid so," I say.

"Come with me."

I follow him through the camp, Gil and Toang tagging right behind. Nguyen leads me into a raised hut, a family of particularly small and black-spotted pigs snorting about the shady earth below floor level.

"We'll be right here outside," Gil announces.

The hut, I observe, is Nguyen's camp-home—a table

with a bench on either side, a narrow monastic cot with a night table, its tiny, tasteless plastic lamp with a broken, off-balance shade, a framed photograph of a woman and a boy, then boxing posters from the Rajadamnern Stadium in Bangkok tacked onto one wall. Even by Spartan standards the furnishings are meager, yet Nguyen appears oblivious of the self-denial crying out from his environment.

Must be that when you learn how to ignore pain you ignore other encumbrances, too, a whole invasive ganglia of attachments most of us invite like lovers.

Alone now with Nguyen, either for sentimental reasons or because I sense the need to sharpen my Vietnamese, I elect to speak to him in his language rather than in mine.

Communicating in Vietnamese is something like talking in cablese. Whatever you can conceivably leave out, you leave out. A typical sentence either has an understood subject or none at all. You talk in abbreviated wisps of thought, in broad concepts, avoiding the cutting edge, hinting at things, suggesting not delineating, leaving room for the mind of the other person to fill in the gaps according to his own perceptions, so that within a matter of five or six minutes, over hot tea, Nguyen and I have succeeded in headlining for each other most of what our letters over the years had failed to convey.

I know without having to ask that it is most unlikely he'll return with me to Vietnam. He is still bitter about the killing of his family, about the disgrace of defeat, especially since he had fought to the end, been captured, then been shipped off to a reeducation camp along with other ARVN officers and Saigon politicians. He has only scorn to this day for the "flower soldiers" of the ARVN, men who paid their superiors to allow them to serve in areas away from the combat zones and for the "gold soldiers" who hired others to serve in their places.

He tells me that in the prison camp he and fellow officers played games with cards and dice they made themselves, the dice molded from bread crumbs, the cards from scraps of paper. They melted tar from the walls of the huts with the occasional cigarettes they were able to buy from their captors. They then used the tar to mark the black spots on the dice. The red spots came from wrappings of the cigarette boxes.

Nguyen and two others managed to escape in the summer of '77, two years after he'd been imprisoned. They crossed Laos to sanctuary in Thailand. In the seven years since, he's succeeded in building one of the most prestigious Muay-Thai training camps in the country. His fighters have won both provincial and national championships.

Now—my turn. I tell him about the foolish game of death I was forced to play in Bali with Mât Vu assassins, about the ambuscade in the South China Sea, about the old crone with the Soviet grenade in the jackfruit, about the motorcycle run-by in front of the American Embassy—and about my son in Hanoi.

It makes one helluva package of complaints, I must admit, but in times when only the improbable can be depended upon, it sounds almost prosaic as I leach it out to its bottom lines in succinct Vietnamese.

"I'm looking for six men,—seven, actually,—to come in with me," I tell him. I hear the words coming now in English, possibly because I still think of the war in Vietnam as *our* war, not *their* war, a ridiculous point of view I've somehow never been able to shake, even though I know better.

"I need a point man, a jungle expert—like you," I continue, watching his face, finding nothing there to cheer me on. "I need a grenadier for the tail. And a radioman, a medic, and two all-around troopies who can step into any one of the other slots if they have to. And I need—don't laugh, Nguyen—a makeup artist to keep me looking Asian."

Bless him! He doesn't laugh. He doesn't even smile. Nor does he say anything. I can see it's all my ball.

"I don't have to tell you," I say, "that in war only the simple succeeds. And in commando ops, only the simplest of the simple ever makes it home. That's how I'm going to do this. Keep it basic, make it swift—insert, attack, extract. This will be a real LRC."

I haven't used that term for years—LRC—long-range extraction—we used to pronounce it *lurk*.

"Any comments?" I ask, for the silence begins to make my eardrums ache.

"You've been away from Vietnam for ten years, Captain," he says at last. "You have no concept of the society as it now exists. Almost everything you learned before is

118

changed. The country will appear as alien to you as the dark side of the moon. Your logistical problems alone will be insoluble. There is scarcely any public transport. Movement from one province to another is difficult, frequently impossible. The police are everywhere. Watchful eyes are everywhere. We are talking about a garrison state, Captain, where children are honored to inform on their parents. Honor is a vanished concept, except as it is applied by the ideologues to the revolution—honor to the state, not to your fellow man. You can trust no one. Absolutely no one! This conversation we are having—if we had such a conversation in Vietnam, we would be doomed!"

"What else can I do but try?" I demand. "If your son had lived—if they were holding him in Hanoi—would you *not* go in after him?"

The obvious answer dances in his intense eyes.

"Where can I find the men I need?" I ask. "Forgive me for putting a price on their help, but I have to offer *some*thing—and I have nothing else but money to offer. I'm paying ten thousand dollars to each man, payable in advance in Bangkok. I provide all the necessary gear and equipment. I arrange for the extraction and deliver the team back here. If any man fails to make it, I will pay an additional ten thousand—to his family."

"I'm sorry, Captain," he says, "but I suspect the kind of men who would agree to go in with you only to earn the ten thousand dollars are not the kind of men you want."

Suddenly I'm reminded of Al Wilson at the embassy and his "take the moral high ground" approach to the crisis situations of the mid-eighties. Nguyen is laying the same cant on me.

But at least he's talking from combat motivation, and goddamn it, he's right. So is Al. But that doesn't get me to Hanoi, does it?

"Who else *but* mercenaries can I enlist?" I ask him, as close to pleading as I've ever let myself come.

"No one," he says.

"Then I'll just have to settle for them. Can you point me in the right direction?"

"I'm afraid not, Captain."

Truly, I must look shocked, for I can feel the sudden

surge in my chest, the expansion of veins and arteries, the watering in my eyes. Nguyen is *what*? Saying no? Saying he can't help? Not even for chrissake *suggest*?

"But what about the KC?" I blurt out. "The Vietnamese resistance!"

"A figment of the CIA's imagination—and a propaganda ploy of the Politburo!"

"But I heard about them from a high-ranking Thai officer. They *must* exist!"

"If you heard about them from a Thai officer, then it's likely they're Thai agents of Vietnamese nationality who have managed to infiltrate Vietnam."

"You're giving me a pretty fucking bleak picture here," I say to Nguyen. It's the bluntest array of words I've ever permitted myself to speak to a Vietnamese, except, of course, to Doan Thi, who, as my enlightened and enlightening lover, demanded consistent forthrightness from me.

"There *is* no other picture, John," he says quietly.

Never before this moment has he used my Christian name.

He rises from the table, crosses to the door, opens and holds it for me.

Through the doorway I can see Gil and Toang waiting outside as zealously as rookie cops.

Rainclouds are bunching up in holding patterns to the northeast, like jets over Kennedy.

"I will pray for you," Nguyen says softly. "I have nothing else to offer."

═══CHAPTER═══

15

As we drive back to Bangkok I don't trouble to conceal from Gil and Toang my depression and growing sense of mania.

Nguyen's rejection ricochets in my mind. I never expected a rose garden, but this traditionally soft-spoken man from out of my past has been almost brutal in his admonishment that I forget about recruiting candidates for insertion into Nam.

"Fuck it!" I say aloud to nobody in particular. "I'll go in by myself! Stupid idea anyway to travel around in there with a goddamn war party!"

Gil tries to console me. "Relax, Shit Hook," he says. "Thailand's popping with jungle fighters. I'll fly you up to the Golden Triangle tomorrow. I've done business with most of the kingpins up there, especially this one honcho on the Burma border. You can take your pick from his private army—some really heavy dudes."

"Thanks, Gil, but that's exactly what I *don't* want—clodos who cock around with their fingers on the triggers. You know a good makeup man?"

"Only the best. Why?"

"When I go in, I have to blend. I better find out if I *can*. How soon can I meet him?"

"Tonight soon enough?"

"Tonight's fine. Meantime, I need to send a telex. Got my own unit aboard *Steel Tiger*. Mind stopping there?"

"I got the best fucking telex setup in Bangkok," Gil boasts. "Just down the hall from you."

"Then let's get back to the club."

I close my left nostril and begin to breathe forcibly through the right nostril.

"Mind telling me what the fuck you're doing?" Gil asks.

"You fart, Boss?" Toang asks from behind the wheel.

"You know goddamn well if I farted you wouldn't have to ask," Gil says.

"I'm producing greater EEG activity in my left brain than in my right," I tell Gil.

"You got *two* brains, Shit Hook?" He laughs. "That why you're so fucking much smarter than the rest of us?"

"We all have divided hemispheres," I say. "One is more verbal than the other—and one is more spatial."

"I wish I knew what the fuck you were talking about," Gil mutters.

"Three years ago," I explain, "trying to see if neuroscience could clarify some of the stuff I keep picking up in Asia from a variety of ancient disciplines, I volunteered at the University of California in San Diego to have measurements taken of my brain waves."

"Christ!" Gil laughs to Toang. "I wouldn't dare sign up for that kind of shit. What if they found I didn't have any fucking brain—left *or* right?"

"During the testing," I continue, for I see that Toang is fascinated, "I found that most of the time I felt depressed it was originating in my right hemisphere. So I learned how to recognize the way the rhythms of hemispheric dominance affect the mind and one's state of being. Simple breathing exercises can alter your mood."

Gil begins to look fascinated. "That why I start breathing heavy when I get a hard-on?"

"No way, man." Toang grins. "That's from right-hemisphere dominance in your balls."

Gil ignores this and concentrates on watching me breathing in through the right nostril only.

"How long you do that?" he asks.

"Five minutes, sometimes longer."

"Is it working?"

"Like magic. It's like a grass high. I can feel my associative feelings shifting into high gear—I can feel all my senses opening, as though an air-lock has been popped open in my head."

Even now, as I continue to pump air in through my

right nostril and see how apprehensively Gil watches me,
I find myself wondering how Bodhidharma ever managed
in the fifth century to come up with the same theories our
neuroscientists are pursuing fifteen hundred years later.
If you're a true student of the martial arts, you'll know
that Bodhidharma was the cat who came from India to
teach in China at the *Shao-lin* temple in Honan Province
and that while teaching there he became troubled by the
inability of many of the monks to remain awake while
meditating. To toughen them both in mind and in body
he devised the exercises which later became the primary
moves of *Shao-lin* temple boxing and ultimately the basis
for much of Chinese martial arts, exercises which later
were spread by the monks as *I-chin ching*. From this came
the Taoist deep-breathing techniques of *ch'i kung*.

I open both nostrils.

I give Gil a smile, wide and free of plaque.

"Seconds ago I was depressed. Now my optimism is
unquenchable. You see, Gil, the best things in life *are*
free."

By now Toang has reached the Thonburi side of the
Chao Phya River. He turns off Wuthakat Road into a
freight area alongside the Mae Klong Railway tracks and
stops directly behind the delivery van that had spirited
me out of the T. and A. Club early this morning. It sits
there in the empty yard, its back panels already opened
and one of Gil's fearsome-looking Sikhs standing guard
at the entry.

"See you back at the club, Skipper," Gil says, grinning.

I jump out of the BMW and into the waiting van.

The Sikh slams the panels after me. A moment later
I'm rattling around in the back as the driver wheels us
into Bangkok.

I'm thinking of Otis Walden, the man who'll be reading
my urgent telex before the night is over.

Since I said good-bye to Otis in New Caledonia not
quite two months ago, I've kept track of him and his five-
million-dollar motor yacht *Reckless Living*, a hundred-
and-fifty-foot Benetti. In late August he steamed out of
Nouméa, avoiding New Guinea, entered the Celebes Sea
via Molucca passage, stopped briefly at Tarakan in Borneo, then poked north into the Sulu Sea for what I'm sure
had to be a brief and timorous look, then west through

Balabac Strait and southerly to Bandar Seri in Brunei, where he's presently docked.

Only last year Otis Walden was dying of terminal pulmonary vascular disease until a team of Stanford surgeons, using cyclosporin-A and other immunosuppressive drugs, performed one of the world's first successful heart and lung transplants, delivering him, just as he turned forty, back to life for a second time around. Now Otis is traveling the globe, using his money and his luxury yacht to fornicate his way into the center of things. He is dedicated to the thesis that sexual behavior is the source of life itself and that the only way to understand any society is by understanding its sexual customs and practices. One of the most prestigious New York publishing houses has given him a two-million-dollar advance to deliver an in-depth nonfiction work documenting his sexual explorations and it was Otis's idea when he met me in New Caledonia that in return for his paying me a hundred thousand dollars I would transform his yacht into a paramilitary haven, so that after he had cuckolded the wives of Muslim sea-killers on the island of Jolo in the Sulu Sea, after he had seduced their daughters while they were away on their rites of piracy, he and the mercs I would have aboard could successfully resist any retaliatory attack the outraged pirates might send after him. At the time he made me the offer, I was amused by the daring of his concept. Certainly it would make exciting and lustful reading in what would surely turn out to be the publishing event of the century. But back in July I had other missions in mind.

Now I need Otis and his yacht.

Various plans and options for getting into and out of Vietnam keep bombarding me, but somehow, from the beginning, I have known that the key to any successful extraction always was Otis and his *Reckless Living*, for his Benetti can outrun anything Hanoi has in its surface fleet.

If he will support my lunacy, I will support his, even if it means helping him despoil the flower of the Sulu pirates' womanhood.

Pillage where pillage is due.

The van has come to a stop. I peer out through the front and see that we're inside the garage of the club, the street doors already closing us in.

The back panels open. The Sikh guard helps me down.

I thank him and hurry upstairs to where Gil is waiting in a communications center more sophisticated than some I've seen on our aircraft carriers.

I fire off my telex to Otis.

AGREE ASSIST YOU OUTFIT RECKLESS LIVING WITH PROPER EQUIPMENT AND PERSONNEL FOR MISSION WE DISCUSSED. FURTHER AGREE TO WAIVE FEE AND PER-FORM SERVICES WITHOUT REMUNERATION PROVID-ING YOU MAKE RECKLESS LIVING AVAILABLE TO ME FOR FORTY-EIGHT HOURS ON OR ABOUT OCTOBER 15. URGENT WE DISCUSS THIS SOONEST. CAN YOU FLY BANGKOK CONFIDENTIAL DISCUSSION THESE MAT-TERS WITHIN NEXT DAY OR TWO?

LOCKE

I include the selcall number for Gil's telex system.

Gil brings me the confidential long-range weather report the colonel has had the Royal Thai Air Force send over.

"Ten o'clock tonight okay to meet the makeup artist?" he asks.

"Sure. Where?"

"Downstairs in the club—I want you to get a look at him first. He's featured in the ten o'clock show. Then you can bring him up here and work out your deal—that's in case you're as knocked out by his makeup as I figure you're gonna be."

Gil seems to be savoring all this more than it merits.

"Not going to tell me any more than that about him?"

"That's right, Skipper. I want you to get the full, undi-luted impact. Like they say, first reactions are the ones that count."

He leaves me with a wink.

It occurs to me that since we've been together he hasn't farted even once. Self-denial? Bowel-wrenching suffering in my honor? Or is he at long last on the road to recovery?

Using Gil's lavishly stocked bar, I make myself a Freddy Fudpucker and settle down with it at the long conference table Gil has installed in the penthouse suite, along with an IBM PC, so I can pile up all the maps and data I've been acquiring and program into the PC whatever I need to program.

I pore through the weather forecasts for North Vietnam, both short-range and long-range. What I'm hoping for is storm-scale weather throughout the tenth lunar month. The Air Force predictions are right down that alley. They indicate a high probability of disaster warnings for the first ten days of October. The new technology used by the military is Nexrad—next-generation weather radar—a computer-controlled Doppler radar system that can measure not only the size and the intensity of a storm, but also its direction, windspeed, and precipitation. It's even able to detect the high-altitude, circular wind patterns that can generate tornadoes and typhoons.

Looking good.

As I savor the Fudpucker, I begin to formulate my shopping list for Laos and Vietnam. Two lists, actually. The supplies and ordnance I'll need to be able to hump across Laos and to avoid enemy patrols and to withstand the ravages of the natural environment during the monsoon rains is one kind of inventory. What I'll need once arrived in Vietnam is something else entirely. Yet there are requirements common to both areas. Problem here is to take everything that's needed, because you can't pop into a handy 7–eleven and buy what you're missing. Yet at the same time you have to keep the weight of what you're carrying down to no more than sixty pounds of gear per man. Too much weight on a man's back will limit the distance he can travel within a single day. Still, there are items that simply have to be carried, for if the moment comes you need one of them, you'd damned well better be able to lay your hand on it, or else die in place. It's the old for-want-of-a-nail-the-kingdom-was-lost syndrome.

Take a simple item of inventory—combat boots. In Laos at this time of year we'll be sloshing through wet terrain and flooded streams. That will bring on what we called in Nam "warm-water immersion foot." Immersion foot doesn't bother ducks, but it plays hell with a soldier's ability to keep humping ahead. Countermeasures include bringing along two pairs of special boots with drainage holes at the base and uppers made of nylon instead of leather. Add to that six pairs of quick-drying nylon socks and at least six tubes of silicone ointment.

Take weapons. Once I'm into Nam it's critical that all visible weapons be sterile,—that is, that they're the same type of ordnance in current use by NVA units. It's not cool to go prancing around Hanoi with an American M–16 slung over your shoulder, even though we left a million M–16s behind when we scuttled out of Indochina. Clearly, you're going to be a helluva lot less conspicuous carrying the standard AK–47. Even though the AK–47 is a pound heavier than the M–16 and has a slower rate of cyclic fire, you have to pay that price to avoid suspicious glances and the inevitable tap on your shoulder. Same problem if you want to bring along a sniper rifle. You'd better pack the Soviet SVD rather than our M–16, not only to blend in but because the SVD weighs five pounds less than the American rifle and those five pounds you're saving on that one item can be applied to other vital equipment. When it comes to selecting your light machine-gun you're stuck with the Soviet RPK. It weighs less than half the twenty-three pounds our M–60 weighs. That part's good, but in return you're losing at least two hundred meters of effective range by bringing it instead of the dependable American LMG.

But those are the tradeoffs.

As I tap them into the PC it strikes me that in the whole wide world of hackers the spreadsheet I'm working up may be the only one of its kind.

For whatever *that's* worth.

Voice from the doorway.

"Almost ten."

It's Gil, with one of those stretch-limo smiles.

His voice has interrupted me in the midst of my inputting the PC with a calculation of how much diethyl-toluamide I should bring on the mission. Diethyl-toluamide is a chemical ingredient used in all the better insect repellents. Since a repellent will have to be reapplied to exposed parts of the body every few hours for maximum effectiveness, and since the rain will be washing it off as fast as I can put it on, the calculation of how much D-T I'll have to bring along becomes an elusive one.

Downstairs, Gil and I are instantly surrounded by six of the club's security guards, who part the sea of tourists everywhere around us and surf us along disco waves of ear-splitting sound toward the sacrosanct corner booth, from which a throbbing neon sign transmits in sizzling crimson the flashing injunction: RESERVED . . . RESERVED . . . RESERVED.

"Like it?" Gil shouts into my numbing ear.

"Stylish," I shout back. "Really stylish."

"Had it made just for you!"

Gil and I settle into the booth, the six guards forming a vigilant semicircle between us and the crowd.

Lek waves to me from the semidarkness. Tonight she no longer struts in her mini-hot-pants. Instead, she wears a classic *pasin* and her black hair is combed out formally as though for a village wedding. She hangs in among a cluster of other dancing girls who are waiting to go up to their assigned platform. Everything about her proclaims her new, elevated status. She is sending out signals to all who care that she is not working tonight or any night remaining in the span of time I, her chosen lover, remain in Bangkok, nor is she available to the surrounding lechery, not even for a quick feel in passing. She lingers among her less fortunate girlfriends with an almost queenly detachment, yet she can't help moving her hips and shoulders to the surge of the music. She radiates the independence of a cabbie with his FOR HIRE sign switched off and windows up, doors locked.

Gil elbows me. I follow his nod, watch the twelve girls on the stage nearest us all stop simultaneously in mid-grind and patter off the platform, laughing and poking at each other as they sweep down the steps in a breeze of conflicting perfume and cologne and into the waiting arms of young men lining the long bar.

An announcer's voice commands our attention. Yet no master of ceremonies is in sight. I assume it's all being engineered from the dance mixer's rainbow-neon-and-glass-encased bubbly booth at the far end of the club.

"Ladies and gentlemen," the voice says, "tonight we are honored to bring you the eight most beautiful girls in Asia. Each of these girls has won her title in her own country as the loveliest flower of her land and we have spared no expense in bringing these magnificent girls here tonight—for *you*. . . . First—Miss Singapore . . ."

A breathtaking creature with her bouncy black hair cut

short flounces onto the stage. She's wearing the sarong kebaya of a hostess for Singapore Air Lines. She takes her place to one side of the stage as the crowd whistles and applauds her beauty.

"Miss Indonesia..."

The applause grows in volume, for Miss Indonesia somehow manages to cause all eyes to abandon Miss Singapore and to concentrate on the newcomer. She takes her place to the opposite side of the stage.

"Miss Malaysia..."

I now find myself among the demonstrators.

Miss Malaysia is—without question, without doubt, without equivocation—the single most beautiful girl I have ever seen.

She floats up the stairs with the grace, yet the vital coltishness, of a young antelope. I could encircle her wasp waist with my hands, fingertip to fingertip. She's wearing a purple chiffon gown which she elevates delicately as she comes up the steps, revealing ankles exquisitely turned, fine and slender, created for Bedouin lords to adorn with diamond anklets. Her entire body is fine-boned and delicate, giving her a wraithlike elegance. Her thoughtful dark eyes look out at us almost pleadingly, as though beseeching us to forgive so much beauty in one person.

Gil's voice intrudes. "So what do you think?"

"Who is she?" I shout into his ear, for the applause has not diminished, especially since Miss Malaysia, as though embarrassed by so much acclaim, gently swings her head and splashes her long black hair over one perfect shoulder.

"Your makeup man," Gil shouts back.

CHAPTER

16

With a sense of anxiety, a mounting nervousness, I await Miss Malaysia in Gil's penthouse.

He has reacted to my slack-jawed astonishment that Miss Malaysia is not female with more sensitivity than I've credited him with having.

"Go back upstairs," he'd said. "I'll bring Arun up as soon as the show's over."

What am I afraid of? I'd asked Gil to find me a makeup man.

Jesus, what makeup artist could possibly ever be more talented?

Am I afraid of having felt a naked and instantaneous sexual desire toward another man, given the circumstances that the image he'd presented was deliberately deceptive, an image which scrambled and confused my erotic senses? And if so, why does my hand still tremble? Because I was so easily taken in? Because my perception of what is male and what is female and what I permit to arouse me and what I deny took a roundhouse kick in the balls?

At the heart of tonight's experience is one of those abiding core truths which every now and then, if we're lucky, leaps out of the darkness and grasps us by the throat and bites us deeply, like a hungry Dracula infecting us with an immortality of understanding.

I ask myself questions I cannot answer. Is sexual attraction toward another human an ordered edict of chromosomes—two X chromosomes in your cells make you female, one X and one Y make you male—and the only ordained formula is XX into XY? Or is the whole sex ritual simply one more of nature's scams, one more ineluctable subtlety we try to flatten out by social attitude?

The sight of a girl's slender ankles invariably warms my groin. Yet I can look at a boy with slender ankles and feel nothing. Why? Because I don't allow it, is that it? Do I by training or by instinct abort the message before it is delivered?

Tonight I looked at a boy with slender ankles, but because I *thought* he was a girl, I would eagerly, given the chance, and still thinking he was a girl, have made love to him. Is that what sexual desire is? The bombardment of acceptable images which trigger our lust for another? And where are those images formed? Are we in no more control of our impulses than the drones that soar into the sky in pursuit of the queen bee's mating signal?

Suddenly I remember a morning on the beach at Coronado Island in San Diego Bay. I'd spent an ardent night away from my father's home with a girl I'd met at a bar. She'd been wearing a high-neck fluffy collar like something out of a Rembrandt painting. We'd gone back to her place on the beach and in the darkness I made love to the image of her chestnut eyes and her petulant lips. No doubt about it, what I'd fucked mechanically that night was not this girl, this stranger, this collection of XX chromosomes. I'd fucked her eyes and her lips. And now at dawn light we woke up laughing and in the semidarkness decided to rush out onto the beach and body-surf until sunup.

Hand in hand, naked as new coins, we ran onto the beach. As we ran, I glanced over happily and discovered for the first time that her neck was thicker than mine. She had the neck of an athlete—a man's neck—the neck of a linebacker. Her head and neck appeared to be one piece, not separate units of anatomy, and the shock of seeing this, the aesthetic violation of my personal taste in women, a taste which, among many other things, calls for a thin, graceful neck, froze me in the dawn sand. I stared at her with what must have been the cruelest candor, indictment radiating from every pore. And I remember with a sense of enduring shame that her hand crept slowly to her neck and as she stared at me tears began to form in her eyes, and I ran back to the apartment, threw on my clothes, and never saw her again.

Gil enters with Miss Malaysia.

Paradoxically, he is even more exquisite here in the harsh real light of the apartment than he appeared in the wash of the stagelights.

Now I see something I'd not even noticed downstairs. He has the breasts of a young girl, rounded and firm and protrusive, not a man's breasts pushed forward by tape. The strong nipples poke the chiffon.

I'm hopelessly confused.

"Skipper, Arun Samphan."

Miss Malaysia bestows upon me a distinctly feminine *wai*, long, tapering fingers upraised below a dainty chin.

"Please," I say, feeling strangely at a loss—a loss for what? Words, actions, attitudes? "Please—sit over there."

The young man crosses in high heels like a princess and settles into a chair. I notice how tiny are his feet, the usual giveaway with a transvestite.

"I'll leave you two alone," Gil says, rather wickedly, it occurs to me. The sonofabitch!

"No!" I cry. If it isn't a cry, it's a definite appeal for help. "No," I say, with more control the second time. "I'd like you to stay, Gil."

I can see how much he's enjoying himself. No way was he planning to leave.

He pulls up a chair, sitting in it with his big chest pushed against its delicate teak back, settling his chin on the carved ebony top, and waits for me to put my foot into anything convenient.

"Would you like a drink?" I ask Miss Malaysia.

"No, thank you."

"Well," I say, settling across from this vision, "I have to tell you, the makeup job you've done on yourself is strictly first-class. But in order for me to—to get a better idea of what you started with—could I ask you to—to show me what you look like—when you're *not* onstage?"

Miss Malaysia glances over at Gil and speaks to him softly in Thai. I can't help noting that the voice quality is more that of a girl than of a boy.

"Shall he take everything off, he wants to know?"

"I don't think that's necessary," I say. "I just want to see what he looks like as a man."

"This isn't going to be too easy on you, Shit Hook," Gil warns. "But you're the boss."

Gil turns to Miss Malaysia.

"You may speak English, Arun. I'd like the skipper to hear how well you speak it. Arun's grandmother was English," Gil adds for my benefit.

"Very well," Arun says.

He stands and first removes the wig he's wearing. It doesn't come free easily, for his own hair, I discover, is shoulder-length, full, and dark, and blended into the fall. Next he slips the gown from his shoulders, letting it fall to his tiny waist, exposing a girlish upper body with a flat, molded stomach and small, but magnificent, French-classical breasts, my mother would call them, like the breasts Noyer paints on his nymphets.

"You see," Arun says, "my own hair I've let grow. And I've had breast implants, so that the upper half is very much a woman."

He starts to wriggle the gown below his hips.

That much research I don't feel is called for.

"It's okay," I say, much too hastily. "I think I know what the rest looks like."

"Unfortunately," he says, "my genitalia are still male. But I've been saving my money for the surgery that will finally let me be the woman I've always been—trapped in a male body."

"Point of fact, Skipper," Gil says. "I told Arun you're paying ten grand to everyone who goes in with you. That's his motivation for coming along—to make that kind of money so he can fly up to Japan and come back with a cunt of his own."

"I suppose that sounds crass," Arun says, "especially since Mr. Hamlin has told me you're going to Vietnam to find your son. But you have no idea the anguish I've felt ever since I was old enough to realize that I'm truly a woman, not a man, and that only some terrible divine mistake put my woman's heart and spirit into a man's body. If I can't be what I know I am, then I don't wish to continue living. So if I am to die in Vietnam, I will die—but trying. And the gods will let me come back next time without being deformed."

"You'd have to go in as a girl," I say after a long moment, for the young man's intensity of feeling looms like a monument among us. "No way you're going to convince anybody you're anything else."

"Just don't take a leak standing up," Gil laughs.

Arun smiles graciously at Gil's grossness. His smile is so soft, so radiant, so womanly, it makes my heart jump. The man is definitely fucking up the order of things.

"So you play a nurse," I say, the idea hitting me out of nowhere. "A Vietnamese army nurse. Can you speak Vietnamese?"

"A little. But I will learn whatever else you feel I need to learn."

"Okay, now the big question. You think you can make me look Asian enough so that I don't stand out like a billboard?"

He approaches me, his bare breasts close to me, and studies my features. He touches my nose with one probing, exploratory finger. He's wearing Opium perfume. His touch, the softness of his chiffon, the heady scent of the perfume, are definite distractions from the norm. He suggests infinite possibilities simply by his proximity. He lifts one corner of my right eye and studies with an almost feline concentration the look of me with a more slanted eye. He peers at my lips. His breath smells of fresh cloves.

"We'll have to make some tests," he announces. "But I think I can work miracles with you. We'll have to make a prosthetic nose, dye your hair, your skin, fit you with brown contact lenses. Only your height concerns me."

"I've been thinking about that," I reply. "With you as my assigned army nurse, me as an officer wounded in Kampuchea—and putting me into a wheelchair—we might have something going, once we get into Nam. At least, I've been toying with that kind of scenario."

"I can start Saturday, if you wish," he says. "It will take a little time to get the nose made. And we should probably make some spares. I'll first need to make a plaster cast of your face. Then I can work from molds until I have something to show you."

I hold out my hand. Arun takes it.

"Thank you," I say. "You give me hope. Not many others have since I arrived in Bangkok."

"You give me hope too," he says. "May I tell you a story before I leave?"

"Certainly."

Thank God he raises the straps of his gown and covers his breasts. My confusions have been in continuous overdrive for too many minutes since he dropped the gown to his waist.

"Many of my transvestite friends find it difficult to understand why I am so determined to have my operation. They shudder at the mere thought of emasculation. I try to explain to them—as I would like to explain to you— that I have no fear of the surgery because I have a higher purpose—for I know that the gods made women to be nobler than men. I always tell them the story of Combabus, who lived in ancient Syria. When Stratonlike, the wife of the Assyrian king, decided to go off on a pilgrimage to build a temple, the king assigned his dearest friend, Combabus, to be her protector on the pilgrimage. Combabus begged the king not to send him, for he was afraid of being alone for so long a time with such a beautiful and tempting young woman. But the king persisted. So before he left, Combabus, in the presence of six witnesses, handed over to the king a small sealed box with the request that the kind would keep it faithfully, since it contained the single most valuable possession that Combabus had. Accordingly, the king sealed the box and gave it to the royal treasurer to safeguard. Then Combabus went off with the queen and everything he feared came to pass. The young woman fell in love with him and he repulsed her advances. Rejected, the queen sent letters to the king falsely accusing her companion of seducing her. The king ordered his friend returned and thrown into prison to await execution. When the day of trial arrived, Combabus asked the king to open the box entrusted to him, since it contained absolute proof of his innocence. When the king found the seal untampered with, he opened the box and found within the embalmed genitals of his friend. The king began to weep and he embraced Combabus and awarded him the highest honors in the kingdom. Later, he erected a bronze statue of Combabus shown in man's dress but with the figure of a female. Since I was a child, I have thought of that ancient story over and over again. But now, thanks to modern surgery, I do not have to suffer and remain a statute. I can be a flesh-and-blood loving woman. Not some verbal little bitch complaining about men, but a true woman. I thank you, Mr. Locke, for giving me the opportunity."

I'm not really up to an adequate answer. A disturbance

outside my door saves me from having to improvise a reply less elegant than Arun's statement of purpose.

The guards open the door and admit Lek.

She growls something in Thai to Arun.

Arun snaps back at her in Thai.

Gil gets up from his chair.

"Okay, okay," he says. "This isn't the time or place. Let's leave them, Arun."

Arun bows to me, hands again raised in a *wai*, then with Gil he slips out as softly as a silk scarf fluttering from a hanger.

"No trust that one!" Lek exclaims as Arun closes the door behind him.

"Why not?"

"If you take shame for what you are, what *are* you?"

"A fighter maybe?" I suggest. "Somebody who wants more than what they're born with—or who wants something different from they have? We call that, in the States, upward mobility."

"You *like* her, don't you?" Lek says accusingly.

"My personal feelings aren't involved here," I explain. "I'm hiring Arun to render certain unique personal services."

"What means 'unique'?"

"Special."

"Make love to you!"

"No. No lovemaking. Not Arun and I. Strictly business."

She continues to appraise me with suspicion.

"We have saying where I come from," she says. "Husband who cheat on wife better sleep on stomach."

Suddenly she grins, the impish corners of her full mouth flashing up like a schoolgirl's arm in class.

"Village I come from, two years ago, wife catch husband fucking other girl. She wait. When he sleep on back, foolish man, she come with knife, cut off his cock. She run to window and throw cock into yard. Big flock of hungry ducks in yard. Ducks fight for cock. Husband screaming he wants cock back. Maybe doctor can sew on again. But too late. One duck swallow cock. Who know which duck? Hundred ducks in yard. Newspaper in Bangkok run story on front page. With big picture. Show one hundred ducks in picture. Newspaper make big X over one duck. Headline say, 'He Swallow It.' But they just guessing."

As she tells the story she is more and more overcome with laughter, until she collapses on the bed and rolls over and over in a frenzy of girlish mirth. I find it hard to join in. Somehow I identify with the poor bastard who lost his manhood to a duck. It ranks among the leading horror stories of the world, one that even outclasses the terrifying output of Stephen King.

Her laughter stops as suddenly as it's begun.

She removes her *pasin*, lets it flutter to the floor along-side Gil's immense bed. Naked, she slides on her knees to the pillows and lifts her hands in obeisance. I hear her whispering in Thai. I am not familiar with this custom, nor have I seen her perform this rite the previous nights she's come to sleep with me.

When she's finished, she glances around at me through the screen of her black hair.

I ask her about her prayers.

"No prayers," she says. "I pay respects to my parents and to the moon. Please, now you make love to me—and don't pretend you make love to Arun."

"Greedy, aren't you?" I tease her. "Not only the body,— you want the mind too. The thoughts, even."

"Yes," she whispers. "So foolish girl."

I feel back in control again.

An XY with a double-X.

CHAPTER

17

I'm awakened by the drilling of rain on the roof.

My first thought is for the sentries Gil has posted up there.

Clearly, the longer I hang around Bangkok, the more of a monumental pain in the ass I'm going to be for a lot of people.

What is this, Thursday morning? Yeh, my fourth in town—Thursday, the fifth of September. I intend to cross the Mekong River into Laos no later than Sunday, the fifteenth. Here I come, ready or not.

Like Arun, I'm in transit, a man long past the point of no return.

I glance over at Lek. She lies alongside me to the left, like a corolla awaiting the first touch of sunlight.

A woman must never, never sleep on the right side of her man, she informed me our first night alone together. I asked her if she knew why. She didn't, but her father had taught her that when she found the man she cared for, she must teach him this if he didn't already know. So I explained the reason—in days of old when you had no one to defend you except yourself, you needed to have your right hand free to draw your sword. You didn't want your arm numb and bloodless from your woman sleeping on it all night long.

I slide out of bed and onto the floor and start to work on my lower abdominals. I lift my legs six inches off the floor and flutter them thirty times, then I cross them back and forth another thirty times, and finally flutter them from side to side thirty times more to fatigue my lower abdomen.

Now, as though working up the steps of a ladder, I lift my legs, toes pointed at the ceiling, and bend my knees back into my stomach. I extend my legs again and reach up with them, aiming at the sound of the rain pounding above me. Never touching the floor, I repeat this exercise fifty times to stress the muscles higher in the stomach.

For the upper stomach muscles I place my feet on the seat of a chair and do sit-ups, elbow to knee, elbow to knee, for another count of fifty until I begin to feel the familiar and rewarding burning in my obliques.

Next, the pulse—alternating push-ups with running in place, then into squats and squat thrusts. When I've got my heart pumping at max, I switch to jumping jacks. These are quite miraculous when it comes to cooling down. Then I ease into a tranquil yoga stretching routine which I cap off by running my meridians with a massaging, probing hand, tracing the fourteen major meridians and popping any energy blocks free.

I conjure up the sensory image that now all my internal systems are flowing in circles, billions of tiny cellular planets within my personal cosmos, each in concord with the circularity of the earth itself as it rotates along its timeless curving track. Since my childhood and my first startled observation of the tiny little water bugs that dwell in the rim of manhole covers, bugs who can roll themselves into hard little ochre peas, I have found this concept of imagining myself in circular motion to be more magical than perceiving myself as some awkward, spastic, linear figure, isolated against space, thrust up like a matchstick in the sand. I've been told, though I have no data to substantiate this, that at the precise instant the male sperm hits the female ovum, the conjoined unity begins a counterclockwise dance, circling and circling until the lifeform emerges.

Quietly I make myself tea, since Lek is volubly enjoying a dream, whispering in Thai, and smiling in her sleep. With tea and toast I take my regular Thursday morning five hundred milligrams of Chloroquine, augmented by Fansidar. Since I find myself mucking about areas where malaria is endemic, this once-a-week dosage is more important than food or sleep. In Nam we used to gulp

down Dapsone for malaria, but I find the newer Chloro-
quine-Fansidar combo more effective, providing you're
not allergic to sulfa drugs.

And so Day Four begins.

Gil personally brings me the telex just in from Otis
Walden in Brunei.

Otis is flying into Bangkok tomorrow.

He'll meet me at the Oriental Hotel. Dinner in his suite.
Eight P.M.

"Toang and I'll take you," Gil says. "Once we deliver
you to his suite, we can make damned sure nobody interrupts you."

"Keep mothering me like this," I say, but not without
gratitude, "I'm liable to get so used to it I'll lose my edge."

The alert light on Gil's elaborate surveillance console
begins blinking like a clown's nose.

Gil flips the appropriate switch. Toang's earnest image
flickers into focus on one of the glass panels.

"Delivery van in the alley—just outside the loading
zone," Toang announces. "Driver says he's got three fifty-
pound sacks of salt we ordered."

"We didn't order any fucking salt!"

"That's what I told the dude. But he said he was told
to deliver the sacks to—and I quote—'*your guest*'."

Gil's eyes snap over, fix on mine. He looks as gleeful
as a black panther with an antelope in its jaws.

"Well, now, does anybody really think we're that fucking stupid we're gonna open up and let 'em haul three
fifty-pound sacks of *anything* into our loading area without our checking out what the fuck's really in those sacks?
They think they can just drive up and lay it on us that
simple, blow the goddamned club off the foundations.
Jesus!"

"I already blocked off the street at both ends," Toang
says. "These mofus ain't goin' nowhere but *down*!"

"Nice move," Gil says, warming to it. "But let's go to
the next step. Have some of our associates bring that
driver inside—the one that mentioned '*our guest*.' I want
you to stick a submachine gun up his ass and hold it there
on rock and roll till I get through asking him some questions. And if he's got any buddies outside in the van, tell
them in whatever fucking language they speak that

whoever moves is dogmeat. Then send Hercules out there to sniff over those sacks. Coming right down!"

"Affirm," Toang says, and disappears from the TV screen. Gil snaps off the power switch.

"Hercules?" I ask.

"My German shepherd. He can sniff out bombs and dope through a cement wall. Sleeps at my feet and never complains when I fart all night long. I love that fucker. If he was a bitch, I'd marry him."

He starts to pound out.

"Gil," I call.

"Yeah?" he says impatiently from the doorway.

"Arty could have sent those salt bags."

"What for?"

"I don't know, but he must have a good reason."

"Well, Shit Hook, I know you're the expert, the master strategist, the fucking brains of the operation, but I'm here to tell you I've been expecting some dumb-ass move from these cocksuckers. They've been trying to penetrate our security ever since you zapped two of their boys in front of the embassy, and they just can't hack it. So now they figure they'll blow us off the map. Poor sorry bastards—playing in the wrong league!"

He hurries out like a kid eager to drown kittens.

Lek is sitting up in bed, watching me.

"My father warrior like you. He fight Communists when he in army. These men who want to kill you—they Communists too?"

"Possibly."

"Gil say is great danger. All of us must keep eyes and ears open. He make me promise I never speak your name when I leave club every day. Say if anybody know I sleeping with you, maybe they try to make me hurt you. I die first."

There it is again, the loops that form around me wherever I go, that form around those who come close to me.

"Gil tell me better I take my baby home to my parents so bad guys don't steal baby, make me bring knife here and cut your throat when you sleep. I take baby home yesterday."

"Your baby?"

"I show you picture when I get up. Now I want to make love again."

"Show me first."

Naked she slips from bed, crosses to a side table where she's left her purse. She brings out a wallet and comes to me, lifting her wide lips to mine. I'm surprised by the freshness of her mouth after our long night of lovemaking. She selects three Polaroid prints from the wallet and exhibits them proudly.

The child is not yet two, I'd guess, a tiny, delicate girl with spindly legs and laughing eyes.

"No nickname yet. Her name Suporn—means good blessings."

"Where is her father?"

"He farm boy. Still on farm at home. No like city. I no like him. But I love my baby. Would you believe I make love with him only once and I get baby? But I don't know then what I know now. No more baby. Just fun. You come back in bed. Good make love while rain on roof."

"Gil will be back any minute."

"Lek make love with *you*, not with Gil. He come back, he wait till we finish."

She giggles.

"Maybe he even learn something."

Her statement has primal logic. In Asia, where things are usually multifaceted, you must learn not to overlook the primal.

I return to bed with Lek.

Our timing is impeccable.

Lek is singing in the shower when Gil returns.

He's holding a salt-covered envelope in his hand.

"No bomb," he announces, scattering disappointment about him in the manner of a dog shaking its fur when it comes out of the sea.

"Only this envelope. Addressed to you."

I open the envelope. The note inside is from Arty.

He's already got the first fragment of information he promised me out of Vietnam. I can only conclude he used satellite–to–ground-saucer communication to come up with anything within the twenty-four hours that have passed since we met at the salt basins. It's critical, his note continues, that he share this preliminary information with me ASAP, since it indicates grave complications. He provides an address and a sketch of where one of the

Agency's latest safehouses is situated in Bangkok. He'll meet me there at noon tomorrow.

I hand address and sketch over to Gil.

"Across the river," he says after a moment's study. "Along one of the principal canals, Kong Bangkok Yai. . . . Why the fuck didn't he just call this in? Why all the hocus-pocus with the fucking salt bags? Shit, Hercules has salt up his kazoo from poking around in those bags."

"Could be Arty was afraid that if he called, somebody might be listening in. Your lines could be tapped, you know."

"Jesus, that's right. I never thought of that."

"I've seen some of the new surveillance devices, Gil, so state-of-the-art they're downright scary. There's this one device that can pick up and translate the impulses from computers in a building across the street. I mean, you can just sit there in your van with your instruments and run off a printout of everything the other guy's putting into his IBM. Arty knows about that kind of shit, so he must have decided to do a real old-fashioned cloak-and-dagger number—and send the note in with some salt bags."

In spite of himself, Gil chuckles.

"Like a fuckin' movie, ain't it?"

"Isn't everything?" I ask.

"Okay, we'll leave here at eleven hundred hours tomorrow. You in the panel truck, Toang and me in the BMW. But this time we won't switch you out of the truck. We'll go straight on to the safehouse, with Toang and me riding shotgun for the truck. Tomorrow sounds promising, huh, Skipper? Maybe the Mât Vu's figured out our little scam by now and will try to fuck us over. Wouldn't that be sweet? Give me a chance to field-test my new Ithaca ten-gauge Roadblocker. Oh, shit, man! Let's just *hope*!"

"Let's hope *not*!" I say with a note of reproach. The bus of my conscience is already overloaded. I have neither seats nor desire for additional passengers. Especially not this exuberant friend.

Gil rushes out to prepare for tomorrow morning's cavalcade.

Above me I hear the rain noisier and heavier, attacking the roof like maddened killer bees.

Lek appears from the bathroom, a towel wrapped around her at the breasts.

She stands a moment, one ear tilted toward the ceiling, and listens to the drumming above us. She glances over at me.

"You go out today—in this?"

I shake my head.

"I'm on stand-down till tomorrow."

"Stand-down?"

"I wait."

She smiles like a kid who's just won the big stuffed pink elephant at the fairgrounds. She drops the towel and playfully rushes across the penthouse and dives into the bed, her laughter louder than the rain above us.

I think, what prodigy! She reminds me of myself in my nineteenth year in Paris when I was trying to fuck everything in sight. My mother admonished me about the condition of too much sex—"*toujours perdrix*," she called it, partridge at every meal. If one continues such excesses, she pointed out, one can soon tire of what can be, approached with more selectivity and less compulsion, a lifelong joy.

But then, my mother is an aesthete and an artist.

She is neither aware nor interested that our biochemists have isolated and identified the peptides that are released into our bloodstreams at the moment of orgasm. She has never heard of a hormone called oxytocin, which is pumped by the pituitary when one goes over the top and acts directly on the mammary gland. The entire number, of course, is choreographed by the dependable old hypothalamus. As even the uninformed are aware, the reflex of orgasm produces a most contented feeling and an agreeable change of mood.

My mother does not know the whys and wherefors of such arcane matters.

Neither does Lek.

The fact that I do, however, in no way diminishes the recurring floods of contentment Lek causes my hypothalamus to order out all through Day Four and the night that follows.

I almost feel nineteen again.

CHAPTER

18

Thursday's rainbursts cover central Bangkok with three feet of water.

By Friday morning, even the gaudy high-wheeled Thai lorries, embellished along their sides with such symbolic Buddhist daubings as prescient blue eyes staring from the middle of raised brown palms, are stranded along the flooded streets. Taxis loll like manatees in the rivers eddying between office buildings.

Gil rouses our war party an hour earlier than we'd planned the night before. He knows a circuitous but comparatively dry route. With a city map he shows the two Sikhs who are to shepherd me in the van how we'll proceed in single entrainment away from the city, southeast on the expressway, then work our way back in a westerly loop until we can head north again once we're on the other side of the Chao Phraya River, when we'll come onto higher ground in the Thonburi section and can make our way toward the Klong Bangkok Yai.

Gil estimates we can negotiate the watery course in just under two hours.

I watch him as he joyously hands over to the two Sikhs a pair of Heckler and Koch MP5 9mm Parabellum submachine guns fitted with silencers. He gives each man three 30-round detachable box magazines.

"Anybody fucks with us," he says, "hose 'em down! If you can't fire 'em up with ninety rounds apiece, I swear to Christ it's off to the Punjab with both of you!"

In the back of the van I find the next two hours an

endless succession of stops and starts, advances and delays, but after the first hour or so the darkness lifts as the rain blows off to the north and a sifting of sunlight can be seen ahead through the windshield.

When at last I feel the final lurching of the van as it stops and the engine is turned off, I move to the back panels. One of the Sikhs opens them and bright noon strikes my eyes.

I step out, the Sikhs now to either side. The BMW is parked only feet away, both Toang and Gil already out, Toang holding a third HK-SMG, Gil with his brand new Ithaca alley-sweeper.

The four men fan out in front of me. I note with approval that under Gil's orders they move like real troopies, properly separated, two of them combing the canal front, two of them surveying an ominously silent two-story Thai residence. Apparently Gil has been able to drive us straight onto the secluded grounds. I take some reassurance from the sight of an armed American in civilian khaki even now securing from inside a high metal gate with strands of barbed wire clustered above it.

The grounds extend onto the canal. A wrought-iron fence seven feet high and topped off with triple lines of wire closes the yard away from the canal. Even from where I stand, well back from the fence, I can both see and hear the busy water traffic sloshing up and down the *klong*. Directly across the canal, framed like a postcard photo in the boatgate on this side, a *wat* stands in the afterwash of the rainstorm, its usually stark red and orange colorings now softened and run into each other like a watercolor left out in weather. To the right of the safehouse, kept at bay by the fence, a grove of coconut palms interspersed with banana trees extends back from the canal deep inland, while to the left huddles a dark and crumbling shell of a factory. Workmen with kerchiefs around their foreheads are bent with muddy hands over wet, spinning forms, modeling and shaping earthen water jars. Other workmen squat in front of the finished product and paint traditional designs onto the clay before the glazing process that follows. Even from here I can feel the hot reach of the fired-up kilns.

It hits me right in the numbers that this is a piss-poor location for a *safe*house. It's a flytrap, vulnerable on three sides, from the waterfront to the sweeping flanks of palm grove and factory.

I can see that Gil, too, senses the danger of ambush. His eyes are scouring the greenery at the top of the palm trees, even as he glances back over his shoulder toward the factory.

"Put the glasses on that fucking roof," he calls to Toang. "Pranay!" he calls to one of the Sikhs. "Get over to the other side of the grounds, down behind that bench, and keep that factory covered. You see anybody pop up with a weapon in his hand and pointing it this way, slot him!"

A horn stabs three times from the driveway outside the grounds. The American guard peers through an opening. Satisfied, he unscrambles the chain he's used to secure the car gate. He walks the metal panels to an open position, admitting a drenched and battered-looking jeep. It speeds toward me, its tires flinging patterned mud chips in all directions. From behind the wheel Arty waves one of his painfully thin arms and slides the jeep to a stop alongside me.

"Been here long?" he asks.

"Five minutes," I say.

He grabs a briefcase from the seat next to him. I have never before seen a worn-out alligator briefcase. Arty's looks as though it's been worked on by sandpaper.

He waves to Gil and Toang, then leads me toward the back veranda of the house.

"Those buddies of yours are really six-checking you," he comments as I catch up to him.

"They're hoping for some action," I say. "If they get it, I hope to hell it's not here. Who picked *this* place as an Agency safehouse?"

"Some dumb motherfucker from Langley," he says, unlocking the glass doors that run along the veranda. "The kind of button-down asshole who's never been shot at."

He vanishes into the dark interior and I follow him.

As he opens the shutters and lets the noon brighten up the parlor, I decide that whoever acquired this particular residence as a trysting place for intelligence operatives is someone I wouldn't trust even to buy a Christmas tie for my worst enemy. There's not even a grand piano to duck under. It's all silk and brocade and objets d'art, like a

Thai cultural center. It lacks only a water font and dancing girls.

"We got troubles, John," Arty announces mercilessly as he snaps open his abraded alligator case and brings out his notes.

"New troubles?" I ask. "Or just more of the old ones?"

"The old ones are bad enough. Let's not even consider new ones. Let's start with your son, okay?"

I feel myself splitting off again, one part of me climbing back up there on the ceiling from where I can watch myself react to a roundhouse kick to the groin.

"Okay."

"If somebody's raising him, it's nobody in the Politburo nor in the Secretariat. That's *confirmed*, John!"

"Then—*who*?"

"We're going to have to work on that one. And it's going to take time. It means our people in the North are going to have to check out every single dust child."

"You're overlooking the shortcut," I say, more harshly than I've intended.

"What shortcut?"

"Thanh Hoa."

"I was just coming to her. We found her."

I'm sure my face lights up. At least, it feels as though it has.

"She's the key!" I say. "You found her, Arty! That's beautiful! *She'll* tell me where I can find my son."

"You told me she's got only one ambition in life—to terminate you. Not with prejudice but with the greatest of joy. Incidentally, I've always hated that stupid phrase 'terminate with extreme prejudice.' Frankly, John, I've never heard *any*body in the Agency—even the lads in wetwork—ever say it."

"No way she can kill me," I say, "unless I let her. I'll make a deal with her—take me to my son, let me at least see him, *then* kill me. If she can," I add.

"There's a complication."

"Oh?"

"Thanh Hoa's no longer in Hanoi."

"So? Wherever she is, that's where I'll go."

"She's in a reeducation camp in Nghe Tinh Province."

I give this the time it deserves, then I ask, "*Where* in Nghe Tinh Province?"

"Thirty clicks west of Vinh."

"I've heard of that camp," I say. "Survival rate in there is not too high."

"Then you have the picture. How long she can last is something our people hesitate to estimate. A month, some think, two months, others say. Nobody would optimize for three. My information is that she's in deep shit with the Mât Vu, so nobody's rooting that she make it back out. Obviously, when she blew it in Bali with you, she signed her own death warrant."

"All the more reason I have to bust her out."

"You realize what you're up against? When your mission was simply trying to get your son out, you were already off the scale of the achievable. Now you're into outer space, John, *without* a life-support system. You're talking about having to fight your way into a place you can never fight your way out of so you can find somebody who wants to kill you the minute she sees you. Doesn't any of that sound just a little irrational to you?"

"No more than the things I did every day when I was in Nam."

"Well," he concedes, "if you want to put it into that context, I have to agree with you. Measured by *that criterion*, you have no problems at all."

The first ripple of automatic gunfire rattles the French doors along the back veranda.

Sounds like two or three AK–47s being fired our way from close range. From the factory.

The answering fire from Gil and his men instantly overlaps the hammering Kalashnikovs. The hideous booming of Gil's shotgun drowns out the crisp staccato of the smaller-gauge weapons. His cyclic rate of fire sounds hotter than that of a machine-gun.

I pitch forward, easing Arty down, as I scamper to a spot away from the French doors. From here I can look out at the grounds. With a life of its own, the Browning is in my hand.

One of the Sikhs lies without moving on this side of the fence adjacent to the factory. The other is behind cover and raking the roofline with his silenced SMG. He fires professionally, short bursts, three or four rounds with each impulse, and I can see silhouettes tumbling down after each burst.

Gil and Toang, I discover, are sheltered behind garden statues on the far side of the grounds. They're picking away at the upper terraces of the palm grove.

The American has collapsed upon himself like a dead spider, his khaki blotted with crimson. Apparently, he'd been trying to dodge his way into the house but had been cut down by crossfire from the roof of the factory.

I see one of Gil's loads tear the top fronds off a tree and a man who'd been up there only an instant before firing down at Gil rains in clots all down the trunk of the tree.

I've about made up my mind to go out the front door, through the car gate, and then to circle around behind the factory and spruce up the environment on that flank, when the glass windows disintegrate and a grenade bores through the parlor and implodes a wall in the adjoining room.

I can just make out the two men with their RPGs across the canal, pegging at us from the temple grounds. A second grenade skims in on the tail of the first round and drops the wall and ceiling of the dining room.

"Let's get the fuck out of here," Arty calls up to me from the floor.

"You have a weapon?" I ask him.

"Christ, no! Remember, I'm in the salt business."

"Okay, then follow me. I'm going out the front—hoping they haven't surrounded us."

Outside, Gil nipping at my heels, we race toward the front gate. I start to unscramble the chain, but a clear voice whispers in my ear. I listen closely. It is the voice that whispered to me so many times when I was in the jungle. It tells me to look out through the slit in the gate. I look.

Just a few yards beyond, two men are setting up a machine-gun on the road, its muzzle pointed toward the gate.

I raise the Browning to the slit. There's just enough open space to let the bore breathe. The distance is less than twenty feet, but the area is in shadow and I decide not to go for head shots. I fire off four rounds, two to each man, dead center into their chests. They drop soundlessly onto the machine-gun.

I rip the gate open, go scrambling and zigzagging toward the machine-gun. I think I see a figure moving out from behind a tree. I send two rounds his way, but don't stop to judge their effect. I dive for the gun, even as bullets chip the road behind me. I nestle down between the two young men I've shot, swivel the gun toward the sound of the firing coming at me, and begin to comb the tree line with steady bursts from the machine-gun.

My ears echo with different levels of gunfire. The sounds mount, higher and higher, slamming at me from everywhere, as though a platoon of fighters has suddenly entered the firefight. Yet no bullets seek me now. I seem strangely isolated. A silence as abrupt as the initial rounds of gunfire has descended like the blade of an ax, severing now from then.

I hoist the machine-gun and its box of belted rounds and, still keeping low, take advantage of the lull to dart back onto the grounds and slam and chain the gate.

I discover that Gil and Toang are half-standing, staring around with the same confusion I feel.

"What happened?" Gil shouts to me.

I look past him and see that the two men with the RPGs on the temple grounds across the canal are fallen. Other men with guns are rolling them over to make sure they're dead.

On the roof of the factory, more men with guns are checking the dead.

These newcomers are not firing at us, and something about them impels us not to fire at them.

Another line of shadows forms up among the palm trees, keeping to shelter, but not shooting at us.

"What the fuck?" Gil says. "Who *are* those guys?"

With the machine-gun I run to what's left of one wall of the safehouse and settle down behind it to set up a clear lane of fire, even though instinct tells me we're all through shooting for today and that we've lived through one more.

A voice crackles from a bullhorn.

"Captain Locke, we are allies. The men who attacked you have been disposed of. We have left no survivors. May I show myself?"

That voice. I know it. I know it.

"Show yourself then," I shout back.

He does.

From the roofline of the factory, standing against the clear noontime sky.

It is Nguyen, my jungle scout from another time, my backup, my wingman—Nguyen, who just two days ago had told me he could find no fighters to come with me into Nam, Nguyen, who had caused me to breathe through my right nostril to dispel the depression his pessimism had caused me.

As Gil always says, what the fuck?

CHAPTER

19

While we wait for Nguyen to come from the factory roof and onto the grounds of the safehouse, we check out our casualties.

The American, about whom Arty knows little except that Washington had sent him over only a few months ago, has at least died instantly, his chest lifted off by crossfire. His mouth is locked open in silent rictal protest.

Arty, shaking his head numbly, begins to clear the man's pockets.

Gil and Toang patter after me as I cross toward the Sikh cradling his fallen brother.

Suddenly the surviving Sikh shouts to us.

"Still alive!"

The wounded Sikh looms up, as though jerked by a titanic spasm, and starts to shamble toward us. He clutches at his eyes and sobs something in a language I don't know.

"He's blind," the other Sikh mutters. "He can't see."

The wounded man collapses at my feet.

Below the cheekbones his face and beard are clotted with blood. But there is no other mark on his body.

I look up at Gil. "Jaw?" he asks quietly. I nod. Both of us have dealt with friends hit in the lower face. The wound often causes temporary loss of vision.

"Stomach down," I say to the other Sikh, and together we roll the wounded man onto his stomach. "Keep him in this position, but hold his head straight, be sure he can breathe."

I satisfy myself that the man's tongue has not dropped

153

back into his throat. "Keep checking his tongue. Make sure you don't let it drift back. Gil, can you and Toang improvise a stretcher? There should be things still intact in the house. What we need to do here is to keep him stomach down, with his head projecting out, but supported at the forehead by a sling. Have to keep his feet higher than his head so he doesn't swallow the blood and choke to death."

Gil and Toang run off toward the house.

"Thank you, sir," the surviving Sikh says.

I feel Nguyen behind me and I turn, looking up from the wounded Sikh.

"There were twelve of them," he says so softly I have to strain to hear him. After combat some men lose the desire, even the ability to speak. Others become shrill. I remember now that Nguyen seldom spoke for hours after a firefight.

"Eight were Thai, probably criminal elements, hired at random from the streets. Only four were Vietnamese— the two across the canal, and the two with the machine-gun. One I know from Saigon. He is high in the Mât Vu."

"*Was*," I correct. "It should have worked," I add. "It was simple enough, wasn't it? Engage us on both flanks, drive us into the house if we lived through the first ambush, blow up the house with grenades. Then if any of us survived and tried to break out the front way, cut us down with the machine-gun. But it *didn't* work. Why? Good simple plan, three-to-one superiority in manpower, total surprise. Why didn't it, Nguyen?"

"You know the answer to that as well as I do, sir," he whispers. "They met men better than themselves."

"Isn't that always the problem? You can have the best-laid plan. On paper it's a sure thing. You got everything taped. Except for the one unknown, the one factor you can't ever be sure of—the other sonofabitch. If he's a better man than you, your plan can turn to shit, and you along with it. It never changes, does it, Nguyen?"

"Thank God it never will," he says with a ring of conviction that springs from some hidden vortex in his soul.

"I guess we need to talk," I suggest. "When and where? You name it."

He glances over at Arty, still occupied with the dead American.

"Here and now, sir, I would think," he replies.

"Why are you here?" I ask. "How did you know we'd be attacked? Who are the men with you? May we start with those three questions?"

"I am here because I did not want you killed. We have double agents planted with the Mât Vu. It was from them I learned only an hour ago you were being followed and were to be ambushed. I was able to move quickly enough to let us follow those who were following you. And so we arrived here. All the men with me are Vietnamese. Like me, they are *khang chien*—the Resistance. All of us are members of the United Front of Patriotic Forces for the Liberation of Vietnam."

"Then why—just two days ago—when I told you I needed to recruit this exact kind of manpower—did you tell me the KC didn't exist?"

"I had to check you out first, sir."

"Me? Check *me* out? Jesus, Nguyen!"

"Who better than a war hero such as yourself, with such outstanding credentials, would be a more perfect double agent for Hanoi? Is it not possible that in return for their giving you back your son, you could be tempted to give them information about us? Is it not possible that all the previous efforts of the Mât Vu to kill you were simply staged to make your story more convincing?"

It's whiplash time all right, but there is no way I can find fault with Nguyen's caution.

"What gives you the assurance now that your suspicions aren't justified?"

"We trust both Thai Army Intelligence and Colonel Katrini of the Indonesian Counter-Insurgency forces. Both sources have within the last twenty-four hours vouched for your integrity."

Gil and Toang appear from the crumpled interior of the safehouse, their arms loaded with silk and two bamboo poles. I watch them running to the two Sikhs.

Arty is coming toward me and Nguyen.

"Does *he* know who you are?" I ask Nguyen.

"He's one of the very few Americans who does. He, too, vouches for you."

"Thank you for an especially timely arrival, Nguyen," Arty says.

"There was little left to do," Nguyen comments. "The

155

captain had already secured the front exit and his four companions had killed five of the eight men on the flanks. We had only one in the palm trees and two on the factory roof to deal with."

"What about the two across the *klong*—the two with the RPGs?" I ask.

"I killed both of them."

"The bodies?" Arty asks.

"Even now being taken out to sea."

"The factory workers who saw it happen?"

"They saw nothing. Heard nothing. We have made a donation to their temple."

"Okay," Arty says. "I'll tend to the dead American."

He smiles at me vaguely. Arty's smiles were always untranslatable.

"What happened to your safehouse?" I ask.

"Leaking gas heater." He grins. "Happens all the time. Well, have the two of you made a deal?"

"We were about to," Nguyen replies. "Am I correct, Captain?"

"Six men," I say. "And, preferably, one of them you."

"Two conditions," he says.

"What are they?"

"We do not want your ten-thousand-dollar bounty for each man on your strike team. But the United Front will accept whatever donation you care to make to our treasury for the purchase of medical supplies and weapons."

"You have it," I reply. "What's the second condition?"

"You will help us plan and carry out a specific military operation in Vietnam. Once that has been accomplished, we in turn will help you find your son and get him out of the country."

"What is the mission?"

"We plan to attack the navy base at Cam Ranh Bay."

"That's insane! Even with all their muscle, Hanoi never managed to drive us out of there. If *they* couldn't pull it off with all their forces, how do you expect to do it with a handful of men?"

"With your leadership, Captain."

"What am I? Better than General Giap?"

"For a small-unit insurgent operation, yes!" Nguyen says.

It's the kind of fool's confidence that can get us all killed and I tell him so.

"Must I remind you, sir," he retorts, "that you won your first Silver Star at Cam Ranh Bay? August of '69, wasn't it? When communist sappers attacked the base?"

"That was then," I say. "This is now."

Nguyen appears not to be listening to me. His eyes shift to Arty.

"He was close to dying—even though he'd been flown in to the hospital—this was the second time he was wounded. He was undergoing blood transfusions to keep him alive when the sappers struck the base after midnight. They broke in through the northern perimeter, then on through the R and R area until they got to the army hospital. Here they attacked the wounded by throwing satchel charges in through the windows and firing into the beds with their AK–47s. The captain disconnected himself from all the IV tubes, knowing fully that by doing so he was condemning himself to certain death, and obtained a weapon that he used to defend the ward, singlehanded, against a superior force—driving them off before he collapsed. His self-sacrificing action saved the lives of more than eighty men."

I look over at Arty.

He's studying his fingernails.

"Are you involved in this?" I ask.

"I'm not even listening," he says.

"You know damn well it's a violation of both federal and international law for an American citizen to go wading into another country and attack its military installations."

"I said I wasn't listening. Besides, I don't think you'll ever have to worry about Washington slapping you on the wrist. If the Vietnamese don't kill you first, the Ruskies at Cam Ranh Bay will. They've got most of their Pacific fleet stationed in the bay, along with Tu–16 medium bombers and fourteen MiG–23 Flogger fighter interceptors, the most capable air-superiority fighters based in Southeast Asia at the moment. Hell, it'd be easier to bust into the Kremlin."

"Exactly my point," I say. "So why go in there?" I demand of Nguyen.

"Sometime within the next month the first Russian aircraft carrier to cruise the waters of the South China

Sea—the largest of their carriers, the *Kiev*-class—is scheduled to dock at Cam Ranh Bay."

"So?" I insist.

"We understand it'll be the *Novorossiysk*," Arty adds, out of nowhere.

"It is our intention to sink it—or at least damage it significantly," Nguyen adds.

I look from Nguyen to Arty. It is not possible to believe they are serious.

"In one ear, out the other." Arty smiles.

"Such an incident would so destabilize Hanoi-Moscow relations that our Resistance could move on other fronts inside Vietnam. It is the powder keg we need to unravel Hanoi and to speed our success."

"What do you know about these *Kiev*-class carriers?" I ask.

"We have detailed plans," he replies.

"Then you know the setup on their weapons suite—everything from antiship cruise missiles to surface-to-air missiles, air-defense gun batteries, tactical sensors, electronic warfare systems, and advanced communications devices. A six-hundred-foot flight deck, both Hormone and Helix helicopters and Forger vertical-short takeoff and landing fighter planes. It's just plain *overwhelming*, old friend, to put it as generously as I can. My need is really very simple. I have to get into Nam and get a little boy out. Nothing more. Not try to sink aircraft carriers and take on the Russians too! You understand, Nguyen. It's just me and my son—not world forces contending against each other!"

"You cannot do it by yourself, sir," he says. "I wish you could. But we both know you can't. Especially now that you have to try to break into an armed camp to free the young woman—the only person who appears to know where your son is to be found."

"Did you tell him that, Arty?" I ask.

"No. He told me. His people got the word before I could. My people confirmed what he already told me."

"*Can* you do it alone, sir?" Nguyen asks.

I don't hear his voice as much as I hear something soundless, something silent and unacceptable, the first stirrings of a growing helplessness I'd sensed ever since I arrived in Thailand and began trying to paste this operation together. What it is, I realize, is the cold flame of possible defeat flickering in my guts. For all my bravado, all my training, all my fieldcraft and soldiering, I'm coming to believe this is one operation I can't pull off by myself.

"No," I finally admit, "I doubt that I can. But that doesn't stop me from trying, does it?"

Nguyen's eyes stay on me for the longest time.

"If you should change your mind," he says at last, "you know where to find me. But may I suggest, Captain, that you not take too long if you do reconsider. With or without you, *we* are going in. Very soon."

He salutes me.

I watch him trot away. I feel I'm watching the cavalry ride off between the bluffs, leaving me alone in Comanche country.

"Smart decision," Arty says. "Poor bastards! They don't have a prayer."

"Would they?" I ask. "*With* me?"

"We'll never know, will we?" he smiles.

20

Gil is certain—and I concur—that whatever dark forces were out there stalking me probably no longer exist, at least not this soon after their noontime bashing. It will take the enemy time to regroup, reconsider, plan a new ambush.

Gil relaxes his guardianship of me to the extent that he sends Toang along with the uninjured Sikh to get immediate medical attention for the man with the jaw wound. He gives Toang special instructions that the man be taken to an army hospital, where Toang is to ask for a particular surgeon.

Gil drives me back into Bangkok in the BMW.

As I'd expected, he shows no elation from the combat we've just been through. I know him better than he knows himself.

Trying to gloss over it, I ask him how the Ithaca worked out for him. How'd the patterns hold?

"Fucking tornado out to thirty yards," he says. "Beyond that I was getting only three or four pellets into the target. And even though she's an autoloader, the three cartridges you get with each loading don't give you a helluva lot of continuity."

"You were sounding good to me," I say.

"All shit, isn't it, Skipper?" he mutters. "Before we got into it, I was like a fuckin' redneck—couldn't wait to sock it to 'em. But when it gets down to hard killing, nothing changes, does it? You think it does, but you're just bullshitting yourself. You start out with this fantastic

160

fucking high, like I used to get when we went out on a recon mission. But the minute you blow the balls off the bastard you're hunting, and he lies there at your feet like a pile of shit and you see the fucking insects already going to work on him—there's no goddamn satisfaction in that, is there?"

"No," I say. "None at all."

"It all came back today. Every fucking second of it came back. And what I remembered as a high—wasn't . . . *isn't!*"

Not much I can add to that.

We're both quiet most of the way in.

"So what's the poop on Nguyen?" Gil asks as he turns us onto Surawong Road, not far from the club. "Who were those gunjis with him?"

"The gunjis I've been praying for. Vietnamese resistance fighters."

He brightens. "All *right!*"

"But Nguyen offered me a deal I had to resist."

"Yeah? What deal?"

"I help him sink a Russian aircraft carrier in Cam Rahn Bay, he helps me get my son out."

"Holy shit!"

"My reaction, exactly."

"I thought you learned in Nam, Skipper, never to try to bargain with a Vietnamese. They make Armenian rug dealers look like the kind of assholes who buy the Brooklyn Bridge. I tell you, let's get the hell up to Burma and we'll line you up however many men you need."

"Maybe it could be done," I say. I assume I'm the one saying it, because Gil is staring straight at me, instead of at the traffic all around us.

"You don't mean . . . ?"

"Yeah, I do."

Oh, it's me, all right. That's my voice.

"Attack a carrier?" Gil demands.

"Maybe we can't sink it, but we *can* attack it," I argue. "It's the symbolism that matters here, not the specific amount of damage. See what I'm saying, Gil?"

"I'll put that on your tombstone, Shit Hook. "Here lies John Locke. Died on foreign soil from a severe case of symbolism."

"I already told him pass," I say defensively.

"Then how come you're still fucking with it? John, I *know* you! Your first instincts are always good. I mean, you *do* know shit from Shinola, right off the bat, soon as you see it coming your way. But then this goddamn thing you got somewhere in your head or in your balls, I don't know which, kicks in and you start figuring the odds. Now, for chrissake, forget it! Don't even *think* aircraft carrier!"

"It's Nguyen I'm thinking about," I say. "With him on point, I can go anywhere."

"Know what you sound like, Skipper? Like a guy the Mexicans hate and the Texans hate even worse. Got that picture? Now the Mexicans want his ass and the Texans want his balls. And you know what he does? The dumb cocksucker fights his way through the Mexican Army to get *into* the Alamo! *That's* what you sound like!"

No doubt about it.

Gil drives into the club's garage.

His security people shutter the street doors behind us.

We sit in the car a while longer, Gil staring at me through the semidarkness.

"Gonna take the shot, aren't you?"

"Do I have any other choice?"

We both know I don't.

═══CHAPTER═══

21

While I'm dressing for dinner with Otis Walden, Lek bursts into the penthouse, runs to me, and clings like flypaper, swirls of tossing black hair hiding her tearful eyes as her body shudders against mine.

I try to calm her.

"What is it?" I ask with deliberate patience.

"You maybe die this morning," she cries accusingly.

"But I didn't."

"They shoot Pranay in face!"

"He's going to be okay. Only an hour ago we talked to the surgeon."

She lifts her head from my chest and stares up at me. Her lips are trembling. "What if they shoot *you* in face?"

"Face better than brain." I smile. It occurs to me I'm starting to talk like Lek, but why not? She's been teaching me Thai over the long hours we've spent in bed together. I'm finding it easy to learn, because of my knowing Vietnamese, also a tonal language, and because Thai offers shortcuts we don't have in English. Verb endings, for example. In Thai, verb endings never change. In English we have five different endings. And when I studied French, my first language, I had to learn thirty-eight different verb endings, a needless overcomplication.

"You face beautiful!" she says. "No shoot!"

"No problem," I say. "Nothing can hurt me. Remember the amulet Dasima gave me? Remember I told you about Dasima? Her amulet is absolutely guaranteed to stop bullets from hitting me."

Her lips no longer tremble. In fact, they now seem locked. Her eyes almost spark, as though someone has bridged them with cable jumpers.

"Lek no want to hear about Dasima!"

"Not another word," I agree.

She discovers I was in the act of dressing when she came hurtling through the doorway.

"Why you put on business suit?"

"I plan to do some business. At dinner. At the Oriental Hotel."

"You go out?"

"Yes."

"They shoot you in face!"

"I think maybe they've run out of shooters. For the time being, at least. Anyway, Gil and Toang are taking me. They'll be right outside the hotel room. Gil says the suite I'm having dinner in is on the top floor. So unless some human fly tries to climb down from the roof, it should be a quiet evening."

"I wait."

"Actually, no," I say hesitantly, but having to say it. More than anything now I must make some hard decisions. To make them I need to be alone. Lek is becoming addictive. I'm finding it more and more tempting to escape into our lovemaking and to push the outside harshness off until tomorrow and tomorrow after that. "I have a lot of thinking to do—a lot of planning," I tell her. I indicate the pile of data the colonel has sent over. "I need time to study all those documents and to make some decisions."

She wipes from her cheeks the residue of her tears.

"Lek sit over there and say nothing. I sit like statue. When you ready, you come to statue. Statue come to life."

"It's not your voice, Lek, it's your very presence. You understand? When you're with me, you're all I can think of. So I want you to go home this weekend—to your parents—and spend the time with your daughter. Take her this . . ."

I open my wallet, bring out a sheath of bahts in high denominations. "Someday you may want to send her to a special school, one of the best private schools. Put this in the bank for her as a beginning—for her education. And I'll see you Monday night."

For a moment I suspect she may be going to spit on

the money, but the thickness of the offering and its unexpectedness overcome any such foolishness. She raises her palms to me and accepts the currency. I know she's dying to count it, but she would never embarrass herself with such unseemly behavior in my presence. Taking my scrotum in her lips in front of her friends would be perfectly acceptable behavior in her world. Evaluating my gift to her daughter in my presence would be unthinkable. How amiably the Thais have adjusted their priorities!

"I leave now," she says with scarcely disguised eagerness to be gone. "I hold my daughter in my arms before midnight and I think of you."

Gratefully she kisses me.

"I be back Monday night," she cries over her shoulder as she runs out.

I imagine her breathlessly counting the money as the elevator takes her down to the club. But not with the cold avarice you'd likely get from the average American or European hooker.

What Doan Thi taught me about the Asian woman's love of frequent and expensive gifts is simply that greed is not the impelling factor in their appreciation. To the Asian girl a gift is simply the pragmatic expression of genuine affection. The greater the gift, the greater, obviously, the affection.

As Gil and Toang drive me to the Oriental Hotel, I feel no sense of imminent danger. Black Friday's shootout has put the Mât Vu into a holding pattern. Clearly, they are going to have to redraw their organizational chart and replace the cadre in charge of blowing ass.

I'm startled by my sighting of the Oriental Hotel. I'd seen it last in '75, when it was still Victorian and echoing with memories. The now-completed ultramodern river wing was then still under construction. In '75 this magical hotel, which was then approaching its one hundredth birthday, was truly the pearl of Asia, with its baroque facade, its limited number of rooms, its flower-bedecked lobby with clusters of soaring bamboo growing alongside the elegantly curving staircases, parting upward to gracious balconies leading to the guest quarters.

Joseph Conrad had stayed at the Oriental in 1888, for like me he needed at that particular period in his life to be within clear and immediate sight of water at all times and the Oriental faces directly onto the Mother of Waters, the Mae Nam Chao Phraya River.

As I get out of the BMW, Gil and Toang already out, looking around like two Secret Service agents, the gusting wind bears the sweet scent of the Gulf directly to me. I miss *Steel Tiger* in that instant. She lies not more than a mile south, on the far side of the river, and I hunger to be aboard her with my son, all this turmoil and darkness miraculously behind us, the two of us, together, learning about each other, as I beat south again toward the China Sea.

Instead, I'm in an elevator speeding up to the sixteenth floor.

Gil and Toang walk out first, eyeballing the long, carpeted corridor. Gil motions to me and I take my finger off the hold button and come out. We advance in file toward the double doors of the suite on the river front of the hotel.

Far down the corridor the door to the Oriental Suite opens as if some sensing eye has triggered an electronic release.

Gil's hand starts to pull the .45 Colt he's wearing in his belt.

"It's cool, Gil," I say. "I know the door person."

It's Kim.

In the doorway of the suite.

Doing a broad send-up of Lauren Bacall, who used to stand in doorways about as well as it can be done. I can almost hear the classic dialogue from another decade: "You know how to whistle, don't you, Steve? You just put your lips together—and blow!"

I'd met Kim this recent July. She stood posed above me on the helicopter pad of *Reckless Living* when I'd tied *Steel Tiger* up at the Club Nautique de Calédonie directly astern of Otis Walden's handsome motor yacht. At the time she was naked from the waist down, the hair of her pubis shaved into a Valentine patch. A T-shirt scarcely covered her breasts. Emblazoned on the front of the T-shirt was the statement HAPPINESS IS A CONFIRMED FUCK.

She'd invited me over to inspect the solid gold pipes in the yacht's crappers, but I took a pass. At first appraisal I read her as a girl in urgent need of rescue from herself, and I was by then already out of the salvation business.

Later, during the bad times in New Caledonia, I got to know her better, but never in the biblical sense. She aroused only pity in me, nothing else. She was a girl who'd come to the big city to see the elephant and they'd broken it off up her ass.

She'd wanted to be the lead singer of her own rock band. But she got only as far as the sequins-and-polyester circuit in a few motel lounges. From that she eased into high-priced hooking, out of boredom at first, she told me, then for the money. She ended up with a really classy operation in Atlantic City, but refused to pay off the right people, and was bounced out of Jersey. But she'd already achieved a rising reputation in the expanding world of porn and she started writing a monthly column of sex advice for one of the glossier jerk-off magazines. This brought her international recognition—and ultimately Otis Walden, who pays her ten thousand dollars a month to act as his procuress and as mistress of ceremonies and stage manager for the sex research he's doing aboard *Reckless Living* as his crew sails him from country to country.

The night I was invited aboard in Nouméa, but had other business which kept me ashore, she had collected six local French girls, three motorcycle studs, two tourist couples from Sidney hot to play switchy, and some friends of mine. As Kim had said when I conveyed my regrets, "You're not missing anything—just another shitty night in Paradise. We'll probably do a little taping, some girl-girl fucking out on deck under the stars, and maybe some anals while we're at it—we've got these great new ni-cad batteries that give you an hour and a half shooting time before you have to recharge."

Tonight, in Bangkok, Kim looks years younger.

"You're doing something different." I smile.

She kisses me softly. "Celibacy," she says. "Been saving myself for you. Nobody else playing kissy-face with me."

Gil's jaw has gone agape. He's been in Asia too long. He'd forgotten what an American sexpot can look like.

I introduce Kim to Gil and Toang.

"Come in, please, gentlemen," she urges. "Otis has ordered up a perfectly fab Thai banquet."

"Maybe you could have them serve us out in the corridor?" Gil suggests.

"I don't understand," Kim says, frowning at me.

"Gil and Toang are my life-support system while I'm passing through Bangkok. Lately some really nasty types have been breathing down my neck," I explain.

"The same people who were trying to kill you in New Caledonia?"

"No. Different crowd."

"You do tend to stir up animosity wherever you go, don't you, John?"

"You've noticed?"

"May we send out something to drink—*before* dinner?" Kim asks Gil and Toang.

"Negatory," Gil says. "Not when we're driving."

Kim takes my arm, leads me into the suite, and kicks the door closed behind her with one slippered foot. She's wearing a high-necked brocade *ao dai*, the traditional dress of Vietnam. In my honor, I daresay.

The Oriental Suite appears to occupy a major part of the sixteenth floor. The foyer is larger than most hotel suites in their entirety. From the near distance, from what must be the living room, I hear Otis's voice as he talks on the telephone with that increased volume most people pour on when speaking long distance, as though sending their voices through some hollow tube directly to the far side of the globe.

Kim stops me in the foyer and places her hands on my shoulders.

"Since you sailed off I've limited my relationships to my mirror. You've been on my mind more than I like. You ever hear from that French fireball you were making it with in Nouméa? What was her name?"

"Rosine. No, not a word."

"Still hung up on the memory of that dead Vietnamese poetess? Doan Thi?"

"Interesting you'd remember *her* name, but not Rosine's."

"I know competition when I spot it—even if it's no longer around. Okay, since you left Nouméa, any new flames? You can tell ol' Kim."

"Why should you want to know?"

"Because I didn't fly all the way from Brunei to Bangkok just to have dinner with you and Otis! I've had the hots for you, Mr. Locke, since I first saw you through field glasses sailing your little toy boat into the Baie de Pêcheurs."

"Suppose I simply say I have not been entirely monastic. Can we let it go at that?"

Before she can answer, I hear Otis hang up. Almost instantly after, he's in the doorway of the living room.

"John!"

He looks thinner than I remember him, and as he hurries toward me he seems to shudder all over. Yet he pumps my hand with a strong and vigorous motion.

"You cut your hair," I say.

"*I* didn't. *Kim* did. Snuck into my stateroom one night when I was asleep and did a Delilah on my Samson."

"His hair got so long it was revolting," Kim says. "No man worth twenty-four million dollars should look like he's still frozen back in time, in the sixties."

"I was hysterical when I woke up and felt my cold head," he laughs. "I was sure that Kim had robbed me of my virility just so she could quit her job—which she's been threatening to do for the last month or so—and so I'd be incapable of performing at the orgy we'd scheduled for that night."

"Ten Japanese office girls," Kim snorts. "Disgusting."

Otis laughs suddenly, a dry, rattling sound I don't remember from the little time I spent with him in New Caledonia. It's as though someone is shaking a pair of maracas behind his back. It hits me he may be racing time, sensing its limits.

"But I was magnificent that night, wasn't I, Kim? This was special research on the age-old question—is it easier for a man to make love to ten women than to make love to the same woman ten times? I taped the whole thing—stream-of-consciousness, what I was feeling with each girl, what they said. It's one of the best chapters in the book, if I say so myself. Which I don't really have to. Kim, I was talking to my editor in New York when John arrived. They are *delirious* with the first two hundred pages. They're already calling it the ultimate book on sexual behavior around the world, the book no anthropologist ever dared write—the first book, actually, on pansexualism. As you know, John, I firmly believe that the sexual instinct is at the heart of all human activity. And my book will illuminate this theory. Well, come in, come in. Let's celebrate your change of mind. The Dom Pérignon is iced and waiting. And a most remarkable public relations lady here at the hotel—a Mrs. Pornsri Luphainboon—has arranged for a special staff to serve us dinner in the dining room—*our* dining room."

He indicates the closed double doors from behind which I hear the stirring of the kitchen staff at work, then he leads me into the living area, an L-shaped array of windows framing the river below us and the lights of Thonburi across the shifting surface of the Chao Phraya, the crisscrossing of darting Thai boats forming soft chevrons in the water, shimmering for an instant, then vanishing into the dark surface.

"Your telex was a shot in the arm, John," he says as he starts to work open the impossibly sealed cork of the Dom Pérignon. After years of grappling with Dom Pérignon corks, I'm convinced the reason the champagne from this winemaker tastes so superb is because of your gratitude for managing finally to separate cork and bottle.

"What made you change your minds?" he asks. "You were dead set against helping me turn *Reckless Living* into a warship so I could pursue my sexual research with the wives and daughters of the Sulu pirates. Why the switch?"

"Necessity," I say. "I need you to pick me up in the Baie d'Along sometime between twelve October and fifteen October. As we get closer, I'll be able to refine the extraction date—right down to a given hour. But not yet. Still too many rivers to cross before I reach that point."

"Where is the Baie d'Along?" he asks.

"In the Gulf of Tonkin."

I tell myself I will remember this moment, for Otis's expression of shock at my mentioning the Gulf of Tonkin is timed perfectly to the instant he manages to free the cork from the hostile bottle of champagne. Only a tiny pop escapes, whether from his lips or the neck of the bottle I'm not certain.

"Isn't that up near Hanoi?" he asks.

"Hanoi is inland. Baie d'Along is closer to Haiphong."

"Forgive my asking, John, but what will you be doing

up there in October? Or at any other time, for that matter?"

"Scrambling like hell to leave the country."

He pours the champagne with what I consider a trembling hand. His buoyancy of a few minutes before has left him. Mentioning Vietnam has taken away all the fun and games. It usually does—to millions of us.

"To the future," he toasts. We touch glasses. The clear ring is Baccarat at its finest tonality.

"Your telex said you expected no remuneration. Why is that, John? I promised you a hundred thousand dollars for thirty days of your expertise."

"I'm asking you to risk a five-million-dollar yacht," I say. "I'm expecting you to steam from Brunei to Singapore this weekend and outfit *Reckless Living* with armor plate and ordnance I'm going to recommend. That will not come cheap. I'm expecting you to hire a platoon of top mercs. Under the circumstances I don't feel justified adding my fee on top of that."

"Risk. You mentioned risk. What risk—other than poking about in an area where American pleasure boats aren't supposed to be?"

"You may be attacked by Vietnamese patrol boats and aircraft. It's highly possible, Otis, that a lot of pissed-off people are going to be looking for me when I leave Vietnam. If they discover I'm extracting aboard your yacht, they will stop at nothing to send you to the bottom. You understand?"

"My God, man, what do you plan to do?"

"Bring out my son."

"You have a son?" Kim asks.

"I learned of it only two weeks ago."

"With Doan Thi?" she asks.

"Yes."

"Well, look here, John," Otis says, as though someone is no longer stepping on his arches, "I am not without connections. I think I can arrange to get your son out so that you don't have to bust in like Rambo and single-handededly take on what I understand is the third largest standing army in the world."

"Unless your connections are with the Kremlin, forget it!" I tell him. "Hanoi's not listening with both ears to anyone else at this time."

"Obviously, my connections aren't with the Soviets, but I am a major contributor to the Quakers. They're back and forth all the time between the States and Vietnam trying to get the Amerasian children out. I can ask them to get to work on your case too."

"I don't want to put you in that position," I tell him, "nor the Quakers either. Somebody in Hanoi's secret police apparatus is devoting full-time to my speedy demise. Apparently, I am not well regarded in certain circles. So any kind of diplomatic or institutional approach would be pigeonholed, believe me, Otis!"

I tell him and Kim about the specific attacks against me, starting with the first in Bali last month and the full-scale shootout this morning at the safehouse in Thonburi.

Both of them are so shocked they fail to hear the soft-spoken Thai butler who appears from the dining room to announce that dinner is ready.

All through the superb banquet, Otis and Kim remain somber and monosyllabic. More sound tinkles from the tableware than from either of them.

"Win, lose, or draw," I say to Otis, "I'm going in a week from Sunday. It would be nice to know that I have a way of getting out. You're my first choice, Otis. Is it worth risking your life to get me to help you do research on the genital standing of pirates' wives? Is a chapter in a book worth having *Reckless Living* shot up, maybe sunk?"

"A man can't always get by on flair alone, John," he says after another long silence. "Now and then you have to make the commitment."

"Like Custer?" Kim asks archly.

"Exactly!" he says. "Does anybody remember who was president of the United States when Custer made his last stand? *Nobody*! But Custer's name lives on—even more than Sitting Bull's! Now that's flair *and* commitment—and I like that. I like that very much indeed! Okay, John, you have a deal. I'll leave Brunei this weekend and steam over to Singapore. You tell me what shipyard can make the modifications and what your contacts are there for weapons and for mercenaries and I'll take it the rest of the way. I'll have *Reckless Living* in the Gulf of Tonkin and at your disposal in the Baie d'Along for mid-October. We'll get you out, count on it!"

SILVER STAR

I feel better than I have in days.

I can see the beginning and I can see the end.

All that remains is the in between.

I allow myself one cognac after dinner. We take our drinks on the topmost balcony of what many consider the world's finest hotel.

Below us the river surges lustily to the Gulf, the tide sweeping the clusters of water hyacinths south. Swarms of *rua hang yao*, the needlelike water taxis, carve the water, hurtling rooster tails behind them. Noiselessly, the stately rice barges slide upriver, towed by tugs.

It is impossible for me to keep my eyes focused on one spot, for the crisscrossing, colliding wakes of so much water traffic compel the attention at one instant off to the right, then the next instant left, then right again as the lives below play out on the ever-changing surface. The smell of the river is borne to us, even up here on the sixteenth floor. It comes interlaced with the odor of boiling noodles and the scent of glutinous rice being fried.

It strikes me that the river is the very symbol of the Thai people. If only I were able to accept their concepts, the avoidance of confrontation, the flowing with life, the belief that patience (water) is stronger than force (rock). *If*.

Yet in whatever direction I look out over Bangkok and its sister city, Thonburi, across the water, I see building cranes and the steel grids of high-rise construction. Of all the world's governments, those of Asia appear to have the singularly most relentless obsession to turn themselves inside out and to become modern. The past is vanishing under the bulldozer. In no time at all the exotic Orient will turn into downtown Tulsa.

For reasons unknown to me,—possibly it's the cognac, possibly it's having finally locked up at least one key element in the overall plan of taking custody of my son, possibly it's this high balcony—I flash on Angie Mihalovich.

He surfaces from the miasma of my San Francisco police years.

Angie Mihalovich—the Tenderloin's leading dipstick.

His field of enterprise was teenage girls, no victim over fourteen. He'd hook them to their eyeballs on freebie drugs, then market them to pedophiles so the girls would have the means to support their habits. He was scoring at both ends of the stick, selling shit to the girls and then selling the girls to wealthy clients.

Only one girl ever escaped his web, a thirteen-year-old from Navato. From a freedom perch high on the Transamerica pyramid she took a last glazed look across the City by the Bay,—possibly she even took the time to look north toward her parents' home in Navato, if you like your six o'clock news on the sentimental side—then she stepped off into the foggy morning and managed to disrupt traffic for all of the twenty-two minutes it took the fire department to tidy up below.

When you're working Vice or Narcotics, you simply can't afford to let yourself get emotionally involved with the flora and fauna on the street. But the incident with the thirteen-year-old truly stressed all of us on the narco squad. Unanimously we arrived at a deep-six verdict for Angie. We couldn't drop him legally. The dude was too artful. And we couldn't walk out and gun him down in broad daylight, much as we itched to do so.

So it was brainstormed that we'd give him the TLC treatment, and I was elected the cutting edge of that policy.

I began to operate Angie personally, all the rest of the squad laying off and avoiding any contact with him.

That first morning I scooped him up and jazzed him around the Tenderloin in my shit-brindle low-rider coupe. In the beginning of my roust he radiated what-me-worry all over my soiled sheepskin upholstery.

"Got nothin' on me," he insisted.

"That's right, sweetheart," I agreed.

"*Y qúe?*" he said, the cholo way of laying a so-what on you. Fascinating, since Angie was Serbian.

"Call this a crash course in behavior modification." I smiled. And kept smiling. And smiling and smiling. I made him sit up front next to me, so all the Neanderthals on the block could spot my sparkling good nature and observe Angie openly fraternizing with the heat.

That first afternoon I gave him a measured fifteen minutes of blue-ribbon camaraderie before I dropped him off in front of a rogue's gallery of loitering hardcases. I flipped him one of those it's-been-grand salutes and breezed off, looking as though I'd just run out of notepaper from jotting down all the hot leads he'd spilled.

A seamless performance, I do recall.

After a few such guided tours, he got so paranoid every time he spotted my low-rider, he'd light up like the tailfins on a '57 DeSoto and go blistering down the nearest alley. He knew I wasn't there to bust him, only cozy up to him, love him right out in plain sight—just the two of us, Angie and Johnny, the dealer and the nark, puckering-up buddies glued together out of the sheer pleasure of each other's company.

So he'd run and I'd flash down the alleys on his tail, sometimes having to park and shag him down on foot. I'd manhandle him back to the car, into the front seat, belt him in, then sally into the sunshine with him.

Whenever we drove past his sidewalk peers, I'd talk to him like the piece of shit he was, although all the while I'd be smiling and showing my keyboard teeth in clean, loving display while he pleaded with me to get off his case. After a few minutes of such public conviviality, I'd spin him back to whatever intersection his peers happened to be jiving at the moment. I'd slide in to the curb, right in next to them, leap out in obvious gratitude, and escort Angie freely from the car. No cuffs, no visible restraints. I'd thank him loudly and profusely for all his civic-minded cooperation, wave adieu till tomorrow, then zip off, leaving him in the snake pit, trying to convince the dark circle of knitted lowbrows he was being set up by this crazy cop who was killing him softly with his love. The more he swore he'd dropped nothing on me, the deeper he buried himself.

It amused all of us on Narcotics to learn one afternoon that his fancy threads had been torn off just five minutes after I'd deposited him among a really mean cluster of motherfuckers. His lips got split, his teeth bent back, one ear bitten off, nose rearranged, left patella pulverized, not to mention an artistic network of flesh wounds obviously sketched on his hide by Ramon the Blade, who was the turf's master of a Filipino knife-fighting technique called *kali*. We even heard there was also severe genital trauma, but since we never took flowers to the hospital, the story about Angie's emasculation might only have been wishful thinking on our parts.

One thing I know for sure—Angie had got himself fucked over good by his fellow Nearderthals simply because we used reverse psychology. I never laid a glove on him, something his associates found unthinkable and therefore unacceptable. The irony of this provided an invaluable lesson at the time, although now I can no longer recall what the lesson was, unless somehow this ties into the Thai concept of "flowing with life" or water wearing away rock.

For two weeks I waited up every night in bed for the tossing and turning to set in, waited for the remorse to hit me, but each night I fell asleep like a winner the second my head touched the pillow.

Putting the lumber to Angie struck me as an achievement comparable in importance only to Kekule's unraveling the structure of the benzene molecule.

No question, Vietnam had prepared me for duty in San Francisco as a police officer. I'd not only become more merciless than the deadliest scumbag in the Tenderloin, I'd turned clever, too, bristling with street smarts.

Clearly, ahead of me stretched a long and brilliant career in law enforcement.

How wrong I'd been to think so!

Now, finishing my cognac, looking out over the lights of Bangkok, I have to ask myself what memories of *this* night I will carry with me—and for how long.

As long as October 15th?

As far as the Baie d'Along?

Kim's voice cuts into my reverie.

"I have to see you tonight," I hear her saying.

I discover that Otis is back on the phone again in the living room. Kim and I are alone on the balcony.

"I'm sorry," I say. "I'm loaded with things I have to do."

"May I tell you why you'll put them off till tomorrow?"

I wouldn't quite classify her question as ominous, but there's some kind of concealed throw-weight in the way she faces me now.

"If it weren't for me, you'd never have got the boat," she says. "Otis may want that chapter on the wives of the Sulu pirates, but not so desperately he'd risk his precious balls. When you told him you needed the yacht in Vietnam, maybe you noticed how his eyes turned to me."

"Matter of fact, I did notice that," I admit.

"And maybe you saw me nod?"

"I saw that too."

"That was the signal. He knew that he had to give you what you were asking for. Or else."

"Or else what, Kim?"

"I've been wanting to quit," she says. "Watching people grope each other every night and supervising the camera and tape crews is just too goddamned boring for me to take any longer—even at two grand a week, tax-free, and living like a queen in my own stateroom aboard a five-million-dollar yacht cruising the exotic Orient. I want out, John! And I've been telling Otis this for weeks. He keeps begging me to stay, at least till he finishes the book—three more months, he figures, then he'll have all the research he needs. So I said okay, under one condition—that whatever it was you might want his yacht for, he had to say yes, or lose me the minute we got to Bangkok. I've saved over fifty thousand dollars already. I don't need this! Anyway, those are the facts, John. You doubt me, ask Otis. He'll tell you!"

Not obligation, not gratitude, impel me to consent, because once past thirty most men are adroit enough to sidestep a mercy fuck. But Kim's approach is so starkly bottom-line that for a second or two she blasts me out of the tower-keep of my malehood and makes me feel what a starlet must feel when the producer points imperiously to the casting couch and unzips his fly.

"I'm staying in Gil's penthouse at the T. and A. Club on Patpong. I'll be waiting."

"You won't be sorry, John," she says.

Somehow I believe her.

═CHAPTER═

22

Without incident or even the hint of assassination, Gil and Toang deliver me safely back into the shelter of the T. and A. Club.

Tonight the disco music is dialed up to the max, a level that would have toppled the walls of Jericho at first blast. The club teems with a smoky deco crowd, except for a solemn cluster of dark-suited young medical students. Gil tells me they're from Singapore. Groups like this come in regularly for the weekend to escape their own sterile, high-rise, sanitized city. Now in wonderfully wicked Bangkok they huddle around one of the dance platforms and peer up as though through microscopes at the grinding mons of a Thai dancing girl teasing their noses with her musky labial scent.

Once upstairs, partly shielded from the pounding of the music, I make three calls—the first to Nguyen at the boxing camp.

"Can we be ready in time to move out a week from Sunday?" I ask.

"Yes," he replies.

"Then that's it," I say. "When and where do we talk next?"

"Not on the phone," he says. "I will handle it."

He hangs up.

I call a second number, one Gil has just given me when we were downstairs.

A recorded voice answers—Arun's soft, girl's voice.

The voice tells me to leave my message at the sound of the tone.

"I'll be in all day tomorrow," I say to the recording. "Ready for makeup."

The third call is to Arty down on the salt farm.

He's out too. I leave a message to the effect that I'm hungry for chicken Kiev and that I need to discuss the recipe for making it. At his earliest convenience.

I congratulate myself on being such a tricky sonofabitch that even if Gil's lines have been tapped and some operative intercepts my chicken-Kiev comment he'll never in a billion years connect it with an attack in Cam Ranh Bay against a *Kiev*-class carrier of the Russian Soviet Federated Socialist Republic.

Suddenly the guards unlock my door and admit Kim.

Clutching a frosty bottle of Dom Pérignon to her hip, she poses in the doorway, one palm sliding seductively up the doorjamb.

She's shucked the black *ao dai* she wore at dinner in the Oriental Suite. Now she's back to basic deck jeans, floppy T-shirt, a nuke mushroom blossoming Satan-red between the outcropping of her breasts, a B–1B bomber scatting across the valley between them—with the caption NOW COMES MILLER TIME.

"You ever just *walk* into a room?" I ask.

She ignores my question. "What does the word *andromania* mean to you?" she asks.

I suspect that in the long, febrile scan of world history no other woman has ever come on before with this particular opening shot.

"*Andros* is Greek for 'man,'" I reply. "We all know about *mania*. So, *andromania*—'crazy for men.' Okay?"

She saunters in, kicking the door closed behind her, as she did at the Oriental. Obviously a new behavior pattern. "You are a smart one, aren't you?"

"In some areas, yeah. In others, a real dummy."

"I discovered that word in the book Otis is writing," she says, "and I simply adore it! It's so much more exact than *nymphomania* inasmuch as I have always preferred men to nymphs. But currently I've developed a case of the hots for one man only. Any guesses?"

"Humphrey Bogart?"

"Shithead!" She laughs and looks around the apartment approvingly.

I can feel the muffled go-go beat pushing up through the ceiling of the club directly below us.

"Good vibes in here," she decides. "I can feel multiple orgasms dancing in the air."

"It's Gil's personal pad. He's a man who puts in his full time fucking."

"These seem more recent. How long have you been staying here?"

"This will be my fifth night. I carve a notch in the wall for every night I'm up here. That's so I don't lose track of the outside world."

"Does he send girls up here for you too?"

"The first night he sent six."

"Poor baby. You must be exhausted."

"No, I managed okay. It's the nights since. There's this one special girl. Her name is Lek."

She tosses me the champagne bottle.

"Later with the champagne," she announces.

She circles the Chinese platform bed with its carved dragon posts and its top tented with lacquered paper umbrellas from Chiang Mai.

She sniffs around the bed.

"Happiness is the lasting scent of last night's lover," she pronounces.

"Profound," I say.

She turns to face me. She unbuttons her jeans from the top down, taking her time, teasing the tight waistband ever lower as she appraises my languid expression.

"I learned still another neat word from Otis's book," she says. "*Gymnophobia*. That means 'fear of nudity.' I do not suffer from *gymnophobia*, my darling."

"I'd never have guessed," I say as she peels herself out of her denims.

Her mons is no longer trimmed into a heart shape. Now she's crafted herself into corn rows set with miniature pearls and colored rhinestones.

She models for me. "Well, what do you think?"

"Ouch!"

"That your *only* reaction?"

"It reminds me of something we were told when I first arrived in Vietnam."

"Oh? How so?"

"They told us that the Vietnamese hated us so much their women all tucked razor blades into their vaginas in case some poor horny grunt should make a frontal assault."

"I'm surprised you still have a dork." She laughs and shrugs out of her T-shirt.

She steps naked onto the bed, turns her hard backside to me, and bends over provocatively, legs wide apart, like a feeding giraffe, her face down between her long, slender legs, her hair tumbling all the way to the satin bedspread, her eyes flashing back at me from between the fall of her breasts.

"Okay," she announces from this compelling stance. "So you knew *andromania* and didn't know *gymnophobia*. Bet you don't know *corpora cavernosa* either."

"No," I acknowledge. "I don't know *corpora cavernosa*. Should I?"

"The corpora," she says, "are the two spongy, tissue-filled cylinders lying on either side of the male urethra. When blood engorges the corpora cavernosa, the penis becomes stiff. You *do* know what a stiff prick is, don't you, John?"

"I'm happy to reply in the affirmative."

"Yours stiff enough yet?"

I decide to serve the Dom Pérignon despite the inherent cork problem.

Kim swings her neck around with the abandon of an African dancer, her hair flopping wildly over her eyes as she straightens. She steps off the bed and advances upon me.

"What are we waiting for?" she demands. "A favorable alignment of the planets? Or don't I turn you on?"

"Too much sex clogs the arteries," I comment. "And this week my in tray has been overflowing."

I continue wrestling with the damned cork. This one has been set in cement.

Challengingly, her fingers lightly explore my crotch.

She finds my corpora fully engorged.

"Your mouth says no, your cock says yes. Do I remind you of somebody you mustn't touch? Your mother, maybe?"

Miraculously I wrest the cork free.

"No chilled glasses," I say. "How about straight from the bottle?"

"But *I* understand you, John Locke. More than you understand yourself. I could teach a postgraduate course in what makes you tick."

"Mind if I audit the class sometime?" I ask.

"You can't see what's driving you, can you, John?"

No way to argue that. "Things are coming together," I manage. "Better every year. Not clearer, but somehow better."

"You're still conning yourself. You think that now you've got a son—once you actually get him—*if* you somehow manage to live through whatever it's going to take to get him—you think that all the rest will automatically be solved. Everything put in place—Doan Thi, the war—"

"Wrong! Knowing I have a son, going in after him—that only makes me vulnerable. *More* vulnerable, I mean. I already know that, for chrissake, Kim!"

"Now you said the operative word—*vulnerable*!"

Long silence as I question her eyes. I still feel the soles of my shoes rippling with the sound waves from the club downstairs.

"You know *why* you go bouncing from island to island, John?" she asks.

"Do I have to have a reason?"

"Of course not. But *you* think you do. You think you have to have a reason. When you don't really have to. But I know what *you* think your reason is."

"Okay, what?"

"A reason why..." She hesitates. Not like her.

"Go ahead, goddamn it!" I insist. "You opened this up. Now finish it!" My voice sounds as though it were the voice of a strident stranger.

"A reason why you deserve to be alive—that's what you're looking for. That's why you keep bouncing from one place to the other. To find out why *you*—unlike all the others—should live, when they couldn't...didn't..."

I let that one hang in there with the reverbs from the stereo amplifiers downstairs until the residual memory of her words has stopped slamming around inside my head.

"You come up here tonight to lay that shit on me?" I ask her finally.

"I came up here tonight to get laid," she says. "I came up here to tend to a basic need—to get off with the guy I've been dreaming about lately. Nothing more than that, John—and nothing less! I'm not up here for your sake, I'm here for *mine*! But every fucking time I see you, I make the same goddamned stupid mistake. Instead of just loving you, I end up in a pissing contest with you! Well, the hell with that!"

She grabs the champagne bottle with one hand, unzips me with the other, virtually tearing the zipper loose with the force of her tugging. At the revelation of my still engorged state, she whistles softly.

"I would definitely say you can walk through anybody's locker room without towel—or apology," she says.

She anoints me with champagne from glans to scrotum, then drops to her knees in front of me. First her lips, then the lining of her puckering mouth, then her yawning throat close over me like successive wraps of wet silk. I begin to feel as though I'm encased within a moist cocoon— spinning, spinning, spinning, worm becoming butterfly. Just as I'm about to sprout speckled wings and fly away forever, Kim stops gently, sliding her mouth free of me, then presses herself up my thighs, along my chest, until her lips align with mine.

"I've thought about nothing else since you sailed away from New Caledonia without fucking me, you sonofabitch!" she whispers. "You want to waste time with foreplay, or do you want to go for it, right here, right now, standing up?"

She guides my hand between her legs, her eyes fixed on mine like two windows into deep space. My middle finger vanishes into her. Her vaginal barrel clasps my finger like a splint, opening and closing.

So be it.

Standing, if that's what the lady wishes.

Her abdomen seems to ripple in waves as I enter her. Even her sphincter muscles tug at me. I feel her spasms over my stomach like miniature tidal waves. Her breasts flatten over mine. I cup her with both hands, clasping her tensing glutes to pull her higher onto me. She sobs and arches and grinds her pelvis into mine and she reddens like a lobster in boiling water.

"Oh, Christ, Christ, Christ!" she screams. "I'm already

coming. Oh, John, shit! Darling, darling, I'm coming apart—unglued—oh, Jesus! Oh, fucking shit!" she shouts.

She shudders endlessly against me. A film of sweat bathes her body as though triggered from every pore.

Strange, I feel no pain from the abrasive pearls and the rhinestone beads.

Lost not in the stars, but in the cornrows.

Later, in bed with Kim, a reading lamp focused on the multiple lacerations around my groin, she tenderly applies tincture of iodine to each furrow in my flesh, using Q-tips she's brought in her purse—for the very purpose, I must assume.

"At least nobody else will be putting too much pressure on this particular patch of terrain for the next few days," she tells me. "Is that going to cause you any problems, John?"

"Not until Monday night," I say. "By then, if there's any evidence I've been mutilated, I know a Thai girl who may cut my balls off."

"I didn't mean to ruin your love life," she laughs, "but I'm delighted I have. I've made an important decision. You're going to be my lover. Not just tonight. But when you come back. You *are* coming back, aren't you, John?"

"I'm going to give it my best shot."

"Historians of the skin trade," she cries to the paper umbrellas above the bed, "make note! September six—dateline Bangkok. Kim Correll, goddess of grunge, mistress of ceremonies aboard Otis Walden's floating round-the-world sex lab, a bimbo who never listened to Mama's warnings, has just made a date with John Locke for—when did you say we're to pick you up, John?"

"October fifteenth—at the outside."

"Well," she says, "I'll be waiting. And between now and then I promise to do my Kegels religiously."

"Your Kegels?"

"For my PC muscle."

The PC muscle—the pubococcygeal, as all new-age girls have now been informed, and as even the dusky belles of ancient Araby were taught in girlhood—is the muscle that contracts the walls of the vagina.

"I truly don't think you need to exercise your PC," I assure Kim. "It's already a blue-ribbon winner. Pump it up too much, you're liable to turn it into a killer clam."

SILVER STAR

She laughs. "Don't be silly. I do only maintenance techniques—a series of twenty three-second squeezes three times a day and three sets of the 'flutter.'"

"The flutter?" I ask. It can't be the leg flutter I do she's referring to, can it?

"That's where I squeeze-release as fast as I can. Then there's the one I always do in the tub—sucking water in, spurting it out. What a turn-on! That's my favorite!"

"I should think so," I agree.

"The fourth—and final—exercise is just a simple sort of bearing down, you know, like you do for a bowel movement—except you put the stress on the vagina, not on the anus. See what you men are missing?"

"Impressive," I concede.

"Back home," she says, "I see all those silly housewives out jogging, trying to strengthen their cardiovasculars. Silly twits should be in the tub exercising their PCs. What man stays with you because you give great EKG? There'd be a lot less divorce if women built up their pussies instead of their pulses."

It's not exactly the kind of advice that gets engraved on the heads of pins or delivered by reverends as Sunday's sermon, but it does have a convincing ring to it, I have to concede, and as the night passes, Kim's PC dexterity makes me feel as locked in as a quarterback who's used up all his time-outs.

No question, I've never been with any woman whose PC muscle is so dominating—or whose need for loving is greater.

Kim must be tuned into my thought waves, for she whispers into my ear in soft justification, "This has to last me till October fifteenth. In the meanwhile, John Locke, don't you dare die!"

"Tonight? Or in Vietnam?" I ask.

23

Day six.

Saturday.

Kim leaves early, while raindrops big as hatchlings pelt the city. She takes with her the packet of instructions I've prepared for Otis, along with two letters, one to an enterprising Australian buddy who knows where to hire men willing and able to fire weapons as sophisticated as Bofors's new Robot 70 missile, the other to a marketing agent for a holding company in Singapore, an arm of the Ministry of Defense, a company that handles exports of Singapore-made weapons, material, and support devices.

Arun arrives shortly after I've finished breakfast.

I smell the Opium perfume through the door even before the guards open it and permit him to enter.

He's wearing his hair in glossy braids. An artist's smock covers his silk blouse and the front, though not the back, of a red miniskirt. A pigtailed monkey perches on his shoulder.

He places a professional-looking makeup kit on the dressing table, then turns to me and brings his palms together.

"I hope I have not kept you waiting," he says.

"Not at all. Who is your friend?"

He nuzzles the monkey's face. "Khai. He's four years old and a champion picker of coconuts. He holds the record in Chumphon—he picked ten coconuts in fifty seconds. I do not wish to sound immodest, but I trained him myself."

He whispers to the monkey in Thai. Without apparent preparation, the animal leaps onto the canopy above Gil's bed, a remarkable aerial scamper of more than three meters to the right of Arun's shoulder and two meters higher than his head.

In Thai Arun instructs him to nap, or so I must assume, for the little creature with its piquant, ebonite face chatters a moment, then composes itself into a silent and obedient furry ball.

Now Arun begins my transformation.

First, my hair. He cuts it short, high along both sides, giving me the typical military look of an NVA officer.

I compliment him on his knowledge of the precise hair style I'll need to pass unnoticed in Vietnam.

"I've been doing my homework," he confesses. "Vietnamese friends have been giving me photographs to study."

Next he dyes my hair jet black.

While we wait for the dye to set, he looks at me openly, without embarrassment.

"Gil told you my grandmother was English, did he not?"

I nod.

"It is the Anglo in me which now emboldens me to say something I feel must be said. We Thais do not express our feelings this boldly. So, forgive me..."

"Please say whatever it is you're thinking," I encourage.

"I imagine that you...find me—*confusing*?"

"Yes. Very."

"May I make a suggestion?"

"I'd appreciate one."

"Think of me only as a girl. It will make things much easier for both of us. While I was cutting your hair, I couldn't help noticing in the mirror that you were trying not to look at my legs."

I grin. "And having one helluva time *not* doing it," I agree. "Your high heels and that miniskirt only set your legs and ankles off more than usual. I might as well come right out with it, Arun. You've got the most beautiful legs I've ever seen on any human being, man *or* woman."

"Thank you. So please enjoy them. Enjoy the way I look. *I* do. I love being a woman. Well, *almost* a woman. Soon I'll be one entirely. So in the meanwhile, Mr. Locke, please don't be ashamed of reacting to me anyway you wish to react. It only flatters me and makes me more feminine."

"All right," I agree. "We'll just go with the flow."

"Wonderful!" He smiles and resumes his work on my hair.

Next he experiments with the shape of my eyes, using tiny transparent strips of tape to lift and tuck and stretch. At each stage he makes Polaroid shots of his handiwork and with each stage he brings me closer and closer to appearing Asian, at least with my hair and my eyes. Satisfied at last with the new shape of my eyes, he claps his hands delightedly.

"I'm going to put a very temporary skin lotion on now," he says. "It's quite subtle. It will, I hope, take away some of your South Pacific tan and give you a more wintered, ivory look. I'm assuming you want to appear as though you're from Hanoi, not from the South."

"Correct."

"Now, this is washable," he cautions, "so it will streak in the rain, which, of course, is a huge problem at this time of year. But the more permanent skin dyes make a person look exactly as though he's deliberately changed the coloring of his skin. I'm hoping that the combination of this temporary dye plus my constantly touching up your makeup as we travel will fool everyone—unless they're examining you close up under bright lights."

The lotion works its magic, and slowly my sun-browned face begins to appear five years older and pale. Incredibly, the dye has leached away the American look of me.

"Have you ever worn contact lenses?" Aruns asks.

"No."

He brings several pair from his makeup kit.

"I bought alternates, since I didn't have a prescription. All dark brown. Pick the pair that works best for you. These will take some getting used to, Mr. Locke. May I show you how to slip them on?"

I find myself staring with unabashed prurient feelings at his full rich lips while his face is close to mine and I feel his breath cool against my forehead.

The third set are God's own. I have my normal, sharp, unobstructed vision back once more.

"Look at yourself now," he says.

The clipped black hair, the brown almond eyes, the ivory skin tone combine into a startling image in my mirror. Aside from my nose, an alien enclave on the continent of my face, I have become Asian.

"Awesome," I whisper. "Arun, you're a genius."

"Thank you, Mr. Locke."

"Call me Linh," I say. "It will be my Vietnamese name from this moment on."

"Very well, Linh. Now I need to make more photos, then a plaster cast of your nose. I'll work from that to create a prosthetic nose we can place over yours, then blend into your cheeks with the dye and makeup. I think it would be wise to have six of them made up, don't you? Wear and tear, you know."

"I'm in your hands, Arun. Order a dozen if you think we'll need that many. But I'm not the only one who needs your expertise."

"Oh?"

"*You* do as much as I. Many Vietnamese girls are quite beautiful, but we're talking your basic North Vietnamese Army nurse. She—that is, you, playing that role—must look scrubbed and puritanical. You think it's possible you can make yourself into the kind of girl men won't stare at?"

"Oh, I can make myself look so pure and innocent they'll want to put me on one of their revolutionary posters. Don't you worry, Linh. I'll blend right in. And I've been studying Vietnamese. I speak Mandarin, you know, and I'm finding so many similar words in Vietnamese. Oh, I'll be fine. It's so exciting. And you mustn't worry about my being able to keep up with the rest of you. I'm a dancer and I've done yoga since I was a little girl. I can run for miles and never even breathe hard."

"Since I was a little girl."

Arun's phrase lingers in my mind even after she—after he—has gone, the pigtail monkey back on her—his—shoulder, and left me sitting alone in the penthouse, staring at myself in the mirror.

I'm still seated in front of the mirror when Gil rushes in breathlessly with a startling companion, a Moorish sheikh, flamboyant in burnoose, hood tied under his bearded chin. I have been speaking Vietnamese aloud to my reflection and trying to evaluate the credibility of each facial expression. The planes of the face shift subtly when you switch languages. I need to make certain that my American persona is not exposed behind the makeup as my lips change shape to accommodate an Asian tonal language.

"It's you!" Gil exclaims.

"*Sans* nose," I add. "Once I get the nose on, I'm hoping it all snaps into place."

Two of Gil's security men bring in what appears to be electronic gear. They hurry right out again, the guards in the corridor closing the door behind them.

"You going to a costume party?" I ask Arty, the man who's bootlegging around the penthouse in the ridiculous-looking outfit from the Atlas mountains.

I've wounded him, clearly, for he rips off the phony beard and unties the hood.

"I've had great success with this burnoose," he insists. "Nobody has ever identified me before when I've been wearing it."

"Maybe they've just been ashamed to tell you," I suggest.

"Well, goddamn it, John, I put it on this morning for *your* benefit, so if the Mât Vu's back on the job and watching this place, they'd never know I came rushing over here to meet with you. Maybe I didn't fool you, but I know it fooled them. Tell him, Gil."

"Man's right," Gil says to me. "We get Saudis and Tunisians and Moroccans in here all the time in the daylight hours. They drive up here in big limos to book their favorite girls in advance."

"I even rented a limo to make it look absolutely authentic," Arty says. "It's parked out front. God knows how I'm going to justify it on my expense account. You do know, don't you, John, that I'm doing all this strictly on my own? Washington doesn't have a clue that I'm personally backing your play."

"You expect me to believe that, Arty?"

"No, but I thought I'd better start getting used to the sound of it, in case any of this blows back in our faces."

"Don't think I'm ungrateful. I just have to get used to seeing you in a burnoose, that's all."

"What about yourself? You think it's easy to adjust to seeing you turn Asian in front of my eyes?"

"So what do you think?"

"I'm immensely impressed."

"Gil, how about you?"

"Fucking A, Shit Hook! I've shot dozens of bastards who looked just like that. You put the nose on, you better shout the password around here or you got glass for an ass, man, that's how right-on you look. I told you, huh?— that fuckin' Arun can turn day into night."

"When will you be ready to leave?" Arty asks.

"Depends on Nguyen," I say.

"He's ready right now."

"I'd like to hear from him first and find out just exactly what his word 'ready' means in my terms."

"You won't."

"What do you mean—I won't?"

"He called me right after you spoke to him last night. He's asked me to act as middleman. So you lay it on me— I'll lay it on him. That's how we'll do it."

"I'm not sure I'm happy with that, Arty."

"Simply in the interest of security, nothing more. He's not trying to usurp any of your authority, John. Even though this is a two-pronged mission, there's a clear understanding on everybody's part that you're the honcho in charge. On the other hand, Nguyen and his men have been in and out of Nam a dozen times—and as recently as an incursion right into Saigon just three months ago. It's been more than ten years for you, John. So Nguyen is going to have a more precise knowledge of what you may or may not need for the mission. Am I right about that?"

"In theory, absolutely. But ten years doesn't change certain givens—the terrain in Laos, the weather this time of year, immersion foot, leeches, malaria. It doesn't change the fact that we have to be prepared to evade one helluva lot more armed men just getting to the border of Vietnam than we ever had to worry about when we were fighting in Laos."

"No problem, John. You give me your list, I give it to Nguyen. You want it, you got it. We're only trying to cut down the traffic flow in and out of here, so the opposition can't vector in. Okay?"

"Makes sense."

"Which brings me full circle, back to my question—when will you be ready to leave?"

"I need at least two more days to digest all the intelligence material the colonel has sent me, then a day to be sure I've committed it to memory. I also need another day after that to wrap up personal affairs—I've got some letters to write, for Gil to mail if I miss the bus home. And Arun needs every bit of those four days to get the noses made and my makeup down pat. Not to mention her own. Incidentally, that's one of the many things we'll need—a nurse's uniform, army issue, along with shoes, hat, insignia, and a cover ID for her. I need a cover too. Make me a major, first name Linh; whatever you invent for the rest of my name is okay with me. Born in Hanoi. Assign me to a combat unit that has recently suffered heavy casualities in Kampuchea in a firefight with the Khmers.... Then I need an hour or two aboard *Steel Tiger*, just to make sure she's okay while I'm away—and to feel a little maudlin about leaving her behind. Then I'll be ready, let's set it for Thursday morning. We can be on site in Nakhon Phanom Thursday night and cross the Mekong into Laos the first rainy night after that."

"Okay, Thursday morning it is. We'll pick you up. When can I get your inventory list?"

"Tomorrow night. It's going to be a long list, Gil."

"From you, John, what else would I expect?"

"It might tax even the resources of the CIA. That is, if they knew anything about this operation."

"Tax away. I'll do my best. Incidentally, we've—I should say *I've*—tagged this whole gaggle Op Sacred Sword."

I seem to recall a previous Sacred Sword operation in Vietnam, back in the early sixties.

"Didn't that go down the tube?"

"To quote you, that was then," Arty counters brightly. "This is now. And the psyops seem even more relevant for this mission. You know the dynamics?"

"No, I don't."

"Okay, back in the fourteenth century a dude named Le Loi—who, incidentally, lived in the very same province where you're first going to hash into Vietnam this trip—organized a resistance against the Chinese Ming occupation. Legend has it that he was out fishing, and lo and behold—he pulled a sword from the lake, the sword he used to lead his country to freedom. When the fighting had ended, he threw the sword back into the lake. But it didn't sink. With a clap of thunder it pulled itself from its scabbard and changed itself into a fire-breathing dragon and flew off to the mountains, where to this very day it waits, ready to assist the cause of freedom."

"Fuckin' gooks ripped off King Arthur!" Gil cries. "That's *The Lady in the Lake*, man! The sword is Excalibur! Jesus, are they ever one tricky bunch!"

"You got that turned around, Gil," Arty comments. "The Vietnamese have had that legend for almost six hundred years. It definitely predates Sir Thomas Mallory and *The Lady in the Lake*."

"Sonofabitch!" Gil mutters. "You learn something every day, don't you?"

"Okay," I agree, "the operation will be known as Sacred Sword—or SS as the acronym. Now, about that inventory I'm working up. I'm wondering if you can turn up some of the items in the next four days or if we need more time."

"Give me a for-instance."

"Well, it sounds like a little thing, but in the long run it's not. There's a San Francisco outfit that packages survival food under the trade names Light Force, Power Pack, and Stress Pack—vitamins and spirulina powder as travel rations where space and weight are critical. We need enough for eight people for the twelve days I'm estimating it will take us to work our way across Laos. Once we're into Vietnam, we can dump a lot of the gear we need in Laos."

"No sweat with that one. I can have it here overnight."

"Gil's got AK–47s right here in the club I can borrow to practice field-stripping. I haven't fired an AK–47 since I left New Caledonia in July. I need to refamiliarize myself with the weapon, especially with the firing-change lever, which, as you know, is on the right side, not on the left like our M–16. I also need to check myself out on the Vietnamese submachine gun. I'd like you to send one over today, if possible, a K50M with the MAT–49-type sliding wire stock and Type 56 pistol grip—and please make sure, Arty, the model you send me has had the forward end of the barrel jacket eliminated."

"Mind if I make notes?"

I hand him one of the pads from the work table and watch him as he jots down *K50M* and *MAT 49* and *Type 56* and *BJ elim*.

When he's got his notes caught up, I ask, "You issuing us claymores?"

"Any objections?"

"If we're going in sterile—and I believe we should—we should pack instead the Soviet *Miny ye Oskolochonym Napravleniem* antipersonnel mine—they call it the MON–50, not to be confused with the MON–100 or the MON–200. It uses a plastic explosive similar to the C–4 in our claymores, but the fragmentation matrix is etched to detonate into rectangular fragments rather than into the steel spheres we use in our mines. We'll need both types of detonators, trip wire *and* electric, okay?"

"How come you're into all this specialized shit, John?" Gil asks,—more impressed, I can see, than surprised.

"Same way you're into pussy, Gil." I smile. "For the money. So what do you think, Arty? Can do?"

"Give me one good reason why you can't just go in with claymores, like everybody else?" Arty asks.

"Okay, scenario. Third night into Laos, right? We've got claymores set up on the perimeter. Some unfriendlies encroach and get blown away. Each claymore fires seven hundred steel pellets out to fifty meters. So we've zapped the intruders and we scoot away over the horizon. But what have we left behind? *American* pellets embedded in trees all over the ambush area. Wouldn't it be better to leave Soviet shrapnel—rectangles, not spheres,—so that any main detachment on our trail is confused as to our true identity?"

Arty makes a note. "I'll get you the MON–50."

I lay a few more highlights on him, since I don't want him to turn overwrought when he takes delivery of the full list of absolutes I've been preparing.

"Well," I conclude, "why don't I have it all together for you tomorrow night, so you don't have to go at it piecemeal?"

He looks relieved.

"All right, now," he says, as though delighted to have his shot at me, "I'm going to show you a couple of goodies I brought you, some really high-tech equipment. I'm willing to gamble one hundred sacks of Thai salt you don't have *these* on your goddamn list."

"I'm sure I don't," I say.

"These are working models, John, and I'm going to leave them right here so you can familiarize yourself with their operation and maintenance. Two identical pieces of equipment will be made available to your team for the mission. Now, this first little sweetheart we call Tiger Eye. It's a telephoto device sensitive enough to be able to let you read a license plate on a vehicle twelve clicks out. Once you get your Asian persona together, you might want to go up on the roof of Gil's club. If no Mât Vu sniper tries to pick you off, you can be a little more relaxed about how convincing you look as an Oriental. And while you're up there you can take this Tiger's Eye and read the menus in some of the top-floor restaurants in the midtown hotels. . . . Okay, this other little beauty . . ."

He opens an olive-drab box in the manner of a magician producing a full-grown white dove from a darning needle. He reveals a compact field radio topped by a state-of-the-art console.

"You'll dig this, Gil," Arty predicts. "You were a radioman, weren't you?"

"Bet your ass," Gil mutters. "So what do you call this? And what does it do?"

"TRANSAT—transponder-satellite replay. To operate it, you have to use this—"

He opens up a small, collapsible dish antenna attached to a tripod. He plugs a cord from the tripod into the TRANSAT box.

"Whatever message you want to send goes out in a millisecond burst. The signal is instantly coded into an infrared pulse, which is picked up by one of our satellites and bounced back to the Intelligence and Security Command Detachment based as the U.S. Army Field Station on Okinawa—Torii Station. They relay it back to us— and we slow it down and decode it. It all happens so fast there's nothing the enemy can triangulate on—no radio signal."

Arty is gloating over his magic box.

Deservedly so, it strikes me. I feel loved and sustained

by such awesome technology. Here in this compact, easy-to-carry box is my voice to the outside world, a voice that travels as fast as lightning.

"Thank you, Arty," I say. "You've made my day."

CHAPTER

24

Gil has given orders to his security force that I'm not to be disturbed until I choose to surface from self-imposed solitude.

The prospect of the long weekend and uninterrupted hours so frees my mind that I'm able to complete the inventory of equipment and ordnance before midnight Saturday, an inventory so finely honed it even includes such items as leather pouches for ammo mags. Over the years of combat I've learned that it's bad policy to drop loaded magazines into your pockets to gather dirt and lint. This kind of sloppy fieldcraft can result in a malfunction precisely at the split second when a firing glitch can cost you your life. Pocket carrying can likewise dent or damage a magazine and lead to feed blockage, so for years I've been carrying my spare mags in a leather pouch slipped over my belt. The inventory calls for the entire team to be outfitted with such pouches.

Sunday passes all too swiftly as I alternate between absorbing the mass of intelligence material the colonel has sent me and handling the Soviet weapons Arty has had delivered.

Thirty minutes with the AK–47 proves more than adequate. When the front end of the firing change lever is in its top position, it locks the trigger and prevents the bolt from being opened to chamber a round. In the central position it allows for automatic fire. When fully depressed, it permits only a single shot with each pull of the trigger. Up, down, middle, top, bottom—I practice thumbing the lever into alternating positions until my thumb feels as though it's melded with the steel.

The K50M submachine gun is more alien to me. I walk around with it in right-side firing position, then left, then lying on my back, then prone, then kneeling, then rolling onto my shoulder with the gun held in both hands, until after a time the weapon begins to feel like an extension of either arm.

The third weapon is a surprise. On his own, Gil has sent over a wild-card Soviet 40mm grenade launcher, the BG–15. I'd never seen a BG–15 until now, although I have been hearing rumors for the past few months that it has surfaced in Afghanistan. It's designed to supplement the firepower of the AK–47 in the same way the U.S. M203 supplements the M–16. This Soviet blooper is short-barreled, scarcely a foot from pistol grip to bore. The launching tube itself is not even six inches long. The whole weapon feels light, probably not more than two pounds. The barrel is rifled, unlike our smooth-bore, and it's muzzle-loading, as opposed to our breech-loaders.

Arty has sent along a sample grenade. It has a perforated tail at its base which appears to contain the propellant charge. Unlike our M79 or M203 systems, it looks as though the entire round is launched at firing, no cartridge case to be ejected, as in our grenade launchers. I find the BG–15's sights overly complex, however, if not in fact clumsy. A series of detents is marked in white as 2 and 3, presumably indicating 200 and 300 meters. There is an extreme elevation detent on the sight marked in red as 42—420 meters, unquestionably the weapon's maximum range.

By Sunday night the discord in my mind no longer sounds like the background noise at a cocktail party, indistinct yet tumultuous. A calm, even a serene silence replaces the chaos. I begin to feel as a mountain climber must when he has surmounted the icy, precipitous rock face of the ascent and has at last achieved the summit from which, now, at last, he can gaze in any direction and behold infinity.

As I fall asleep I project myself into Laos.

I'm moving along the creviced scar of a road leading east across a checkerboard of rice paddies, the lavender mountains beyond shrouded in mist. I pass a cluster of houses on stilts. Rain explodes on their thatch roofs; ill-fitting doors bang open and closed in the wet gusts. Banana trees in the bordering fields whip-dance insanely in the monsoon wind. The more the merrier, I'm thinking, the wetter, the windier, the better. Covers the sound of my passing. Washes away my tracks in a matter of minutes. Keeps the guards huddled in their barracks.

Now I steal through the silence of a bamboo grove. Directly ahead a green bamboo viper hangs head down, coiled and ready to strike. I circle him, stepping away into underbrush, and am besieged by mole crickets and tiger beetles. A leech plummets onto my shoulder. I flick him away with a long splinter I carry for the purpose. The sawlike dive of a lone mosquito tickles my eardrum.

Ah, Laos! Lovely, soft, green—deadly. How I have thought of you these last ten years!

And while I'm running Laotian memories, miraculously Sunday night becomes Monday morning.

Day Eight brings Arun with my nose.

For the longest time I stare at myself in the mirror and say nothing once she's stepped back with a tiny sigh of completion and allowed me the shock of discovery.

My reflection is no longer that of the face I remember nor of the jawline I've shaved all these years. The man looking back at me now from dark, impenetrably narrowed eyes has a flat nose and a scar along his upper lip—one of Arun's last-minute strokes of inspired theatricality. The man in my mirror is dangerous-looking and implacable. I would not care to meet him under adversarial conditions.

"Do I have to look quite so—mean?" I ask Arun.

"Smile," she suggests.

I smile. I have seen prettier smiles on the faces of Colombian hit men.

"Well, at least nobody will be inviting me to any dinner parties in Hanoi, will they?"

"Are you pleased?" Arun asks.

"More than pleased. I'm almost scared, looking at my Asian self. Somehow I pictured myself as more benign. What I'm seeing here is a real jungle killer."

"Possibly, Linh," Arun suggests, "you are finally seeing your true self. Or possibly I *wanted* you dangerous-looking."

I let it go at that and call downstairs for Gil.

I observe that he's genuinely stunned by the wonders Arun has wrought upon me. But almost immediately his surprise turns into excitement.

"Goddamn it, Skipper, you're just liable to pull this caper off after all! Tell you the truth, when you first asked me about getting you a makeup man, I thought you were crazy. But not anymore! Okay, so you're three or four inches too tall, more like a Manchu than a Viet, but otherwise you could be just one more fucking slant. No offense, Arun."

Arun *wais* Gil forgivingly with upraised palms. She appears even more ecstatic about her handiwork than Gil.

"No longer is he *farong*," she says.

Farong is ethnocentric Thai for Westerner, Occidental, whitey, honky.

"Got to test it, Gil," I announce. "I need to get out now—onto the sidewalks—among other Asians—and see how it plays."

"Some fucker waiting out there will blow you away, that's how it'll play!" he shouts at me. "Jesus, Shit Hook, this close to jump time, you gotta start gambling?"

"If I can't fool some half-ass secret police agent in Bangkok, how the hell am I ever going to fool trained army cadres in Vietnam?"

Twenty minutes later, Arun having given me a final touch-up, the Browning snugged into my shoulder holster, I saunter out of the T. and A. Club and onto Patpong Street as cool as a pimp.

The morning air smells of rain, but the sun-textured sky over Bangkok ripples like pastel silk banners. I walk up Patpong to Surawong Road and turn to the right toward Rama IV, my feet steel springs, coiling and uncoiling with each step I take, bouncing me along effortlessly, a man with a new identity, a man named Linh whom no one is hunting, a man moving now among the streams of Asians as though obeying a different law of gravity than those around him.

The city lies caught like a panther in a net, cars, buses, trucks, *tuk-tuks*, and *songthaews* tangled in growling mid-morning captivity. I walk past them all, as liberated as the bent old man I see paddling his sampan along a canal which bubbles from shore-to-shore with detergent escaping from an upstream laundry. Oblivious to the traffic above him, he passes under the bridge I cross.

Soon enough I find myself drifting into Yaowaraj, Bangkok's vast and sprawling Chinatown, where I am swept by the currents of humanity along wide, boisterous streets until at last I'm swirled into the eddy of one narrow, twisting lane between New Road and Suapa Road.

Nobody appears to be taking notice of me. I have vanished into the quicksand of anonymity. Elbow to elbow with Asians, I merge and blend and flow without challenge. In passing, I turn to glance back at an American couple. Lord and mistress of the civilized world, they have staked out their own, not-to-be-invaded space in front of one of the antique shops of Nakorn Kasem. In what I guess is a Kansas accent, they are debating the probable price of a rosewood screen displayed inside the window. The man's pockets bulge with Fielding, Fodor, and the Far East Economic Review's *All-Asia Guide*.

I wonder—am I seeing them now as Asians see them? As Asians see us? Or am I seeing them out of the knowledge, and the guilt, that for all of our good intentions, all of us—all races—when we come to see another country, come as sojourners, as voyeurs, with the security of credit cards and return tickets.

Is this how I am perceived around the China Rim in my role as John Locke, sailor of fortune? As an itinerant?

Well, certainly! How else?

Look at me—son in Hanoi, father in San Diego, mother in Paris, woman I love buried in Vietnam, girl who loves me waiting in Bali, *Steel Tiger*, my only home, lying to ties across the Chao Phraya.

Now, that is one fragmented son of a bitch!

Suddenly I feel overwhelmed by the separation from everything I have ever known. It is as though the makeup on my face has torn me away from everything I have ever loved. What violence will this new persona, this man Linh, do to whatever singularity I might once have had? And yet how else can I claim my son? Already he lives in my mind. I need him to live in my heart. I need the sense of purpose that caring for him will give me. What else but purpose endures? What else of us can possibly remain intact?

What are *these* questions? Who is today's ventriloquist?

I find myself passing the open-front gold shops of Yaowaraj. I spend all the bahts and traveler's checks I've brought with me. I buy necklaces, bracelets, and anklets of gold for Lek. I do not bargain with the bent Chinese shopkeeper. Even though she assumes that I'm Asian, she will not grant me a lower price than she will any passing *farong*, for she knows that I know that the price of gold is fixed by the government and that her prices are identical with the prices at the dozens of other gold shops glittering wall to wall along this particular block.

My buying spree allays my identity crisis. Weighted down with gold chains, I manage to restore my illusion of self.

I call Colonel Chutai at his headquarters.

I'm in luck. He's at his desk. He accepts my call straightaway.

I explain to him that I'm wandering around the city on my own at present and since I'm not more than minutes away from *Steel Tiger*, could he arrange for the dock guards to permit me to come aboard, say, thirty minutes from now? The reason for all this, I tell him, has to do with the fact that the guards will not recognize me in my Asian persona.

He assures me the arrangements will be made at once.

His aide waits at the gate to the navy base as my taxi drops me. The young lieutenant's eyes pass over me without interest, even though I approach him and stop only a few feet from him.

"How does that popular song go?" I ask. "About the entertainment girls in Thailand?"

His eyes snap around, bore into mine.

"That's right," I say. "It's John Locke—underneath the greasepaint."

He has trouble with it.

"Didn't the colonel tell you?"

"No, sir. He simply ordered me to wait at the gate for you."

"Good," I comment. "His way of testing."

"Sir, it's—it's remarkable! I saw you get out of the cab, but—then I looked away. You were not the person I was waiting for."

"What was your first impression when you saw me get out of the cab? Did you notice me in particular, wonder about me—or simply dismiss me from your mind?"

"I felt that—well, that you were somebody important. But then I went back to watching for the next cab, and for Mr. Locke."

"Important?"

"Yes, sir."

"No more than that?"

"Well, I could feel—a certain forcefulness. Even a slightly . . . dangerous air that you gave off."

"I have to work on that," I say, more to myself than to him. "Have to tone that down."

"Please follow me, sir."

He leads me past the sentry gate and the guards.

Once inside the walls of the base I spot *Steel Tiger*'s mainmast ticking back and forth in the wash of passing river traffic like the blade of a metronome.

Colonel Chutai himself waits on the wharf, the two navy guards patroling either beam of *Steel Tiger*.

I salute him. He returns the salute with a smile.

"You really don't have to do that, Captain," he says.

"Possibly that's why I like to." I smile back.

"Let me look at you," he says.

He walks around me, appraising me from every aspect.

"Incredible," he says at last.

"Thank you, sir. And thank you for all your support. I could never have hoped to make it, even across Laos, without the intelligence data you gave me."

"When you come out, Captain, you can repay us with a few hours' debriefing, so we can update that data."

"I shall plan on it, sir."

"Especially if you pick up any information about the Vietnamese dry-weather plans for harassing our borders."

"Understood, sir."

"Well," he says, "I know you have things to do aboard. Take all the time you need. When you're ready to go back, the lieutenant will handle your transport. And be assured your boat will be kept under constant guard."

"I'm very grateful, sir."

Most un-Thai-like, he extends his hand, as he did when I first met him. I take it.

"The gods be with you," he says.

I watch him stride away, then I turn to *Steel Tiger*.

Times before when I've left her, I could sense her rebuke or at least a certain petulance. Now she feels settled and secure.

I climb aboard, absorbing her welcome through my soles. It's as though I'm standing on the living back of a leviathan, savoring its beneficence.

I switch off the intruder-alarm, unlock and unboard the companionway, and scamper below.

In the salon I feel that instantaneous back-to-the-womb wash of security a loving boat gives you. Each of *Steel Tiger*'s little sighs and sounds, the very smell of her, indicate that all is well in her world.

I take off my jacket and go to work on the few things that must be tended to in order to keep her this contented for the month or more I'll be gone.

I close all the sea cocks on her through-hull fittings.

I inspect all hose clamps for tightness and examine each hose-to-metal joint for any evidence of leakage. I move from one raw-water hose to another until I have felt each one for its resilience.

I check the power operation of the float switch on the automatic power-driven bilge pumps.

And finally I inspect, clean, and burnish the output leads and terminals on the automatic battery charger.

I board up the companionway as I leave, lock the hatch, and activate the alarm system.

The colonel's aide returns me to the corner of Patpong and Surawong Road. I walk the short block to the T. and A. Club.

Gil is waiting at the bar with an anxious-looking Toang.

"We been sweating your case all afternoon," Gil grumbles.

"Spot any dudes following you?" Toang asks.

"Nobody noticed me. You were so right," I say to Gil. "Arun *is* a genius!"

I bring him upstairs and write four checks on the funds I transferred from Singapore to Bangkok.

"This check goes to Nguyen for the Resistance," I say. "Please send it over with Arty, so Nguyen and I don't have to deal with it one-on-one. This check's for Arun. She should deposit it before we take off."

"Why the fuck do you keep calling Arun *her* when it's a *he*?" he demands.

"Like Arun, Gil, I'm living for the future, okay? This third check is for the security guys here—break it up among them however you feel is fair. The fourth check goes to the two Sikhs who fought alongside us."

"You know, you're a stylish motherfucker," Gil says. "The guys won't forget this."

"I won't forget them."

"Fifty grand," Gil comments, totaling the checks I've written. "Business is that good, huh, Skipper?"

"I got lucky in New Caledonia. But even with this, I still have a few bucks left in the bank in Singapore—enough to keep me cruising for the next few months anyway. Speaking of cruising, Gil, if I don't get back, keep an eye on *Steel Tiger* for me till my old man can fly over and sail her back to San Diego. I'll be writing all my sign-off letters tomorrow and Wednesday. But I don't want you to mail them unless you get definite confirmation my makeup ran while I was on hang-time in Hanoi."

"They haven't yet invented the motherfucker good enough to drop you, Skipper," Gil says. "When you come back, we'll burn your letters and scatter the ashes in the river when the tide's on the way out."

Later, when the nighttime disco beat begins to shake the penthouse floor, the guards admit Lek.

Apparently no one has told her about my transformation.

She looks at me, past me, then around the apartment.

"Where Mistah Locke?" she asks suspiciously. "Who you?"

"Right here, Lek, looking at you, baby."

She comes to me slowly, incredulously, staring hard at my features, touching my lips with her fingertips.

I kiss her and she knows I am the person I claim to be. She skips around me with a little dance of delight.

"You more handsome as Asian!" she cries, clapping her hands together. "I think Lek in love with you now!"

I start to hang gold on her as though decorating a Christmas tree, around her neck, her wrists, her ankles, until she is weighted down and has summoned into her lustrous eyes tears of gratitude appropriate to the weight of the gold.

Gil pounds into the room as though being pursued by Martians.

"Change of plans!" he announces. "Arty just called. That chicken Kiev arrived ahead of schedule. Nobody knows how long it'll be on the menu. So everything moves up. Arty suggests you write those Dear Johns at your next stop. He'll get 'em back to me."

"How soon's he want to leave?"

"Fifteen minutes. On the roof."

"The roof?"

"Chopper."

I reach for Lek. She has not fully understood our conversation. She's been too preoccupied with the comforting warmth of the gold against her satin skin.

"This is a good-bye kiss," I say.

"Good-bye? Lek just get here!"

"I'll be back before the end of October."

"I cry six days after you go."

"Make it seven." I smile.

And she kisses me so that I will remember her. I keep wondering if we'd had tonight in bed whether she'd have discovered the havoc Kim's cornrows did to me.

She leaves with Gil and ten minutes later I'm packed.

Gil returns with Toang precisely as I hear the single most remembered sound in my memory bank—the thwuck-thwuck-thwuck of rotors above us.

Toang takes my gear. I follow Gil and him up a flight of stairs and onto the roof.

Gil's guards ring the perimeters.

City lights glitter on all sides of us.

Arty's pale, birdlike face peers out from behind the bubble of the slick. He sits thinly at the controls and urgently waves me aboard.

I hold Gil in my arms a moment, then Toang, until I break off, feeling that I'm leaving one more chunk of me behind, one more fragment torn away. I run in a wind-buffeted crouch to the chopper and pile in as I've piled in God knows how many times before, and while I'm still strapping myself in, Arty pulls pitch, wrenching us up and away.

By the time I manage to look back down I've already lost sight of the roof of the T. and A. Club, of Patpong, of Surawong Road, and discover that we are elevating past the blazing windows of downtown skyscrapers.

For an instant I succeed in catching sight of the Mother of Rivers and the approximate area where I have left *Steel Tiger*.

And then we are clattering northeast, the diadem that is Bangkok falling away behind us.

═CHAPTER═

25

Arty follows Highway 21 northeast.

He zips down at Nakhon Ratchasima to refuel, then lifts off again and once more tracks 21 toward the airport at Khon Kaen, an hour and a half's flight time closer to our destination.

No man looks more natural in a cockpit than Arty does. He, not the machine encasing him, is flying, his movements instinctive and graceful and sure, none of the twentieth-century-executive look, the dapper silver-haired, steely-eyed four-striper jockeying a 747 across the sea. Arty was born to fly in small planes, to operate out of truncated jungle airstrips, to pitch through narrow valleys. I wouldn't be surprised if his bones, like those of birds, are alive with air, not with marrow.

He sits strangely, one side slightly higher than the other.

"Don't tell me you still have it!" I say.

"Never leave ground zero without it."

"How about letting me touch it? Maybe some of the magic'll rub off on me."

He slips the book he's sitting on out from under him, a battered copy of Norman Vincent Peale's *The Power of Positive Thinking*. The AK–47 round an enemy had directed his way back in the late sixties when he was zooming in and out of some pretty dicey LZs is still lodged in the book's hard cover.

"Beats the hell out of sitting on a steel helmet." He grins.

Two thousand feet below us, rice *sawahs* lie like blackboards chalked with streaks of moonlight reflected by paddy waters. We loft along, ghosting through the scribble of clouds, toward the thin, infertile plateaus of Thailand's northeast provinces—known as *Isaan*, from the Sanskrit name for the Mon-Khmer kingdom Isana, which flourished here centuries earlier. Not too distant from our flight path the late Chester Gorman and his team of University of Pennsylvania anthropologists excavated the remains of the world's oldest agricultural society and bronze culture, centuries older than similar cultures in China and in the Tigris–Euphrates valley.

Arty interrupts my reverie.

"Nguyen and his men believe Arun is a woman," he says out of nowhere. "I figured it was better to leave it that way. And Arun agrees. I thought you ought to know."

"Thanks for telling me," I say. "How'd Nguyen react to the idea of having a woman on the team?"

"Not well. You don't know what I had to go through this afternoon. I took Arun over to the boxing camp and had him run an obstacle course with the jungle fighters Nguyen is bringing along. He beat the shit out of the whole pack, so that was the end of Nguyen's beef. At least about a woman not being able to keep up with his men. But he's still unhappy, even though he knows Arun has to come along to keep you looking Asian."

"I'll settle his mind," I assure Arty. "Tell me about the men he's bringing."

"State-of-the-art guys, all of them," Arty says. "You'll see."

We refuel once more, this time at the airport outside Khon Kaen.

"Nguyen, his men, Arun, and all your ordnance and equipment were flown in by transport to NKP. That's where I'm dropping you."

"NKP?" I ask.

"It's what we call the Royal Thai Air Force base—twelve clicks west of Nakhon Phanom. We flew rescue and recon missions out of there during the Indochina War. Now it's a listening post for radio and electronic sensor devices. It'll be your staging area."

"Was that very adroit, Arty? Flying us all in? Can't that be traced back to the Thai Air Force? Or to the CIA?"

"Just a routine training exercise. Hell, John, it happens

all the time. This July we staged Operation Cobra Gold, a joint exercise—Thai forces with our participation. We airlifted an entire U.S. infantry batallion and six Green Beret Special Forces teams straight from Hawaii and Okinawa aboard C5 Galaxys and C141 Starlifters. Our people spent a month exercising with Thai forces in Songkhla Province before the big climax—an amphibious beach assault involving two thousand Thai troopers and U.S. Marines. We even tossed in six F15 fighters for air support, so who the hell's going to take any notice of a handful of people getting off aircraft at NKP?"

"Strikes me you keep pretty busy out here, Arty."

"Way to go, John, way to go. Besides, the CIA is an equal-opportunity employer. Hell, we'll work with *any*-body!"

An hour later, as we pass above Lake Lahan, still a hundred kilometers from the border, I sense a silhouette of mountains appearing dimly on the horizon beyond the long whip of the Mekong River. They rise out of Laos subtly, like whispered fables once told at night in long-vanished kingdoms.

"Too bad I can't just fly you across to Keo Neua Pass and the Nam border," Arty says, picking up my thoughts. "But that tranquil-looking countryside across the river is a beehive of fortified missile sites. The Vietnamese have close to fifty thousand troops in a country where the gross national product is nothing more than two million orgasms a month. You any idea how paranoid the Thais are about the Vietnamese driving across their border?"

"What would that get Hanoi? Except more problems?"

"Oh, I admit it's an unlikely scenario. But between you and me, John, Hanoi could do it, if they wanted to. I think the Thais could hold them long enough to give us a chance to get back into it. Can you imagine the shitstorm *that* would kick off in the States? And you can bet that Beijing would pour a million men into North Vietnam. The whole enchilada could make our war in Nam look like the prelims to the main event. But that's how touch-and-go it is out here. And that's why shifting the hot potato to Hanoi is so important—like, say, a sudden, spontaneous uprising of the Vietnamese people against the Soviet presence, say in Cam Ranh Bay, say an attempt by the people to sink an encroaching imperialistic, colonialistic Soviet carrier. That's what the ol' doctor ordered. So—enter John Locke, looking for his little boy. Next thing we know Captain Locke has become the linchpin of a geopolitical ploy so secretive, so tangled, it becomes unthinkable—and therefore doesn't exist. Yet a Kiev-class carrier damaged at Cam Ranh Bay is the hair trigger of a gun pointed straight at the heart of Hanoi."

I look over at him. He's slipped Norman Vincent Peale's book back under his glutes. He reminds me of an eagle circling a rabbit warren.

"I have to tell you," I say to him, "that I'm not in sympathy with trying to destabilize Hanoi, not the least little bit. We had our shot and we blew it. We left their country in shambles. If we can't help them rebuild and find their way back into world society, the way we did with Japan and Germany, at least we can leave them alone! I also want you to know that I am feeling personally blackmailed. Somebody in the Mât Vu is using my son to get back at me. And my own side is using me to get back at Hanoi. I wish I were in the position to say fuck all of you, but I'm not. So I'm in. But don't pretend for a second that you don't know I'm goddamned pissed about one helluva lot of things!"

"I know how you feel, John."

"The fuck you do!"

"Maybe I even agree with you. But the outfit I work for has a different set of drummers and I'm a team player. You're not."

"Did you know that the Thais invaded Vietnam?" I ask him abruptly.

Skeptically, he looks over at me.

"The Thais?"

"That's right!"

"No way, John! They're a peace-loving people. Oh, sure, they've had to fight for centuries to defend their borders, especially against the Burmese. And they had to juggle the French against the English, but how else could they have remained the only Asian country the Europeans didn't take over? Invade Vietnam? Come on!"

"Two hundred years ago—20 January 1785—a Siamese expeditionary force of fifty thousand men aboard three hundred warships sailed up the Ha Tien River to attack Vietnamese headquarters at My Tho. But the Vietnamese, under the command of a brilliant thirty-two-year-old field commander, Nguyen Hue, sucked them in and waited for a change of tide and wind, then ambushed them at precisely the right hour. Only a handful of Siamese escaped. All the rest were annihilated and died in the swamps near Rach Gam."

"I knew you loved Vietnam, John, but I didn't know you were a history buff."

"Doan Thi taught me," I say. "She taught me to love her country, even though I was shooting her people. And she taught me something about its history."

"But not enough," he adds. "None of us knew enough. If we had, we'd have stayed out. So what else is new?"

"I have a confession to make, Arty."

"Lay it on me."

"I *want* to go back."

"Back to Nam?"

"Yes."

"Well, sure. How else you going to find your son?"

"Even if I didn't have a son."

"Okay. I can handle that. A lot of the guys who fought in Nam feel the same way. I know this French importer who was a paratrooper during Giap's siege of the French at Dien Bien Phu. He makes these romantic pilgrimages back to the valley where he damn near died in '54. You came to Nam like most of us did, John,—jolly green giants, still wet behind the ears. Hell, I hadn't been shaving that long when I flew in. We left the best of us in there. We gave up the sense of immortality nineteen-year-olds have, the belief we could live forever. Everybody loses it sooner or later. But it was fucking *blown* away from us before we were ready to let go of it. Still, I'm warning you, ol' buddy, don't mythologize this little caper. It's not some pilgrimage to find the Holy Grail. What you were then, you're not now. What your enemy was then, *he's* not now. And Doan Thi is dead. Gone, all gone, John. Unless you think of this as a SLAM mission—search, locate, annihilate, and monitor—unless you go in hard and fast, without emotion, you won't come back alive. It's that goddamned simple, my friend."

All at once the lights of Nakhon Phanom appear below and beyond, radiating in crisscross patterns along the Thai side of the broad, black Mekong River. Laos lies, dark and unlit, just across the waters, in touching distance.

Arty lowers to rooftop level over Nakhon Phanom and skims the TV antennas sprouting everywhere from rusty tin roofs. We are so close to ground level I can see a sound truck with its full-color posters on either side as it waddles along one muddy street and in exhortative Thai blares a commercial for a kung fu movie now playing at the local theater.

Inexplicably, relevant lines from Kipling come to mind:

> At the end of the fight is a tombstone white
> With the name of the late deceased.
> And the epitaph drear: "A fool lies here
> Who tried to hustle the East."

Moments later, we skip over a grassy knoll outside of town and I am looking down at the isolated Royal Thai Air Force base.

At NKP.

Arty drops us toward the tarmac.

Time now to hustle the East.

We've been quartered in a facility unused since American recon pilots scrambled home from here years ago. Nguyen and his men, with Arun's help, have policed up the environment in the hour they've been here.

In the small building we've been given, the team has already made up two rows of cots in one area of the cavernous barracks room. At the far end, in ringing isolation, they've strung a wall of army blankets to provide privacy for Arun, as the group's only operative female.

Arty marches me in as the group is completing the housekeeping duties.

Instantly I'm struck by the look of the men Nguyen has brought with him. All five of them are young, none more than twenty-five, I judge, which would have made them impressionable teenagers when they suffered the wrenching loss of their homeland. In their silence I can hear a hundred tragic stories. On their somber faces I can read no happy endings.

As we enter, I see their eyes turning to evaluate me. How good is this American Nguyen has ordered them to trust and to follow?

Life in-country these days, I know, can be described only by a single Vietnamese word, *cuc*—very tough, very rough.

These are *cuc* faces, no question about that.

Since Vietnamese, even those you have been close to, as I have been to Nguyen, do not welcome embraces or handshakes from those outside their families, I simply nod to Nguyen and wait for him to introduce his men to me.

Tran first, our radioman.

"Tran was a buffalo buy," Nguyen announces, "in Lam Dong Province. When he turned eighteen, the Communists made him join their army. He served his three years and fought Khmer guerrillas in Kampuchea. He became one of the NVA's best radiomen for combat patrols. But when he was ordered back to Vietnam, he deserted and drove a herd of six water buffalo from Kampuchea across the border into Thailand, despite heavy pursuit by a Vietnamese regiment from which he'd stolen the animals. Since each *trâu* was worth more than twice the yearly earnings of a North Vietnamese peasant, he came to Thailand as a rich young man."

Tran raises his palms to me.

"Welcome aboard," I say to him in Vietnamese. "I seem to have read somewhere that one buffalo boy grew up to sit on the imperial throne in Vietnam."

"Ah." He smiles, pleased not only that I should know, but because I am speaking to him in the northern dialect that Doan Thi had taught me. "Indeed, Captain, he was the founder of the Dinh dynasty."

Next I meet Le, our machine-gunner.

"Le escaped when he was still sixteen. His parents were killed in the evacuation south. Wisely, he elected to head west to Thailand rather than flee with the other refugees to Saigon. He has served in the Thai Army and is today considered one of the two best Thai-style boxers in all of Asia. He has the strength of Tran's water buffs and at night he has the eyes of a tiger."

I accept Le's *wai*.

"Van, our grenadier," Nguyen continues. "He, too, like Tran, was conscripted after the war by the NVA and made to serve in Laos. He knows its trails and ridges as well as I do."

Finally Nguyen introduces me to Pham, our expert on camouflage, trail-deception, and booby traps. "Pham lives only to return to the village where he was born—near Pleiku. Not on raids, but permanently, as a free man."

I meet Vo last. Of all five young men he is the only one who has the look of a killer on his face. Hatred is stamped into the vitreous body of his eyes. As I suspected he might be, Vo is our weapons expert and team sniper.

At the end of the lineup of men Arun waits.

As I come to her she brings her palms to her lips and smiles at me. She is wearing cammies and jungle boots, her hair in tight braids.

As she had promised me she would, she blends—to a degree. At least she's wearing no makeup and mercifully she's dispensed with the Opium perfume. But I realize now, seeing her out of her woman's clothes and without cosmetics, that her beauty lies in the incredible perfection of her cheekbones and in her gentle, pondlike eyes, lacking malice.

Nguyen leads Arty and me into an adjoining quarter where khaki canvas bags and sealed boxes of weapons and ammo have been laid out in precise rows.

"We stowed everything in here," Nguyen tells me. "Whenever you're ready, we can check it against your list."

"Okay if we check it out first thing in the morning before I head back to Bangkok?" Arty asks. "I feel beat, guys. So if nobody objects, I'm going to flake off."

"Good night, Arty," I say.

"Night. Night, Nguyen."

"Good night, sir."

Arty starts out, but stops in the doorway and looks back at me.

"You left two items off your list," he tells me. "Otherwise you were four-oh, Numbah One!"

"What two items?"

"Griseofulvin for fungus infections."

"You're kidding?"

"Nope. That's one you blew."

"What else?"

"Plastic polymer."

I let that one sit there for a moment.

"I was just trying to be optimistic," I say finally.

215

For plastic polymer is a tissue adhesive for controlling bleeding and for repairing organs lacerated by bullets or land-mine fragments.

"I certainly don't mean to be a killjoy," he says, "but just for the hell of it I added it to your inventory. The spray guns are already loaded with the tissue adhesive."

He waves to us over his shoulder and leaves us alone.

I run my eyes over the boxes and bags almost filling the room. How seven of us, with some help from Arun, are going to hump all that inventory nearly one hundred miles across Laos through Indian country, God only knows. Have I fallen into the typical American oversupply trap?

"How about you?" I ask Nguyen. "Want to hold off till morning? It's okay with me if you do, because we need quite a few hours to lay all this out—and I've got some letters to write before Arty flies back."

"Tomorrow then, sir. We're still more than forty-eight hours ahead of schedule. Do you still rise at sunup to do your exercises?"

"Afraid so."

"May I join you? With the men?"

"By all means. Ah, there *is* one thing, Nguyen. I'd like to clear it up as soon as possible."

"Yes, sir?"

"About Arun."

"I understand your need to bring her, so there is nothing that has to be clarified. She's made you look like an Asian—and that is a critical element toward our success on these missions. Whatever objection I had to her coming along I dismissed the moment you walked in—as an Asian."

"Well, that's reassuring. I was afraid your objection might be based on her being a woman. And I was going to remind you about the famous Tiger Lady of the Delta. She was adjutant of the Forty-fourth Rangers, who were commanded by her husband. She was a formidable soldier. Decorated three times for bravery before she was killed in action in 1965. Then there was that VC girl who commanded a company of one hundred men."

"Huynh Thi Tan," Nguyen says softly. "But they were Vietnamese women, Captain, and our women have fought beside us for two thousand years. Only thirty-nine years after the crucifixion of Christ, two sisters, Trung Trac and Trung Nhi, warrior queens, led the revolt against the Chinese invaders. They gave Vietnam four years of freedom, then they were defeated, and drowned themselves rather than be captured. But we are talking about Vietnamese women, sir. Arun is a Thai."

"Well, we can't have everything, can we, Nguyen?"

He doesn't answer immediately. I can see that he's churning something in his mind. Suddenly his eyes lock onto mine.

"Just as you cleared your doubts, sir, I must clear mine. I am aware that you love Vietnam. And I know how much one particular Vietnamese woman meant to you. But I think—if you will forgive my candor—that you may have permitted these romantic memories to soften your hatred toward Hanoi."

"I never hated Hanoi."

"Are you not anti-Communist?"

"The issue isn't that simplistic."

"Ah, you see!"

"See what?"

"You are still deceiving yourself with the same illusion many of us had when liberation came. We thought that once the fighting was done we could live at peace, we could devote our efforts to rebuilding our fatherland, we could start after so many terrible years to live a prosperous and happy life in an independent country at peace with her neighbors. But we were so wrong, so tragically wrong! Instead of letting us live in peace, the brutes from the North applied to their own people the most inhuman and vengeful rule ever known in the history of our country. They have turned Vietnam into the poorest and most miserable nation in the world. The people have become slaves to the tyrants who pay tribute to their Soviet masters. More than a million of our compatriots have had to leave their homeland. Knowing this, how can you *not* hate the Vietcong and the communist cadres?"

"Maybe because I've learned that hate is like the nuclear policy of mutually assured destruction. Nobody can survive it—not the one hating, not the one being hated. Believe me, there are stronger motivations."

"I have found none, sir. Hate will keep a wounded man on his feet long enough to kill his enemy."

"Well, neither of us," I say, "is any less dangerous to our enemies because we have different points of view. But I ask you to remember, Nguyen, that I didn't have the moral justification you did when I fought in your country. I wasn't defending my front yard. You were. I still have feelings of guilt about many of the things I did. You never had that problem. But I'm glad you brought this up. Matter of fact, if it's okay with you, I'd like to use a North Vietnamese technique with our team."

Nguyen looks a me with high-chill factor.

"What technique is that, sir?"

"*Kiem thao* sessions every sunset when we break patrol. Both self and group criticism of everybody's individual performance——full and open discussions of any weaknesses or failings during the day——as well as a thumbs-up for duty well performed."

"*Every*body's performance, sir?"

"Yours and mine included," I say.

Nguyen's hard face relaxes for the first time since I've arrived tonight.

He brings his palms to his face and awards me the kind of *wai* reserved only for priests.

Then he leads me back into the barracks.

I discover that Arty is already huddled under the blankets in one of the cots and is dead to the world, sleeping the sleep of the innocent, a salt merchant from the south of Siam, nothing more.

26

"**C**hung ta di di!"

Nguyen's whispered command to the team comes to me like a voice from out of the past. It has been years since I've heard the Vietnamese for "let's go!"

Nguyen is first to jump from the Thai patrol boat onto the muddy riverbank.

All Tuesday morning Arty and Nguyen and I had devoted to checking out my list of requests. Everything was on hand and accounted for. Arty had pocketed the letters I'd written to my mother, to my father, and to Dasima, and had flown out before noon. Then Nguyen and I had laid out our route and our timetable for the Laos crossing—ten miles a day made good for ten days—and we'd be at the border into Vietnam four days ahead of schedule.

Now we cross into Laos like smoke under a door, eight of us in a war party, all in thin, baggy Vietnamese field uniforms, belted at the waist, all wearing pith helmets, standard headgear where we're going, strapped tightly under our chins against a rainstorm so fierce the down-pouring water howls like wind.

Thai border police have glided us silently and without running lights in their river-patrol boat across the Mekong ten kilometers northeast of Nakhon Phanom's grid, the Laos town of Thakhek well downstream of us.

"Night like this," their CO had shouted into my ear as we crossed during the deluge, "they'll all be under cover. They'll never look *this* direction, not tonight, not even when they're patrolling their riverbanks in good weather. They only look *inland*. To keep people from escaping. Who in his right mind wants to go *in*?"

They wave good-bye to us and we climb like weighted robots with all our gear from the boat onto the slippery shoreline. They cover us with their machine-gun and a searchlight at the ready as we scratch our way up the slimy embankment through mud splattering sharper than shark's teeth and disappear from their sight.

Once into the shelter of waist-high grass two hundred meters inshore, we form up, Nguyen taking point, I tracking in second position five meters behind him, Arun spaced behind me, then the others in turn, with Van, our grenadier, assuming the tail-gunner position and trailing the rest of the lineup by ten meters.

I've given the order that our movement procedure for tonight is the old Rogers' Rangers rules—never move straight to the target; zigzag as much as time, terrain, food, and water allow. Our compass course is north by northeast, our objective Keo Neua Pass.

Since we plan to sleep at night and to move only during daylight, we need tonight's rest for tomorrow's hump. I limit distance to be traveled tonight to a remove of only five kilometers in from the Mekong.

We set up camp within a grove of kangaroo trees, where the undergrowth rises knee-high and the trees form a solid canopy above us, partly diverting the beating rain.

Pham, who had spent the day familiarizing himself with the Soviet-made MON–50s, peppers our perimeters with anti-personnel mines. I locate Le and his machine-gun on one flank, place Vo on another, to give us instantly positioned enfilade fire in the event we are attacked, and locate the rest of us within an interior sleeping circle, our simple green and black nylon hammocks slung between the trees so that one tug on their slippery nylon ropes will whisk them down and free. I double-check that everyone's hammock is draped with mosquito netting.

"How do you like it so far?" I whisper to Arun as I look over her situation.

"I'm so excited I doubt that I'll be able to fall asleep," she whispers back.

"After tonight," I warn her, "you'll be asleep before you can climb into your hammock. Good night, Arun."

"Good night."

Settled in my hammock, the Browning Hi-Power under my poncho but lying with safety off in its holster on my stomach, I take a last look around our campsite. I like what I see. Everything, everyone, in his place.

I am surrounded and sustained by young warriors with two thousand years of combat in their genes.

I fall asleep with Doan Thi's ineffable face, her dark, eternal eyes appearing from out of the crisscross pattern of the mosquito netting to watch over me.

Shortly before dawn I'm awakened by Nguyen lightly pinching my ear.

"Trouble," he whispers.

I slip the Browning free.

"Not that kind," he whispers. "It's Tran."

Instantly I'm out of the hammock and lacing up my boots, a matter of seconds.

The rain has blown off, but it's too early to predict the weather we're in for this morning. Semidarkness still clings to our campsite like coal dust, so that when I look over to where I've positioned Tran for the night I can scarcely make out what he's doing, except that he's out of his hammock and huddled like a shot animal, twitching in pain along the earth.

I slip with Nguyen through our still-sleeping team to where Tran squirms with his baggy uniform pants pulled down over his knees. He holds the shaft of his penis with his left hand and in his right hand I see his combat knife. He looks up at me with agony blurring his eyes, his forehead mottled with sweat.

"A leech," Nguyen informs me. "It crept up his penis."

I kneel beside Tran. "Give me the knife!" I order in Vietnamese.

"I have to pass water," he whispers painfully. "But I am blocked. I will explode soon—unless I cut myself open. What else can I do?"

"There's a trick the Kachins use in Burma," I say. "You just hold on!"

In anguish, he nods and I take his knife from him.

I cross to a cluster of nearby bamboo and swiftly cut two long slivers and smooth them with the knife until they are slick from tip to end.

I return to Tran and Nguyen.

"Hold your penis," I tell Tran, "and keep it extended."

He obeys me.

I insert the two slivers into his urethra, one to either side of the red, bubbling buffalo leech that has crept more than three inches into him. When I feel the slivers have passed around the leech and beyond its head, I close them firmly over the leech and slowly draw it out, tail first, then head and suckers, and fling it away.

Blood and urine pour from Tran's penis at the instant of release and a vast sigh escapes from his lungs.

"Stay in fetal position for the next thirty minutes," I instruct him.

He rolls himself into a ball on the earth and Nguyen covers him with a blanket.

The rest of our team has snapped into wakefulness at the sound of our whispering, but no one has stirred.

Nguyen and I move off a few yards away from Tran.

We squat under a kangaroo tree.

"How could it happen?" I ask, keeping my voice low enough so that no one else can hear it. "I specifically ordered that every man wear a protective cup while we were crossing Laos—for this very reason, Nguyen—*and* elastic diapers!"

Nguyen's eyes reflect a personal shame. "Tran admitted to me," he says painfully, "that during the night he uncovered himself and was looking at the girl as she slept. And that he masturbated as he watched her. He fell asleep then—and the leech entered him."

"What girl?" I ask.

He looks at me with some surprise. "Arun."

Shit, I say to myself. Who ever figured *this* scenario? And why didn't I? Look how *I'd* reacted, even *knowing*!

"Well, goddamn it, what can we do about that?" I ask, wondering for one explosive second how'd they all react if I were to ask Arun to stand up and show them *her* penis.

"I would urge that we do not discuss this in front of the others," Nguyen says. "Certainly an incident of this nature should not be a part of tonight's *kiem thao* session."

"Agreed!" I say.

Thirty minutes later, having sipped tea and eaten our glutinous rice balls, we slip our hammocks free and remove any evidence that eight people have spent the night on this site, including Tran making sure he has left no spilled semen under his hammock on the leafy forest floor.

We move out in a long column, Tran walking like a man given new life and apparently already recovered from his deadly intercourse with a raping leech.

Before we broke camp, I'd taken him behind a tree and examined him. Leeches excrete an anti-coagulant in their saliva, a substance much like heparin, which affords them, as they engorge themselves, a painless and ready flow of blood from their prey. Even after they drop away from their host, their anti-coagulant remains, causing blood to continue to flow from the wound they've inflicted.

Tran has been fortunate. He is not bleeding from his urethra and I can find no early evidence of ulceration. I treat him for infection. Shamed to the roots of his soul, he looks away as I powder him.

What joy, were he still alive, the father of fear-of-masturbation would take from Tran's freak accident. I wish I could tell Tran that it was a Swiss physician named Samuel August Andre David Tissot and his 1758 book *De l'onanisme* that gave worldwide credibility to the nonsense that masturbators are doomed to pus-filled boils, impotence, gonorrhea, chaos in their bowels, sluggish conduct, dull comprehension, withering spines, hair on the palms of their hands, epilepsy, fatuity, dyspepsia, dimness of sight, vertigo, and eventual cringing death. And now leeches!

Assuming that our Vietnamese uniforms will arouse no suspicion, we move along briskly for the first two hours, staying off roads and trails and keeping the Lao military encampment near Ban Na Ngou well to the west of us.

At this point the countryside is open, the rice fields knee-high with lush green clumps glistening with the rainwater they've captured during the night. Wind fans across the meadows, bending the tips of the plants, the gusts chasing each other like ripples on an emerald sea.

In this moment my heart opens and I sense something of the happiness and contentment Doan Thi once told me only the rice farmer can ever know, a happiness that comes in the evening when the sun is low and he leads his water buffalo and lets his son settle onto the broad back of the animal for the trudge homeward. As they ride, Doan Thi

223

told me, the boys often sing while their fathers play their flutes. The sunset, the nodding rice stalks ready soon for harvesting, the meadows bounded by lithoid mountains like headstones of dead giants, the idle swaying of the buffalo, the lifting cry of the flutes,—these things the Indochinese peasant holds as the center of all happiness.

Fifteen meters ahead of me Nguyen halts, raising his arm.

Our file freezes in place. We are strung out in a single column the length of a football field.

Ordinarily such listen-stops are standard ops when you're into a hostile area, often as long as ten minutes of stark silence, standing where you last placed your feet, weapon pointed in whatever direction your eyes are searching. Then, assuming you feel secure, and the point has signaled his okay, you move forward for ten more minutes, then once more stop for ten, off and on, advancing, listening, advancing, listening until you arrive at your RON site.

But we are not yet into that kind of oppressive terrain.

I can hear or see nothing threatening anywhere about us, yet obviously Nguyen does.

We wait.

Now I hear something.

The excited voices of children.

I spot Nguyen's hand signal—forward—we file ahead.

Two minutes later I catch sight of what Nguyen, far before I was able, had heard, seen, or sensed, a cluster of buffalo boys gathered around a grass thicket and beating at the grass with their headbands in the manner of American boys snapping ass in a school locker room with their towels.

Nguyen approaches the boys. They stop what they're doing and turn quietly to stare at him.

He waves the rest of us to him.

When I join him, he is talking to the children in Lao. Then, as though suddenly become their leader, he takes one of the older boy's headbands and expertly begins to snap it into the grass. He pounces upon something he's dislodged, cups it in his hands and carefully drops it, kicking, into a box one of the boys holds out to him.

I see the thing he's caught. It appears to be a giant

water bug. It smells as pungent and as unpleasant as underarm odor in a crowded New York subway in July.

But Nguyen, joined now by Arun and others of our team, has become as involved as the Lao boys. He orchestrates their snapping attack on the grass clump, coordinating against one particular stalk, until the group has succeeded in flushing out three more of the bugs and placed them into the box, already rattling with the creatures. Soon our entire war party, all, of course, but me, is flailing away at the grass. I stand back, watching this insanity, the alienated European baffled by the childlike spontaneity of my Asian comrades and these Lao children, and a line by Pascal, from his *Pensées*, if my memory serves me correctly, appears from my mother's teachings: "What is this chimera called man? What novelty, what monstrosity, what chaos, what contradiction, what prodigy!"

Children catching insects with the help of armed men in an occupied country, Thailand surrounded by Marxist nations, the Soviets and the Americans contending for control of the China Sea, I made up to look Asian, on a do-or-die mission,—and here we loiter, collecting water bugs!

Indochina—how I love thee, I think. Why can't it be like this everywhere? Nobody singing "This Bud's for you!"

Nguyen waves good-bye to the children, making them a gift of all the bugs our party has beaten free for them, and once more we file out toward the looming mountains. But not until I have insisted on an explanation for the incident.

"After a storm," he explains, "the field water bugs appear. People of all classes find them irresistible."

"You mean, you *eat* them?" I ask.

"You pull them apart,—taking care, however, for they can sting you with a tiny dart in their mouths. Then you pound them up with pepper sauce, or if you prefer you can pickle them with fish sauce. And if that troubles you, may I remind you that Saint John, one of Jesus Christ's teachers, is said to have enjoyed eating grasshoppers dipped in honey."

We advance, the men exhilarated by the hunt for the water bugs and the bell-like laughter of the Lao children.

We avoid ridgelines and the crests of ravines, forging boldly across open meadows and past farmhouses on stilts. Three women squatting in the shade under their uplifted house are spinning silk as we file by. Not one of the three looks up at these Vietnamese conquerors passing in solemn silence. Only one man dares lift his eyes to ours as we slog past his house, the last in a village adjoining the forest area we're heading toward. He has built his hut on top of tree stumps in a jungle clearing in order to survive the monsoon floodwaters. He is a carpenter working with a *coupe-coupe*. He watches us narrowly as we pass, the heavy blade gripped strongly in his hand, his eyes tracking each of us until Van, coming last, has caught up with us in an area lush with elephant leaves. We stop long enough to funnel the fresh, clean rainwater from the giant leaves into our mouths, drinking until our thirst has gone, refilling our canteens, then dousing our hands and faces with the sparkling water.

Here in the forest the earth is spongy with leaf mold. The tall vines and grasses are coated with water droplets from last night's rain. We slip into our ponchos so that every move we make through this stretch of wilderness will not bring cold showers down upon us.

Heavily screened by foliage overhead, the sunlight barely sifts through. Watching Nguyen ahead of me, I see him flickering forward as though in a Pierrot clown suit, half light, half black shadow.

Suddenly he points up, holding two fingers spread, our signal for aircraft, but since he continues moving ahead, none of us loses a step.

Now I hear the engines,—jet interceptors, two of them, as Nguyen has signaled,—high above us, slicing south toward Kampuchea. Through a hole in the canopy above us I catch the afterimage of their passing—MiG21s.

When we stop, forming a protective circle, for our lunch break of rice, vitamins, and spirulina powder with our tea, I take a compass bearing and X our present position on the route map I've laid out to snake us between the various Lao and Vietnamese troop locations pinpointed for me by Thai intelligence. We're still four days south of Lak Soa and the point where we will have to cross busy Highway 8, which I intend to do at night. Yet

I feel a growing sense of the nearness of patrols in the area directly ahead.

Nguyen, too, admits he has the same feeling.

We dispense with the linear advance and roll forward for the next two hours in a widely dispersed circle, constantly observing a nearby military secondary road from hidden positions and each of us climbing, from time to time, into the highest trees to sweep the road with our field glasses.

On one such sweep I pick up the glint of metal in my glasses. A second later the glint materializes into the first of two M113 APCs flying the Lao red flag. The armored cars speed imperiously along the muddy groove through the forest, less than a click away from us.

Deliberately I look around to locate Vo. I put my binos on him.

I can see his tongue moistening his lips, his arms raising his Soviet SVD with its PSO–1 scope. Every cell in his body appears to be urging him to fire into the open hatch of the lead car. I watch him control his need to kill his enemies.

The cars are gone as quickly as they have come, the sucking of their wheels in the mud no longer heard.

In view of the growing proximity of hostile forces, I decide to use a countertactic I often employed in the war when we had to bivouac in disputed areas.

Two hours before sunset, having traversed fourteen miles instead of the target ten on our first day into Laos, I select an ideal overnight position, a large, semicircular area almost two hundred meters in radius, with waxy-leafed plants forming the jungle floor and a surround of giant *yang* trees with great bare trunks rising more than a hundred feet, all crowned with leathery foliage.

Now, having decided this is where we shall sleep, I signal Nguyen to continue advancing beyond it, to keep going until he has led the team half a kilometer deeper into the trees.

Here, as night closes down on us, Pham places his anti-personnel mines and trip-wired booby traps. When I'm satisfied that we're centered within a circle secure out to five hundred meters, I gather the team together and we hunker down in the flanking shelter of two massive tree trunks to share our first *kiem thao* session, aimed at rooting out any faults either in our individual performances during the day's march or in our thoughts.

"Nguyen and I will speak last," I tell the group in Vietnamese. "Le, please begin."

"Although I joined in and enjoyed it greatly," Le responds, "I feel it might have been a mistake for us to stop and help the children catch water bugs."

"Why do you feel it was a mistake?" I ask.

"Because they will tell their elders about the incident. It could arouse suspicion."

He glances at Nguyen. "Why did you signal us to stop and why did you decide that we should help the children?"

Nguyen shows no sign of resentment that one of his men, a much younger man, should question his command decision.

"To ignore the children," he says, "would have been unnatural. They would have told their elders that a heavily armed file of Vietnamese soldiers had passed, neither stopping to make friends nor to assist the children. The elders would have wondered what military action might be threatening so close to their village to make the soldiers this duty-bound, since the elders know of no guerrilla action in this province. They would certainly have gone to Lao Army headquarters and asked who these soldiers were. That would have caused headquarters to investigate."

"Thank you, Uncle," Le says respectfully, calling Nguyen *chu*, for "uncle." "I have much to learn."

Next I call on Pham.

"I have no criticism of the leadership today. I will follow it to the death. But I do feel shame for myself. Many times today I became impatient. I wished we could move even faster, though I knew if we did, we would tire ourselves. I wished we could seize an armored personnel car and ride to our homeland—not to avoid walking, but because I hunger to be in my own village again and to attack the Soviet carrier as quickly as possible, since that may cause our people to rise up and take our province back from Hanoi. I know that such thoughts are reckless and that we must be prepared to give years to our struggle, and I know that these impetuous thoughts could endanger my comrades. So I will try to control my impatience."

228

"Do you understand why we did not ambush the armored cars?" I ask.

"Yes, sir. We might have suffered casualties and endangered the missions. And even if we had taken them without any of us being killed or wounded, we are risking being stopped at a roadblock and being suspected. It is safer, even if it is longer, to cross Laos on foot, using trails that are seldom used."

Without my asking him, Vo raises his arm.

"May I speak, sir?" he asks.

"Please."

"I share Pham's shame. I, too, am impatient. I wanted to attack the armored cars. For a moment I held the head of the driver in my sights. I wanted to see his head burst open. But had I shot him, I would have shot each of us as certainly. Why am I so filled with hatred for my enemy?"

"Can anyone answer Vo?" I ask.

"Of all of us," Pham intercedes, "Vo has the least personal reason to hate the North. True, he is an orphan, but his mother and father died of malaria when he was very young, not at the hands of the enemy. Possibly this is why his hatred is so strong. It is not men he hates, since he has already killed many Northern soliders, and his hatred does not lessen. It may be the *idea* of defeat he hates."

"I am *not* defeated!" Vo cries out.

"Not in your heart," Pham says, "but you have to admit we no longer have our country. What good is a passport issued by Saigon. Saigon no longer exists. Maybe you feel like a ghost. An angry ghost."

I can see that Vo is charged with inner fury, the more painful because he has not been able to isolate or comprehend its specific cause. I decide that over the course of our time together I'll try to help him dredge it up. Talk about the blind leading the blind! I've got similar pains, but I've learned how to push them down under the surface, the way you use your spoon to keep a marshmallow submerged in hot chocolate until it melts and you can blend it with the chocolate.

"I suffer from similar feelings," I tell Vo. "I've lost many friends in your country. I lost the only woman I have ever loved. I told myself for many years that I hated the enemy for doing all this to me. But then I began to ask myself. What had I done to them? Until finally I understood that hating is an endless, self-perpetuating circle. It'll spin you around and around until finally, inevitably, it will kill you. But the question still remained. If I were to stop hating, how then would I be able to deal with my enemies? I thought that the minute I gave up my hatred, my enemies would rush in and crush me. But that's where the deception lies. It is not necessary to hate a man to be able to defeat him. Le here, I'm told, is one of the best boxers in Asia. Do you hate your opponents, Le?"

"Never," he says. "I feel compassion for them. And gratitude."

"Gratitude?" Vo asks.

"Yes. I am grateful to them for giving me the opportunity to use my skill against them. Without these opponents, whom could I challenge? How else could I test myself?"

I can see that Vo is, at least, considering the point.

"Van, what are your feelings about this first day's march?"

"Good feelings, sir. I am proud to be with such comrades. Proud to be a part of these missions."

"Tran," I say.

"I have little to say, sir, but much to think about before I permit myself to speak. But I can say this much. When I was in pain this morning, you helped me. If you ask me now to walk into a mortar, I will obey you. And I thank all my comrades for their silence. My shame is great enough without having to speak of it to them. I can also say that it will be a great moment when we strike at the Soviet carrier, but to me an even greater moment will be to see you and your son united—as my country someday will be."

Nguyen—who is Catholic, I suddenly remember—crosses himself. Catholic *and* Buddhist. East *does* meet West.

"Thank you," I say to Tran. He has touched me deeply, not alone by what he's said, but for the effort I know it took him to make any reference to this morning's incident. All during the day's long march he must have been bombarded by thoughts of the others—how much do they know? Why are they so carefully avoiding asking what happened?

"Arun," I ask, telling her to speak only in Vietnamese. We have been careful to keep our voices subdued, and nobody can get through the mines to overhear what we're saying, but sometimes voices carry in a forest and a Thai accent is the last thing I want bouncing from tree to tree deep in Lao territory.

"I feel no fear," she says. "Only exhilaration."

"Good." I turn to Nguyen. "Any comments?"

"Only that if I'd had a lifetime to select the men to come with us on these missions, I would not have chosen any others."

"Well," I conclude, "I agree with that. And I give our first day a four-oh. Everyone was on his toes. I liked especially the fact that nobody slipped up and forgot the order—guns to be carried at all times, never slung over the shoulder. My feeling is that if we had been attacked, our counterattack would have started within two seconds. We made thirty percent more mileage today than we were scheduled to make. That's good, because tomorrow's terrain is a lot tougher—heavier bush and some uphill humping."

We take our final meal of the day and prepare to bed down, should anyone have been observing us all through our *kiem thao* session and our dinner. But when the darkness is total, we open a lane through the mines and creep back with total noise discipline to the position I had selected earlier, some several hundred meters removed from where we'd taken our evening meal.

Again Pham sets up a circle of protective mines and we string our hammocks, break out our nets, and turn in for the night.

I remember one time, just beyond Muong Nong in Laos, when my Black Mamba team was on a mission, that this precaution of establishing a false RON saved our lives, since, unknown to us, some really smart jungle killers had been following us for hours. But they closed their ambush not around where we had moved to, unknown to them, but around the camp where they'd patiently watched us eating. When we heard the claymores going off, we hugged the earth within our separate area and watched the enemy desolate the deserted site. They mortared and machine-gunned the area where they imagined we were sleeping, then fired grenades in as frosting on the cake.

We waited until they'd expended their firepower and went rushing in to finish off any survivors at point-blank range. Then we closed our own circle and counterambushed them, killing them to the last man.

But that was in a no-quarter war.

This is in a pacified area.

Still, I prefer that we not gamble, that we conduct ourselves as though we are an endangered species.

Happily, nobody attacks us on our second night in Laos.

Nor on our third or fourth.

But on our fifth day, while we are scampering from rock to rock across a high limestone plateau buttressed with sharp ridges and pocked by yawning sinks, something foreboding happens. I slip and go belly-clawing down the face of a karst hole. I manage to grab at a brake of bamboo and arrest the humiliating slide. But when I climb back up to rejoin the team and to assess what damage the equipment I'm carrying all over the front of me may have suffered, I discover that the protective amulet Dasima had sent to me, the stout ceramic phallus I've been wearing inside my uniform and around my waist, has been shattered during the accident. The shaft is missing. Only the testes remain.

At that instant, I, John Locke, a fullygrooved twentieth-century Western pragmatist, feel the searing of a primitive dread. The pagan in me—which has become the most of me since I sailed into the Pacific—warns that I've carelessly destroyed the animistic spell which until now has driven off devils, djinns, and enemies.

Premonition jangles like a firehouse bell.

The trees, the rocks, the rain-fattened streams, may all turn against us now, exposing, not sheltering us.

Instinctively I know that despite all my careful planning and all my hopes to the contrary, we are never, never going to be able to make it across Laos without confrontation.

Without the obligatory sacrifice—the shedding of blood.

Ours or theirs?

CHAPTER

27

Three days shy of Keo Neua Pass, our threshold into Vietnam, we emerge from a sweaty two-hour passage, hacking a pathway through muscular elephant grass, and trickle out in combat lineup onto the bald peak of an escarpment directly overlooking the turbulent Theun River.

I give the order to reduce our highly visible silhouettes and we snake ahead on our bellies to the eastern edge of the escarpment overhanging a long, turbulent stretch of the Theun River as it races northwest to empty into the Mekong at Pakkading.

Through binos, we take our time surveying the stretch ahead of us, for a major Vietnamese Army command is headquartered in Lak Sao, not quite twelve clicks distant. We lie on our stomachs in a frontal line a hundred meters long, each of us combing the tangled brush between our present position and the banks of the Theun.

As I would have expected, Nguyen is the first to discover the faint zigzag of what appears to be a long-unused trail stepping down the face of the ridge and disappearing into the trees along the riverside.

He elbow-crawls over to me and points. I track through my glasses and observe that the trail comes out into a stand of palms.

I must not be able to conceal my concern.

"What troubles you about that way down?" Nguyen asks.

"Those palms."

"What about them?"

"They're *nipa* palms."

Nguyen raises his glasses and restudies the trees, giving them a revised evaluation.

"Shit!" he exclaims.

"I see that you're getting your English back." I smile. "Look what happens when you hang around me."

"I remember what they used to tell us in jump school," he replies, and suddenly imitates a Georgia-cracker accent. "If you wanna run with the big dogs, you gotta learn to piss on the tall trees."

We lay our glasses back onto the palm grove and rake the trees from one end to the other. What has me concerned here is that I've mapped this particular spot as our crossing site of the Theun River. None of my Thai intelligence maps shows a village anywhere in this area, and yet the *nipa* palm seldom grows wild in such profusion as it's doing in the grove below us. These trees favor brackish water and often form colonies along riverbanks, yet nine times out of ten they're planted by man to produce the raw material for wickerwork and to yield a much-prized sap used in making rice dessert.

"Suppose there are villagers," Nguyen proposes. "Even if they see us crossing the river, what will that mean to them?"

"They'll wonder why we're not using the bridge on Highway Eight—less than an hour's walk from here."

"If any villager should see us, I'll assign Pham to talk to them. His Lao is perfect and he comes from a small village. They will feel a bond with him—and believe whatever he tells them."

"Which will be what?"

"That we are engaged in a training maneuver."

I roll over on my back to read the sky.

Colorless as aniline.

"Can't expect rain for hours," I comment to Nguyen. "And it's suicidal to try to cross the Theun in the dark. I'd like to put Lak Soa behind us before we make camp tonight. What do you think?"

"I think we cross now."

"Okay."

Nguyen signals for everyone to form up in their given positions, but to keep low. He points toward our objective, the almost imperceptible break in the brush which opens into the downhill trail.

The team is up, ready to move out, when I notice that Arun is not rising. She remains stretched out on her stomach. She appears to be paralyzed.

I duck-walk to her, only a distance of ten meters, and see that she's holding up one palm toward me, as though trying to warn me. I squat lower and stare at her. Her eyes pivot to one side. I look the way she is looking.

A black-and-yellow-banded *krait* is coiled less than two feet from her temple, its bulletlike head raised, eyes fixed on Arun as though there is nothing else in the universe.

In Nam we called the banded *krait* the "widow snake." Its bite kills in a matter of minutes. We also called it the "shoe snake" because it creeps into a soldier's boots at night, but then, an alert jungle fighter never takes his boots off when he sleeps, simply unlaces them.

"I'm not going to move," I whisper to Arun. "There's not going to be any of that bullshit you see in flicks where I make a quick slash and cut the snake's head off. For obvious reasons of security, I can't shoot it either. So— we're going to do something entirely different. You're going to keep on doing exactly what you've been doing, which is especially intelligent of you—that is, *not* moving. Until you hear what kinds of moves I'm going to ask you to make. Meanwhile, don't answer. Don't speak. Don't even breathe too heavily. I'm going to assume you're hearing every word, that you understand me and that you will follow my orders. I am also going to assume that you already know a great deal about this particular kind of snake, that it is not by nature vicious, even though it is very deadly. It strikes only in self-defense. I assume you know this, Arun, because you have wisely avoided frightening it. Okay, here's what you're going to do. Very, very slowly you are going to lift your left arm, the arm that's farther away from the snake. You're going to point your fingers up—keeping them together, palm toward the snake. And you're going to make sure that he sees your palm, that he concentrates on it. And that he turns his head to follow it. When you're certain you have his absolutely undivided attention, bring the arm closest to him, your right arm, up very, very slowly, off to the side and behind his head, making sure he never loses focus on your other palm. Then slowly lower your right hand until your index finger is about to touch the back of his head. Okay, moving swiftly now, push down on his head, not in panic, but firmly, as though you are simply guiding his head down to the ground. This move has to be fluid, Arun, and natural, as natural as if I were to toss you a mango and without thinking you'd simply and reactively catch it. You understand? When his head makes contact with the ground, suddenly increase the pressure of your finger, making sure that he is firmly pinned down to the ground. At that point I will catch him by the tail and toss him away from us. All right...calmly now...empty your mind of everything except your compassion for this snake. Know that when I catch him I will not harm him. Know that both of you deserve and will have long and happy lives. Know that he is less fortunate than you. He has never been to Bangkok and lives way up here in the middle of nowhere with few friends. Let him feel you are not afraid of him, that you understand that the two of you can coexist without reason to harm each other."

As I talk I see Arun's left arm lift like a wand. I watch her fingers rise delicately and then her palm is facing the *krait*, as though in salutation. She glides her palm farther away. Following the whiteness, the *krait* swivels its head, eyes glittering.

Arun permits the snake to focus on her palm for what seems an endless time before her right arm, index finger extended, begins to elevate like the neck of a curious swan, up, up, and behind the *krait*'s head, then down without hesitation, now about to make contact, then contact flowing into a firm, downward push.

The *krait*'s head seems to collapse, as though an unsupported veranda were toppling from the facade of a house. Arun pins him to the ground and I pounce forward, grasping his tail, finding him thicker and heavier than I had estimated. I fling him away like a discus toward a nearby stand of bamboo. As he whips through the air I am able to see that he's more than six feet in length.

Arun is up, trembling, and into my arms.

"Well done," I say.

I discover that I'm not holding or comforting her as I would a woman, even in her distress still conscious of her breasts and flat stomach against me, yet making it clear with body language that the embrace is humanitarian, not sexual. I find instead that I'm holding Arun in my arms as I would hold Vo or Pham. She is no longer androgynous in my mind, but has become a comrade, a human being without need of sexual classification. I believe Otis and his theory of pansexualism are off the mark. Other things make the world keep ticking, even though I haven't a clue what they might be.

We descend the trail to the river warily, yet we still maintain a brisk pace, for despite its bushed-in, unused appearance, Nguyen has found tracks made recently by the sandals of a peasant.

To come down such precipitous slopes I was taught by a mountain tribe in Vietnam how to lean backward to counteract the tug of gravity and to absorb the shock of each down-plunging step with an equal upward force coming from the knees and the quadriceps. Using this rhythm—flex, release, flex, release—you can descend effortlessly hour after hour with a hip-swinging jog more like a trot than a walk.

The descent is made difficult by a profusion of giant worms underfoot. They stretch lazily everywhere across the trail, a world of them as far as we can see, their foot-long, thick orange bodies agleam with slime, spiny horns protruding from their backs and heads. I am pleased to find that none of our team regards these plump, tubular creatures as one more esoteric food source and that everyone takes care to toe-dance between them. And so we go skittering down the cliff face like children skipping cracks in sidewalks.

Nguyen arrives first at the foot of the trail. He signals for a listening halt.

We freeze in place.

From my position I can hear nothing but the gentle seething of the river eating at its overflowing banks. I hear another sound directly above me, a rustle of movement. My eyes and the front gunsight snap to the source. A brilliantly colored frogmouth tilts its head and looks out at me from the opening in her spherical nest which hangs from a branch above me. The bird's head is black, her throat yellow.

Nguyen motions us forward.

We enter the grove of *nipa* palms, the river a hundred

meters beyond. I point Le and his machine-gun to our left flank, Vo with the RPG and his sniper rifle to the right flank, and Van, our grenadier, back up the trail, to afford us elevation and at the same time to cover our blind rear-side.

I examine the palms. These are old trees, most past the fecund years. None has been touched or worked for some time. The Thai maps may be correct, after all. A village may once have been near this place, but the danger of flooding, so close to the Theun River, must have caused the villagers to relocate.

Nguyen and the others, except for Le and Van and Vo, who maintain their vigilance, help me prepare for the river crossing.

I shed all the gear I've been humping except for the Browning Hi-Power, which I zip into a waterproof bag, along with an extra magazine. I secure the bag to the belt of my uniform. I take off my jungle boots and slip into the swim fins I have brought for exactly such crossings, then into the buoyancy-compensator vest. I snap it around my torso and inflate it while Nguyen finishes tying the stout nylon cord we've unpacked around my waist, Pham laying out the rest of it in big coils on the bank. There is no need for talk, since Nguyen and I had long since settled the matter of which man on the team is the strongest swimmer.

At this point the river closes in on itself, like a collapsing vein, providing the advantage of less distance, but the disadvantage of a swifter flow as it crowds between its banks. To the team's thumbs-up I wade into the river, my whole being charged by the pristine excitement I always feel slipping into unexplored water. The sudden chill shoots up my thighs and tightens my scrotum. I relax my muscles, opening to the cold, and move out waist-deep into a powerful stream sweeping me off my feet. I go with it, exhilarated by the forces beating around me.

I've set myself a landing point some sixty degrees downstream, my course a broad reach crosscurrent toward the far bank. The fins drive me across the surface, even as the river tosses me straight ahead.

Too much air in the BC. I deflate it slightly so I can lie flatter on the skin of the river. I begin to powerhouse across, arms in crawl-stroke, legs churning the fins. No longer am I in Laos, but back in time to another place—the sea at Point Loma in Southern California, where I grew from child to teenager every six months I spent each year with my father, sharing the year with my mother in Paris, who took possession of me from January through June. From July through November I was my father's child. Came December the two of them farmed me out and met in neutral territory to make love for December's thirty-one nights, then my mother would return to her atelier in Paris, since she detests the United States, and my father would return to his yacht-design factory in San Diego, since he prefers beaches to cities. But much as I loved the intellectual and artistic stimulation of my mother's world, it was in my father's world, in the Pacific Ocean, that I came to know the true meaning of personal joy and freedom.

Before I'd turned eight I was swimming off Point Loma in the backwash from spuming sea caverns, diving from the cliffs into the fetch as it swelled cliff-high,—a great way to learn timing—then letting myself be swept out by the retreating combers, a lesson in inevitability, out to where the water lay deep and green.

By my tenth birthday I'd managed to stroke my way miles out to sea, from Point Loma to an anchored freighter five miles offshore, its decks lined with day fishermen brought out early each morning by motorboat. I was welcomed aboard by the astonished skipper, hearing everyone shouting that a boy had swum all the way out. I was given a free lunch, then escorted back by the knobby old salt in his personal launch. He delivered me to my father and suggested it was poor evidence of parental responsibility to permit a ten-year-old to swim five miles offshore. I recall my father suggesting that he move his freighter two or three miles farther out to sea, since a five-mile swim was hardly a challenge for his kid. He had personally taught me how to survive for hours in the sea, and off Point Loma it was hardly a problem, since the sea was blanketed with kelp beds and I would slide up onto them whenever I'd feel tired and stretch out as though I were on the arms of branches growing out of the bottom.

Just ahead now I see the bank I've aimed for. Six strokes more and I'm touching sand, gliding in out of the driving current and once more standing firm.

I look back across the river to the palm grove.

Nguyen has raised one arm in an approving signal.

I slip off the fins and walk along the bank to a nearby beached tree trunk. I secure the rope I've swum with to the trunk, tying a sturdy bowline and turning to watch Nguyen and Pham pulling the line tight at the other side, giving us the bridge of rope we need to guide our inflatable across with all our equipment aboard.

I hear the snap of safety catches being unlevered.

I turn, looking as casual as I can force myself to look under the circumstances, for that pagan warning I'd felt when Dasima's amulet got broken is back now, up and down my spine like dancing radiation.

I confront a somber-faced young Vietnamese lieutenant. Four other young men stand in a line behind them, all with AK–47s, not quite pointed at me, but unmistakably in a state of instant readiness.

"Pardon me, Major," the lieutenant says to me in Vietnamese, and I can see his eyes raking me over, checking out my uniform, my collar-tab insignia, "is there some problem?"

"None, Lieutenant," I reply in Vietnamese. "We are conducting an amphibious exercise. If you have no other immediate duty, you may assist me."

"Gladly, sir. What are your orders?"

"Is this your entire detail?" I ask.

"The rest of my men are back on the road."

I glance off, behind him, as though fully aware I know where the road is. On my Thai intelligence reports, there is no road indicated in this area.

"Very well," I say. "I doubt that we will need them too. The purpose of this maneuver is to determine the feasability of small guerrilla units being able to carry enough equipment through hostile territory and to cross swollen rivers during monsoon seasons. As you can see, the pathfinder, in this case myself, must first swim across the river using nothing more than a flotation jacket and fins and carrying with him the line that is needed so that an inflatable raft can be hooked onto it, all ordnance and supplies loaded aboard, then brought across. If your men will keep the line taut, I will begin the exercise."

He turns to his men and orders them to form up along

the line and to keep it snugged in as tightly as they're able.

While he's half-turned from me, I unzip the waterproof bag and slip the Browning free. I flip off the safety and push the gun into my belt at the small of my back.

I signal Nguyen to start the raft across.

Our plan has been to unpack the inflatable Nguyen has been humping in its deflated, folded state, blow it up, then load it with all our equipment, link it by painters fore and aft to the cross-river line, then to hand-to-hand it across with one man aboard the raft and two in the water astern, one to either side, to steady and to balance it.

Nguyen starts across, he in the raft, Pham and Tran in the water.

The lieutenant comes over to stand next to me. He smiles, obviously enjoying this unexpected afternoon encounter with fellow warriors. But suddenly his smile dies. I catch the subtle change deep in the pupils of his eyes as something he sees about me for the first time sets off an alarm in his mind. Jesus, I think, did my nose come loose while I was swimming across? Can't be. Arun and I had tested to make sure the tape would hold.

He steps back, starts to raise his K50M toward me.

But I've pulled the Browning the instant I detected the change in his eyes, several ticks before he steps back. I shoot him between the eyes before his SMG has lifted a single inch.

I drop to one knee and, steadying the pistol with both hands, kill the two soldiers farthest from the riverbank before they can react to the unexpected turn of events. I don't have to worry about the other two. Echoing within my first two gunshots I hear the clean, powerful thrusting sound of Vo's sniper rifle. His opening round spangles the forehead of the third soldier, then spins the lone survivor around before the man can release his AK–47 in my direction.

I scoop up the lieutenant's SMG in one hand, one of the fallen AK–47s with the other, and hightail into the bush, creeping in a few meters, but staying under cover. I hear the crashing of men running toward the river from behind me. I wait.

Six of them jam past me, jogging pell-mell toward the place where they've heard the guns stuttering.

I wait until they pass, step out directly behind them, and using selective fire rather than rock-and-roll, cut them down surgically from back to front, dropping them in their tracks with spine and kidney shots before they can whirl and return my fire.

I circle around, running low, checking the rounds still in the SMG magazine, and happy to have the AK–47 with its full box of thirty as a backup. I come out onto a rutted road and a parked Soviet BMP–80 infantry fighting vehicle.

The Soviet Army is a mechanized army, lacking our traditional "leg" infantry divisions. The Soviets prefer motorized rifle divisions. Every squad has its own APC or, in this case, an IFV. Obviously, the Vietnamese are adopting many of the Soviet military practices.

I slip around the IFV, sniffing for signs of life. But the vehicle stands alone and isolated, without its human cargo, squatting there in the mud with its 73mm cannon, a SAGGER antitank guided missile and a 7.62mm machine-gun, all as worthless now as a computer without software.

Nevertheless, I have to make sure. Staying close to the steel turret, I slide up and peer into the open hatch.

Nobody home.

I decide it might be dicey to go charging back to the river at this particular segment of time.

Not with Vo on the far bank with that sniper rifle. He's too deadly a marksman, and at this distance he may confuse me in his crosshairs with one of the bad guys.

With confidence that Nguyen will know what to do, I climb down into the IFV to wait.

I check my wristwatch. Four minutes more for Nguyen to reach this side of the river, thirty seconds for him to check out the dead and to make sure nobody's still left alive on the ground to shoot his men in the back, then two minutes more to move through the brush from river to road, adding another thirty seconds to check out the six soldiers I've tumbled between here and there. Seven minutes, let's say.

Ten seconds short of my estimate I see the bushes moving. Knowing Nguyen, I know he is not there, that he has simply moved the bushes to misinform anyone waiting.

"All clear!" I call out from inside the IFV. Sure enough,

Nguyen emerges ten feet to one side of the bush that had moved. "I'm in the vehicle," I add.

He crosses toward me, Pham well to his left, Tran to his right. They move like cats, I think, and my admiration for them grows in that instant of watching them cross toward me.

I look up and grin at Nguyen's thoughtful face in the open hatch.

"I checked their fuel," I say. "Three quarters full."

"What are you saying?" he asks.

I climb out, slide down to the road, Nguyen after me.

"I think we can accelerate our timetable," I say.

"We agreed it would be too risky to capture a vehicle here in Laos," he points out. "In Vietnam, that is different. We will need to commandeer our transportation. But not in Laos."

"We have all the IDs we need," I say. "We'll promote Pham to lieutenant. Put him into the uniform of the dead lieutenant. I believe you'll find his tunic is intact. I shot him in the head, not in the chest. Then distribute other IDs to each of you. That will leave only Arun and me without Laos papers. Hell, Nguyen, we can roll right up to Nape, the last checkpoint between here and Keo Neua Pass. We'll abandon ship five clicks south of the checkpoint, take to the trees again, and have only fifteen kilometers to make good."

"You were feeling unlucky when you lost your amulet. Apparently, you now feel like gambling."

"Right!" I agree. "I feel all that's behind us. First, the snake. We came through that one. Then those goddamned worms. Finally, the river crossing—and the firefight. That's three in a row, so my instincts are that we've got clear sailing between here and Nape. And much as I hate sticking myself into a tin can on wheels, I have this hunch that we ought to go with the flow. What's your feeling? You want to go for it—gain a couple of days? Or just keep humping the hard way?"

Nguyen studies the formidable vehicle with its cannon, its missile launcher, and its machine-gun.

"Let's piss on the tall trees!" he agrees.

"Okay," I say. "We'll tidy up first."

He leaves Tham and Tran staked out to guard the IFV and we slip back toward the river.

"What happened?" he asks me. "We saw you come ashore, and then they came out of nowhere. We were ready to target them, but then we saw you had them under control. They were actually assisting you. But suddenly you shot their officer. Why?"

"I don't know, Nguyen. One minute he was a pussycat. The next something clicked in his mind, something he saw in me—or I should say, saw *through* me. He started to go for it and I had to finish him."

Nguyen stops and moves in closer to me, looking me over. He lets out a silent breath.

"No wonder!" he says. "Your left contact lens is missing. You must have lost it in the river."

"Jesus! No wonder the poor bastard freaked out. One brown eye, one blue—not your run-of-the-mill Vietnamese major. Hell of a reason to have to die, isn't it? Because of a missing contact lens."

"You have spares?"

"Yep," I say. "Arun brought along six pairs, just in case."

We move out again and come to the riverbank. Nguyen signals to the rest of our team on the far side to cross over. He and I hold the rope taut for Arun, Le, and Van to cross, one at a time, leg looped over the rope, their backs just out of the water, pulling themselves along until they reach our side.

Last man across is Vo, as we have planned. He slings his rifle, now encased in a waterproof plastic bag, then frees up the nylon line, which has been secured to a tree trunk on his side. He ties the line around his waist and steps into the river. We haul him in like a flounder.

Our team and equipment now across, we police the site, stripping the dead soldiers of their identification and issuing the cards to our own people. We ease the bodies into the river and heave their weapons into the water, since we can't afford the extra weight. I check the area for the three casings I've expended in the firefight and quickly scoop them from the sand. We sweep the bank into a natural state, covering the footprints and the outlines of the dead. We bear the six other casualties from where they fell on the trail to another section of the riverbank and consign them to the surging water. We clean-sweep that bank as well, return to the trail, and collect all the casings from my ambush, twelve in all. We deflate the raft, repack it and all our equipment, so that we can once again shoulder it in a matter of a minute or two when that time comes, then set off like a winning ball team in the IFV, Van at the wheel. During his three years in the North Vietnamese Army, Nguyen tells me, Van had been trained in the care and handling of armored personnel carriers.

Well before sunset, a measured five kilometers south of Nape, the last major military center in Laos before Keo Neua Pass, we abandon our transportation on a deserted stretch of Highway 8. We have made good in two hours' time and without incident a distance that would have taken us two days to hump. We have gone rolling fat and happy past other military vehicles, Vo sitting up in the open hatch and doling out casual waves, like a true comrade in arms.

Here in the shadow fall of the Annam Cordillera Mountains, Phu Xai Lai Leng to the north of us, a towering peak almost nine thousand feet high, Rao Co to the south, reaching up seventy-five hundred feet, we have no problem selecting a dropoff platform for the IFV. Together we shove the IFV over the shoulder of the road and watch it tumble into green oblivion, not burning, since we have drained it of fuel. We brush the shoulder of the road to remove the tracks, then we cut off into high ground and blend into the heavy forest, Nguyen tracking along the compass course I've laid out to guide us to a campsite near the entrance to the pass.

Because of heavy military traffic through Keo Neua and the bristling border checkpoints, I decide that we'll flank our way through at night.

We sleep only until midnight, then we awaken the team. I lead everyone through a sequence of *wushu* exercises, then, stimulated, our spirits soaring, we set off precisely at twelve minutes after twelve, a sentimental concession to me, for it was at twelve minutes after midnight that I left Vietnam.

April 30, 1975.

Avoiding checkpoints, border troops, and ranging patrols, we cross over from Laos into Nam and come out into Nghe Ting Province.

The first people we see are Tho indigs, the men in

baggy trousers of white calico falling to their ankles, black robes reaching their knees, turbans of violet crepe, the women wearing blouses split in front with a row of buttons, tight sleeves, and sides cut like those of the Viet indigs. The men all carry a fiber-woven bag slung over their shoulders. They watch us impassively as we descend the faces of giant basaltic rocks and angle ourselves down toward a distant expanse of ricefields, polished as malachite by day's first sunshafts.

I stare out at the country I left ten years, four months, and seventeen days ago.

Without knowing why, I kneel.

I find myself whispering a couplet Doan Thi taught me during those other years, whispering it in Vietnamese, as she had first spoken it to me:

> *Sôn hà thâu chính khí,*
> *Nhât nguyêt chiêu đan tâm.*

When men and women die for their country, "mountains and rivers absorb their righteous life-sustaining spirits, and the sun and the moon shine on their true-red hearts."

If only we had understood before we came crashing in that the Vietnamese think and feel about their country in a special way! To them, the national territory is not just the physical space in which they live. It embraces a supernatural cosmos where the spirits of rivers and mountains are the souls of the heroes who, defending their country over two thousand years, have lived and died for a place where the soil is sacred and the people, down to the lowliest peasant, are heroic.

Who in his right mind chooses such people as enemies?

Suddenly Nguyen, Pham, Le, Vo, Tran, and Van are kneeling around me, Arun standing off to the side and watching us with tears in her eyes.

We have come home at last.

CHAPTER

28

The ricefields have ripened early, even prior to the tenth lunar month.

As Nguyen leads us in centipedal column across an endless mud ridge, I see that already the farmers of this district walk the *sawahs* with bamboo poles and press the plants down right and left, forcing the stalks to lie in flat, divided rows, like hair neatly combed away from the part, so the rice can be reaped more easily. If the farmers neglect this laying of the rice and leave the plants to fall upon themselves as wind and rooting pigs direct, the stalks become tangled and difficult to reap. "To have a drunken husband," peasant girls once sang for Doan Thi and me, "is like reaping rice beaten down by pigs."

I observe that these stalks are being laid toward the west, indicating that the farmers are already planning to harvest this area during morning hours, so they'll be able to keep their backs to the sun. For afternoon harvesting, they would be laying the rice toward the east instead.

It strikes me that I have a junkyard mind, littered with tufts of trivia. Put most anyone else down in the middle of a patchwork of rice paddies and he'd simply see farmers using poles. Ask him what he thought they were doing, he would probably tell you they were obviously pressing the stalks down. But would it occur to him that the stalks were being pressed to the west, rather than to the east, and if so, would he ask himself why?

Why does trivia fascinate me so? Or *is* it trivia? Combat teaches you that survival depends on your constant observation and interpretation of the inconsequential, a pinched leaf along a trail where no one else but you is thought to be, the sudden downwind scent of a burning cigarette, the clunk of a gun stock against rock or tree. Yet I find that since we descended out of the mountains four hours ago I am lowering my level of perception almost instinctively, still aware, yet joyously headlong, like a trail horse smelling the stable. With each step bringing me closer to the village in Tho Xuân district, where we are to meet a backup troop of Nguyen's resistance fighters, I'm feeling more and more transcendent, a god descending to earth, dampening his divinity, yet still aware of his inner power and self-confidence. For it was not too far from here in these forests that I was forged, on this very Trân Ninh Plateau, where all my pubescent dreams and visions were torn away from me by the mutilation of friends and specter enemies, here in this place where their deaths symbolically fused with my own, day after day, the recurrent universal death, which died often enough, ultimately gives you back your lost immortality, since living or dying no longer has intrinsic value one way or the other, except for the muted and somewhat sad certainty that dying is much easier, because what is due has finally been paid and you can no longer be dunned by vulpine landlords.

Nguyen signals for us to halt.

Beyond him, less than a kilometer off, a village within a compound fenced by bamboo borders a hillslope riotous with tropical grass. Through my binos I scan the cluster of houses, all one-floor thatch dwellings built with a framework of bamboo and wood and roofed with straw, except for one roof of tiled saddle ridge, marking the residence of the village leader.

Nguyen motions us to kneel. We kneel and wait.

From somewhere nearby the whinny of a horse startles a flock of hens and from the center of this disturbance a blue kite skitters upward, its knotted white tail fluttering higher and higher until it dances well above the treeline.

Apparently this is the signal Nguyen has been awaiting, for he motions us forward on the double. We trot across the small savanna toward the village. Its sturdy gate is already being swung open for us, permitting me to see for the first time the assemblage of villagers waiting inside, women and children unspeaking behind the alert vanguard of twenty armed men dressed as rice farmers.

Their commander detaches himself from the others, steps one pace forward and salutes Nguyen.

Nguyen introduces us.

"Captain Locke, Le Danh. These are his men, this his village."

Le Danh salutes me too. His right hand is missing middle, fourth, and little finger. It is apparent they have been cut away, one at a time, rather than blown off with a single burst. The columella of his nose appears fused, as though a bullet has sealed his nostrils. Yet his black eyes remain undaunted.

"Welcome," he says to me in Vietnamese. "All my men are not yet here, since you arrive many hours earlier than we expected you."

"Nguyen moved us across Laos in record time." I smile.

Proudly, Le Danh leads us toward his men, who have formed into a smartly dressed line. They snap their assault rifles into salute position as we pass.

The women and children open before us, alternating their stares and whispering between me and Arun, clearly finding each of us worth study and comment.

We follow Le Danh to what at one time must have been the Chinese *tap hóa* shop, the general store. On the porch a shelved wooden chest still stands with stoneware bowls and tureens on the upper shelves. On the lower shelves mugs of fish sauce, *Phan-thiết* and *Phú-qúôc* are on exhibit. Brooms lean against one side of the chest, and next to these hang brushes made of bamboo roots.

We enter the store, which is lined with rows of shelves reaching to the ceiling. Bottles of beer, orange juice, and Vĩnh-hảo spring water are displayed along with other left-over canned foods. In one corner a small altar of Kuan-Kung juts out into the room.

Le Danh has cleared off the top of a pinewood platform in the center of the room and on it I see maps.

"The Chinese who once owned this shop fled four years ago," Le Danh tells us, "leaving all his merchandise in his hurry to leave the country. Now all of us own his pots and pans, his brushes and brooms. We do not drink the beer or the spring water in these bottles because they were already old when he was still here. We leave them on the shelves as a monument to the poor old man who bought his way to freedom with eighteen lang of twenty-four karat gold paid over to the security police—everything he had managed to save in the twenty years he did business in this village. Now we use his store as a meeting place to plan our own revolution against brute masters who trade human lives for gold."

He leads me to the pinewood platform.

"These maps are accurate down to each rat hole," he tells me. "The camp where the girl Thanh Hoa is being held is officially named Trai Sán Xuât Và Tíêt Kiêm—we call it Trai Dàm Dùn. It is an old camp, dating back to the Viet-Minh."

How euphemistic, I think, that the camp's name translates into English as "production and economy-drive camp." Who are the faceless drones who work for governments all over the world to supply the officialese, the mitigating phrases, the softening, deceptive words, turning "death camp" into "economy-drive camp"? Why don't we have camps for *them*?

"As you see, the camp covers an area of five hectares on the edge of a wood that once was part of Dàm village. It is isolated from the outside world by a double wall of bamboo stakes planted in link-style, so thick and so close that not even a field mouse can squeeze through. Outside the bamboo are lines of barbed wire. Inside is a deep trench three meters across bristling with punji stakes. And here, at each corner, are the watchtowers occupied twenty-four hours a day by two guards armed with light machineguns."

"Where is the girl being kept?" I ask.

"Our contact within the camp told us only yesterday that she has been shackled in a connex until now, but he heard a rumor that the commandant is ordering her placed in *les fossés habitées* as of tomorrow."

My brain burns from the words *connex* and *les fossés habités*, words I haven't heard for ten years. The dreaded connex boxes are the metal or wooden air freight containers we left behind. Over the years of our supplying the South, thousands of these crates were put to odious use as ready-made confinements for prisoners. The condemned were shackled into the boxes "butterfly" style—one arm elevated over the shoulder, the other pulled around the trunk of the body, thumbs lashed together behind the back, then in that unyielding, painful position the prisoners were stuffed into boxes which had once contained air-conditioning units or Dodge motor blocks and left to bake in the tropical sun.

Les fossées habités, imported by the implacable French invasion forces who preceded us in Indochina but came without our subsequent technology, are "living ditches," deep trenches each seven feet in length, but deliberately kept narrow. Prisoners are manacled and forced to sit in these trenches, knees crunched into chests, for days at a time, their urine and excreta matted around them, attracting flies and insects.

"What is her physical condition?" I ask.

"She is suffering from dysentery and general debilitation, yet in spite of this her will remains strong."

He glances at Nguyen, as though awaiting approval to continue.

Nguyen nods. "The captain is aware of the girl's feeling toward him."

"She speaks all day and night, over and over, the same prayer, 'My dear God, I will serve you forever if you give me the strength to survive until he comes.' *He*, Captain, is *you*. The other prisoners consider her mad. But she insists an American *will* come. That he will liberate her. And that once he does—she will kill him."

"I am not among her favorite people," I admit. "But as long as we keep her unarmed, I'll take my chances. Why are they treating her so harshly?"

"She is a beautiful girl," Le Danh says. "And it is well known throughout this district that the commandant at Dàm Dùn is a collector of women. The wives of prisoners come to him at night so that he will give their husbands extra rice. When this girl arrived from Hanoi, he saw himself in possession of a rare jewel. He sought her sexual favors at once. It is told around the camp that she kicked him in the groin and then fell upon him, coming close to killing him with her empty hands before the guards beat her unconscious. She was then thrown into a connex to die, but she continues to live, to the amazement of all."

"Just waiting for me." I smile.

That's Thanh Hoa, I remind myself. Pure jungle cat. I remember that night in the mountains of Bali under the lashing of rain, hardly a month ago, when she and six guerrilla fighters tried to terminate me. When the firefight had ended in my favor, she came crawling over broken rock toward me, crabbing through the mud, her neck torn open from my grenade, and begged me to kill her.

"*Tôi múôn chét*," she said without emotion. "I want to die."

"Why should I do you the favor?" I asked.

I managed to get her back to a hospital in Denpasar in time to save her life.

"How large is the defending force?" I ask.

"Forty men, no more."

"How many prisoners?"

"Two thousand."

I look at the map again. I can see only ten barracks indicated.

"Are these drawings to scale?" I ask.

"They are."

"But—it's impossible to jam more than a hundred—if that many—into buildings this small!"

"Not for the commandant at Dàm Dùn," he replies.

"I am going to kill the man," Nguyen announces. "I have intended to for some time, but we had more pressing business elsewhere. For that matter, I should tell you now, Captain, that it is our plan to kill all the guards, except the one who has been our inside contact and source of information."

"Negatory," I say. "The mission is to extract one prisoner. There is no way we can engage a force of forty armed security men within a fortified position without suffering casualties. And I did not come to Vietnam to get people killed."

"If we were to free only Thanh Hoa," Nguyen says, "think, sir, how simple we would be making matters for the Security Police. They would search everywhere for her and in a country where children are taught to inform on their mothers the authorities would find us before we could get her to help you locate your son. Your enemies in the Mat Vû would certainly associate her escape with your arrival in Vietnam—and the net would close faster than it would if they had nothing on which to pinpoint their search. Suppose instead we liberate two thousand political prisoners, give them the chance to scatter across

Vietnam, to seek freedom over the border however they may. Think of the consternation in Hanoi. For days nobody will be able to sort out what happened at Dàm Dùn, where the attack came from, who is behind it, until we have accomplished our missions and left the country. Believe me, sir, this is the only way to confuse and mislead them."

"I'm convinced," I tell him.

Nguyen awards me one of his rare smiles.

"Thank you, Captain. Coming from you, that is a conviction to be treasured."

"What is the camp timetable, its routine?" I ask Le Danh.

"The prisoners are locked into their barracks from five at night until six every morning—except for those in the connex boxes and those in the ditches."

I study the sketches Le Danh's people have made of the inside of the camp.

"These barracks," I say, referring to the sketch of a typical barracks, "have they no windows?"

"None," Le Danh says. "The prisoners remain in the dark, without windows, without heat."

"I don't see drain pipes. Aren't there any toilets?"

"Two one-hundred-liter drums to each barracks, one at either end."

"Counterproductive way to reeducate anybody, isn't it?" I suggest.

"*Amoindir, avilir, affamer, aneantir*—these are the true purposes of Hanoi's reeducation," he says bitterly.

To diminish, to debase, to starve, to annihilate.

"What happens to the prisoners at six A.M.?" I ask.

"They are released from barracks and given a bowl of hard corn for breakfast. Some prisoners are given uncooked rice as a punishment. Then they empty the drums of human waste and are marched off to their eight hours of labor. At Dàm Dùn presently they are still clearing the nearby jungle and planting corn. Lunch is brought to them in the fields—rice mixed with sliced cassava. Then they are marched back to the camp at the end of the day."

"Where are the guards all this time?" I ask.

"Twenty are on duty while twenty stand down. Those on duty are stationed in the watchtowers—eight men altogether. Two guards watch the prisoners in the connex boxes and two patrol the trenches to make sure none of the prisoners below ground change their positions. Of the remaining eight guards, one stays at the main gate, and seven are in the fields."

"With all those prisoners?" I ask.

"The seven surround the field with mortars and machine-guns. No prisoner could take four steps without being cut down or causing the deaths of his friends."

"What about support personnel—cooks, clerks, drivers?" I ask. "How many of those are in the camp?"

"Another fifteen or twenty, some women, but they are mostly militia, with little combat experience."

"So tell me, Le Danh, when does anybody get time to be reeducated?"

"There are regular nighttime study sessions which focus on self-criticism, on government policies, and on Communist party history. Time is given to each prisoner to write his autobiography and to disclose his financial assets. Twice a month each must write down the story of his own life, of his father's life, his mother's, his sisters and his brothers, his children, his grandparents, listing all their possessions, past and present, including what make of television set or camera they might have owned, even if that were twenty years ago, what books were possessed, what books read and remembered. If the authorities find out you have left something out, then you are in grave trouble. You must write new confessions many times a day and still make up your work clearing the forest. When the authorities have accepted your written confession, then you must make your public confession before the camp authorities and other prisoners. The more 'crimes' a prisoner confesses, the more he is praised as 'progressive' by the camp authorities."

His words slam into me until I no longer hear him. I am thinking of Doan Thi, who died two years ago last March in the reeducation camp Gia Rai Z30, died watching—what? An empty wall? No window? "Beloved," she wrote—her last words ever—"this morning the curtains steal across the sill—reaching south. Shall I ever again see you? Touch you?" Thanh Hoa had brought me her note, as part of the entrapment that almost got me waxed in Bali. And I had bought it, lock, stock, and barrel, because the note was in Doan Thi's handwriting. Now, realizing how stark, how savage these camp barracks are, I have to question when and where Doan Thi penned that note to me. Or did she, because she was so great a poet, lie there dying on a wooden pallet and gazing at the windowless wall make herself see an opening, see curtains stealing across the sill and the fresh morning wind making them dance for her imagination?

Suddenly I yearn to be at Dàm Dùn behind an advancing vengeful wall of gunfire.

"When will you have all your men here?" I ask Le Dahn.

"Before dark."

I begin to use the calipers on the overall map to chart the distance from here to there.

"Ten hours," Nguyen tells me. "I've humped it twice before from here."

"Then I suggest we move out at eighteen hundred hours, putting us on site tomorrow morning at oh-four-hundred. We will rest and observe. During stand-down time, while everyone is at lunch and the prisoners are in the fields, we will attack simultaneously on two fronts—one attack against the guards in the fields to achieve the release outside of the camp of the general mass of prisoners, the other attack against the watchtowers, the front gate, the connex, and trench guards, taking down whatever resistance remains inside the camp. Agreed?"

Nguyen and Le Danh both salute me.

Wordlessly.

Of the three of us I am no longer sure which is the most frenzied.

By the time Le Danh's village begins to soften in the long evening shadows, all his men have filtered in from neighboring hamlets.

They stand before me now, Nguyen and our own team alongside me, while Le Danh proudly introduces each man, making it clear that all are trusted fighters for the Resistance and that no man among the fifty assembled has not killed at least one enemy in hand-to-hand combat.

"How many of your weapons are silenced?" I ask Le Danh.

"Only three."

He beckons three of his men forward. One is carrying a Soviet Dragunov sniper rifle with a PSO–1 scope and a suppressor, identical to the one Vo carries for our unit. Another man bears a Type-64 Chinese silenced SMG. The third has a U.S. M–21 rifle with a Sionics Noise Suppressor.

With Vo's Soviet SVD and suppressor, along with my silenced .22 Hi-Standard, that gives us five silent guns.

"We'll take out the guards in the watchtowers with the two SVDs, the M–21, and the 64," I tell the assembled men. "Four of our people to hose down eight sentries from midrange. At the moment these sentries come under fire, four teams of four men each will attack the watchtowers with automatic weapons, in case any of the guards have survived the initial sniper fire. Each team will send two men up, while the two remaining on the ground give them what covering fire they may need to reach their objective. Once in place, these two-man teams in the watchtowers will take over each of the four machine-guns and use them to sweep the camp. Anyone seen carrying a weapon is to be shot. Le Danh, you will please select the sixteen men to secure the watchtowers. Now—and this is critical—no one is to fire until he sees the guard at the front gate fall. That will be the signal for the attack against the watchtowers and the camp."

"Who will kill that one?" Le Danh asks.

"I will," I tell him, "with the silenced Hi-Standard. Now everyone must understand this, okay? The signal to attack is the man dropping—not the sound of gunfire. There won't be any sound from my gun. It is especially silent. Is that clear?"

I look around at the encircling eyes.

"It is understood," Le Danh says for all of his men.

"The second the guard at the gate falls, the four snipers will kill the first four of the eight machine-gunners in the watchtowers. They will work out among themselves which enemy they are each to target. I expect the second series of silenced rounds to kill the remaining four—all within a matter of no more than three seconds from the time I've dropped the guard at the gate. If the teams can get up and into the watchtowers without requiring supporting fire from their ground forces, so much the better. At my signal, once I see we have secured the watchtowers, we will enter the camp in force. If anything has happened to me, the signal will be given by Nguyen, who will be with me at the gate. We will enter the camp with a force of twenty-one men, three units of seven men, my unit straight across, cutting the camp in two, each of the other units peeling off to either flank and cleaning up from the center out to the far walls. Our remaining seventeen men are to eliminate the seven sentries guarding the prisoners in the forest. This attack will begin five minutes before I kill the man at the gate. I am hoping it can be carried off in silence, but if not, at the first sound of gunfire I will kill the guard at the gate and launch our attack against the camp. Which of your men, Le Danh, are most skilled with the knife?"

Good-naturedly, his men turn to elect those among them known to be their deadliest hand-to-hand fighters.

"We need seven men," I say.

Five are pushed forward by their comrades with a good deal of smiling and encouragement.

Two step forward on their own. I observe that nobody challenges their volunteering.

These two have the same burning in their eyes that Vo has.

The seven assemble in front of me.

I lock in on one of the two whose eyes are as merciless as the eyes of the bronze whaler shark that attacked me last year off Australia's Great Barrier Reef.

"Please show me how you would kill a sentry with your knife," I say, and turn my back to him. "*Without the knife*, if you don't mind," I add over my shoulder, and get the first laugh of the evening from the grim assembly of young warriors.

He moves softly, swiftly, without announcement, coming in behind me, gripping me vigorously over the mouth with his left hand. He starts to pull my head back and to simulate a slashing motion with his right hand across my jugular and larynx, but at the instant I feel his left hand grasping at my chin I slam my right hand over his and turn my shoulder left into him, driving my left elbow into his chest even as I hip-throw him over my left leg, which I've planted just outside his line of attack.

Astonished, the air pumped out of him, he falls, but I hold him and help him land uninjured.

He leaps up, eyes firing.

It is apparent I have not made a friend, but I have made my point.

"Too many things," I announce to the group, "can go wrong with the classic throat slash. We were all taught that technique in special ops, along with the stab into the carotid artery or into the kidney, but I lost some good men before I learned there's a more reliable way to take down a sentry with a knife. What was your name again?" I ask the young man who lurks before me now, measuring me for revenge.

"Tran Van Ninh," he says.

"Okay, Ninh," I say. "This time *you* get to be the sentry. I'll attack you. My right hand will be the knife."

He turns his back to me. I see how he waits, every nerve coiled to do to me what I've done to him.

I move on him soundlessly and simply bring my palm down smartly on the crown of his head in a vertical chop.

Ninh whirls on me, even further humiliated.

"What kind of attack is that?" he demands.

"With the proper knife I would have split your skull open like a coconut."

"What if I'd been wearing a helmet?" he demands.

"Turn around."

He turns.

I whip out my hand and strike a horizontal blow at the base of his neck.

"That would have cut your spinal cord—sometimes it even decapitates."

I face the men.

"Either attack will do two things instantly—silence and kill. These are attacks against the nervous system, not against the circulatory system. Split a man's brains, he has lost his capability for speech. Same thing when the spinal cord is cut. Believe me, cutting your enemy's throat is *not* the quickest nor the quietest way to take him down. If you happen to pick a strong opponent, you're going to be spending all your energy trying to hold on to him. The secret is not to touch him—except with your blade . . . with *these* blades . . ."

I motion to Nguyen, who produces the unique parrot's-beak knives we've brought with us from Bangkok—part of my special weapons inventory.

I hold one up to let them see the weapon I've selected for sentry takedown.

"This," I announce, "is a *kukri*—the weapon of choice

among the British Gurkhas. It has tremendous chopping power. With one blow it will split a skull or sever a spinal cord."

The knives distributed and every man assigned to a specific duty on either of two separate attack groups, our timetables and orders of assault worked out to the last detail, I visit Arun in the hut which she's been sent to share with three other unmarried village girls.

She gives me a final touch-up while the three girls squat to one side of us and watch in whispered fascination.

"I'm coming with you," she announces as I study my Vietnamese face in her hand mirror.

"Sorry. You're staying with the girls. I can't afford to let you catch a stray bullet. We'll be back by this time tomorrow."

"Suppose it rains," she says. "Ninety percent probability."

"Then I'll turn into an American."

"It could happen at the wrong time—and turn you into a dead American. I'm coming!"

"You ever fired a weapon?"

"I took basic training in the Thai Army. I was also a monk for a full nine months. All Thai young men must do both."

I laugh. "Forgive me. I keep forgetting the other half of you."

"I'm glad you do," she says, and touches my cheek softly with the palm of one hand.

"I'll get ready," she says brightly, and turns away before I have to show any reaction to her touch.

Ten minutes later we move into the forest, fifty-seven men and one in transition, our destination ten hours to the northwest.

═══CHAPTER═══

29

We march in farmers' clothing, Nguyen and I, together with Arun and our Bangkok team, blending with Le Danh and his Resistance fighters, each man issued an orange headband to wear when the attack is launched so that we don't blow away our own people in the inevitable criss-crossing firefight.

I ask Le Danh how he will manage to isolate and spare the cooperative guard who has been his source of information from the camp.

"He was told at the time of our last contact to be absent on leave all this week."

Arun is right about the rain.

All night we slog through forest bent under wind and water, our ponchos unable to keep us dry.

My makeup, even part of my waterproof Asian nose, is scoured away by the downpour. I can feel myself exposed for all to see as the Great White Hunter, primary target.

Shortly before oh-four-hundred hours we arrive on site, half a click in from the area where the prisoners will be marched out to clear trees in a little more than one hundred and twenty minutes from now.

Here we set up our perimeters, sling hammocks, and permit the main body of men two hours of rest while Le Danh leads Nguyen and me off on a recon probe of our objective.

En route to the camp I spot a nearby hill and despite Le Danh's protest that I'll be unable to see anything from its peak, I lead him and Nguyen up its slippery rise until we achieve the summit.

I break out the Tiger Eye telephoto device Arty had given me in Bangkok, and sighting through it I take a cool tour of every square inch of Dàm Dùn. I watch one of the tower machine-gunners picking his nose and it occurs to me with icy comprehension that he will soon be as inanimate as the fragment of himself he has just plastered onto the bamboo pole next to his gun while his fellow guard was looking elsewhere. I zoom in on all three of the long, dark slits inside the camp and the soldiers guarding them, even in the rain, and wonder which one Thanh Hoa occupies this miserable night, hunched down in mud and shit, struggling to hold on to whatever humanity may still be left in her, kept alive only by her passion to kill me. I consider how her will would shift into overdrive, her eyes regain their fire, if she knew that soon I would be sliding down into her trench to scoop her up in a replay of that night in Bali when I pulled her from the mud. Finally I work the Tiger Eye over a hundred other images and details inside the camp before I pass the lens to Nguyen.

I am ready. More than ready.

I feel the blood ticking in my veins, marking the minutes.

What back in Bangkok had seemed so distant, so insurmountable a goal, now lies at my feet.

Thanh Hoa first.

Then the Soviet carrier.

Then my son.

Here we come, ready or not!

I feel as though I'm a strip of film, the end of one scene, the start of another, spliced head to head, an instantaneous switchover, no long dissolve from one moment to the next, but this image of me on the hill overlooking Dàm Dùn, the next image of me lying in the grass thirty feet from the front gate of the camp, rain still driving down, splattering the runaway mud trail down which Nguyen and I and the others lying to shelter all along the front of the camp have just watched two thousand ravaged prisoners march with their seven guards spaced out like yapping sheep dogs along either flank of the long, silent column. It is a raw look into the reptilian heart of mankind, this sighting of the helpless herded by armed men, made even more unredemptive to me by my knowledge that all over the world other ragged lines of doomed people are being shuffled in one direction or another by those with superior power.

Five minutes earlier we had cut the phone lines, hoping the commandant wouldn't be placing any calls at six in the morning or that if he did he'd assume the storm had taken out his lines.

He has SSB-radio equipment in his office, Le Danh has told us, and we've assigned Le Danh and his team who will be rolling up our left flank to give first priority to silencing any outgoing transmission.

Arun has agreed with me that keeping my Asian face intact under the given weather conditions is impossible. She has wrapped my head with wet rags so that only my eyes show. Not that our attack plans call for survivors, except for the absent guard, but Nguyen agrees that the longer we can confuse the Mât Vu about my presence in Vietnam, the better our chances to extract.

I watch the second hand on my Memosail flipping past the numbers like the pointer on a wheel of fortune—round and round it goes, and where it stops . . . *we* know!

Four minutes of the five-minute lead time we have allotted to our men with the *kukri* knives have elapsed. Still no betraying burst of gunfire from the nearby fields.

I slip the Hi-Standard free. Its long barrel made longer by the suppressor comforts me at thirty yards, giving me the illusion that I'm using a rifle instead of a hand gun.

The guard at the gate slops back and forth in the mud, probably debating to himself whether he can keep drier if he remains in one spot or whether he should move between the slanting downpour and stay drier. I cannot see his face too clearly in the wet slate light, but he looks young. How appropriate! Why should he be an exception? It is the fate of all of us when we are young to be brought to places like this to face the possibility of death at the hands of strangers.

Thirty seconds.

I watch the second hand until it has only five more ticks to go, then I concentrate on the target. One wrist braced into the mud, gripping my extended right wrist, I count five backward and as I reach one I exhale softly and squeeze five rounds into the boy at the gate, just as he turns my way, patterning them upward along his centerline for maximum shock and directing the sixth into his forehead before he can slump.

He lowers to his knees like a wearied horse and topples in slow motion into the mud.

I look up at the nearest watchtower in time to see the young man who'd been picking his nose two hours ago lose the top of his head.

I count off three more seconds and observe that two of our men are already scrambling up the ladders of the nearest watchtower.

Still without a sound.

I rise to my knees, watch the other three teams ascending. I signal along the line. All twenty-one of us jump up and go sloshing in three columns to the gate.

Just inside the gate to my left a guard appears. He stares at our oncoming grayness and claws for his slung AK–47.

Le Danh unzips him across the chest.

The first gunfire I've heard.

It triggers a firestorm. Our teams in the watchtowers comb the camp with controlled bursts of intersecting fire.

Nguyen and I run toward the nearest slit trench and prepare to kill the guards, but they appear to be dancing away from us, whirling obscenely as bullets from above pound into them.

Nguyen and Tran stand cover for me as the rest of our team secures the center line. I peer down at the sodden heads of six prisoners in the trench at my feet. They sit with their hands over their heads and push themselves deeper into the mud as though trying to bury themselves from the death they hear everywhere above them.

Thanh Hoa cannot be one of these. She would be looking up, facing whatever it was.

We slide twenty meters right to the second trench, stepping over the bodies of the dead guards, already sinking into the wet earth.

The ripping of gunfire comes to me now less fiercely. It has the sound of winding down as targets become harder to isolate.

I stand at the collapsing lip of this second trench and look down at this group of prisoners, like the others in postures of pitiable retreat, heads drawn deep into shoulders, fearful turtles, hands clasped over glistening skulls.

Except for one face. Pinched with defiance.

Thanh Hoa. Staring up at me.

In that first instant of seeing her again I know nothing has changed. I still perceive her as the living substitute for the woman I lost, as Doan Thi's replacement, as the fusion of the real with the memory.

I slide down into the trench. With my Randall I cut her wrists and thumbs free, then her ankles. I bring her immobile, stricken left arm forward slowly, rubbing and massaging the shoulder. Then I lift her. She feels even lighter than she felt when I lifted her into the back of that truck in Bali. She feels so light I despair that she may not have enough life left in her to acknowledge my coming, to realize that the final victory has been hers after all.

And to tell me where I can find my son.

"Sorry it took so long to get here," I whisper.

I climb out with her.

Already the rain is starting to dribble the mud from her swollen ankles. She feels as though she's melting away in my arms.

For a moment I believe she has died.

Desperately I put my face to hers. Her breath touches me gently.

I have no idea why I stand there in the rain, Thanh Hoa in my arms, and begin to weep.

CHAPTER

30

I bear the girl across the spectral killing ground, Nguyen guiding me to the stilted, open-sided hospital hut. Carefully I ascend the bamboo steps, taking care not to slide in the terracing blood of the camp medic, who has been machine-gunned at the entry.

Silence has lowered upon the camp, the silence which for me inevitably follows the final stutter of a no-quarter firefight, a silence that drains away the last of your adrenaline and deadens your hearing until you can *slowly* notch back down from the high. Voices from here and there about the compound waffle toward me, but only faintly, without meaning or involvement.

Though Thanh Hoa lies airy in my arms, my feet feel leaden as I cross with her to one of the filthy wooden slabs in the hut and lay her onto it. She looks as inert as an African mud doll.

I check her airway and her pulse.

Airway clear, pulse acceptable, no sign, at least, of cardiac decompensation.

Along her neck the skin is welted, still red and angry where it heals from the fragment of my grenade fired last month in Bali. Typical hypertrophic scar. Six more months and it will have blended with her natural skin tone.

I ask Nguyen to bring me fresh water, but minutes seem to pass before he returns. Abruptly, I hear gunfire, a three-round burst not more than a few yards away. It brings me out of my dream state. I peer out across the still-smoky camp and observe Nguyen approaching with two buckets, clear water slopping out of each as he hurries toward me.

"Sorry for the delay," he apologizes. "But Le Danh was holding the camp commandant for me. The dog demanded a trial."

"I heard your judgment," I comment.

"Too merciful!" Nguyen says. "But he'd been trying to conceal himself in a latrine pit. He almost succeeded, since he blended so naturally with the feces. Nobody volunteered to fish him out, so I had to shoot him where he lay. It will not make a pleasant memory!"

I wash down the girl's arms and legs. The skin on her ankles and feet is pocked with festering insect bites. Lacerations from the shackles ring her wrists and lower legs. The bottoms of both feet are as swollen and as split as overripe pomegranates.

She's been beaten repeatedly on her soles. I cleanse these areas and apply corticosteroid lotion.

Examination of her scalp reveals no contusions or lacerations. I rotate her head, watching for evidence of "doll's eye" response, but she comes through this with flying colors. Her abdomen remains pliant to the touch, without spasm or rigidity. I find no signs of muscular twitching or of convulsions.

"Simple case of beating and primary inanition," I tell Nguyen. "How they managed to starve her into this condition in three weeks, God knows, unless they gave her no food or water at any time."

Nguyen says nothing. His silence is confirmation enough.

"They take out the radio?" I ask.

"They did."

"What happened in the fields?"

"All seven guards died by the knife. I have had to promise the village fighters who killed them they could keep the knives we brought."

"By all means. What about the prisoners?"

"It's taking them time to adjust to the sudden change in their condition. But some are starting to wander in now, looking for food. Others haven't yet been able to understand we've set them free. They remain in the fields. But Le Danh is organizing everything now. You must be sure to keep your face covered when we leave. No witness should later be able to tell the authorities an American led this attack."

"Better send Arun in here to check me out."

"I've already sent for her."

I open my rucksack and bring out a packet of formula, forty-two percent dried skim milk, thirty-two percent edible oil, twenty-five percent sucrose plus K, Mg, and vitamin supplements reconstituted to give fifteenth-percent–strength dried skim milk. I mix it with water from my thermos, and lifting Thanh Hoa's head from the slab begin to spoon-feed her.

As I feed her I study her immobile yet still-lovely face. I remember that I saw her first as a ten-year-old girl fifteen years ago when I led my SOG Black Mamba team into her village shimmering in heat. I knew instantly we'd poked into Indian country, for there were no men to be seen anywhere. Then I spotted a defused bomb not quite concealed under a pile of brush. Only trained cadres were capable of defusing our magnetic bombs. But what made me dead sure we were in the TZ was my sighting a village girl just as she threw away an empty bottle and leaned a broom against the side of a hut.

I signaled my men to freeze in place, some thirty feet separating each of us, and I called the girl to me. She was seventeen, I guessed. In Vietnamese, which surprised her, I ordered her to walk ten paces directly ahead of me through the village. The team followed as we started in single file down the hard-packed dirt track separating the rows of huts. But halfway into the village the girl broke to one side and ran.

Four meters off I killed her with the Swedish gun I carried back then—killed her from escaping to the VC waiting, I was certain, just outside the village.

Then, at the point where she'd wheeled off, we found the telltale cluster of mines she'd buried just before our arrival. The empty bottle I'd seen her drop was what she'd used to roll the earth after she'd planted the mines. The broom she'd used to give the ground a natural look. It never occurred to her that a stupid American soldier could possibly equate an empty bottle and a worn straw broom with death waiting underfoot.

We rounded up every woman and child in the village and tied them securely.

Long after, I remembered one little girl of ten. She started at me more intensely than any of the other prisoners. I didn't know then as I tied her thin wrists together that she would grow up to be the striking-looking girl lying here now on the wooden slab.

We moved out, leaving the villagers tied up so that no one could zip out and warn the VC we were leaving.

We were less than an hour out when the first enemy mortar round struck well outside the village. Then came a measured interval of five minutes before the barrage began, a full-scale bombardment of 81 mike-mike, directly into the village. The VC, believing that we were camping overnight in their hamlet, were obliterating it—and theoretically us along with it. They were operating on the belief that their families would have fled at the first warning mortar burst and that we, reacting, taking cover, would not have stopped the women and children.

Fifteen years later that ten-year-old girl found me in Bali. When she and six trained Vietnamese jungle fighters put me on "trial" in the mountains there, she held out a crumpled paper for me to study. On it was a sketch tinctured with what appeared to be faded watercolor, a childish sketch, obviously drawn of a young American officer in cammies, his cheeks sunken, his eyes ravenous, giving him a terrifying post-holocaust aura. I recognized the subject of the sketch.

Me. Back then.

Thanh Hoa had drawn it, using the blood from her wounds, to capture my face so she could never forget the man who had shot her sister, then brought a rain of death upon the hamlet. For only three women and children survived the mortaring.

Thanh Hoa's failure to kill me in Bali has now brought her here, to this camp, and to this morning in September.

By the fourth spoonful of formula her eyes open.

She continues sipping as I feed her, but her stare is fixed on me unwaveringly.

Do I imagine this, or is some of her earlier intransigence muted? Or am I again, with typical American mirror-imaging, deceiving myself that her gratitude will overcome her hatred? After all, this is the second time this year I've saved her life.

"Are you allergic to penicillin?" I ask her.

She shakes her head.

I dig into my ruck for the V two-fifty-mg penicillin capsules and feed her one.

Suddenly Arun is kneeling beside me and checking my disintegrating nose.

"We can kiss *that* beak good-bye." Arun laughs. "But never mind! Nose number two is right here in my makeup kit. This the girl we came for?"

"She's the girl all right."

Arun bends closer. Thanh Hoa's eyes fix on her.

"A jungle cat, isn't she?" Arun exclaims.

"More dangerous!" I say. "Just be sure when you're near her she doesn't get hold of anything lethal. For *both* our sakes."

"A jungle cat is one thing," Arun says. "A city cat is another. And I am a city cat. You make a move to harm Captain Locke, I will cut your throat from one ear to the other!"

Out of nowhere Arun produces a knife with such legerdemain that both Nguyen and I are startled, not so much by her unexpected dexterity as by her silky ferocity.

Thanh Hoa appears unperturbed by the theatrics. Her eyes move from Arun to me.

"Thank you," she whispers.

I try to arrest it before it escapes, but I'm too late. I still hear myself saying "I beg your pardon?"—not believing what I've heard.

"Twice you've given me back to life," she says. "Why *you*, of all men? How can I forgive you for killing my sister? Yet how can I ignore what you've done for me?"

She begins to cry, silently at first, then it all wells up, and her wasted body shakes in my arms.

How can I possibly let myself believe her? In Bali I deceived myself into believing that she was Doan Thi's Sister Fourth. She had dangled the Brooklyn Bridge in front of my nose—the Bronx-Whitestone too—and I bought the package, tollgate and all, hoping to bring Doan Thi back from the dead in the body of a younger, surviving sister. Certainly she is pretending all this now, this melodramatic act, saying this to disarm me so that later, when she's regained her strength and I've let my guard down, she'll find the weapon at hand and make her move. Yet, until then, what else can I do but play along, pretend,

pretend, when God knows I yearn to believe her more than anything else I can think of?

"I need only one thing from you, Thanh Hoa," I tell her when she is finally calm. "Just tell me where I can find my son."

"If I tell you, you will be very sorry," she says. "Sorrier than you've ever been in all your life."

Instantly, I'm alarmed, not by her words alone, but by the feeling I sense behind them.

"Why should I be sorry?" I ask. "Why else do you think I've come all this way?"

"Once you know where he is, you will learn other things you will wish you'd never learned."

"Is something the matter with him?"

"No," she says. "I saw him only a month ago. Such a beautiful boy!"

"Then—why shall I be sorry?" I insist.

Her hesitation seems real enough, not staged, but genuine. "I thought that telling you this would be the greatest fulfillment of my life," she says quietly. "Hating you all these years, wanting to kill you, I finally realized I might never have the chance. Then as they starved me and I got weaker, I thought you might never get here, and I would die—without seeing you again. I became too weak to be able to kill you, even if I had the chance, so I began to dream of how else I could hurt you—and I kept imagining your face when I told you."

"Told me what?" I demand.

"But—something happened to me. I don't hate you anymore, Captain Locke. I finally understand that what you did that day in my village, any North Vietnamese commander would have done in the South. Look what my own people have done to me! In spite of all my loyalty!"

The canthi of her eyes fascinate me. They have caught the sudden welling of her tears and now cloister them in each magnificently curved corner. I marvel that anyone can maintain tears of such depth without them running over.

"The man next to me in the ditch," she whispers, "chewed in his dreams. His teeth grinding together reminded me of locusts in the trees at night. Even after he died I could still hear him chewing—or so I imagined."

Her eyes flood over, streaking her gaunt cheekbones, but she appears not to feel the spill, even when it reaches the corners of her parched lips.

"I waited in that trench to die," she says, "and I lost all feeling—except for the thought of food."

She shudders in my arms. I feel her fingers clasping at my arm as though she is trying to remind herself of something before the memory of it escapes her forever.

"Please," she whimpers. "Hold me!"

A spasm takes her. She feels like a runaway vibrator in my arms. Nguyen tears the bloodied shirt from the body of the dead medic and hands it to me. I wrap it around Thanh Hoa's feet and bundle her even tighter into my embrace. I find myself rocking with her, giving her my own body heat, sharing it and letting her feel the terrible calm that lives deep within my own faultlines.

In a while Thanh Hoa is still again, but she feels so light in my arms I have this irrational fear that she may simply vanish before she can tell me what I have come here to learn.

She is muttering now. I can scarcely hear her with her head tucked into my chest. I ease her back, her face to mine again, her lips near my ear.

"I'm waiting, Thanh Hoa," I say. "Just tell me where he is. Then you can sleep."

"In the trench," she says softly, "I lost my hate. You would think it should be otherwise—that I would learn only to hate even more. But I began to remember moments in my life—bright moments, not the dark ones I'd lived with for so many years."

I look up at Nguyen. My desperation must show, for his eyes caution me to be patient, to wait, to let the girl release her anguish.

"I remembered the morning you brought me to the hospital in Denpasar. You placed a blossom in a dish of water—and covered it for a while. Then you uncovered it and placed it close to me. I could smell the fragrance, strong as smoke—and you said, 'When you see my son, tell him his mother used to do this for me before we fell asleep together. Tell him his mother did such beautiful things, not only wrote Socialist poetry.'"

I feel her fingers crawling toward my collar. For a split second I suspect she may be going to try for the trachea, a sudden finger-jab, but I manage to reject the alarm reaction.

She clings to my collar with one hand and stares into my eyes.

"Can you imagine that such a simple, sentimental thing could affect me so? *Me*—whose heart danced with joy whenever I could kill an American!"

I have no comment. Of course.

"I told myself that if I no longer had the strength to kill you, at least I still had the weapon to crack your heart. But now I have no desire to use it against you."

"That would have to be some weapon, Thanh Hoa," I say. "You can't crack what's already been blown apart."

"Oh, it is. It is!"

"Okay, give it your best shot!" I say.

She looks straight up into my eyes. I can find no enmity in hers. Not anymore. Or at least, not as deep as I can see.

"Your son is in Hanoi. He is being raised by his grandfather."

"Grandfather?"

"Yes. Doan Thi's father."

"She never spoke of her father. He was dead, she said."

"That was the public story."

"What do you mean—the *public* story?"

"To deceive everyone. All the top members of the Politburo go to great extremes to keep their backgrounds and origins shrouded in mystery. They took many different names. All from the need to deceive the French during the early days of the Resistance."

"Are you saying that Doan Thi's father is a member of the Politburo?"

"Not the Politburo. He is the head of the Mât Vu— the director of our secret police."

Her words drill into me like a round from a silenced gun. Yet at the instant of impact, soundlessly, the universe expands. Black holes are abruptly illuminated. Meteors light the darkest reaches of my personal cosmos.

No wonder Arty and all his agents in place could find no record of my son. The boy is not known as just another *con lai*, a half-breed, a dust child, but rather as the honored Vietnamese grandson of an influential and powerful communist official, one who deals in secrets, master of the game. And no wonder the vendetta has been so unremitting. Not only is the man seeking revenge upon the crass American who dared to conduct a public affair with his daughter, but he is making goddamned sure that same American never makes it back to Vietnam to try to claim the disputed child.

I feel a sudden bonding toward my enemy. Our blood is joined in a nine-year-old boy.

"Thanh Hoa, I thank you. What you've told me explains so much, so many things. Why did you think that this information would destroy me?"

"I haven't finished yet," she says. "But it is no longer necessary to continue. What I've told you is enough for you to find your son. I am willing now to help you, to take you to the place he lives, even to his school if you wish. But you must promise to take me out of this country which has turned against its own people and make certain I get to France or to America."

"Agreed," I say. "You'll come out with us. Now—tell me the rest of it."

"Why?"

Do I read pity in her eyes?

"Why should you keep it bottled up? Dump it, Thanh Hoa! It's all part of the cure—of your new life."

"Doan Thi betrayed you," she whispers. "She was never what you believed she was."

"We loved each other!" I hear myself saying defensively. "There was no one else for either of us!"

"I didn't say she betrayed you with another man. How unimportant! Her betrayal was much deeper."

We stare at each other, she still hesitating, I still demanding, no matter the cost.

"She was high in the ranks of the Liberation Front. She was your sworn enemy. All the time you knew her—and were with her—she was working for Hanoi in the South."

Gently I lower Thanh Hoa onto the pallet.

I find myself dream-walking again.

I am vaguely aware of Arun, of Nguyen, of their eyes, mirrors of my shock and rushing despair.

I move to the bamboo steps. I trip blindly over the body of the dead medic and fall out, sprawling into the mud at the foot of the ladder.

I lie in the rain, wanting never to move from this spot, wanting only to sink into the earth. I envy the camp commandant, already turning into excrement, his passage paid.

I bury my face in the mud and cry out silently to all my dead comrades. God forgive me, I ask them, did I ever, while loving this woman I will always love even though she was my enemy, it turns out—did I ever say anything to her, reveal anything she might have used against any one of you?

Can you hear me? I cry without sound into the earth. Can you answer me?

Can you *help* me?

CHAPTER

31

"Shall I carry her? Or do you wish to?"

Nguyen's voice. Compassionate, yet urgent.

I look up from the mud.

He is holding Thanh Hoa in his arms. She appears to have slipped back into unconsciousness, her head drifted down.

Arun is kneeling beside me, checking me out.

"With all that mud on your face," she says, "I think we can dispense with makeup until we get back to the village."

How long have I groveled here? How long has Nguyen allotted me to deal with Thanh Hoa's revelation that the only woman I have ever loved, the woman who has haunted every waking and sleeping moment of my life since I watched her leave me in Saigon ten years ago, was an enemy officer?

I discover that the rain has stopped and that the first wave of prisoners is advancing into the compound like protozoa, extending about us through the primal act of prolongation, surrounding us without apparent movement, rows of faces numbed by suffering, ranks of apathetic eyes scanning us blankly.

I know only that in the poultice of the mud I have wandered feverishly back into the past like a drunken man searching a vast parking mall for the car he's parked somewhere he can't remember. I have tried to rethink what memories of Doan Thi and our love affair I can still call up vividly, tried to realign them within the context of this new reality. But crucial connective tissue is wanting. Somewhere back there, past the edges of my remembering, are clues, tonalities, textures that are critical to summon up if I'm ever again to mold any coherence of vision, words and phrases and whole sentences whispered to this woman I adored while lying in darkness with her, one leg numb between her relaxing thighs still wet from our lovemaking, hearing the enchantment of her softening breath as the night passed.

But what did we *say* to each other? Did she ever *ask* me anything? Did I ever tell her where I was going? Ever talk about an upcoming mission? Talk about tactics or objectives? Not that I can remember.

On the contrary, I was usually tonguetied in her presence. She was magical. Her words were wands. When she spoke of alleyways, they became broad avenues. Hamlets she turned into gleaming cities. She transformed ugliness into beauty for me. She made the agony almost bearable. She was always teaching me, showing me, opening the country to my deeper perceptions.

Possibly she had decided to exempt me from the grim business of intelligence-gathering, to treat me as her toy, and in the process, I must believe, she became as enflamed as I by our mutual passion. She had dared to put a toe into forbidden water and had slipped in, over her head, both of us swept away in the same flood tide, both of us daring to claim a private life for ourselves during a time when history was being written in body counts and when only a collective life was permitted. We were all engulfed within the pain of Indochina, Americans and Vietnamese alike, so that any individual pain seemed insignificant and therefore acceptable when measured against the mass pain. Doan Thi and I were thrown up on the same tidal wave and we made love along its impossible crest before it broke and crushed us under its debris.

So then, where is the betrayal? How could she have possibly told me except in the ways she did? When we made love among the areca groves in a stilt house on the bank of the Perfume River in Hué and she asked me "Is happiness such a crime?" I thought she was speaking in the broad sense of stolen moments within a war. But she meant something other than that, I see now. Something much more profound. She was speaking out of her own frame of reference as a Northerner, perceiving herself as rational, efficient, hot-tempered, aggressive, and warlike. I should have grasped it even then, for Vietnam is a badly divided society and has been so over several millennia, with distinct regionalism in North, Center, and South, and Doan Thi somehow never blended in my mind with the South Vietnamese I met.

She once told me that living is the unconscious discovery of joy within the fabric of endurance and that endurance means letting it all count, all experience, permitting oneself no aversion to the worst of it nor celebration of the best of it, taking it as it comes,—cadaverous moons, rude red mornings, harsh whisperings in the reefs, the howling in the night, all of it, the stuttering nonsense and the awesome silences—finding new existence in all of it, day by day—existence, my love, not meaning, she whispered to me, never looking for the meaning, for there is none. There is only the existence, one more morning, if it is granted to you.

Not a South Vietnamese philosophy, by any means. Yet neither is it Marxist-Leninist.

Later, I tell myself. Deal with this later. Too many unnumbered doors into the past to try to open all of them right now.

I retreat into the simplest of sanctuaries, into the immediate reality.

I take Thanh Hoa from Nguyen, settle her into my arms.

"On the far side of the compound," I tell Nguyen, "there are two trucks. Collect all the weapons and ammo and load them into one truck. Let Le Danh take responsibility for disposing of it once he's delivered the ordnance to wherever he chooses to hide it. Our team will take the second truck. What are our casualties?"

"Two dead, three wounded."

He sees my pained reaction.

"How the hell did that happen?"

"None from our team," he adds. "These all happened when the left flank took the barracks. I ordered Le Danh to rocket the barracks and to stay under cover until he was sure every man inside had been burned or shot trying to come out, but his men insisted on taking it head on. But how else are they going to learn?"

"Bring the dead and wounded with us. Along with two dead from the camp personnel. Intact as possible, please."

Nguyen's eyes widen.

"They will serve us," I say. "You'll see."

Nguyen hurries off. Suddenly from nowhere, as though filling the vacuum of his leaving, two of our team appear, Le and Van, stepping in on either flank to watch over Arun and me.

We cross the camp toward the motor pool I had spotted from the nearby hill before we attacked.

A wall of prisoners converges raggedly before us.

An old man shuffles free of the group and kneels before me, bowing his head gratefully. One by one the others fall to their knees. They, too, lower their heads.

"You are free," I say to them in Vietnamese, "free to leave this camp. I must warn you it is a matter of hours only before the authorities come here to find out why their telephone line has been cut and why the commandant's radio does not answer. Before then, each of you should try to get as far away as you can. I am sorry we cannot take you with us. But we need the trucks to bear our wounded and to carry away the weapons we have won here this morning so we can fight again in other places. Long live the Resistance!"

I have no idea why I have added that bardic warcry except that like these pitiful victims I, too, feel trapped in the theater of the absurd and sense the need of a ringing exit line.

Our team assembled and augmented by ten of Le Danh's men, our casualties stabilized and loaded into the back of the truck next to the dead, Van at the wheel, Nguyen and Vo up front with him in the cab, I in back with Arun and the half-conscious Thanh Hoa, we point south down a flooded road. The Song Ca River rushes noisily along our left. The steep, inhospitable rise of the Annam Cordillera dominates our right. We have lined the back of the truck with sandbags to serve as a breastworks in the event we meet NVA regulars or militia before we abandon the camp truck some seventy clicks south, only two hours' uphill hump into the rain forest and Le Danh's friendly village.

We cross overflowing tributaries of the Song Ca River as we roll south, flinging mud from the tires and thumping across pontoon bridges. I remember during the war seeing these same bridges, but detached from one bank during daylight hours so the whole structure drifted downstream and lay parallel to the bank under mangrove branches to make the bridges less visible to our air observers.

We pass sodden hamlets, seemingly dissolving in the rain, which has swept in with newfound ferocity. Some of these villages perch precariously on the eroding levees; others stand daringly on their stilts along the river front, muddy crests of water swirling around their foundations.

After two hours we turn onto a secondary road, little more than twin ruts, and begin to grind upland into the waiting forest.

When we left camp, I wrapped Thanh Hoa in a blanket and covered her completely with my poncho, but as we lurch along and I find myself staring down at her immobile body, her covered face, causing her to resemble the dead we carry, I can no longer endure that perception of her. So I tuck the poncho around her neck and expose her face to the rain. Even its incessant drumming on her cheeks and forehead does not awaken her. She sleeps next to me with a splattered face, her hair dribbling off in wild rivulets.

I study her magnificently rounded forehead and watch the streams of rain roll off it. I watch the flicker of rain on her high cheekbones. I see it fill the sockets of her wide closed eyes, glisten on her full lips with their tiny, upturned creases on either side, proof that she can smile, given reason, and I recall that first day in Bali when she found me at COIN-OPS headquarters and I met her at the gate, saw her step toward me as I marveled at her grace, her delicate beauty, her fine-drawn waist loosely cinched by a belt of seashells jangling as she approached me. And I remember her teasing me sexually as I drove her into the mountains. "Are you afraid you might begin to feel toward me something of what you once felt for Doan Thi?" "*Still* feel!" I'd reminded her. "Do I remind you of her? Even a little?" Something had made me stop the car. The afternoon was fragrant with *tjempaka* blossoms. She didn't move. She appeared to be waiting, eyes widening, lips parting slightly, and on her face suddenly I saw Doan Thi's face, lit by that ancient, enigmatic Asian sexuality flashing for a trillionth of a second in acknowledgment and acceptance of a white lover. I placed my lips lightly against hers. I inhaled her breath. Then I heard what might be a muffled sob as she cupped both her hands over the back of my head and pulled my lips abrasively against hers. With an abruptness that I later found out was totally premeditated, she released me and moved her lips a measured inch from mine. "One way to deal with fear," she whispered, "is to confront it. You've confronted it. Are you still afraid of me?"

Am I?

I wasn't then. In Bali. Where she set me up.

Question: How about now, in Vietnam, on her home turf?

I feel Arun's hand on my arm. I glance over. Arun leans in close to my ear.

"When I was a kid," she says, "my mother used to sing a song to my baby sister. Obviously, I took it as *my* song. I remember it went like this: 'A woman is like a drop of rain. No one know where it will fall—into a palace, or the mud of the ricefields.'"

"There *is* a punchline, isn't there?" I ask her.

As I expected, Arun has tuned in on my fascination with Thanh Hoa.

"This girl," she whispers, "does not belong in the ricefields. Do you agree?"

"I agree."

"Has it occurred to you your son will need a mother?"

"I was thinking of offering *you* that spot." I grin.

"Think you," Arun replies softly, "even though you don't mean it."

"Don't sell either of us short," I say. "You're so fucking beautiful, any man would kill to have you. And I'm a pretty flaky guy, okay?"

"Please don't joke about that," Arun says, suddenly more serious than I've known her to be. "Not about our friendship. I would never hurt you, John. Or cause you to have to reject me. I'd die first."

"Okay. Bad joke. Sorry."

She looks at me from under her long black lashes.

"But maybe next year—when I'm *fully* qualified—I'll find you, wherever you may be, and I'll apply for the job. That's if Thanh Hoa doesn't work out."

"*Next year!*" I repeat, savoring the words, holding them

up before us like a fine wine caught in Baccarat. "Those are two good words, Arun—like *hope* and *tomorrow* and *dreams*. You ever wonder who thought up all the good words—and who thought up all the downers? Same guy, you think?"

"Yes, John. I *know!* There's no happy without a sad, is there?"

"I'm still working on that," I say.

Vo slides the truck to a stop.

Nguyen is suddenly outside and motioning the fighters to scramble out.

"Far as we can drive," he tells me, "without giving the enemy a sense of which way we've gone from here."

"Okay."

I climb out. Pham lifts Thanh Hoa down and into my arms. She moans slightly, but doesn't awaken.

We unload the wounded and our two dead.

The truck is now abandoned except for the two enemy dead we've brought along, both slumped in the flatbed.

"Move them into the cab," I instruct Nguyen. "One behind the wheel. Then fire up the truck. Let's leave the impression they were ambushed. It might add to the confusion when the security people try to sort all this out. Or it might not. But what the hell?"

Nguyen orders our grenadier to do the honors.

Van, making sure the rest of us are well into the clear, takes his position one hundred meters off and lays a single HE round into the gas tank of the truck. The shock wave of the explosion and its fireball fans over us. For a moment we watch the truck consumed by flames, taking the two enemy dead on their Viking voyage, then the insistent rain battles with the fire. Smoke begins to rise from the hissing contention of the two elements.

We place Thanh Hoa and our casualties, both dead and wounded, on bamboo litters. Taking turns at the poles, we cross the countryside, making a best effort to obscure our trail. With each step we climb higher toward the stately sack trees towering into the roiling sky.

Two hours and ten minutes later we approach Le Danh's village.

He has arrived just ahead of us and has already scattered his men to their distant hamlets, each unit bearing away its share of captured weaponry.

We deliver his dead for burial, his wounded for care, and let him lead our team two kilometers deeper into the mountains, through a rain forest of *cho chi* trees carpeted with grass.

We follow him into a labyrinth of rock ridges lining the face of a cliff. He pulls aside undergrowth and exposes the entrance to a deep cave.

Inside we are amazed by the spaciousness of the cavern. His men have built campfires which are drawing nicely, their smoke disappearing into natural air vents high in the ceiling of the cave. To one side of the campfires sleeping mats are laid out. To another side is a wide, low table, with mats around it. Deeper back into the cave I can see a row of brown water jugs.

Two village women are preparing what appears to be a feast for us, hovering anxiously over the rice. I watch them with fond amusement, realizing that in all the world nothing is more important to these two than their domestic proficiency, measured in this part of the world by the ability to prepare rice properly and in precise quantities. Should a young wife spoil the rice by overcooking or burning, it is regarded as a bad omen by her family. If she has not prepared enough rice, she is said to be miserly. If too much is left over, she is scolded as a spendthrift. These two chosen by Le Danh to pay honor to us and to celebrate our joint victory must certainly be the two best cooks in the hamlet, otherwise Le Danh would not have trusted them to cook our rice.

Le Danh produces with considerable flourish a bottle of treasured *lua moi*, a variety of Asian vodka more corrosive than the fiery Chinese *mao t'ai*. He pours each of us a finger of the drink, all but Arun, of course. As we raise our glasses, I catch her eye. But she has become so complete a woman that not the slightest hint escapes from her that she resents being omitted from this male ritual toast.

"To Captain John Locke," Le Danh proposes. "A leader with a cool heart."

"Hear, hear!" Nguyen adds, giving me one of his rare smiles.

We drink, if one can ascribe so painful an experience to the simple act of swallowing. I can feel the liquid plunging through me like mercury dropping in a barometer.

There is more liquor with dinner, this rice alcohol flavored with lotus flowers. The rice served is cooked to perfection, glutinous, regarded as a food of special purity and even served as an offering on the altar of the ancestors. The soup is a masterpiece of campfire cooking, combining vegetables and some unidentifiable portions of meat. The fish sauce is superb. The boiled pastry is filled with chopped and seasoned meat wrapped in banana leaves.

We are almost finished when I discover than Thanh Hoa has revived. Arun sits next to her, feeding her soup, the two of them looking like copper goddesses in the flickering firelight.

"When will you leave?" Le Danh asks.

"The moment Thanh Hoa has regained some of her strength," I tell him. "Another day. Two at the most."

"When will we have the transport?" Nguyen asks Le Danh.

"Our unit in Do Luong has promised it by tomorrow."

"Possibly then we can leave tomorrow?" Nguyen suggests to me. "The girl can recuperate while we are driving south. It is a journey of six hundred miles."

"South?"

Thanh Hoa's voice cuts into our meeting without apology or deference.

I look over to where Arun is still trying to feed her.

"You will not find your son in the South, Captain," she says.

"I have one more thing to do before we go to Hanoi," I tell her. "You will have to come with us."

"*What* thing!" she demands.

"Classified information." I smile. "Anyway, you'll find out once we get there."

I ask Tran, our radioman, to break out the TRANSAT box he's lugged all the way from Nakhon Phanom and to follow me outside with it.

Rain still whips down. We work our way up the dribbling faces of druid stones until we come out onto an escarpment with nothing above us but the sooty afternoon sky.

I open the collapsible dish antenna attached to the tripod and plug the cord from the tripod into the TRANSAT box.

Somewhere up there above the clouds a satellite waits in clear space.

Let's see now. No reason to be too cute, because nobody's going to be intercepting a millisecond infrared pulse, but when it's relayed to him in translation Arty will appreciate a slight obfuscation, I'm sure.

So how about "SACRED SWORD FIRST INCISION MADE. PLAN SLICE CHICKEN NEXT NINETY-SIX HOURS. TELL SINGAPORE ADVANCE ON SITE SCHEDULE BY TEN DAYS. LURK NOW ESTIMATED FOR FIVE OCTOBER."

The words vanish instantaneously.

I know that by the time Tran and I have lowered ourselves gingerly back down the slippery rock face, some young American radioman at Torii Station on Okinawa, sitting in a clean, dry shirt, nobody especially seeking his lifeblood, will have picked up the satellite bounce and have relayed it back to Thailand, and that tonight Arty will be ordering a KH–11 to cover Can Ranh Bay with its twenty-foot focal length telescope and its Perkin-Elmer mirrors and its "real-time" capability to transmit radar images onto the Company's TV screens.

If I am to die at Cam Ranh Bay before I can even reach my son, it may as well be recorded for whatever posterity deals with KH–11 transmissions.

There is some comfort in knowing that an X will mark the spot.

Better an X than no X.

CHAPTER

32

It passes midnight, but I cannot sleep. I cannot sleep in a cave, apparently, not a matter of claustrophobia, but simply that as a blue-water sailor I am accustomed to a more open theater of the night, to stars performing above me, to the dance of wind on my face, to the ballet of the sea around me. Only with all that busyness am I free to surrender myself to sleep.

The two campfires have burned down to ember beds. In their twin glowing I can make out the huddled forms of Arun and Thanh Hoa to one side, then the discreet space separating the men from the women, with Nguyen and the others spread out as though on a checkerboard, not in a row, for I never allowed my teams to sleep in tidy rows during the war, accessible to simple raking gunfire. Vo lurks in deep shadow near the mouth of the cave, his AK–47 at the ready, and I recall that Nguyen has assigned him the midnight-to-oh-four-hundred watch.

I rise from my mat and cross to Thanh Hoa and Arun with the medical kit.

Thanh Hoa, too, is awake, staring up at me.

I kneel beside her, examine the soles of her feet. The swelling has diminished. I apply more corticosteriod lotion.

"I begin to understand," she says after a long moment while her mind seems to be racing, "why Doan Thi wrote love poems to you."

I savor this for a minute or two.

"Nicest thing you've ever said to me, Thanh Hoa. Thank you."

"I am confused about so many things," she whispers. "Before, everything was so clear—so simple. Why is my revolutionary morality so weak that it failed me when I needed it the most?"

"Because you let yourself say 'A' to what you've been taught. Once you say 'A,' soon enough you'll find yourself saying 'B.' Incidentally, that's a direct quote from something Trotsky once said to dissident members of his Leninist sect. And when you've taken that step, Thanh Hoa, you've already become a counterrevolutionary. Unless you swallow the Party line, hook and sinker, and never question it, never deviate for one instant, unless you give yourself to it body and soul, ready and willing to die for it, the system itself will ultimately destroy your faith in it. Because no totalitarian regime can exist without totalism—and totalism is antihumanistic. Nobody can live through a whole lifetime of suppression without rebelling—in his heart, silently, if no other way."

"How else could we have driven you out of our country—unless we put the historical interests of the proletariat above our individual desires? How else can we ever achieve a perfected humanity?"

"There is no such animal, Thanh Hoa. Neither under your system nor under ours. But if I'm sure of anything, I'm sure that given an opportunity in an open society, *some* people are going to strive for perfection on their own—stumbling and making mistakes along the way, but a few of them coming close. But under this system, as you can now see, there is only the ruling elite and its military forces—then a mass of intimidated and sullen people."

She studies me thoughtfully.

"I wonder how I would have felt if I'd succeeded in killing you in Bali?" she asks.

"Good. You'd have felt good. You'd have come back home and they'd have pinned a medal on you. None of this would have happened—not the camp, not my coming for you, not your doubts about Marxist-Leninist ideology. Life would still be simple for you."

"I couldn't do it now," she says softly. "Now that I've come to know you better. You are a very complex person, John Locke. Not like other Americans."

"You don't know us, Thanh Hoa. Any more than we know you. That was the problem, wasn't it?"

"Do you trust me now? Just a little more than before?"

"No," I say. "I can't afford to. At any moment you might replay that day outside Quang Tri when I had to kill your sister. You might grab a weapon from one of us and lay the full clip into me. You might even be sorry afterward. That much is possible. But I'd be waxed for good. Not that I'd especially mind, Thanh Hoa, if I didn't have a son. But I do. So if I find at any time, on the way to getting him, that you are lying or leading us into an ambush, I'll kill you without a second's delay. Don't make me do that. Please!"

I feel her hand in mine.

I am comforted, though not persuaded.

"Good night, Thanh Hoa."

I kiss her lightly on her forehead. It is cool, not feverish. Suddenly her neck arches back, her lips search for mine. She finds them and opens to me, one hand carrying mine forcefully to a small, firm breast, rising to my clasp. Her whole gaunt body seems to levitate from the floor of the cave, seeking mine.

Then she falls back, exhausted, but her eyes appear to burn through the dark like the eyes of a panther on the branch just above you.

"Why?" I whisper.

"It is my *tü vi*," she whispers back.

I have not heard the phrase for years—"Destiny chart."

"If I was not born to kill you, then my horoscope tells me I must love you," she says.

"Good night," I say.

I leave her.

I join Vo at the entrance to the cave.

His fine, delicate, almost feminine profile is backlit by fragments of moonlight breaking in through the outside underbrush. He puts me in mind of a North Vietnamese propaganda film I'd seen when I was taking my training for the Studies and Observation Group—a black-and-white film shot in Hanoi by a Cuban photographer. One sequence has remained in my mind all these years—a shot of a regiment of young NVA soldiers marching out of the city on their way to the South. As they march out, they all turn, as if on cue, halfway, from their waists, smiling back at the camera over their shoulders, like a column of magnificent elk with dark, luscent eyes, teardrop shaped, the cameraman's light shining from hundreds of innocent, youthful faces. And as I sat there alone in the darkness of the screening room looking at my enemy, I became so depressed I had to stop the film. Jesus Christ, how could I go out and shoot kids like that? I had to remind myself that I'd been looking at a propaganda film designed to arouse exactly the emotion I'd felt. I had to remind myself that they were no younger than I,—smaller, yes, lighter in weight, yes, but those were AK–47s they were carrying and I was their target, I and thousands of other American nineteen-year-olds. And nobody had lovingly taken movies of us leaving Omaha or Indianapolis or San Francisco, looking back and smiling good-bye for the cameras as our families cheered us on.

I stay with Vo, neither of us speaking, until Le relieves him at oh-four-hundred, then I stay with Le until the moonlight has been replaced by the sunrise.

I sleep through most of the new day. Nguyen awakens me by mid-afternoon.

"We're ready," he says. "They've brought our transport here."

"Wasn't that risky?"

"Apparently they didn't think so. All the local forces are tied up at Dàm Dùn, trying to figure out what kind of unit it was who wiped out the guards and released all the prisoners. The district militia is out looking for those who escaped. It is an ideal time to leave."

I see that Arun is tending to Thanh Hoa, redressing her abraded ankles.

"Are you able to travel?" I ask Thanh Hoa.

"I can't walk yet," she says. "But I feel much stronger."

I go out with Nguyen.

Le Danh has concealed the military ambulance among underbrush outside the village.

This is the vehicle of choice we had planned for back in Bangkok. Thanks to the efforts of the Resistance, here it waits, fully materialized, no longer a dream on paper, but a solid, Soviet-built no-nonsense double-wheeler, painted in battle camouflage, yet showing the international red cross symbol, with stretcher-space inside for six wounded and jump seats and equipment for two medics.

"We have all the necessary papers," Nguyen tells me, "and all the proper uniforms."

"Okay," I say. "We'll try to make it all the way to Cam Lam before we abandon it. With luck we should be able to reach Cam Lam by—when—forty-eight hours? Are the roads that good?"

"Not until we reach Highway One. There the delays will come at the bridges and at the checkpoints. I'm estimating seventy-two hours."

"That puts us in on September twenty-second. We'll need a day's rest-and-rekky time before we take our shot at the carrier. So let's set it for September twenty-third. That give you time to get your southern KC units on site by then?"

"They already wait for us, Captain."

"Then we go," I say.

Within the hour, Arun having done her most masterful touch-up yet on my Asian persona, the new nose firmly in place, we take our positions in the ambulance as we had planned, Thanh Hoa and Arun in back, both in army nurses' uniforms, I in my major's combat clothes, my right leg bandaged, and Vo, Pham, Le, and Tran, each in soldier's uniform, each bandaged as though badly wounded.

Van and Nguyen are assigned to the cab, Van to drive, Nguyen to ramrod us through the checkpoints. Nguyen dresses himself in the full uniform of an NVA senior captain, with his shoulder boards blazing with the four silver stars of his rank, his cap insignia a star surmounting a gearwheel segment, the background red, the disc bordered by rice stalks. He looks formidable, especially with his campaign ribbons and his medals, the Victory Decoration for outstanding military service during the war, the Dien Bien Phu Medal for outstanding service after the war, together with the Ho Chi Minh Medal and the Combat Medal.

"I always thought the Gold Star Medal was Hanoi's highest award for combat valor," I comment. "Why didn't you give yourself that one while you were at it? God knows you deserve it for the way you fought against them!"

"The Gold Star Medal is among *your* awards, Major,"

he says with a perfectly straight face. "Along with the Illustrious Soldier Decoration. Who will dare to stop such a badly wounded hero on his way to treatment at Cam Ranh Bay?"

I embrace Le Danh.

"*Chúc may mán!*" he says, wishing us good fortune.

"*Chào anh,*" I say, and climb into the back of the ambulance, where the others already wait.

Nguyen closes the panels. I slide into my place in the bottom litter on the right side of the ambulance. A narrow window slit permits me an elongated view of the outside world.

The village falls beyond sight. I see only a blur of trees as we bounce down the mountain trail, *vu huong* trees used in the making of furniture, wild fig trees, and jackfruit with orchids wound in pastel tentacles around the lower branches.

I turn to see Thanh Hoa watching me from the jump seat next to my tier.

"Already," she says, "I begin to forget what you look like as an American. You are very clever to disguise yourself so."

"Arun gets all the credit," I say. "She should be working in Hollywood."

"And this is a most intelligent strategy, this ambulance, all of you pretending to be wounded. It is a sure way to disguise your height."

"As long as some smartass doesn't come in here with a tape measure," I say. "Tell me about my son."

"I don't know much really," she says.

"You know more than I do. I'll settle for anything. Like—how tall is he?"

"To my shoulder," she says.

"Eyes, hair?"

"Blue eyes. Like yours. Already wise. And brown hair. And he has a bearing—the way he walks and stands. He could be an emperor's son."

"What about his education?"

"I understand that he's a year ahead of the others, in fifth grade, although he's still only nine. This will guarantee that he will enter Level Two."

"You mean there's any doubt of it?"

"You joke, of course."

"No. Who stops at the fifth grade?"

"Attrition rates between levels are very high. Only fifteen percent of Level One students enter Level Two and only ten percent of those attending Level Two ever graduate to Level Three. Only graduates of Level Three schools may enter academic institutions of higher learning. Mostly only the children of Party members."

"With a grandfather who runs the secret police, he shouldn't have any problem there, should he?" I find myself saying with self-punitive cynicism.

"All subjects, including those in the natural sciences, must be presented in an ideological context," she replies. "Otherwise Party education policies would not be properly implemented. In my instance, my Level Two school was awarded the title of 'pilot school' for carrying out Party policies in an exemplary manner while still contributing to the local economy. We maintained fishponds and small ricefields for our biology students. Even though I was a liberal arts student, I took part in these activities. I attended the University of Hanoi and became one of the young teaching cadres immediately following graduation. Of course, my army service was important in getting me into the university. I'm sure your son will advance much faster than I did because of who he is. He is one of a select group of children being especially trained for the Secretariat."

"It seems a pity to deny him so much opportunity," I say. "With his connections, he could even end up some day on the Politburo."

"Indeed he might," she agrees.

"Thanh Hoa!" I cry. "Are you listening to this nonsense—to what we're saying?"

She catches herself, covers her mouth.

"I'm taking him the fuck out of all that in less than a week. You understand good basic American? I said the *fuck* out of all that! Clear?"

Suddenly she is smiling at me.

"You are a very complex man, John Locke. I said it before. I say it again. Very complex."

I look away from her, take a bearing on the outside world through the window slit.

I see cattle grazing in fields still littered with scrap metal, mines, and unexploded ordnance, for we are already below the old DMZ, I discover, near Gio Linh, not too far from the area where fifteen years ago I had first met Thanh Hoa as that haunted child in a doomed hamlet, huddled there, watching us leave, mute, uncomplaining, her child's mind already plotting vengeance.

The ghosts of war linger everywhere.

This sector and the nearby town of Quang Tri were obliterated by our 52s when the NVA overran it in 1972, our bombers flying in cells of three, too high to be seen from the ground, their passing proclaimed only by the shuddering triple thunder roll of their bombloads as each flying cell saturated a target box two miles long and half a mile wide, the shock wave of the carpet bombing slamming out in a circle twenty-five miles wide.

We slow our speed.

Through the viewing slit I see an army of peasants in conical hats working in the rain, digging out silted irrigation ditches by hand and forming a mile-long human chain to transport rocks being used in repairing the road.

Then abruptly we come to a stop.

I hear Nguyen getting out, slamming the cab door, his voice raised imperiously.

From this position I can scarcely see him and the young lieutenant with whom he is arguing. But I do see half a dozen armed men of the Public Security Force and beyond them a checkpoint with other soldiers on duty.

I motion to our team. Vo, Thom, Le, and Tran now stretch out on their litters. They pretend quiet suffering, as though they had taken an acting course in the anatomy of pain. Possibly it comes naturally to them. I don't know. But they do look convincing, lying there, their AK–47s tucked under them. I have the Browning in hand, slipped under my right thigh. Thanh Hoa and Arun cover us with blankets.

Nguyen is visible now, directly outside my viewing port. He is showing a passenger manifest to the lieutenant.

"But why are they being taken all the way to Cam Ranh Bay?" the young officer insists. "Why not to the hospital at Hue—only minutes from here, not hours to the south?"

"They have already been stabilized," Nguyen explains. "But they require special surgery for their wounds. Only at the base hospital at Cam Ranh Bay can they get the care their bravery merits."

"This manifest indicates the major has earned the Gold Star Medal," I hear the young officer say.

"He has killed more Khmer Rouge bandits than any officer in Kampuchea," Nguyen brags.

"I have never met a man who has won so high a combat award," the lieutenant says.

"I am sure the major would like to meet you. He is very weak from his wounds, but I know him well enough to know that he would welcome you."

With too much flamboyance for my taste, even under the circumstances, Nguyen heads toward the back of the ambulance. A second later the panels swing open.

"Major," Nguyen calls softly, "forgive me, sir, but there is a young officer here who would like to greet you."

Stoically, I pull myself up on one elbow, in the process deliberately tugging the blanket up to expose my bandaged and bloodied leg. Clamping down on my jaw as though suppressing the pain, I grunt in Vietnamese, "Let him come."

But the young man is so stricken by the sight of five of us lying wounded inside, men fresh from the combat he has been spared, that he stays outside, drawing himself to stiff attention and saluting me.

"Forgive this intrusion, sir. I wish you a speedy recovery. You and the others."

"Thank you, Lieutenant," I say.

Nguyen closes the panels.

I ease my finger off the trigger of the Browning.

A moment later I feel the movement of our ambulance and we roll through the checkpoint, heading south into the oncoming night.

We pass the Imperial City of Hue in darkness.

From Highway One I cannot see it, but I know that nearby Nam Giao Hill still rises. Doan Thi had taken me there where emperors once watched the spectacles staged in Ho Quyen arena, with tigers pitted against elephants in fights to the death.

We pass through fields from which come the most highly prized rice in Vietnam, an cuu. Doan Thi always carried a cloth tube of this rice with her wherever she traveled. It returns to me now what it was we talked about the morning after our first night together. Not about the war, not about my long-range patrols, not even about her poetry and her fame as Asia's foremost poetess of this century. We talked about food, I remember. She told me that from the countryside around Hue, in the center of Vietnam, the seat of the emperors, came the finest fruits, thin-skinned tangerines from Huong Càn, sweet oranges from My Loi, longanes from Phung Tien, grapefruit from Nouyêt Bièu, and lotus seeds from Tinh Tam Lake.

We stop for the night south of Danang along the southern bank of the Thu Bon River.

Pham rings our encampment with mines connected by trip wires as I scrutinize the area around us with the Tiger Eye.

We are alone here except for a family living two kilometers downriver aboard the burned-out bow section of a sunken American LCM Monitor patrol boat. In the flickering light of a fire they're nursing in the forward gun turret, a young girl assists her mother with the cooking. I can still read the boat's white bow numbers—M, 11, a missing number, a dash, then what could be another 1—abraded and muddied, yet still enduring more than a decade after the boat met its end.

Another ghost. The living dead.

Once more I begin to separate from myself, to peel away. Somewhere out there in the night the young man I used to be still ravages the countryside. I had thought that by returning to Vietnam I might be able to call him in, tell him it was finished, that he could come in now, become a part of me, and if he could do that we might even manage to blend, like some glorious hermaphrodite, and produce a shining, singular better us—hopefully, even an I, not an us. But I cannot see him with the Tiger Eye. He is not wreckage on a landscape. He is as invisible as yesterday, as vanished, and as irretrievable.

Regret and remorse and hopelessness engulf me. I sit apart from the group, my poncho over my head, the rain unremitting, and give myself totally to despair, letting it course through me like a fever, until finally I begin to consider how I must look to the others, a portrait in black by Goya, an incantation of the night.

I slip the poncho from my head and let the rain purge me. I see Thanh Hoa bending through the wind, crawling on her knees across the muddy riverbank until she arrives at my side.

"What has happened?" she asks. "The others are concerned, but they hesitate to ask."

"You could never have killed me, Thanh Hoa," I tell her. "No fucking way! I was already dead when you looked for me in Bali."

"What are you saying?"

"I just realized that somebody I came for is gone forever. Like Doan Thi. I can't get him back any more than I can get her back. Why have I been so foolish all these years to think that I could? But you see the problem's much deeper than that. I'm still trapped back in the seventies. I kept hoping that when I returned to Vietnam I'd break out at last, be able to bury it all. But I can't seem to. It only gets worse wherever I look. It's all coming back, Thanh Hoa, stronger than ever!"

"Then don't go to Hanoi! Your son belongs to the future, not to the past! Do you want him for himself, or just to remind you of his mother?"

I can't answer her.

She crawls away from me. I want to reach out and stop her, try to make her understand.

But I don't.

And I can't.

Make her understand.

Because *I* don't—and can't.

CHAPTER

33

Today's bright and rainless sky does nothing to alleviate my sense of growing foreboding the deeper we roll south.

Crossing the Central Highlands I lie wordlessly in my litter and stare out bleakly at the lunar landscape, still pitted with bomb craters. Twenty-five million craters, I remember reading in one Air Force assessment, a billion cubic meters of earth displaced.

We pass living trees bordering the highway. Particles of shrapnel are still embedded in their bark. We drive for endless minutes through forests scorched by napalm, the trees putting me in mind of matchbooks that have flared up and remain only as bent ash.

I look out at the same countryside where a little more than ten years earlier Hanoi's armies had rolled up the last of the ARVN defenders. Hanoi drove south behind tanks and their unequaled Soviet 130mm artillery, which outranged the best we had by six miles and dominated the battlefields.

The towns we drive through look strangely demure. No wonder. Bars that once catered to troops on R and R have been converted into sedate coffeeshops. The whores are no longer to be seen. They have fled the country or else gone to cover, facelessly, in Ho Chi Minh City, their miniskirts burned, their high heels kicked off for good.

I feel I am a stranger in a familiar place, an adult come back to the hometown of his childhood. The land is unchanged, still the wasteland we created with our bombs and our herbicides and our napalm and our bulldozers and our cannon. But the people look different, even in their body language, silent and withdrawn, imprisoned within themselves.

At the intersection of Highways One and Twenty-one we are once more stopped at a military checkpoint, this one bristling with gun positions and two parked tanks. The OD meticulously checks each one of our police permits, turning them over and over, holding them up to the late-afternoon sun. He takes his time reading through our orders of transfer. He is the perfect young bureaucrat, the cutting edge of every revolution, one of the street people elevated to power and born to abuse it. Eventually he clears us through, but his harsh, suspicious face clings to my mind as the new countenance of Vietnam.

Fifty miles north of our objective we pass at sunset through Nha Trang. Here my sense of detrition almost overwhelms me, for through the window slit I catch sight of the dirty faces of three Amerasian children among a crowd of street urchins staring impassively at our speeding ambulance. The Amerasian children turn back to what they'd been doing before our sudden arrival interrupted them—back to collecting garbage from the gutter. I see one of them biting into a clotted handful of refuse and I turn away on my cot, my stomach knotting.

Who was it, I wonder, who gave them the name *bui doi*—the dust children?

For they, more than the bomb craters and the steel-studded trees, are the lasting residue of war, the dust that settles after the combat.

By nightfall we arrive outside Cam Lam on the western edge of Cam Ranh Bay.

Thanh Hoa has not spoken a word to me, nor even looked my way, since she blistered me last night, nor have I spoken to her. She is now playing big sister to Arun, who is more amused by the game than Thanh Hoa will ever know. I do not intend to give Thanh Hoa the satisfaction of admitting she was right to say what she said about me and my attitude toward my son. Yes, indeed, I had better shape up. No doubt of it. But the girl already has too much self-assurance for someone who was almost dog meat only a few days ago, and if I ever do decide that I can trust her, if I ever do follow up on the clear signals she's been giving me about her acceptance of me as a lover, about her replacement of Doan Thi in my affections, I'm goddamned if I'll go into the relationship giving her the kind of edge she seems to expect.

We park the ambulance between two sand dunes.

I send Le up to the top of the southern dune with the RPK machine-gun and Vo to the top of the northern dune with his night scope and sniper rifle. Pham lays out a perimeter of mines behind us while Nguyen and I snake across the sand to the shoreline.

I put the Tiger Eye on the whole lash-up, sweeping it all in, this place I remember so well, from the lights of the town of Cam Ranh to each and every installation at the military base, the hospital at the far north of the peninsula, the air base with a ten-thousand-foot cement runway now bristling with Soviet Tu–16 Badgers and MiG–23 Flogger fighters, the ready ammo storage, the massive POL steel tanks, the laundry, the various barracks, the milk-reconstituting plant built by Meadowgold Dairies, the land-based generators, the Marine maintenance shops and Navy Com Center, the barge facilities, the long piers reaching westward toward us.

Our forces began to build up this facility back in 1965, when elements of the 35th Army Engineer Construction Group were assigned to work with two private construction companies, Raymond International, and Morrison and Knudson, using the physical labor of thousands of South Vietnamese war widows called "the little tiger ladies."

Some two billion dollars later the base housed twenty thousand officers and enlisted men and spread over an area fifteen miles long and five miles wide, ringed by high hills and blanketed with hundreds of sand dunes.

Now the Soviets occupy it, without so much as a letter of thanks, and Nguyen tells me there are reports of the Soviets opening fire on Vietnamese fishing boats that have ventured too close to the base.

I can see that since I was last at Cam Ranh Bay the Russians have built additional hangars, oil depots, and storage bins for air-to-ground missiles. It also appears they have upgraded their local ground stations for satellite communication.

Now finally I train the Tiger Eye on what we've come for—the third of the Kiev-class aircraft carriers, what the

Soviets refer to as *takticheskoye avianosny kreyser*—tactical aircraft-carrying cruiser.

She lies alongside pier Number One, her stern to the west, directly toward us, the *Novorossiysk*, I read, with her six-hundred-foot flight deck which can accommodate both Hormone and Helix choppers and Forger V/STOL attack aircraft. Including her flight deck and sponsons, she is more than one hundred and fifty feet in beam, almost nine hundred feet long from bow to stern, home to twelve hundred officers and seamen and to her air groups.

I study her missiles—four twin SS-N-12 SAMs, two twin SA-N-3, and two twin SA-N-4 missiles. I mark off four twin 76mm guns and eight Gatling 30mm mounts, along with one twin SUW-N-1 and two twelve-barreled RBU launchers forward. I count ten torpedo tubes.

Four Helix helicopters sit on her angled flight deck. Two Yak Forgers are parked on her afterdeck.

"Insane," I mutter, and hand the Tiger Eye to the eager Nguyen. "Just pure fucking insanity!"

"That's exactly what makes it possible," he says, concentrating on the carrier with the Tiger Eye.

"This is going to have to be split-second timing or nobody's coming home. I want you to study that main radar array. We have to take that out. You see that big one on the right? That's their air surveillance radar. We don't have to worry about it. It's that smaller Top Steer 3-D tracking radar that's got to go first. Now, study the after part of the island superstructure. You see the twin gun mounting just aft?"

"I do."

"Okay, now moving forward along the superstructure you'll see the SAM launcher. Got that?"

"Yes."

"Aft and to port, just above the launcher, you see the Owl Screech gunfire-control radar?"

"Mmm."

"That sucker has to be taken out at the same time the tracking radar goes. How do you like it so far?"

He drops the Tiger Eye, rolls over, and faces me.

"Everything that I have ever learned has prepared me for this, Captain. Believe me, nothing will stop us."

Not the words, but something in his eyes brings all my

sense of foreboding rushing back. I'd forgotten it for a few minutes while I was cataloging the base. Now it's back, giving me a chill.

I wish I could dig into Nguyen's mind at this second and pull out his thoughts, but he rolls back onto his stomach and peers again through the Tiger Eye.

"A lot of people are going to die, Nguyen," I do manage to say.

"So be it," he says evenly and with less emotion than a mantis closing on its prey.

We slide back to the others waiting in the ambulance.

I watch Nguyen, for he has changed perceptibly.

It's as though he's had two hits on a Colombian stick. His usual dour self has been shucked somewhere back on the beach overlooking Cam Ranh Bay. I get the feeling he might start tap-dancing at any second, despite the ankle-deep sand.

He consults his watch.

"In ten seconds our units should make contact," he says.

He counts, putting it to the test. At ten, he looks up to Vo silhouetted on the northern dune. Vo is waving.

Nguyen calls to Pham to open a path through the mines.

I see them first as distant filaments in the night, then they begin to materialize as a heaving kaleidoscope of men, a long double column of armed troopers in black pajamas, almost a hundred, I estimate, coming toward us from inland, silently except for the soft shushing of their sandals.

One man strides in advance of the others. He is almost as tall as I. His left arm has been shot off at the elbow some time ago, for as he and Nguyen greet each other with slight bows and with their *wai*s, the man's left stub moves toward his upraised right palm. I cannot recall ever seeing a more bizarre physical gesture than this—of a one-armed man attempting a *wai*.

Nguyen leads the man to me.

"My old comrade Colonel Van Minh," he says. "This is Captain John Locke, sir."

Again the *wai*, this one for me.

"We are at your command, Captain," he says.

"Thank you, Colonel."

I look over his men. Among the hundred there is not

an extra pound of flesh. Nor is there mercy in any eye. Clearly, these men have come to fight. I could be standing among a troop of NVA fifteen years ago. These are their successors, as motivated now as the NVA was then— same war, but then it's been the same war in these parts for two thousand years.

"We'll rest tonight," I announce, "and go over the attack plans until every man knows exactly what his mission is—and when. Tomorrow night—at the change of watch, at midnight—we will hit them."

"Very well," the colonel replies. "Follow us and we will bring you to our camp."

"What about the ambulance?" I ask Nguyen.

"It will be driven away—and used again."

We load up our supplies from the ambulance, all our ordnance and maps, and we move out with the colonel and his men.

I find Thanh Hoa attempting to walk.

"Hold it right there!" I say to her. "You go in a litter."

"I walk!" she says defiantly.

She makes it for ten agonizing paces in the sand, then she stops and looks at me. But there is no concession in her eyes, no begging for assistance. Just that long look.

"If you're really planning on coming out with me," I say, "and going back to America—not just saying that to set us up—then you'd better start learning some elementary American vocabulary. For example, right now, any good American girl who couldn't walk and who has to be carried by somebody who's pissed her off would automatically say, 'Oh, shit!'"

She continues to stare at me.

"So *say* it!" I demand.

"Shit!" she says.

I scoop her up and follow the others into the night, Arun alongside, checking my nose.

Five clicks beyond the southern basin of Cam Ranh Bay on a beach washed by the South China Sea, Van Minh leads us into a fishing village, dark except for a naked light bulb here and there in a few of the huts which are stepped out over the gentle surfline on mossy piles.

Most of Van Minh's men disappear, as though through trapdoors.

Thanh Hoa and Arun are given a small hut to themselves along the line of beached boats and drying nets.

Nguyen and our Bangkok team follows me with Van Minh and his key officers into the largest of the structures, apparently the communal center of the fishing village.

I break out the photos of Cam Ranh Bay Arty had given me when we left Bangkok, photos made from radar pulses transmitted by one of our KH–11 remote imaging satellites.

I point out to the group our initial objective, the area adjoining what used to be the U.S. barge and LST facility on the inland tip of the northern pincers that close in the bay.

"This is where we make or break—right here," I tell everyone. "This is the most critical phase of the operation—taking control of these two Shershen-class torpedo cutters. These two boats are under Vietnamese, not Soviet, command. They're two of the eighteen attack boats the Russians transferred to Hanoi, so we'll be fighting with Vietnamese sailors, not Russians, at this stage of the operation."

I break out the photos and deck layouts of the Shershens.

"Each boat is armed with four deck guns. And with four torpedo tubes. As you can see, they also have A/S weapons in two DC racks. Each boat operates with three diesel engines and three shafts, turning up twelve thousand horsepower. The normal complement aboard is twenty-three officers and men, but the chances are many of them will either be off duty and ashore—or sleeping below. It's usually only a two-man deck watch, so taking them out shouldn't be too tough."

I turn to Van Minh.

"Nguyen tells me you have a number of ex-navy personnel among your group—helmsmen, boatswain's mates, engineers, and torpedomen. I'd like to meet with each one of them, to be sure we have the right man in the right job. We're talking about a boat here that's more than a hundred feet long and capable of forty-five knots."

"They're standing by to meet with you, Captain," Van Minh says. "Although we are still not clear what your plans are for these boats. Once we have them."

"Okay," I say, "once we've secured them, all torpedo

tubes are to be loaded, all guns made ready for firing before we start engines. I will give the signal to start engines—and hopefully that will be the first sound anyone else on the base hears. All the enemy personnel aboard are to be dealt with using silenced weapons only—preferably knives and garroting wire. Once we have engine warm-up, we will cast off and commence the attack. From the Shershen docks to Pier One and the Soviet carrier is less than a mile. We'll be alongside the carrier two minutes after we leave our dock. We will make three passes—I repeat, *three*—no more, at the exposed starboard side. The first pass we'll use our guns to shoot out their radar and prevent them from an immediate counterattack from their deck guns and missiles. On the second pass we will fire eight torpedos—four from each boat—into the carrier at point-blank range. On the third pass we will fire eight more. The attack should require no more than four minutes from beginning to end. And if sixteen torpedos don't cripple or sink her, then I have to tell you the Soviets make a pretty lousy torpedo. We are not going back in for a fourth run—by then they will be in a fully defensive and counterattacking mode. We will head straight out to sea, but bearing close—and I mean close—to the southern peninsula and Pointe de Ba Tien."

I pull out a nautical chart of the bay and indicate precisely the spot I'm talking about.

"These boats draw only about five feet, and the water is eight fathoms here only thirty meters off the point. Every man will abandon ship at this exact spot, going over the starboard side and swimming straight to shore, while the boats continue out to sea on automatic pilot at flank speed. Hopefully, the enemy will scramble everything he's got to chase them and will sink them well offshore, giving us a bonus of two North Vietnamese torpedo boats on top of the carrier. While everybody's busy trying to sink us, we will be long gone into the night. Okay, that's it. It's clean and simple and surgical, and it's wild enough to work. The hardest part of it, actually, is our getting onto the base in the first place in order to commandeer the two Shershens."

I lay out more photos and schematics, these from Thai intelligence.

"Electronic surveillance on all land approaches. The

beaches are all fenced in and electrified. Sentry positions along the perimeters, and these other areas are heavily mined with trip wires everywhere. The chances of getting onto the base from land are nil, unless you have artillery and tanks and a division of men willing to accept heavy casualties. So—we come in by sea, each man using a small bamboo float. It's going to be a long swim going in, so anyone who's not at home in the water or worried about sharks is disqualified. Comments?"

Nguyen and Van Minh glance at each other. Van Minh smiles at me. "Would you like to hear what we had planned?"

"I'm wide open," I say. "Maybe you've got a better way to go."

"Ours was to be a suicide mission," Van Minh says. "Every man with us has pledged to die in order to attack the Russian carrier."

"Each of you is more valuable than that goddamned hunk of machinery," I tell him. "Believe me!"

"Thank you," he says solemnly, "but we knew no other way to accomplish the mission. We have three trucks ready, each loaded with C-4 plastique, enough to blow up any city block. We were planning to attack the main gate with mortars and machine-guns, killing the guards, then driving the trucks through with covering fire from two armored cars we have managed to acquire, through the base to Pier One, then straight into the carrier."

"Deep shit!" I tell him. "Look at this!"

I show him another KH-11 photo of the base. I put my finger on an area near the POL jetty.

"Tanks! Four of them. The best and the latest models Moscow could ship in. At the first sound of gunfire from the main gate—*six miles* north of Pier One—you'd have a thousand Soviet Marines blocking your way—and these tanks would be firing on you. Before you could get too far into the base they'd have gunships up rocketing you from topside. You might kill a few people—in return for sacrificing your entire group—but you'd never reach the carrier."

"You have given us our lives back," Van Minh says softly. "Now I will call in the men you need to meet with."

I look over at Nguyen. He is staring down glumly at the KH-11 photo of the tanks. His eyes lift to mine.

"Why didn't you show me this before now?" he asks.

"Because we've been taking it a step at a time," I say. "And it doesn't pay to overload too far in advance."

Again I feel the gnawing sense of foreboding. I swear to God Nguyen looks almost disappointed, as though I personally have stepped between him and some terrible destiny.

Three hours later, the meetings wearily finished, everyone given his orders, I am shown to a hut over the water and left alone. I strip off my clothes, remove my makeup and the contact lenses, and lower myself into the shallow water lapping around the stilts of my hut. It's piss-poor policy to go paddling around the South China sea at midnight, even this close to shore, but I feel shark-proof tonight.

I swim parallel to shore, back and forth, in chest-deep water, trying to forget the statistic that the majority of shark attacks usually occur in shallow water. Instead, I make myself recall that time back in '69 when the VC attacked the hospital at Cam Ranh Bay and I was much more reckless that night than tonight, pulling out all the IV tubes the nurses had stuck into me and rolling out of bed and managing to find a weapon so I could counterattack the guerrillas. It was hardly a matter of bravery. You're lying there, hovering between life and death, already shot up from some earlier nonsense out in the boonies, and some bastards come in out of the night and start killing people around you. Do you lie there and get shot at or do you get off your back and shoot back? For that simple decision I was awarded my first Silver Star. Strangely enough, not too far from where I'm now swimming, just up the bay a few miles on the airstrip, they pinned the medal on me only ten days later simply because some heavy brass from the Pentagon flew in on a fact-finding mission and the PR people decided an awards ceremony was just the ticket for the six o'clock news back in the States, so they choppered troopers in from all over Nam—Army, Navy, Marines—and they hauled me out of bed, shaved me, cut my hair, covered my wounds with an intact, not-shot-up uniform, and marched me out with the others. Some major from MACV announced with a Mississippi accent the bottom line for each of our citations, then the general passed down the line, not pinning each medal on every tunic, which would have chewed up all afternoon, but clipping the medals onto our pocket flaps with those big black clampers they install on clipboards. He shook every hand, looked each man in the eye, and said "Congratulations." All the while the newsreel cameras were rolling. Apparently I was the hot item that afternoon, for my father wrote me from San Diego that I actually got a full one minute on the evening news, a brave young man who got off his deathbed to drive away a superior force of determined enemies. What nobody apparently chose to deal with was the fact that if I'd stayed on that goddamned cot any longer, the VC would have blown my ass. Mine was hardly a heroic act, but rather a reasonable one, since I had no alternatives. They seldom give medals for reasonable acts, for if you were really using your reason, you'd never get yourself into a position like mine to begin with.

Refreshed from the swim, I walk naked out of the sea to discover Arun watching me from the shadows of my hut.

"Thanh Hoa asked me to bring you to her," Arun says.

"She all right?"

"Ask *her*!" Arun says somewhat petulantly.

"Hey!" I say. "You my buddy or what?"

But Arun will say nothing more.

I slip into a pair of jockey shorts and hurry off the way Arun has pointed me.

I find Thanh Hoa lying in darkness on a bedmat in the small hut, open at its front to the sea. She appears more like the adumbration of herself than flesh and blood, an astral spirit glowing in the night. Or is it the slivered moonlight banding her just so?

"Arun told me that—"

"Yes!" she interrupts.

Her voice sounds almost fierce.

I come to her, squat alongside her like a patient fishmonger, the way I remember them squatting in the back streets of Saigon, down on their haunches for hours at a time, with the lid of a garbage pan turned upside down and filled with water and languid catfish for sale.

"Why are you doing this?" she asks.

"Doing what?"

I am told that you are leading an attack against a Russian aircraft carrier."

"Let's hope you don't have a wireless hidden in your pajamas." I grin.

"You still believe I'd betray you?"

"You could make some heavy points with the Mât Vu if you blew the whistle on this operation."

"You believe that I could do that now—after what they did to me?"

"I believed in Doan Thi. But according to you, she betrayed me—and *she* loved me! How the hell can I expect more from you than from her?"

"I know more about Doan Thi than you *ever* will!" she challenges. "Her country came first, you second. Are you any different? Had you known who she really was, wouldn't you have had her arrested?"

There she has me.

"The more I learned about her," Thanh Hoa says, "the more I came to revere her. She was a true revolutionary. She, of all of us, was the voice of the women of Vietnam, not only the women of this century, but for all our women since we first became a people. Do you know what I regret?"

"I couldn't even guess."

"Not being able to finish the work I was assigned by the Bureau of Culture—completing the library in Hanoi that will someday contain all Doan Thi's important poems and essays. In collecting all her personal effects, her journals, and papers, I came across some letters she wrote to you but never mailed. I have them hidden in Hanoi. Would you like to see them?"

What torment now? I ask myself. I refuse to dignify the question.

"Then don't do this foolish thing tomorrow night! Why should you fight against the *lin zo*? It is enough that the *khang chien* attack these Soviet invaders."

"I made a deal. I help them, they help me get my son."

"I will help you do that. I have told you so!"

"Thanh Hoa, even if I let myself trust you, you and I can't do it alone. We need weapons. We need a safehouse in Hanoi. We need friends to get us out. *These* people are my friends."

"Arun told me," she says, sitting up now so that her

hollowed face is close to me, "that you have shown them how to attack the carrier. She heard the men talking. She says it is not necessary for you to go. They have enough force to carry out the operation without you."

"I have to go."

"*Why?*"

"Because I made a deal—one aircraft carrier for one nine-year-old kid in Hanoi."

"What if you don't come back tomorrow night?"

"Then I cut a lousy deal."

She reaches her arms out to me, puts them around my neck, her lips close to mine.

"In Bali—when I told you I was Doan Thi's Sister Fourth, the deceit was only partial, for I had come to feel I was truly a sister to her. Over the months as I worked to collect her poems and to learn everything I could for the history Hanoi is writing about her, she began to replace my real sister, the one you took from me. Doan Thi loved you—this I know. So I have decided to love you, too, as much as she did; more if I can—as she would have wished, had I been her younger sister. But she is gone. And my sister is gone. Only you and I remain. Now am I to lose you too? What a waste of love!"

It's not a bad performance if you believe in pots of gold at the ends of rainbows. For a moment Thanh Hoa's tearful recital transforms the dark shabby fisherman's hut into a painting by Norman Rockwell speckled with golden fairy dust.

But only for a moment.

I leave before I let myself start believing Thanh Hoa means what she said.

Outside, Arun huddles, knees pulled back against her breasts, a lone figure on the crude steps.

Do I see tears in her eyes too?

"What's your problem?" I demand harshly.

"Why won't you listen to her?" Arun sobs.

"You pulled a fucking knife on her only a couple of days ago. Or have you forgotten?"

"She and I have something in common," Arun says. "Neither of us wants to lose you."

"Christ!" I cry. "I needed this!"

CHAPTER

34

By midnight 23 September we bear north in the South China Sea past Mui Da Vaich, the southern point of Cam Ranh Bay, four fishing boats with running lights, as though with nothing to hide, seventy Resistance fighters aboard, with me, Van Minh, Nguyen, and our Bangkok team, a total strike force of seventy-seven men in breechcloths, each of us thickly greased for the sea to conserve body heat.

Coming up to portside and abeam we can see the narrow entrance to one of the world's finest deep-water harbors, known to European and Asian mariners since the days of Marco Polo. But we avoid steering toward its entrance, instead maintaining a course well out to sea, as though our little fleet is making its way past the narrow sandspit that reaches down from the north to close in the bay. We are blips on any number of radar screens blazing inside the harbor as we pass, but as long as we continue our northing, no radarman is going to push the panic button.

We are waiting until we draw dead abeam of the harbor range lights before we slip over, each man with his own bamboo raft.

All this day I had avoided Thanh Hoa and Arun, spent the time field-stripping and cleaning both the .22 and the Browning, then sharpening the Randall. I had decided to go in with knife and handguns only, since the hairy part was all going to be at point-blank range.

While I was wrapping my weapons and extra clips and

309

tucking them into a flotation bag, Arun brought me a message from Thanh Hoa.

"She asked me to tell you that in heaven people eat freely with their hands from bottomless bowls of rice. But in hell people starve because their hands are chained to chopsticks six feet long, too long to bring the rice to their mouths."

"Simple solution," I respond. "All they have to do is feed each other."

"Exactly!" Arun says with whispered triumph. "We were both hoping you would see that. Since you insist on making your life a living hell, you should at least let others feed you. Or truly, John, you *will* starve to death!"

That had been the extent of it. I stayed in my hut. They stayed in theirs. And when I left with the men there had been no good-byes. I had not turned back to see if either of them was watching our departure. We simply boarded the fishing boats and took off without ceremony.

Now I stare off at the harbor range lights.

Three more minutes, I estimate.

Right on schedule the reliable juices start to pump. Jack the Giant Killer, about to climb the beanstalk. One more soar, Merlin, old friend. I find it exhilarating to be experiencing a role-reversal. During the war when we attacked enemy hamlets, the press frequently accused us of committing atrocities. Now I am a unit of a partisan freedom movement, striking from moral high ground, and it's as though at last I'm wearing full body armor. Looking about me at the men awaiting my signal to plunge into the sea, I am swept up by an almost divine belief in the power of the human will to overcome physical obstacles. I remember reading somewhere that Ho Chi Minh's People's Army was formed in December of 1944: thirty-four men armed with nineteen antiquated rifles. From that original core that sprang from the Vietminh the North grew to be able to absorb all the slings and arrows of the world's mightiest military force and ultimately to sweep us from Indochina.

Forty years ago this month, with little more than a dream and unable to foresee that he could ever win the war against the French, Ho Chi Minh had proclaimed the independence of the Democratic Republic of Vietnam.

"All men are created equal," he declared, quoting the

American Declaration of Independence. "They are endowed by their creator with certain inalienable rights. Among these are life, liberty, and the pursuit of happiness. In a broader sense this means: All the people on the earth are equal from birth, all the people have a right to live, to be happy and free. The Declaration of the French Revolution made in 1791 on the Rights of Man and the Citizen also states: 'All men are born free and with equal rights, and must always remain free and have equal rights.'

"These are undeniable truths. Nevertheless, for more than eighty years the French imperialists, abusing the standard of Liberty, Equality, and Fraternity, have violated our Fatherland and oppressed our fellow citizens. They have acted contrary to the ideals of humanity and justice. In the field of politics they have deprived our people of every democratic liberty. They have enforced inhuman laws. They have set up three distinct political regimes in the North, the Center, and the South of Vietnam in order to wreck our national unity and prevent our people from being united. They have built more prisons than schools. They have mercilessly slain our patriots. They have drowned our uprisings in rivers of blood. They have fettered public opinion. They have practiced obscurantism against our people. To weaken our race they have forced us to use opium and alcohol—"

"Time!" I go over the side first, keeping the hull interposed between my splash-in and the naval base, in case night glasses are trained on our passing fleet.

From each of the four boats the men lower themselves into the sea, sliding in silently with scarcely a ripple.

We form into preassigned units and glide through the temperate sea toward the distant range lights as the fishing boats continue north, the thump of their engines soon lost to us.

If Ho Chi Minh could do it, we can do it, I tell myself. Why should the Russians be in here on a pass, any more than the Chinese, the Thais, the Japanese, the French, or the Americans?

The night lies benign on water smooth as grape skin. I set a relaxed pace, using flippers to propel myself forward, my arms extended along the short raft, my shoulders and upper chest buoyed by it. I have estimated it will take us between two and three hours to cover the distance, but this time period is open-ended. We will certainly arrive well before the oh-four-hundred change of watch—or if the Shershen crews are on dog-watch rotation, after the oh-two-hundred changeover.

Our arrival splits the difference. We come in at seven minutes after oh-three-hundred hours, gliding in under the pilings of the barge-landing area, scattering black crabs in every direction. We stack our bamboo rafts and break out our weapons.

From behind a piling I peer out at the two torpedo boats lying to their lines less than a hundred yards away, the ropes groaning slightly with the heaving of the hulls in the water. I adjust the M–802 night-vision goggles Arty issued to me in Bangkok. They turn you into an extraterrestrial with their lenses protruding out of a boxlike frame. But they also turn night into day—and why not, for seven thousand dollars a copy?

I focus in on two seamen standing duty aboard the nearest Shershen. They are posted just aft of the forward torpedo tube.

I give Van Minh the signal he's been waiting for. Instantly he moves out with a unit of his men to board the first boat. Nguyen and our team hunch along the waterline toward the second Shershen. The rest of our force spreads out ashore to intercept anyone who might wander on site.

We creep around the high freeboard of the first boat as Van Minh and his men patter aboard over the stern and begin easing midships toward the two sentries. We duck low and move through ankle-deep water toward the second Shershen tied up less than twenty feet from its sister ship.

I sweep the deckline through the N/V goggles. No sign of sentries. The stern is clear.

I climb onto the deck, working my way forward past the mine racks, Nguyen and Vo taking the starboard side, I to port with Le. Tran, Van, and Pham fan out behind us, watching the superstructure for any sign of movement.

I smell cigarette smoke. A sentry sits forward of the aft gun turret, a cigarette between his lips. I squeeze off a single round into his right ear with the silenced Hi-Standard and motion Le to be sure he's terminal. Le assures it with a stroke of his knife. Suddenly from nowhere a shadow looms—the second sentry, coming out of a hatchway. His mouth springs open as he literally bumps into me, so close he can't unsling his SMG before I slash his throat with the Randall.

Nguyen signals to me from the bow—nobody on his side. The deck is ours. I wave to the shoreline. Two dozen of Van Minh's men sweep forward in response. Within seconds, without sound, they are aboard our Shershen. They spread out as planned—one team to the bridge, others inboard and below to the cabins to kill any officers or crewmen unlucky enough to be sleeping aboard this September night.

Nguyen remains topside with me. I have no taste for killing men in their sleep. I suppose you could challenge this sensitivity as an arrant piece of bullshit, since I seem able to stomach killing men who are wide awake.

Nguyen is acting strange again, distracted, even absent, his thoughts elsewhere. I have never known him to be so uncentered.

"Anything we should talk about?" I ask.

He looks at me as though from a mountain peak.

"If anything happens to me tonight," he says finally, "please be sure my boys get back to Bangkok. Le has a championship bout at Rajadamnern Stadium on October twenty-third."

"Look," I say, "if you've got any premonitions, let's deal with them—right now!"

"How?"

"You remember that one radioman we had with us on the Black Mamba team for a few missions—Higgins?"

"What about him?"

"You remember we were about to saddle up for that exploratory around Sa Moi? And I ordered Higgins to stay behind. You remember that morning?"

"I remember."

"You ever wonder why I made him stay behind?"

"I wasn't sure."

"Well, I could see him with his guts spread all over the landscape—just as if he'd been blown up right in front of me. It was in his eyes—the precognition of his own death, but he was too ballsy a guy to admit it. So I grounded him—*before* the fact. He made his year and flew home in one piece. I still get letters from him. Thanking me.

We both knew he would have bought it on that mission. It was written all over him—like something's written now all over you, except in this case I don't get a clear picture. So talk to me, Nguyen! We haven't come all this way together to get you iced over a fucking piece of Soviet equipment. I can keep you off the deck or put you inside a gun turret where the armor plate's heavier than anywhere else aboard. How about it, dear friend? Just for the Gipper."

"Thank you, John. But I intend to stand alongside you when we take it to those Russian bastards."

Suddenly he grins and I have him back again.

"You know what we call the Russians?" he asks.

"Tell me."

"Americans—without money."

Vo returns from below with the others. His hands are bloody. He stares at me for a long moment, as though seeking advice, but not daring to ask for it. I detect that the killing fever in his eyes is gone, displaced by something else. Sorrow for the sacrificed, shock at the banality of slaughter, the terrible realization of his own mortality? I see myself in his eyes and remember when I crossed over, even as he is doing at this moment.

Van Minh is waving to me from the first boat.

I give him the load-up signal.

His men begin to lever torpedos into their tubes and to arm the deck guns.

Aboard our boat Nguyen issues the same order.

Eight minutes later both attack boats stand ready for combat, every man at his station.

Another signal to Van Minh, this one to start engines aboard his boat. I start ours and watch the gauges until I'm satisfied our propulsion system is warm and happy. From his boat Van Minh waves he's ready aboard.

I follow the sweep hand on my wristwatch. When the minute hand touches three-thirty on the nose, I drop my arm. We cast off lines, zoom straight out, both boats cutting the water side by side. I advance the throttles and steer us sharply to starboard. We skim toward the carrier looming less than two minutes distant on a course that will sweep us five hundred yards off her beam and take us past her from bow to stern while we concentrate all eight guns on her radar.

As we race closer I pull ahead of Van Minh's boat so that we can make our first run in file, Van Minh streaming in our wake.

"Commence firing," I order.

The night is split open by the violent thrusts of sound bursting from the 30mm guns.

Through the goggles I see shells exploding into the tracking and fire-control radar aboard the carrier.

Underneath the pounding of the cannon I hear the tiny rip of light machine-gun fire. Instinctively I shrink behind the helm, until I observe that the fire comes from our deck, stitching into the two Yak fighters on the flight deck. As we zip by, one of them explodes, lighting the surface of the water around the carrier.

I roll out and at flank speed drive the Shershen in a wide loop away from the *Novorossiysk*. I imagine I can already hear the wailing of the General Quarters alarm, a commendably rapid response time—if in fact I am hearing, not simply imagining, the expected sound.

Van Minh's helmsman stays right with me, and as I turn back toward the carrier for our first torpedo run he's churning up the water a hundred yards to starboard and only a few yards astern.

"Fire torpedos!" I shout into the com tube.

The carrier stretches dead ahead, little more than two football fields distant.

The swish of the firing buffets at my ears and I make out two watery tracks to starboard and two to port, spreading out like an extended Y toward the lofty freeboard of the carrier, and then I spot four more burrowing out from Van Minh's boat like rabid moles.

I spin the wheel to port as Van Minh's helmsman spins to starboard and we split apart, thundering back into the bay as all eight torpedos drive home, brightening the night as they rip at the seams of the carrier and explode in a line from stem to stern.

We rocket back on our final run.

Ahead of us now flames streak up from the waterline and I can see antlike figures scurrying across the deck.

We drive in and fire eight more torpedos into the *Novorossiysk*.

This volley rocks her.

I lay us over on our ear in a fast turn, for the first

whistle of deck cannon screeches toward us, heaving up a waterspout directly ahead. I steer straight through it, the water and foam cascading down over us. We zip out toward the harbor opening, the *Novorossiysk* burning in a dozen places and streaking the night with crimson and orange light. Van Minh's boat rides our stern as we dart free before they can launch their missiles.

I set the bow to bear one-ten, lock the course into the autopilot, then hurry down from the bridge, yelling at Nguyen to follow me as the Shershen swings toward the main channel exit

On deck I wave everyone to the starboard railing and point ahead to our jump point. It rushes toward us, the shoreline only yards away.

I make a quick last-minute check of our target now two miles behind us.

Jesus, they've already got one chopper airborne!

"Jump!" I shout.

I tuck my head into my chest and flip over, hitting the surface like a skipping stone and I think, My God, I'm going to go bouncing right up onto the beach. But I crash down and plow under. When I come up, I'm less than ten yards from the reefs off Pointe de Ba Tien.

I turn in the water to count heads.

Dear God! What am I seeing now?

Only one boat is still driving out to sea! Van Minh's boat.

Ours has turned back.

Nguyen!

I scream across the water after him.

But he has made his decision. It strikes me that he must have made it way back in Bangkok. It must have come to him in that quiet, irrevocable way it comes that he had lived long enough with the loss of his wife and son and that tonight he would seek them, wherever they might be across time and space, even as I had set the example of seeking my son.

The carrier's gunship tracks him, firing its missiles as he bores in toward the *Novorossiysk*. But he is not to be denied tonight, not by me, not by the Russians.

He steers toward the rudder of the carrier and drives the Shershen and its remaining twelve torpedos directly into her.

The fireball of his entry hovers over Cam Ranh Bay for at least two minutes.

I pull myself ashore in its dying glare.

Around me the others come wading in.

Van Minh, water streaming from the stump of his missing forearm, stumbles toward me, squats in the sand beside me.

We sit there, it seems, forever, watching everything in slow motion through a filter of sorrow.

Five miles out the second Shershen is blown out of the water by the pursuing Soviet gunship.

Back within Cam Ranh Bay, explosions rack the *Novorossiysk*, each more violent than the one before it.

"He was not a happy man," Van Minh says at last.

══CHAPTER══

35

"**W**e must move you out before morning," Van Minh counsels as we trot back along the beach to his fishermen's hamlet. "The Public Security Forces will be searching every coastal village from Hao Da in the South to Song Cau in the North looking for the four fishing boats that passed Cam Ranh Bay at midnight."

"Where are those boats now?" I ask.

"One to the north, in a remote cove of Hòn Tré Island. Another even farther north—anchored off Hòn Lồn Island. The other two turned far out to sea to evade the Cam Ranh Bay radar, then went south to Cu Lao Hòn Island. Please have your people ready to take off as quickly as possible."

It occurs to me I've been leaving all the backstage arrangements to Nguyen. Without him I feel as though I'm floating in deep space with a ruptured survival suit.

"How do we get to Hanoi?" I ask. "Nguyen and I never discussed that leg of the mission."

"We have a truck. We'll drive you to Da Lat, then put you on a train which now runs from Ho Chi Minh City to Hanoi. It is an exhausting journey, three days crowded into cars that were old when the French were here—eight hundred and fifty miles from Da Lat to Hanoi. You will go disguised as peasants with your ducks and chickens for sale in Hanoi. But you must make the two women older and uglier, or they will attract too much attention."

When we've returned to the hamlet, I collect Le, Pham, Vo, Tran, and Van while Van Minh's men begin to scatter.

"Van," I announce, "you will move up to replace Nguyen. You'll be our point man, our eyes and ears, our main liaison with the Resistance as they support us here and in Hanoi."

"Very well, sir," he agrees.

I make eye contact with each of the other young men standing in a semicircle around me.

"Anyone else feel he can do a better job than Van?" I ask.

They shake their heads.

"We will obey Van, sir, as though he were Nguyen himself," Pham says for the others.

"Does anybody want to say anything about what Nguyen did?" I ask.

Le appears to be the most deeply affected, but even he is reluctant to speak about his feelings.

"Le, I know he trained you to become one of Thailand's best boxers. He made me promise I would have you back in Bangkok for a match on October twenty-third."

Le turns away to hide the sudden rush of tears to his eyes.

"It is not easy to lose one's *sifu*," I say. "I know. I lost mine, the man who taught me how to survive. Now he sits behind a desk in Bangkok, but he might as well be on a mountain peak in Tibet."

Only Vo dares to ask. "Why?" he demands. "We carried out the mission successfully. Why did he destroy himself after we were extracting?"

"His heart was dead," I tell Vo. "It died years ago. He was one of the walking wounded, bleeding from the inside. But psychic wounds take a while to kill. This morning they caught up with him.

"Okay, let's agree that whatever we've done up to this moment has been accomplished because of dumb luck. From here on we've got to be smarter than our enemies. We're going right into their center. One mistake from any one of us, and all our good work so far goes into the shithouse. We must become one person now, read each other's minds, feel each other's feelings. Then I will be able to bring all of us back to Bangkok."

I reach out for Vo first, since he is the neediest and I can sense his inner carnage even as I can sense my own

319

unabated emotional attrition, and I pull him to my side, then I reach out for Pham, bringing him into the cluster I have started to form with Vo.

The young men seem somewhat confused by the personal contact, at the emotionalism, for they are Vietnamese, and such embraces among men are usually unthinkable.

"Le, Tran, Van, come in here with us," I say.

They do, awkwardly at first, but then as the six of us put our arms around each other and hold to each other in a tightknit core, they begin to feel the magic of our brotherhood and the strength of our unity.

I notice Thanh Hoa sitting on the steps of her nearby hut. She has probably seen and heard all of it.

"What we feel at this moment," I say to my team, "we must continue to feel until we have all returned to the Mother of Rivers in Bangkok two weeks from now. *All* of us! Together!"

I break the circle, grin at them.

"Okay, let's get ready to move out. Van Minh wants us looking like peasants. So everybody into wardrobe!"

Solemnly they salute me, then move toward the central building, where Van Minh waits.

I walk over to Thanh Hoa.

"Well, I'm back," I say.

"When are you going to let *me* into your little circle?" she asks.

"It's not a *little* circle! It's a big circle and it's got room in it for just about everybody. I can't think of anybody—aside from my son—I want to ask into it more than you. But my instinct for survival keeps going off like a smoke signal every time I see you watching me. The hairs on the back of my neck keep rising whenever I get close to you. Why do you think that is, Thanh Hoa?"

"Guilt?" she asks. "Or just inability to accept the truth? I don't know. You tell me."

"How about something as basic as self-preservation?"

"I heard you talking about Nguyen. How did he die?"

"Instantly," I tell her as I come up the steps past her and enter the hut.

Arun is asleep on the rough planking overhanging the lapping waterline.

"Arun!"

Her eyes open. Seeing me, she sits up and starts to reach for me almost joyously, but aborts her embrace as she realizes the impossibility of our situation.

"I knew you would be back before daylight," she says. "I let myself fall asleep."

"We're checking out," I tell her, "taking the train to Hanoi—going as peasants. But we can't leave until you do a makeup reconstruct on yourself and Thanh Hoa. I'm talking major old and major plain, right on the boundary of ugly, like forty years planting rice. Got it?"

She's become so much of a woman in my presence she can't resist using the moment to tease me.

"That should take a lot of the pressure off you," she says, flirting, giving me a sidewise glance from her striking, almost violet eyes.

"Stop being so fucking seductive!" I warn her.

"Oh, I didn't mean me!" she insists. "I meant Thanh Hoa. When the two of you are together, I can feel the heat wave. It's a real turn-on."

"You got half an hour to do both of you," I tell her. "Then *I'm* going to need some work."

I go outside. Thanh Hoa is still sitting on the steps.

"Thirty minutes!" I say crisply, and cross toward my own hut.

With dawn less than an hour away, Van Minh loads us into a lopsided Russian-built truck, its flatbed stacked with rice bags and heaped with vegetables. He puts us in the back with the produce and hands up six splenetic ducks and four protesting chickens, their legs bound. Two of his men take over the cab.

"Your train tickets," he says, passing them up to me, "and your police permits to travel from Da Lat to Hanoi. We have given all of you new identities. Here on this paper are the names—your village and your dead and living relatives. Learn them, then destroy the paper. When you leave the train in Hanoi, you will be contacted by a man selling a book that contains the legend of the Sacred Sword. He will take you to our people."

He hands me a pair of crutches.

"Your right leg was injured in an accident in Ho Chi Minh City last week," he tells me. "Here is a copy of the hospital records and the name of the doctor who treated you. He is one of us. Do not walk anywhere without these crutches. They will reduce your height as you bend over and keep suspicious eyes from following you. I wish you luck. May you soon be united with your son."

We rattle off as the dawn begins to creep out of the South China Sea behind us.

Arun has done a masterful job with herself and Thanh Hoa. The two of them put me in mind of bag ladies.

"I said ugly," I tell Arun, "not disgusting."

"Beauty is in the eye of the beholder," she replies.

"There *are* exceptions," I insist. "Even a blind man will turn away from you two crones."

"Oh, my God!" she laughs. "Nobody ever called me a crone before!

We arrive in Da Lat without incident two hours later and join a throng waiting for the Hanoi-bound train.

In our straw luggage we carry only three pieces of equipment: the night goggles, the Tiger Eye, and the COMSAT box. Back in the sands south of Cam Ranh Bay we have buried all the rest of our weaponry and equipment and burned all the satellite photos and charts. I have retained my two handguns and my Randall fighting knife, and each of the men has kept his TT–33 Tokarev pistol, a combat knife, and two grenades.

We have come a long way and shed a lot of fat.

All to bring me face to face at last with a child I do not know and who does not know me.

Fear expands within me like one of those packaged Japanese toy flowers that swells in water, with a life of of its own, and blooms riotously and seemingly without end.

What, if anything, has he been told about his father? Is he aware I exist? Did they tell him I was blown away with the rest of the invaders? Certainly they had to tell him something. His grandfather must have been forced to invent some kind of plausible explanation for the boy's blue eyes and brown hair. And what did Doan Thi whisper to the infant, to the growing child, to the maturing boy? She has been dead now for only two years this March; she lived until he was seven. I have to believe she told him that she loved me, that she wrote me forty-three love poems, the final one when she left me in Saigon. But two years have passed and he has been in the custody of his grandfather, a man who must have done his utmost to poison the child's mind and to indoctrinate him with the most rigid kind of Marxist–Stalinist conformity.

In Hanoi you don't drive up alongside a boy in a flashy convertible and offer him a Mars bar to induce him to jump into your car. There aren't that many cars to begin with in Hanoi. The best you're going to come up with, if you're a high Party official, is a Soviet Volga—which any self-respecting American kid would pay twenty dollars not to have to ride in. It's mostly bicycles up there in Hanoi. I have this sudden, irrational concept of pedaling up to my son as he walks to school and calling out, "Hi, there. I'm your dad. Hop on! I'll run you back to the States."

We wait at the station most of the day until the chuffing of an ancient steam locomotive breaks into my fears and I look off to see the train screeching toward us.

I hobble aboard on my crutches, the five young farmers with me carrying our shabby straw and bamboo luggage and our unhappy ducks and chickens, two peasant women dutifully hobbling behind us. We manage to find seats together, four of us facing each other on one side of the aisle, half on the other, our luggage and livestock wedged in among us, our rice tubes and thermos bottles filled for the long journey. We are surrounded by women and children and infants, yet I hear no crying from the babies, one of the remarkable silences I recall from the war, when village children would only stare, never speak, never cry out—unlike the street kids of Saigon, who were seldom quiet.

The rattling ride north thumps into the core of me and becomes a kind of existential journey. The quest nears its end, even though the end is unforeseeable. I have attacked the castle and freed the maiden all forlorn. I have entered the dragon's den and slain the fire-breathing creature in its lair. Now one last trial by arms. But this is what frightens me—that this last trial is infinitely more than by arms. I cannot use the Tiger Eye and evaluate the terrain and plan to come in and hose down the defenders. This is a matter between two enemies—a father and a grandfather—and a child who, for every possible reason I can conjure up, might very well prefer staying where he is rather than being uprooted by a honky with meat on his breath.

Even though I close my eyes to blot out the sight of the ravaged countryside and the thousands of men and women still digging out with hand tools a decade after the guns were stilled, depressing images keep wheeling across my retina. Most depressing is the knowledge that I was one of the predators and that wars are invariably carried out by people like oneself—not by evil mutants, but by ordinary people, some of whom are vegetarians, not strung out on coke, men who pet dogs, not those who bayonet babies, but men who usually attend church and sleep badly after they machine-gun an enemy they can scarcely see, a transitory flick among the foliage like a blinking image in a video game that has to be zapped with the fingers of your left hand on the buttons, while your right hand is moving you up and down to avoid the laser flashes.

Can it be that rationality has its dark side, too, even as irrationality does? For the first time I begin to comprehend that true understanding is not some seamless, golden caul but is a worn and patched and restitched garment forever in need of repair. You learn something so that you can learn later on that what you learned when you were younger was not really true—none of it, possibly—and that there is a higher truth beyond that, and still other truths, yet higher, to be learned.

Without asking permission, simply assuming that I expected her to do so, Thanh Hoa falls asleep with her head on my shoulder.

The touch of her cheek, despite the wrinkles Arun has creased into her face, feels warm on my upper arm. I realize that it is not only my concern about confronting and winning my son that has churned me up, but the fear than Thanh Hoa will turn out to be just one more entrapment of the Mât Vu.

Two rainswept nights and a final lyrical morning later we approach Hanoi, having crossed the Song Ma river sixty-five miles south of the city.

At our last stop vendors had come aboard and passed up the aisle selling the fragrant *com*. I remembered Doan Thi commenting how sad it was that the war wasn't over so she could take me to Vong, a village on the outskirts of Hanoi where, during the October rice harvest, the people broil the still-tender sticky rice and put it on sale wrapped in lotus leaves and tied with pieces of straw.

When made with young rice, she told me, it is to be eaten with bananas. When made with mature rice, it is mixed with sugar and eaten as a cake. At the time I felt it was a curious, almost nostalgic statement to come from a woman of South Vietnam, but I had dismissed it since Doan Thi was the poetess of all Vietnam, of the North and Center and South, and I assumed she was speaking from that position.

We pass gnarled stands of mangroves along the flooded coastal fringe of the Red River delta. Here the lowlands are flat and fertile, intensely cultivated, with waterways crisscrossing everywhere, the clouds blazing on their surfaces, sampans and cargo junks nosing into the reflections as they cut across the countryside in a silent but energetic ballet of transport. We pass bicycle convoys along the roads and long columns of women with their *don ganh*, their carrying poles, balanced on one shoulder.

Closer to the city I observe that the swampy areas I remember from our military maps have now been drained and filled, that factories have been built on the fill, and that blocks of new flats run endlessly across the quarters of Kim Lien and Trung Tu.

We clatter in toward Central Station and a huge poster of Ho Chi Minh hoisting barbells catches my eye. It exhorts all citizens to do their exercises faithfully every morning.

The train seems to muster up a final burst of power as it rolls into Hanoi, a center which has endured for almost a thousand years, once called Thăng Long, the City of the Soaring Dragon.

My energy rises to match the energy I feel now all about me as we penetrate the living heart of the nation.

We wait until most of the other passengers have squeezed out before we collect our bedraggled poultry and all our baggage, then descend onto the long, crowded platform like peasants arriving wide-eyed in the big city.

In that first moment of stepping down I catch sight of a commotion only a few yards away from our car. A man with a strangely gibbous belly, rare for a Vietnamese, has apparently started toward us through the press of people. At least, I have the feeling he's singled us out and is moving toward us.

I see a book clutched in one of his hands. Can this man

be the contact Van Minh had told us to look for at the station?

Abruptly he whirls away from us and runs in the opposite direction, bowling over passengers impeding his flight.

Four Public Security Force noncoms materialize out on nowhere and surge after the man.

I know they are not from the regular Army nor the People's Police Force, because their shoulder boards have the telltale green base of Security instead of the more common gray of regular-army noncoms.

They seize the man and drag him away.

No one seems to be paying the least attention to the arrest and I whisper to our team to ignore the incident as well. We are pushed forward in anonymity by the crowd in the direction the Security Police have gone.

My right crutch strikes something on the platform.

A book.

Was this the book the man had been holding when I first saw him?

I can't remember seeing that he was still holding it when the officers closed in on him.

I bend to retrieve it.

It is a collection of ancient Vietnamese selections.

One of the pages is folded back.

To the legend of the Sacred Sword.

We have just lost our Resistance contact in Hanoi.

We are alone—cut off and isolated in the City of the Soaring Dragon.

Yet I feel exhilarated.

Maybe because I know we won't go hungry. After all, we've got the six ducks and the four chickens.

Just kidding, son.

I'm on the high of my life because I'm in the same town you are.

Coming to take you home!

36

We come out of the terminal in time to hear air-raid sirens warbling across the city.

Incongruously enough, I stare up at the glassy winter sky as though expecting to see the specter cells of our bombers still imprinted on the fabric of the stratosphere.

"The noon hour," Thanh Hoa tells me. "We make use of everything in Hanoi. Even the wartime sirens."

The street where we linger while I try to get my bearings is devoid of cars but overflowing with cyclists. At a nearby intersection I watch a traffic officer at her task. Her long black hair spills out from her undersized brown-and-red military cap as she stands dutifully high on a white metal barrier drum planted in the middle of the intersection. Decorative wire reminding me of Persian script rings the top of the drum. A green arrow is daubed across its face to point the permitted direction to be taken by the streaming bicycles. The girl is enveloped in a severe brown uniform, a no-nonsense Sam Browne belt, and white gloves. It strikes me that in her robotic posturing all Hanoi is symbolized, for the city lies hushed and silent about us, with none of the street vitality which, I'm told, still throbs through the boulevards of conquered Ho Chi Minh City.

"I've been given a contact here," I tell our group, "but he'll have a heart attack if he sees all eight of us come trooping in on him. So we split up. Vo, you stay with me and Thanh Hoa. The rest of you break into two groups, but stay within eyeshot of each other. Divide the poultry and get over to the Dong Xuan market, but don't be in a hurry to sell everything. We may need these props for tomorrow too. Hopefully, I'll be able to send Vo to bring you all in by eighteen hundred hours this evening. You take the COMSAT box with you, Tran. If Vo doesn't come for you today, assume we're still out looking for a safehouse. You'll have to figure out a way to take shelter tonight without getting the police or the Security Force on your tail. Return to the market in the morning and wait for Vo to come for you. If he fails to make contact by tomorrow evening at eighteen hundred hours, send a final message on the COMSAT that you're moving toward Ha Long Bay. Then work your way north to Hon Gai and out to Pointe des Mines, our extraction site, and wait for the exfil sometime during daylight on October fifth."

I sense that Arun is reluctant to leave my side.

"You'll be fine," I reassure her.

Surprisingly, she's smiling. "I was just playing out a wild scenario," she whispers to me. "Can you see their faces if they were to take me into headquarters and do a body search?"

"Perish the thought!" I grin. "Think of the poor bastard who would have to write up *that* report in triplicate!"

I watch the six of them blend into the flow of pedestrians, and soon enough I lose sight of them.

"Okay," I say to Thanh Hoa and Vo. "Let's go get lucky," and swinging along on my crutches, bent forward to reduce my profile, I move off toward Restored Sword Lake in the center of Hanoi. We pass through the European sector of the city at the southern end of the lake and along broad avenues and past spacious grounds occupied by two-story villas built by the French, weathered and in need of refurbishing, occupied now by Eastern-bloc diplomats.

Slowly, adjusting our pace to the timing of the people everywhere around us, we wander along the lakeshore and gaze out at the willow-patterned water with its dreamlike reflections and its small island on which the legendary Turtle Pagoda stands. Of the twelve-storied Bao Thien tower built in 1056 only a few remains can be seen. Young men and women stroll along the banks, laughing together, yet hushed, like the city itself, as muted as the winter noon. In the shallows, Chinese cranes here to winter in

Hanoi doze one-legged, their gaunt images shimmering along the surface in attenuated white spangles.

The waterfront cafés are crowded, but even here there is no rattle of dishes, no loud voices raised in argument or debate. The pungent scent of *gio lua*, pounded pork pressed and boiled, and of *pho bo*, a vermicelli soup with beef traces, a soup which is as vital to the Northerner as chicken soup is to a Jewish grandmother in the Bronx, reminds me we haven't eaten since dawn. I motion us to an available table and sit, Thanh Hoa and Vo to either side.

"Have you ever tasted Hanoi beer?" she asks.

"They weren't pushing it down south when I was incountry."

"It's the best beer in Asia," she says.

"Not better than our Thai beer," Vo states, speaking up in behalf of his adopted country.

I order *pho bo* for three and beer all around, then I see Thanh Hoa catch sight of two approaching police officers carrying SMGs slung over their shoulders. She pretends she hasn't seen them. I pay for the beer and the soup with the *dongs* Arty had given me in Bangkok, using my left hand for the transaction. With my free hand I grip the Hi-Standard with its silencer. I'll have to take out Thanh Hoa first, dismal though it may be, the end of the dream—then the two officers, scooping up their submachine guns and with Vo making a run for it. I spot a nearby bicycle rack with scores of bikes slotted into it.

The beer comes before the soup.

Superb!

Even Vo has to concede it is world-class.

Meantime, the policemen saunter by, laughing at something one of them has said.

Thanh Hoa, thank God, has not betrayed us. At least, not yet. Not this time anyway. Maybe she noticed my hand slipping inside my ragged farmer's blouse and decided not to risk it. Or possibly she recalled the warning I gave her in Bali that if she wished to wax me, she could never pull it off inside three hundred meters. She's good, I'll concede that, but not good enough at close range. I advised her then to get herself a good sniper rifle and a dependable scope and lie out beyond five hundred yards on a fine day when the wind was right and the sun was in my eyes.

I watch an old man perched on his heels on top of the backrest of a poured-concrete park bench. He squats there like a sleeping parrot. The old man, like everything else about me, seems a fusion of the real and the surreal. Here in the center of Hanoi, I feel like a man from another planet, *Ngùòi tū hành tinh khác dên*, expecting at any second that someone will point at me and start shouting.

But the waiter who brings us our *pho* questions me with sincere concern about the injury that has reduced me to crutches. I tell him I was grazed by a Volga driven by a drunken Russian when I last took produce into Ho Chi Minh City. He becomes angry in my behalf and curses the Russians. He tells me that the cigarettes he would sell to me for two hundred *dongs* he sells to the Russians for three hundred. He asks me where the accident happened and assures me he knows Ho Chi Minh City as well as he knows Hanoi.

I remember Van Minh rehearsing me on this very point. "It happened on Dong Khoi Street," I tell him, and luckily for me, since it turns out he brags he was among the Northern forces who poured into Saigon in '75 and was still on duty there when Tu Do Street was renamed Dong Khoi—the Street of the Simultaneous Uprisings. Had I said Tu Do Street my credibility would have vanished and the man's suspicions would certainly have been aroused.

We move out, refreshed, my spirits soaring again, and advance toward the ancient Vietnamese section, which I recall from my map studies lies northeast of the lake. This quarter is all that remains of ancient Hanoi. Here the streets are laid out as in European Middle Age cities, on the basis of the crafts which are practiced along each street. Thirty-six of them still remain, a street for workers in ivory and jade, a street for braziers, for tinsmiths, for leather workers, for weavers of cotton and silk, for lacquerers, for those who specialize in embroidery.

I tell Thanh Hoa we are looking for Hàng Bac—Silver Street.

She guides us into it.

The houses squat along the narrow street precisely as Doan Thi had described them to me in a poem she wrote about Hanoi, the lower floors sprung out like an open drawer in a cash register, the upper floors set back, a single window in each house looking onto the street from upstairs. I remember her telling me that feudal law forbade commoners to build houses higher than those of kings and mandarins, so even these two-level houses seem squashed, pushed down by ancient decree. It occurs to me there is no heritage of democracy in the North. Historically the northerners have accepted benevolent despotism. How can a people miss what they've never known? But then, what business is it of mine?

I am looking for a potted dwarf plant growing in a polished silver vase set in an upstairs window.

For a man named Pham Van Ky, the name Guntur gave me when I was aboard the submarine, a man who is Indonesia's top agent in Vietnam.

"There," I tell Vo and Thanh Hoa. "That house."

The three of us stare up at a silver vase so bright it gleams, even in the harsh noontime light, like a beacon.

I lead the way into the open shop where two wrinkled men are tapping delicately on silver urns in the making.

"Ky?" I ask one of the men. He motions with his hammer toward the semidark interior.

I tell Vo to stay with Thanh Hoa. I advance into the shop. A man is bent over a crude desk. He is sketching the outline of what appears to be a chalice. But even as he sketches I am aware that his eyes are evaluating me. Birthmark-brown bags cling puffily below his eyes, diverting attention from the eyes themselves, which are as cutting as a straight razor.

In Vietnamese I tell him that of all the vases along Hàng Bac, his appears the brightest and that I had been told that only an artisan named Pham Van Ky is able to create such sparkle from silver that I would be drawn to his shop as though to a magnet.

"Who told you that?" he asks.

"A friend in a distant place," I reply.

"What language do they speak in this distant place?" he asks.

"Bahasa Indonesian. But my friend also speaks three forms of Balinese and English."

"How is he, this friend of yours?"

"The last time I saw him he was in fine spirits. He suggested I look you up."

"I suggest we retire to the upper floor."

We do.

Ky leads me into his monastic bedroom, gestures me to a seat. He moves to the window, looks out cautiously. Apparently, he observes Thanh Hoa and Vo waiting below.

"They are with you?"

"Yes. Plus five others presently selling ducks and hens at the market. I've told them I'll be in touch by eighteen hundred hours."

"*Eight* of you?" he asks, as though trying to deal with the impossible.

"There were nine of us. We lost a dear friend at Cam Ranh Bay."

He crosses to me gravely.

"Word of what happened there has spread like the plague," he says, giving me no hint of whether he approves or disapproves. "Yet understandably there has been no mention of the incident in the controlled media. Cam Ranh Bay is under the strictest military blockade. The carrier rolled half over and is now resting on the bottom in forty-five feet of water, her superstructure exposed like a monument to all the Soviet aspirations in the South China Sea. Moscow can say nothing. Hanoi can say nothing. But heads will roll. It remains only for somebody to decide *whose* heads. Moscow has sent in their top agents from the GRU, despite Hanoi insisting that no foreign intelligence service will be permitted to operate in Vietnam. Yet taskers continue to arrive daily. So now we have not only the KGB, but the GRU. I cannot begin to conceive what consequences all this will precipitate. You are a formidable opponent, Captain Locke. God help you if you fall into their hands."

He sits down opposite me and studies me as though he were an anthropologist observing a new kind of man.

"Today's only September twenty-seventh," I say. "We're to be taken out on October fifth. After today, that leaves me eight days to get my son out of Hanoi and to move my group to our liftoff site almost two hundred miles northwest of Hanoi. That's almost too wide a time frame. I'd prefer being down to seventy-two hours, so what I need right now is to reestablish contact with the local Resistance people so we can stay out of sight. We need additional weapons—we had to dump almost everything after Cam Ranh Bay so we could travel here by train as peasants. And we need transport. I just can't go hobbling endlessly around the city on crutches. Everything had been set up for us, but just as we arrived this morning the Public Security forces arrested our contact. He had enough presence of mind to break away without leading them to us, but by now they've certainly managed to make him talk, so we have to get out of these clothes and change our appearance as quickly as possible."

"I can reestablish your contact with the Resistance," he says. "It may take an hour or two. Meantime, better bring your friends upstairs."

"I have to send Vo to the market," I say. "But I don't want to risk putting him on the streets in those same clothes he's been wearing."

"Bring the two of them up here," he repeats. "I can send him out again as a corporal in the People's Police Force. What have you learned about your son's whereabouts?"

"He's living in the home of the director of the Mât Vu." The man is startled.

"How can that be?" he asks.

"If I had married the boy's mother, the head of the secret police would have been my father-in-law," I say. "He's the boy's grandfather."

"Dang Van Thuc is your son's grandfather?" he asks unbelievingly.

"Is that his name? In all my time so far with Thanh Hoa I never got around to asking. So much I don't know yet, but we haven't had much chance to talk."

"Can you trust this girl?"

"Not out of my sight."

"Well, bring them inside. I have much to do in the next two hours."

CHAPTER

37

Thanh Hoa and I are alone in the upstairs room over-looking Hàng Bac Street. She has washed herself in a basin of water Ky has brought her and shed the old-crone makeup. Color has returned to her cheeks. They've even filled out slightly.

Vo has been sent off to the municipal market in the shadow of Long Bien Bridge. I watch him stride away as though born for the uniform Ky has provided and feel secure he will not fail us. Ky goes off into the afternoon by himself, as though passing into a secret world of his own.

"Tell me about Dang Van Thuc," I say to Thanh Hoa.

She stands at the window and watches Ky's bent figure go crabbing away on the street below and she strokes her long straight hair with the brush he'd managed to find for her. She glances at me over her shoulder.

"I never spoke his name to you. Never."

"Do you remember everything you do or don't tell me?"

"Every word," she says. "Every thought."

"Why?"

"Because I feel you watching me, judging me, always evaluating every word—and every motion"

"I don't enjoy having to do that, Thanh Hoa."

She turns away, continues pulling the brush through her hair as she stares down at the street echoing with the soft tapping of dozens of tiny hammers. Her voice sounds as distant as the hammering.

"When we were sitting by the lake, you thought I was going to call the policemen, didn't you?"

"I thought it was possible you might consider it."

"What must I do to make you believe in me?"

She turns back to me. In the interval she's managed to fill her eyes with tears, a valiant emotional achievement that leaves me as unpersuaded as ever.

"I even offered myself to you the other night when we were in that cave, but you rejected that too."

"You were still feverish. Besides, we weren't alone."

"We're alone now. I am no longer feverish."

"What would it prove if we did make love?"

"I have nothing else to offer you. No other way to soften your harshness toward me."

"My son."

"You no longer need me to help you find him. I have told you he lives with his grandfather. Now you know his name. You know he is the director of the Mât Vu. Anyone in the Resistance can tell you where he lives. If you can attack a Russian aircraft carrier, you can easily overpower the few guards he keeps at his residence and take away a helpless nine-year-old child."

"Why is it important that I should believe in you?"

"I ask myself that every second since you came for me. I don't really know. Possibly because I hated you for so long. Now that I see I misjudged you and wasted so much emotion, I feel that I must make it up to you. And to myself. Maybe mostly to myself. It's as though I'm coming out of a long darkness. I want to live again, and laugh—I must have laughed when I was a child. And to love. Better you, John Locke—whom I've known since I was ten, you who have never left my mind all these years—than some transient stranger."

I permit myself to close the distance between us.

Maybe together Thanh Hoa and I can manage to free each other from all the excruciating carnage of the war years.

Her lips are close. They no longer appear split and shredded from thirst but have already healed as smooth as I remember them from Bali.

"I have never been with a man before," I hear her whispering. "What more proof can I give you than this—that I will not betray you?"

"Virgins aren't capable of betrayal?" I ask.

"How could I take you as my first lover, then bring harm to you?"

Her earnestness arouses me as I cannot remember being aroused since that first night with Doan Thi in that other lifetime, for it is not a sexual need she's expressing, but a need for life, for existence itself, for purging joy to cleanse her of all the long, dark, oppressive years of discipline and denial and death. Both of us reach out for redemption.

I am not tender with her, no more than one is tender with a victim whose heart has stopped. Revival is a violent treatment, an assault against nullity. But as fierce as I am with her, I find her even fiercer with me, her teeth, her nails, her hard young body and strong arms and legs, her demanding lips, all combining to overpower me. As she senses I am close to ejaculation, she clamps me deep within her to prevent me from withdrawing. I have to use all my strength to escape from her in time. I splatter the top curve of her seeking mons with my flooding sperm and she reaches for me to thrust me back inside her. But I roll away from her in order to deal with the rush of feelings that shudder through me.

She lies on Ky's narrow cot with my whiteness on her belly, circling her finger in it, then bringing it to her lips. The gesture is so childlike, so pristine, I can no longer sustain my disbelief in her.

I kneel on the floor beside the cot.

I look at her for the first time.

I no longer see Doan Thi.

I see another girl, younger, different, a girl named Thanh Hoa, who in a matter of a few blinding, soundless moments has put an end to all my searching into vanished years, has released Doan Thi from the terrible prison of my memories and let her escape into some trackless place from which at last I can no longer recall her at will.

I kiss her gently, as though for the first time, kiss her as Thanh Hoa, not as Doan Thi.

And at this moment all the love I have felt for Doan Thi seems to shift inside me, like cargo in a storm, and to center on the son I have never seen.

I know now that I will have the inner power when I see him for the first time to be able to project my love for him. Without a word being spoken, he will sense it. He will know instinctively that I am his father. And he will come with me.

"When you make love," Thanh Hoa asks, "is it always like this?"

"Only once or twice in a lifetime," I tell her. "But the other times can be almost as wonderful."

"With us," she says, "it will always be as though it is the first time."

Having viewed the world so long with such cold understanding, I find it difficult now even to smile the false reassurance that such miracles do occur between people, yet I grip Thanh Hoa's hand and turn all my disbeliefs into pretended certitudes. She has asked me to believe in her. How bizarre that she should believe in me! I remember the haunting, tragic cry made by Itzhak Zuckerman, one of the leaders of the Warsaw uprising, a man who like myself had seen the vapid face of horror. "If you could lick my heart, it would poison you."

"You asked me about Thuc," she says unexpectedly. "He is more dangerous than anyone suspects. He is a purist, denying himself the least deviation from Lenin's teachings. He is ruthless and relentless. His sole ambition is to keep the cadres mired in ideology and self-criticism. His only imperative is absolute and unquestioning conformity. He believes that Vietnam must follow the Albanian path and stand alone, isolated, against the world, purifying its people until every man, woman, and child believes as he believes. He uses the Mât Vu as his personal army to deal out death or imprisonment to any revisionist elements in the Secretariat. I know he is waiting for you, that he has made his plans. The moment he learned I had escaped from the reeducation camp, he knew that you had arrived in Vietnam and would be coming for your son. By now he has set all kinds of traps and surprises for you."

"Then what was all that you said a while ago?—if I can attack a Soviet carrier, I can easily overpower a few guards and waltz off with my kid?"

"That was before we made love—when I was feeling you had no further need of me. Actually, John, your attack against the camp and the carrier were much easier than getting your son is going to be. Neither the camp nor the carrier had any warning. You took them by surprise. You will not take Dang Van Thuc by surprise."

Soon after, I learn how right Thanh Hoa is, for Ky returns, muttering to himself, shaking his head back and forth with some curious inner rhythm of concern.

"Everything is much too subdued," he tells us. "It is almost as though the police have been ordered to look the other way. Under the Basic Decree promulgated on the twentieth of July 1962 by the National Assembly Standing Committee, the Police Force is empowered to search homes without warrants, seize and detain suspects in the streets, and do whatever is necessary to combat counterrevolutionaries and other criminals. And yet no homes are being entered, no suspects are being seized, except your contact at the train station. And this is the most unsettling development of all. He has already been released."

"Why would they do that?"

"Either he told them everything he knew shortly after they brought him in, or they set him free to lead them to the Resistance—and to you. My informants tell me that the officers who arrested him were severely reprimanded and that apologies were made to him. This is so unlikely a procedure that it baffles all logical thought."

"Thuc is behind this," Thanh Hoa says. "This is the sort of thing he does. The unexpected. Then—while you are pondering what it means—he pounces."

"Very possible," Ky says. "This is not the response I would have predicted in view of the incident at Cam Ranh Bay."

"Can you give me a bottom line?" I insist. "What do you think it means?"

He looks at me gravely.

"They know you're in Hanoi," he says. "They're waiting for you to make your move."

CHAPTER

38

"At the moment," Ky informs us, "your friends are being contacted at the market by a man who can be trusted. He will take them in a truck to a small factory in the suburb of Kim Lien, just outside the city. This will be your haven until you leave Hanoi. You will rejoin them this evening."

"How do we get there?" I ask.

"I am arranging uniforms for each of you, regular army, and identity papers to match. They should be here soon. You will travel across the city to Kim Lien by bicycle, like everyone else. Even members of the Secretariat arrive at work on their bicycles. By six o'clock this evening, the beer parlors and lakefront cafés will be crowded and the streets packed with hundreds of thousands of workers returning home on their bicycles. This is the best time for you to travel. In this way you will become simply two more anonymous figures among a mass of anonymous figures."

"What about you?" I ask. "Have you been compromised in any way by our coming here?"

"It is a risk I live with," he replies. "It keeps me young."

"How can I thank you?"

"By avoiding arrest—by living."

Soon after six, Thanh Hoa, in corporal's uniform, and I, as an army captain, pedal off on the bicycles Ky has provided. I look back as we wheel away, up to the lone window on the second floor, up to the silver urn now burning in the sunset, and I marvel that in all the world, across all its seas and on its infinite islands, in all its continents and countries and provinces and cities, in all the places I have searched, that here, in this alien silver shop, on its matchbox second floor, in an austere bedroom, on the narrow cot of a stranger who has done me a kindness, I found the stage to act out at long last the hope of these last ten years, that I could accept the love of a woman other than Doan Thi and dare to believe we might even have a future together. It strikes me that we live our lives within vivid fragments, times we don't anticipate, places we don't know, yet these times and these places mark our way and light our memories. Everything else in between is forgotten.

We come out onto Silk Street, one of the main thoroughfares in Hanoi, and enter the gentle flow of homeward traffic.

"Where are all the one-man bomb shelters that used to line the street?" I whisper to Thanh Hoa, peddling along beside me, her eyes almost heart-stopping with their shine of newfound love and kittenish morning-after smile.

"Filled in," she says. "But we have left other reminders."

She indicates the Botanical Gardens coming up to our right. I see a huge heap of B–52 debris lying in a chained-off section, on permanent exhibit, one of the twenty-three B–52s brought down over Hanoi.

An arrogant sounding of horns from behind us causes the cyclists around us to wing off toward the curb. We follow their example. A convoy of military trucks rumbles by. I recognize them as the big two-and-a-half tonners turned out by the Likhachev factory in Moscow.

I let Thanh Hoa set our course. We roll along Hàng Dào Street, the main commercial avenue, lined with private shops selling Chinese procelain, Levi's jeans, and counterfeit Camel cigarettes. From a nearby street I hear a strange metallic clatter—three streetcars linked together like something left over from the twenties, quaint and antiquated, a faded blue color with a long red stripe running under their windows.

Thanh Hoa turns off on Hai Ba Trung Street. From my memory of Hanoi's street grid, we have now turned away from the Kim Lien suburb.

"Why are we going this way?" I ask her.

"To show you something," she says. "And to tell you what you need to know."

"Show me what?"

"The Temple of Literature."

"Tell me what?"

"About Doan Thi."

Thanh Hoa stops at the entrance to the Temple of Literature and dismounts. She walks with her bicycle toward a row of stone stelae spaced about the grounds.

I catch up with her.

"The Temple of Literature," she tells me solemnly, lowering her voice as though in the presence of ghostly ancestors, "was built in the eleventh century. It was the first university in Vietnam."

As she leads me past the individual pillars, I observe that each bears an individual name in Vietnamese.

"Each column carries the name of a doctor of literature," she informs me, "starting with the fifteenth century and ending in the eighteenth. Eighty-two writers. In our entire history these are the only ones so honored. And here, at this spot—"

She stops at the end of one row of stone columns.

"—the eighty-third stele will be added in December. On it will be placed the name of Vietnam's greatest poetess, Doan Thi—the eighty-third person to be so honored, the first writer to have her name added since the end of the eighteenth century."

She turns to see how I accept this awesome information. I'm having trouble equating a stone pillar to the flesh-and-blood woman who came into my life almost sixteen years ago when I was serving as the One-Zero of a Bright-lights caper we'd code-named "Steel Tiger." Doan Thi had appeared out of nowhere to recite poetry to a team of South Vietnamese Rangers who had been sent up to reinforce us. I thought then—and still think—she was the most exquisite woman I had ever seen. But when I was introduced to her that night I could not look straight at her, much as I hungered to.

"Why are you not able to look me in the eye?" she had asked with the kind of directness I learned to expect from her at all times.

"Because I'm killing your people. That's what I do. I kill Vietnamese."

"Is that your only purpose here? *Only* that?"

"God, no!" I had cried.

"Then what *is* your purpose? Why *are* you here?"

I was too immature in the early months of that year to be able to answer her. I'm not sure that even now I could.

"When you *do* know," she had said, "come and tell me."

"Where do I find you?" I'd asked.

"Wherever you can find friends. Or enemies. I am in both places."

It all breaks from me in one terrible cry.

"Why did they send her to a camp if she's so god-damned important to them?"

"Thuc ordered her sent away," Thanh Hoa says.

I stare at her for a long, long moment.

"His own daughter?"

"Had she not been his daughter, she might not have had to go."

"Jesus Christ!" I shout, probably the only raised voice in all of Hanoi this evening. Suddenly I want to kick down all eighty-two stone pillars.

"He had to make an example. He likes to tell the story of an ancient Roman king who went into battle after he had ordered his generals not to advance or to retreat without his personal command. Once the battle was joined, one young general saw an opportunity to turn the enemy's flank. He ordered his troops to attack. He routed the invaders, giving the victory to the king. It happened that this young man was the king's own son, heir to the throne. But, with tears in his eyes; the king, with all his armies and officers assembled to watch, struck off the head of his own beloved son—to make an example. Nobody is above the law, even the son of the king himself. Thuc is famous all over Hanoi for telling this story. He continuously reminds anyone who will listen that Rome conquered the world *because of* this kind of dedication and that it fell when it became depraved and corrupt."

"But what did she *do*?" I demand. "Aside from loving me and bearing my son?"

"She began to write revisionist poetry," Thanh Hoa says. "She began to suggest that now that we had won the war, we should win the victory, make peace with the West, especially with the Americans. We should forgive the Americans, she hinted, and try to understand that they were not invaders as the French had been, and the Japanese and Chinese before them. But that they had fought a *political* war. Although we were its victims, it had not been directed against us. We were simply a line in the sand. The Americans were saying to the Chinese and to the Soviets, we will not permit you to advance one more foot beyond this line. Well, you can understand the effect such a suggestion had upon our leaders. They were more embarrassed than outraged, because Doan Thi had behind her a body of published work vehemently supporting the revolution. She had been trained at our most prestigious school, Nguyen Ai Quoc, during the time it was headed by Truong Chinh, a high-ranking member of the Politburo, and she had been his personal favorite and protégée. For a time, during the most dangerous period for the Viet Cong infrastructure, when the Phoenix program was in full effect and twenty thousand cadres were assassinated or executed in the south, she bravely took command of the Viet Nam Cong San and rallied it to resist while she was convincing the South that she had defected from Hanoi. It was an extraordinary feat, to convince Saigon that she had put her revolutionary past behind her and still at the same time operate covertly as the commander of the VC forces. She was the only woman awarded the War Medal and the Victory Decoration. Aside from her love affair with you, John, her record of service and dedication was peerless. But even that relationship—and having your child—was forgiven in Hanoi as one more of her clever and sophisticated strategems for deceiving the Saigon puppet government. When we achieved reunification and she began advocating rapprochement with America, she was perceived as a counterrevolutionary whose purity had been subverted by her time in the South and by her relationship with you and her half-American child. It was at this point, a little more than two years ago, that her father took action against her, even though nobody above him ordered him to do so. He sent her to a reeducation camp and took her son away from her. As you know, she died in the camp."

"I will not leave Hanoi," I say, my voice trembling, "until I have killed Dang Van Thuc with my bare hands."

Thanh Hoa leads me, tense with hatred for my enemy, out of the grounds.

We mount our bicycles and swing back into the stream of cyclists going our way, this time toward the suburb of Kim Lien.

After a moment Thanh Hoa pulls off to the curb and slips out of her seat.

I stop alongside her.

I discover she is laughing to herself.

"You find what I said back there amusing?" I demand.

"I'm laughing with joy," she says expansively.

"About what?"

"The way I hoped I would. Do you know I haven't laughed since I was nine? I now remember that morning. I was watching two crows in the ricefields. They looked so silly, pecking at each other, jumping up and down, I laughed and laughed."

"I asked you what you're laughing about *now*."

She leans close to my ear and whispers. "I can hardly sit on the bicycle seat. Where you made love to me hurts so wonderfully. It still throbs. And I'm all swollen. Oh, John, I want you inside me. Right now! I do love you!"

Of course, you do not indulge such fantasies on the streets of Hanoi, particularly in our situation.

Gritting her teeth, but laughing, Thanh Hoa gets back on the bicycle seat and we pedal off toward Kim Lien.

CHAPTER

39

In darkness we approach our destination, an unlit cinder-block building, one of many identical blacked-out structures in this industrial area outside Hanoi. Thanh Hoa tells me that frequent outages are the norm, and that whole sections of the city and its suburbs are regularly without electrical power. But this is a minor inconvenience, a small enough price to pay for the growth of a nation struggling to rebuild itself.

"Under French rule," she says as we roll in, "we were dependent on the invaders and their colonial administrators. We were forced to import all our necessities from France. They made us become a nation of consumers, not producers, for their own profit and our enslavement. But now that we are free we have built almost three hundred factories in Hanoi alone, and five hundred handicraft cooperatives, forty market-gardening cooperatives supplying Hanoi with a hundred thousand tons of vegetables, four pig farms, one cattle farm for the rearing of purebred strains totaling half a million head, one dairy farm, one poultry farm, and three state-run farms."

I get off my bike, lift her from hers, and pull her into my arms in the shadows lying like a moat around the bleak little building.

"You're delightful!" I tell her, and nuzzle at her neck.

"Why do you say that?"

"I'm a traditionalist. I admire anyone who can be unashamedly proud of his country's accomplishments. Don't ever stop being Vietnamese, Thanh Hoa. Especially when I take you into a junk-food culture."

She kisses me. "I never will stop being what I am. I never could."

Vo's voice calls softly.

"In here, Captain."

We bring our bicycles with us, through the steel door he's holding open.

Inside, only half-revealed in candlelight, our group awaits us—Tran, Le, Van, Pham, and Arun. Vo bolts and chains the door behind us. I see they've all discarded their peasant disguises and that each is now dressed in NVA uniform.

Arun hurries to me, pretending that the urgency is the need to check my makeup. But I know better. I can see in her eyes, even in this semidarkness, something else— her relief and her caring. I do not find this disquieting in any sense.

"Forgive us, sir," Tran says, "but we disobeyed your orders."

"How so?"

"You asked us not to sell all the poultry today. But when Vo came to the market and told us we were about to be contacted before dark by the Resistance, our capitalistic indoctrination could not be ignored. We sold all the poultry."

He shows me a sheath of crumpled *dongs*.

Thanh Hoa appears impressed.

"What is this place?" I ask, not being able to see beyond the few candles our group has centered at this end of the factory.

"Here we make bicycle frames," a woman's voice replies from the darkness. "But we are a private factory. I have only a few workers, all loyal members of the Resistance. You are safe here."

I peer into the shadows. Out of them materializes an elderly Vietnamese woman in trousers and Mao jacket, her hair calcium white, dark glasses obscuring her eyes, like a sideman in a dim cabaret. Arun whispers to me, "She's blind."

"I am Khanh Chi," she says. "Whatever you need, I will do my best to see that it is provided, if it is possible."

"Thank you," I reply. "Do you know why we're here?"

"Yes," she replies. She snaps her fingers. Two boys appear from behind her, one carrying cups, the other a gallon-size Japanese thermos decorated with lacquered lotus blossoms.

"Tea?" she asks.

"Thank you," I say.

While the boys serve us, Khanh Chi says, "I know you must be eager for information, the floor plans of Thuc's residence, his security arrangements, your son's time-table. We will attempt to help you determine all these factors."

"Thank you," I repeat. "I have a critical decision to make: Do we make our move at the residence? at his school? or en route to his school? Or at some event that may be coming up in the next six days—something he'd go to: a concert? a field trip? Once we've decided the time and place for our strike, then we have to lay out our escape route and line up our transport."

"This will take a few days," she says.

"At the outside we have six days," I tell her. "After that, we have forty-eight hours to liftoff. I'd like to plan Thursday, October third, as our strike day."

"Then we should start at once, tonight," she says. "I suggest you send your own people out to make separate observations, but never send more than two together. And once you've seen one place, do not return to it. I shall be having our people doing the same thing. We will combine our observations with yours and tell you everything we have learned. Then you can make your decisions."

"Thank you."

"I will bring you blankets later. We have running water and toilet facilities in the back of the shop. I am sorry we have no place you can cook, and I hesitate to bring food in for fear someone will wonder why I bring rice for eight people to a factory that is temporarily closed. We're waiting for machine parts already ten days overdue."

"We'll manage, thank you. We have plenty of money to buy something to eat when we're out scouting around."

"I shall return later with the blankets."

She seems to have faded out rather than to have walked away—one minute there, the next gone.

We gather around the clustered candles so I can lay out our moves.

"Tell us about Hanoi's rhythms," I ask Thanh Hoa. "So far all I know is that from around four-thirty in the afternoon until seven or seven-thirty we seem to be relatively safe on the streets because of all the people out there. What are the other time frames?"

"In Hanoi," she says, "people rise at five in the morning and retire at nine-thirty at night. Except for tonight, Friday night, Young people will be in the streets and in the parks. And the same tomorrow night."

"Until when?"

"By eleven o'clock the streets will start to empty."

I look at my watch. It's almost seven-thirty.

"Okay, that gives us a good three hours. So let's make some preliminary runs tonight in teams of two. Thanh Hoa will tell us how to find the place my son is living. Don't ever forget that his grandfather is head of the Secret Police. He knows we're in Hanoi. Getting his hands on any one of us will make him a hero with his bosses—and with the Soviets. So remember, he is nobody's idea of a nice guy. He will most certainly have agents on the streets all around his house, watching anyone who passes, and they probably won't look like agents. They can be little old ladies or vendors selling *pho*. Don't talk if you can avoid it. Only two of you have northern accents. And Arun, keep your lips sealed. The Thai shows through. If you get hungry, want to order something, *point*. When you pass my son's school, observe without appearing to be observing. Just don't plant yourself down out front and look like you're making mental notes. Trust nobody, talk to nobody. Not even schoolgirls. Thuc is capable of recruiting seven-year-olds into the Mât Vu. You have to put yourself in the frame of mind of a bomber pilot making a target run into the teeth of a missile site. You're on their radar and you're being watched. So it's in and out. Just stay frosty. Okay?"

Their intense young faces tell me they've received the message.

"We'll break up into teams. Thanh Hoa will go with me. Vo, I want you with Arun, and I expect to see you both holding hands and looking like all the thousands of young couples out there in the park tonight."

Tran, with a little giggle, protests courteously.

"I would like to volunteer for Vo's place," he says.

"Vo is so stern-looking, nobody will believe he likes women. I will be much more convincing as Arun's friend."

I remember Tran's masturbatory fixation on Arun and the incident with the leech. No question he's paid his dues.

"How do *you* feel about that, Vo?" I ask.

"I agree with Tran. He will be more convincing."

Vo looks over at Arun.

"You are very beautiful and I mean no disrespect. But I know that I look too serious most of the time."

"So it'll be Tran and Arun. Vo, you and Le go as a team."

"Thank you, sir," Vo says, nodding to Le. Le nods back.

"That leaves you, Van, to team up with Pham. Let's move out of here at ten-minute intervals as soon as Thanh Hoa has briefed you on the two locations. Meantime, Arun will give me a touch-up. Any questions?"

Van raises his hand.

"Yes?"

"In the event any of us is suspected—and they try to arrest us—what do you expect us to do?"

"Each of you still has his pistol, his knife, his garroting wire, and two grenades. Use them only as a last resort— only if you're certain you're about to be taken into custody. Hose the place down, then hop on your bikes and get the hell out."

"And go where, sir? We can't lead them back here."

"Any ideas, Thanh Hoa?" I ask.

"Head to Western Lake," she says, "past the Mausoleum of President Ho Chi Minh. There are thick lily ponds and many reeds in the water where you can hide. When the search has moved on, you can work your way back here."

"Okay," I say. "Ten minutes. Van, you and Pham move out first."

I pick up a candle and separate myself from the others, Arun coming with me, bringing her makeup kit, Thanh Hoa settling down with the men to draw them a street map.

Arun opens her kit.

"I am happy for you," she says.

"Thank you. It's almost over, isn't it?"

She goes to work on my face.

"I wish I could have watched."

I turn to look up at her, but she pushes my chin back into line with a commanding finger and continues to smooth out my nose.

"She's a very passionate girl, "Arun comments.

"You don't miss much, do you?"

"Oh, I miss a lot of things."

"Not for much longer."

"No, not for much longer, thank God. I plan to fly straight to Japan the minute we get back. She loves you, you know. Can you accept that?"

"Yes," I say. "Finally."

"Then I am truly happy, John."

I reach up and clasp her hand. For a moment, she rests her chin on the top of my head. Then suddenly she gets very businesslike, polishes off my Asian look in a matter of seconds, and pronounces me once more fit for the streets of Hanoi. A few minutes later she leaves with a smiling Tran. In all the city tonight there will be few couples more handsome.

Thanh Hoa and I are the last to leave.

At the door I feel her tugging on my sleeve. I look back to discover that she has slipped out of her uniform tunic, letting it fall to her feet, and that she is easing the straps of her undergarment from her shoulders.

"Is it possible to make love standing up?" she asks, her eyes glittering with an abandon I have seldom seen before.

"In lovemaking anything is possible," I say. "If you care for each other, there are no limitations."

"Show me," she challenges, stepping out of her khaki tousers.

"We have a long way to go tonight," I say, "and not much time. On *bicycles*. Do I have to remind you?"

"I am used to pain," she whispers, her lips almost on mine. "I am not a soft Western girl."

"I have no condoms with me," I tell her, hearing my voice get huskier by the second. "Left them off the inventory."

"You will not impregnate me," she announces. "We are taught to understand the natural rhythm system of birth control. For the next ten days I am safe."

Famous last words!

But she's kissing me and one hand is fondling me so that abruptly all my resolve, all the urgency of my mission, goes on down-time. We press together in the dark factory and I lift her onto me, my hands cupped under her yielding buttocks, her legs locked around my waist, her arms around my neck, her lips lost on mine, until we are spent.

"What if I had died without ever knowing this?" she sighs, kissing my eyes and ears and mouth over and over again.

We leave the factory and together pedal into Hanoi, Thanh Hoa glancing seductively at me from time to time, keeping me in a state of semitumescence, so that it seems only seconds between the time we left the factory and our turning onto a broad tree-lined avenue near Thong Nhat Park.

The girlish playfulness has vanished. The guerrilla in her is back in the driver's seat.

"On our right, half a kilometer ahead," she says, "is Thuc's home. You will not be able to see much from the street. A high wall runs along the entire front of the grounds, but as you pass the gate you can look through its bars and see the house set back on the grounds."

We wheel closer. The avenue is crowded with cyclists and pedestrians. Everyone is in motion, nobody is lingering.

Now we are almost there. My heart literally jumps against my rib cage.

The gate is high, ornate, probably made in France in an earlier century, black wrought iron, and through it now I finally see the villa, two stories high, lights on both floors.

My son is in that house! In one of those rooms!

I have to force myself to keep pedaling. To go past the gate. To leave him in there for even one more night.

But then we are past. One swift look and we are past.

"Strange," Thanh Hoa remarks. "I saw no guards inside the gate."

"He's probably got them spaced out on the grounds—out of sight."

"He always keeps two guards just inside."

I mark the time. "Eight-thirty—no guards seen inside

the gate. Okay, duly noted. What else struck you as unusual?"

"Usually there are several official cars parked inside. There are no cars tonight."

"Maybe he's not home."

"He is always home. He operates out of there."

"Then where was *his* car?"

"He does not have one. Either he is picked up by a driver or he travels by bicycle."

"How does my son get to school?"

"On his bicycle or by car—depending on weather. He is always preceded by agents in one car and followed by agents in another car. Sometimes, when it rains, he rides in the lead car."

"Do all schoolchildren get that kind of protection?"

"Only the grandson of the head of the Mât Vu. Since Thuc has so many enemies, this precaution has been authorized."

"Where is his school from here?"

"Not far—near the Army Museum."

We ride away. I cast one quick glance back at Thuc's residence and note the trees alongside the walls to either side.

Within minutes we are flashing past a French colonial building adjacent to Ba Dinh Square, where Ho Chi Minh read his Declaration of Independence forty years ago this month.

The building faces directly onto the street, far more accessible for entry than Thuc's residence, yet it is totally exposed to public view and to the swift response of police officers in this, the cultural heart of the city.

All my instincts, even without supporting evidence, start telling me the best chance we have to carry out the mission with some element of surprise and concealment is to operate against the comparative privacy of Thuc's villa, despite guards and electronic sensors.

By ten o'clock all the members of the team have returned to the factory.

None of them has been able to detect any movement within the walled estate. Nor did anyone notice cars parked inside.

We agree to make additional reconnaisance runs in the morning, despite Chi's warning that we should not risk going over the same ground twice. It is unlikely that any observers Thuc would have had on the streets tonight will still be on duty tomorrow morning, and even so they'd have to be inhumanly sharp-eyed to identify passing cyclists in the night as having returned by daylight, not with the thousands who've gone wheeling by tonight.

Chi has brought us blankets while we were out. We divide into boys and girls for the night, despite Thanh Hoa's whispered cajolery. I tell her that since I'm the honcho in charge, I have to set an example—and heavy breathing in the dark is not the example a leader should set.

I have trouble sleeping. A boy's face hangs luminous above me. He entreats me, asking *what*? I cannot hear what he says or even distinguish what language he's speaking. His mother would certainly have taught him some English, possibly even some French, in the few short years he was at her side. In the past two years Thuc would have certainly thrust Russian upon him. The lips in the darkness are not speaking Russian, that much I know. When I do sleep, if I do, my dreams are chaotic, their sound tracks out of sync. Long before dawn, I'm up. Rain thrums on the metal roof. I do my exercises to the staccato beat of the torrent outside.

Before I go out with Thanh Hoa, Arun fastens a new nose in place and checks my contact lenses. I throw a poncho over my head and soon Thanh Hoa and I are gliding in company with the silent stream of men and women on their bicycles, most with umbrellas, a stunning movement of hexagonal blackness over each cyclist, like endless rows of dark petals twirling along a drowned and infinite garden row.

We pass Thuc's residence precisely as the gate opens and two sedans slosh into the street. Two men in the first car, two in the second, men with those standard expressionless and mutant faces assumed by all men who are hired to protect others.

In the backseat of the leading car, through the slashing rivulets on the window, I see Le Hoang Hai, my son, on the way to Saturday morning's half-day of schooling.

Le—a surname suggesting he is one of the direct descendants of one of the ancient liberators of Vietnam.

Hoang—meaning "princely" or "golden."

Hai—meaning "sea."

He sits alone in back, isolated.

I am not more than three feet from his window.

Suddenly he looks over.

His eyes are so faultlessly blue, even through the wash of rain against his window, I have trouble steering. His gaze is so pure, so direct, so much the look I remember from old photographs of myself at his age, that for a moment I almost believe I am pushed back in time, a boy again, given new life, a second chance, and that I am sitting in the backseat of a Russian sedan in Hanoi and looking out without foreknowledge at the passing stranger I will be twenty-five years from now.

And then he is gone, the car's rear wheels splashing me in the haste of its departure.

CHAPTER

40

By Tuesday night, the first of October, we have as much intelligence about Thuc's private citadel as we're ever going to get. I've decided against trying for my son at his school. It's bad karma to go charging in with guns where children are being taught about the constructive aspects of mankind. I don't want to earn my son at the cost of another father's child, and surely, so close to central military and police headquarters, we would draw a swift response from armed units. A similar risk exists in going for rollout on the street when Le Hoang Hai is being driven to school. Too many innocent bystanders in the streets. As I have known from the beginning, we'll have to move against Thuc where he expects us to.

Several baffling givens have emerged from the continuous, though transient, surveillance we've managed to maintain in the four days since I caught a glimpse of my son.

Inexplicably, no guards stand duty at the gate or anywhere about the grounds.

Yet until now, I am told, there have always been armed men on duty around the villa.

The Resistance scouts have reported that they have seen no identifiable agents on the street outside Thuc's home, no cars parked casually down the block, no loitering cyclists.

Except for a truck that made a food delivery just yesterday, no other vehicle has entered or left the grounds—except, of course, Le Hoang Hai being picked up by the two sedans yesterday morning, Monday, and taken to school, then returned yesterday afternoon, a routine repeated this morning and afternoon in the steady rainfall.

But one of the Resistance observers has reported that when the food supplies were unloaded yesterday, there was a noteworthy abundance of food delivered, far more than a boy and a grandfather could eat in a month, even allowing for the cook and the housekeeper we've determined are presently inside the residence.

The house waits there, opaque and lifeless, a silent world of its own, an inhuman, baleful silence overhanging it, unspeaking menace behind its shadowed windows.

I can sense Thuc waiting for me, lurking in there like a grotesque, oversize spider, his web spun, his plans made.

In candlelight I convene our group for a strategy session in the far corner of the factory, where we have set up our clandestine headquarters.

"Why else would he have withdrawn all his guards unless he was trying to suck us in, then blind-side us?" I ask. "And consider all that food that was delivered yesterday. Doesn't that suggest the guards are hidden *inside*?"

"Easier to dispose of them," Vo replies.

"He's got something going," I say. "But God knows what!"

In the guttering candlelight we pore over floor plans and the layout of the grounds we've managed to piece together from blueprints a Resistance worker managed to copy from old records in the Office of Registry, Hanoi's Sô Trước Ba. Matching these up with the observations we've made about the patterns of light in the windows at night, we've arrived at a consensus about which upstairs bedroom is Thuc's and which is my son's. Plans for additions reveal the installation within the past four years of a sophisticated computer-and-communications center on the ground floor, and all of us have taken notice of the array of antennae thrust up from the rooftop.

"He must have men in that com center," Tran says. "At least two, possibly even four. Then if you allow him another four staked out inside, we're probably talking about no more than eight people."

"It takes only one of them, with his finger on a button, to hit the panic switch when we come through the windows, and from somewhere not more than a few blocks away he could have tanks and APCs swarming out front in a matter of five minutes," I say, playing devil's advocate.

But it's something Thanh Hoa told me when we swept by on a run yesterday evening that has suggested the one crack we might slip through—the power outages in Hanoi. She'd mentioned that they do not occur at random but are in fact scheduled to conserve energy and that each section and suburb of Hanoi has a specific downtime, so those temporarily without electricity can plan accordingly.

"What about this area?" I'd asked her as we wheeled past Thuc's residence.

"I think this area's only out from midnight Wednesdays until five in the morning on Thursdays."

I'd asked Chi to verify this and this afternoon she had confirmed Thanh Hoa's recollection.

"It's narrowed down to this," I tell the group. "Tomorrow night at midnight Thuc will be without power. His com center will be off the air until five in the morning on Thursday. We'll go over the wall at oh-three-hundred hours. If he has men on duty inside the house, we'll take them down. We'll assign one man specifically to do nothing else but track down a possible generator, in case Thuc may have put in a back-up power system that these blueprints don't reveal. Tran, please ask our friends in the Resistance to assign us a volunteer who's an expert electrician, somebody who would know how to hunt down a generator real fast. We have to make damn sure no signal gets to the outside world from that house."

"Yes, sir," he says.

"We'll need one more Resistance man to cut the phone lines before we go in, okay?"

"Affirmatory, sir."

"Okay, we'll enter over the walls on either side of the villa. We're out of sight of the street from back there. Weapons will be silenced SMGs. Chi is providing them."

"What about the cook and the housekeeper?" Vo asks.

"If they surrender, tie and gag them. If they resist or try to escape, kill them. Once we've secured the interior, I'll take custody of my son. But not until we know for certain Thuc has lost all his backup. Chi is giving us ten men. Five will patrol the grounds. Five will come in with us. We have to remain on site until the two cars come by on Thursday morning to take Hai to school—that's at zero-six-four-five hours, right?"

They all nod, for each of us has observed the morning pickup and afternoon return and noted that the time doesn't deviate by more than a minute or two.

"We will have to get the cars into the grounds. I will attempt to persuade my son to help us accomplish that. Once they come in, the drivers and guards will have to be terminated. We will then take the sedans and leave with Hai. Van, you and Le and Pham will take the lead car. Vo and Tran will come with Hai and me in the second car. Arun and Thanh Hoa will be waiting in the truck on the other side of the river across Long Bien Bridge."

"Chi tells me that tomorrow they're expecting heavy winds and rain," Arun says. "If you have ever needed me to be with you to make sure your face doesn't wash away, this will be the time."

"No, Arun," I tell her. "I want you across the river waiting in the truck. This time I'm going in as myself. When my son sets eyes on me, I want him to see me as I am."

"Isn't that risky?" Van asks.

"If any of the bad guys get close enough to look into my eyes, we're all in trouble," I tell them.

"But what about the next morning, when we leave?"

"I'll stay down on the floor in the backseat," I say, "until we get to the truck. Then Arun can put me back into shape for the trip to Hon Gai."

"All right," Arun agrees reluctantly.

"*She* may wait across the river," Thanh Hoa announces suddenly, "but not I. I am coming! I have more combat experience than any of these men."

They all cock their eyes at the girl. She stares back at them defiantly. Finally they look away. She turns her eyes on me.

"I have been inside Thuc's house more than once," she says. "Have any of you?"

"How can we trust you?" Van asks. "This could be what you've been waiting for all along. To lead us into the trap and then alert Thuc just as we enter."

Van—and the rest of us, for that matter—discover that Thanh Hoa is suddenly holding a silenced pistol, its front sight fixed on Van's forehead. I have no idea where she got her hands on the weapon nor how long she's had it.

"If I had wanted to," she says, "I could have played that game many times since I've been with you." She slips the pistol back into her tunic as swiftly as she's produced it.

Van lets out a quiet breath.

"Besides," she says, not taking her eyes from mine, "I have more reason, more right to kill Thuc than any one of you. Even more right than you, John."

"Well, I could debate that all night long," I say.

"He condemned me to certain death when he sent me to that camp."

"That doesn't even put you in the ballpark," I tell her, "compared to the times he's tried to deep-six me!"

"I am not killing him because he tried to kill me. I will kill him for betraying the revolution. For preventing the few leaders we have who understand the need—to do what must be done if we are ever again to join the world community and not stand alone."

"Okay," I agree. "You can come with us. But we can't promise you an exclusive on Thuc. He's hardly going to sit there while we draw lots about who collects his ass. The first of us who gets a clear line of fire will blow him away. Let's get that very, very clear."

"I accept that," she says.

I marvel that this is the girl I am falling in love with, for I can see the duplicity swirling in her eyes like chemicals mixed by a mad scientist in a test tube, then it occurs to me that this very duplicity, this strength and ruthlessness, is one of her fascinations for me. I have to admit we are two of a kind and that I like steel under a woman's softness.

"Now that we have that settled," I continue, "the Resistance fighters who come over the wall with us will leave when we leave. They'll scatter on foot and by bicycle and blend in with the crowds going to work Thursday morning. I have to tell you it's not much of a plan, but it's all we've got. Special Forces would lay a low readiness rating on this operation, a C–3 at best."

"What is a C–3?" Vo asks.

"Marginally ready. If that. The three absolutes for a successful commando strike are stealth, speed, and a quick getaway. Okay, we'll hit Thuc with all the speed and stealth we can muster up, but our getaway is pretty shitty. We have to sweat out that long stage-wait in order to get those two sedans."

"What if we changed just that part of the operation, sir?" Van asks. "I mean, we go over the wall at three A.M., take everybody down, grab your son, then back over the wall and away—all within five minutes while the power is out and no alarm can be sent."

"Van, I wish we could. That's what I had laid out to begin with, but Chi and all her Resistance people tell me it's a sure way to commit suicide. As you know by now, nothing—and I mean nothing—moves on the streets of Hanoi at three A.M.—except the Security Forces and the military. Chi tells me the odds of our being spotted at that hour are one hundred and fifty percent! No, we have to wait till morning, so we can blend in with the street crowds. Same thing applies to our taking up attack positions outside Thuc's walls tomorrow night. We're going to have to move into place as soon as it gets dark, get around to those side walls, and hunker down out of sight—and wait. That's another big time-slot when anything can go wrong. Somebody might spot us lying there. But that's a risk we're going to have to take. We don't have any other options."

Later, sitting in the dark by myself in a distant corner of the factory, I assume a meditative yoga position, acknowledging that this is the last night in this lifetime I shall ever be sleeping in this place. I try to lock my thoughts into single entrainment, reaching out into the space that surrounds me for all their ricocheting substance, trying to bring the exterior world into the interior world of my being—into the CPU, so to speak, says a random and mischievous thought, the central processing unit, the CPU, my mind-brain structure like a one-megabit random-access memory chip—and I attempt to play out Thursday morning's hot-potato caper, unreeling it second by second. But my thoughts romp and tumble disobediently, picking up invasive static from the past. An irreverent mantra overrides my concentration, a song title, one of my all-time favorites, this one by Jimmy Buffet, "If the Phone Doesn't Ring, It's Me." *It's me! It's me!* I hear my inner voice echoing. Why not call the sonofabitch on the phone by the time I get to Phoenix and say, "Look here, Thuc, you old asshole, I want my son. Now, are you going to play ball or do I have come over there and kick your butt?" Then suddenly I'm seeing a bubble-gum machine on the black ceiling above me. My son is imprisoned inside the glass bowl, trying to crawl over gumballs. One of George Lucas's special-effects geniuses has made him toy-size, and I have no small change to activate the retrieving claws inside the glass to pick him up and swing him over to the escape chute. Then I hear my stomach wamble. Shit! What kind of meditation is this? Now I even hear Thanh Hoa's voice whispering in my ear.

"Where'd you get that fucking pistol?" I ask her.

"From one of Van Minh's men, back at the fishing village. He was a boy I knew—from my village. He understood my need for self-protection."

"You had it all this time?"

"Yes."

"You know what I told you in Bali—that you weren't good enough to take me out inside three hundred meters. I was wrong. You're something else!"

"Something else? Am I not what and who I am?"

"That's some more American slang—something else. It means—like 'too much.'"

"Not for you I'm not," she whispers. "John, I'm sleeping by your side tonight. I don't care what anyone thinks. They all know anyway. This could be our last night."

"Could be," I admit. I bring her into my arms.

Who needs to meditate? Holding each other, we fall asleep.

The rush of wind outside awakens me just after dawn. Its force is such that I can feel it driving in through the pores of the cinderblock walls. The tin roof creaks and wavers.

I go to the door and ease it open. The wind almost tears the door from my grasp. It whistles ominously through the suburb, tumbling debris along the street outside. Dark, menacing clouds race by. I can almost smell the onslaught of hail. I push the door closed with a feeling of sudden reassurance and hope. If this continues until we go over the wall something like twenty-two hours from now, the gods are with us. Make it worse, make it worse, I whisper to the unseen forces. Give us a typhoon, a cyclone, a tornado. Give us all the piss in heaven. Pour it on us!

I remember a verse by Baudelaire: "I have felt the wind of the wings of madness pass over me."

Because only madness will bring us through.

41

All Wednesday thunderstorms rattle Hanoi, causing me to wonder if those who endured our bombings are not now reliving the detritus of the past. Winds lash at the telephone wires, whipping and looping them like children's jump ropes. Blinding sheets of rain turn to hail, which piles up in successive unmelting sheets outside the factory. But this is the only whiteness in the city. Everything else outside appears gripped in the sky's relentless black talons. We cannot tell day from night, and if we had no watches, we would now know that the time has come for us to move out.

We leave by twos, ponchos tenting us over, since umbrellas, even if we had them, would have been torn from us or blown inside out in seconds. We lean forward low on the bicycles to reduce our windage as we pedal through the storm, wraithlike figures here and there about us angled into the jets of rain.

By eight o'clock Wednesday night we lie in position along both flanking walls of Thuc's phantom fortress, its high antennas snapping back and forth in the wind, water guttering down in massive strands from the overflowing roofline spouts, seven of us from my team, along with twelve Resistance fighters Chi has sent to rendezvous with us, ten of them assigned for fire support, one to cut the telephone wires, probably an unnecessary precaution in this storm, one to demolish a generator should he find one on the premises. The men bring us our weapons, Chinese Type-64 silenced submachine guns. The marking on the receiver of the gun I'm given indicates it was made at Factory 66. The fire-selector markings are etched into the steel in Chinese characters, full automatic to the back, single shot fire forward. I thumb my weapon to full auto and bring it under my poncho with me, cradling it as we wait.

I empty my mind until I am pastless and futureless and am able to enter that vast zone of immediacy where time no longer exists. I can no longer recall, even if I were to try, any of the great transforming moments of my life until this moment. There is no future either. There is only the beckoning edge of the cliff as I wait eagerly to step off into space.

As we wait the storm grows fiercer. Roiling black thunderheads hopscotch across the night.

Precisely at oh-three-hundred my body seems to rise unbidden from the trench of muddy water where I have stretched out since we first took our positions.

The wind rips at me as I stand, but I resist it and wave down the dark sprawling line of men along the base of the wall. I see them rising and I heave up the grappling hook with its knotted line. I anchor with first throw. I soar up the wall, my blood pounding in my eardrums, every sense abruptly tuning in. Broken glass is embedded in the top of the wall. I blanket it with my poncho, slide over and drop lightly to the inside of Thuc's garden, the SMG ready now, for clearly this operation is going to be one of those point-and-shoot operations.

Faintly, through my spacy night goggles, I can make out the blur of our people coming over the far wall on the other side of the grounds. I sense someone behind me. It is Thanh Hoa, lithe and deadly.

"I love you!" she shouts against the wind. If I were more than three feet away from her, I would not hear her.

I look along the inside of the wall I have climbed.

Nine of us already over. Across the grounds I count the eight on our far flank.

I beckon us forward, hoping everyone can see the obscure gesture against the pitchblack downpour. We move to our preselected entry points, four of us scaling up to the second floor on our side, our other five advancing to ground-floor windows at the front and back of the house.

I'm trusting that a similar division and placement is happening simultaneously on the far side of the house.

I look down and discover the electrician has hit gold. He has found the generator in a shed near the back of the estate and is already cutting the lines. One for our side!

Realizing we could never coordinate a visual attack signal in this storm, we are operating strictly on clock time. Entry is to commence at zero-three-oh-five. I crash through the window of Thuc's bedroom as my sweep hand hits the mark and I land, rolling on my shoulder, then onto my knees near his bed, my finger hesitating on the trigger for fear he might have my son in the room with him.

The night goggles tell me I am alone in the room.

I slip over to the door and ease it open. I come out onto the upstairs landing. Thanh Hoa appears from another bedroom just down the corridor. Beyond her I spot two of our Resistance team kicking open another door. They begin firing mutely into a bedroom. They disappear inside.

I start toward the door I know leads to my son's bedroom.

Below in the reception area I see the darting muzzle flashes of silenced guns. Disembodied forms of a faceless enemy appear to be twisting and falling grotesquely, as though caught night-walking—Thuc's guards. I could be watching a silent movie, flickering black-and-white images, but no sounds.

Now I am at the door.

At the threshold of a new life—or at the edge of an abyss.

I try the knob. The door is unlocked.

With my toe I push it open and flatten back against the outside wall.

I see flickering light dancing along the one wall visible to me from out here.

Candlelight.

"Come in, Captain Locke," a man's voice says. "I promise you, I am unarmed."

I whip in, low and ready for the worst, just praying to whatever dieties might be tuned in tonight that I don't have to take Thuc out anywhere close to my son.

Thuc is settled into a rocking chair beside my son's

bed. Le Hoang Hai, wide-awake, sits cross-legged on the bed. He is wearing silk pajamas.

Keeping the SMG in line with Thuc, I ease my night goggles back with my free hand and kick the bedroom door closed behind me.

Someone starts to open it. Must be Thanh Hoa.

"Stay out!" I order, my eyes never leaving Thuc.

Since man's beginning, our most authentic mode of speech has always been silence. Eloquently now, the unspeakable grips me as I stare at the old man and the boy. In this awesome moment of first sight I see and understand so much, even though I am unable to articulate it. Thuc is dressed in scruffy trousers and a worn shirt that once must have been blue. He sits in his rocker and chain-smokes, the ashtray on the white wicker side table beside him a pyramid of stubs. He squints at me through the smoke. He has, I see, a nervous tic above his right eye that causes the eyebrow to arch up constantly like some sinister antennal play of a hungry insect. In contrast, Hai studies me fearlessly, his thin face almost quivering with the awareness that he and I and his grandfather are all locked together within a living myth.

"Do you intend to kill me?" Thuc asks me in Vietnamese.

"Yes," I tell him.

"Do you hear that, Hai?" he says to the boy.

I can literally feel the boy's stare piercing me.

"Have you considered the effect this will have on your son?" Thuc asks. "Seeing his father kill his grandfather."

"No," I admit. "I have not thought of that."

"I have," he says, lighting a fresh cigarette from the one he has only half-smoked. "Even if you were to succeed in taking him away, you could never erase that memory. Could you?"

"God damn you!" I say in English. "You're a fucking monster!"

"Your son understands English, Captain," he says, shifting over to that language. "Out of some absurd need of her own imagining, his mother taught him. You do realize, don't you, that you and the people you've come with will never leave Hanoi alive?"

"Don't bank on it," I say.

"It was typical of you to come when the power was

out. I anticipated you might. But by now my radioman has already sounded the silent alarm. Forces will be surrounding the house at any moment."

"If you're counting on that backup generator to get your signal through, don't!" I tell him. "We took it out before we came in."

He blows out more smoke than usual. For a moment I can scarcely see his face in the enveloping cloud.

"I see," he says quietly. "Well, then, that was clever of you, wasn't it, Captain Locke?"

I divide my attention now between him, though I watch his hands, and my son, sitting like young Buddha on the bed.

"Then you know I'm your father," I say to Hai.

He does not answer me.

I repeat the statement in Vietnamese.

Still he does not reply.

"It is a painful subject to him," Thuc says in English. "He knows that you raped his mother. That he was born out of violence, that his own mother was invaded even as our nation was invaded."

He sits there smoking away and twitching that goddamned eyebrow as though inviting me to cut him in half.

"Is that what you've told him?" I ask.

"He knows she died of syphilis contracted as a result of your assault on her."

This one almost gets him blown away, but I cannot, will not, take his life in front of this sensitive child. Thuc is right about that. That's been his game plan from the moment he knew I'd come to Vietnam. If I did manage to get this far, he knew that his secret weapon was this ultimate cruelty, and he knew enough about me to know that I'd be a sucker for his play. Well, by God, he's not so fucking brilliant after all, is he? Thanh Hoa is waiting outside for her turn at him. All I have to do is pick up Hai, move him out of the line of fire, and invite my lady to step in and waste this sonofabitch.

I turn for the door and in that instant I sense I may have made a fatal mistake.

From under the pillow I catch in my peripheral vision the glint of a submachine gun being whipped out of concealment. I whirl to fire, but discover that Thuc is not holding the weapon.

Hai is.

He holds it as though he has been taught how to use it.

He holds it on me.

I see his delicate index finger on the trigger. There is nothing tentative about the poise of his finger. I stare into the muzzle of the gun as though into the eye of God. I know this is the end, but what can I do about it? At least, I came this far, almost the distance.

"Your son is considered the finest marksman in Hanoi for his age. He has been taught by experts. He has waited, as I have, Captain Locke, for this moment. To even the score. To avenge his mother's suffering and her untimely death. Have you something you would like to say to him?"

I face Hai.

"Only that I love you."

I drop my weapon at my feet.

"At least I saw you. Until now I have fought against death for the privilege of seeing you. But I cannot fight against you."

He looms up onto his knees, the gun ready, but unexpectedly he half-turns, facing his grandfather, and fires point-blank into the man.

Thuc jerks like a puppet in the splintering rocker, his chest expanding in a shapeless mass of lacerated, still trembling flesh.

Behind me I hear the door snap open, Thanh Hoa rushing in with Le and Vo.

They stand as transfixed as I stand.

Expertly, Hai releases what remains unfired from the magazine, clears the chamber, and drops the gun on the bed. He slips off the bed and barefooted patters to the dressing table. He picks up a framed photograph and brings it to me.

Still stunned, unable to deal with what has just happened, the stuttering of the gunfire still blocking my ears, I accept the photograph. It is a picture of Hai when he was six. He stands on the seat of a cement bench along the shoreline of Hoan Kiem Lake in Hanoi, his arms around Doan Thi, their lips almost meeting. It is a captured moment of such ineffable love I feel the hot, spontaneous rush of tears to my eyes.

He reaches up and shows me a tiny lever on the back

of the frame. He eases it down. A section of the silver comes free. He waits for me to bring out the things I see tucked away inside.

I pull out a worn and many-times-folded square of paper. Then a medal.

My Silver Star—the one I gave Doan Thi as a keepsake.

Through my tears I have trouble reading the note.

It is written by Doan Thi to her son, a final testament, it seems. It tells him that he is a special child, born in a war to enemies who were lovers, a Hanoi revolutionary and an American officer, that he is a star-child, wanted by both of us, merging the best of each of us, created out of adoration in the final weeks of the war, that he is the living embodiment of hope for tomorrow—the longed-for reconciliation.

Someday, Doan Thi had written, your father will come for you. When that day comes, you will go with him, without question, knowing that I loved him as dearly as I love you, helping him to see life brightly, with all the beauty there is everywhere about us.

A tiny photograph of me is clipped to the letter.

Hai stares up at me. His chin begins to quiver.

He forces himself to look over at the man slumped shapelessly in the disintegrated rocker.

The boy starts to sob. "He killed my mother," he cries. "And I've waited all this time to kill him. But I didn't dare to until you came."

I gather him into my arms.

EPILOGUE

Between the moment I hold my son against me and our arrival hours later along the moonscape of Pointe des Mines in Ha Long Bay, I float like a phantom, leaving behind me the Vietnam in which I have been rooted for so many years, but from which now, mercifully, I am at last released, a place no longer remembered in sorrow, but pacified and redeemed, finally accepted and put behind me.

Everything that happens now follows magically, from the prompt, unsuspecting arrival of the two sedans at six forty-five Thursday morning, Hai waving them into the grounds. We have all had enough of killing. We lead the four guards inside and tie them. Hai stands before them, bowing slightly and asking their forgiveness.

"This is my father," he tells them, nodding toward me. "Where he goes, I go. This was my mother's choice. It is mine too. I thank you for all the care you've taken of me. Good-bye."

I huddle low in the backseat as we drive through the flooding streets of Hanoi and cross Long Bien Bridge, then transfer to the waiting Soviet truck.

Arun throws her arms around me, then embraces Hai. She is astonished by his bearing. If she only knew what he has been through these past few hours! These past few years!

I thank Chi and through her all those who have risked their lives for me. I wish her well, though both she and

I know how awesome the odds against the Resistance are and will remain.

The wind tosses our truck around the road as we work our way to the northeast. Trees are stripped of their bark, telephone poles are toppled by the rampaging storm.

By twilight, close to our destination, a dreadful noise rolls toward us, tumbling everything before it. Around us village huts are swept away and the earth looks freshly plowed.

But then, abruptly, the storm veers and as we come out onto Pointe des Mines the sky shifts with a sudden spasm and sunset is revealed for a blinding second.

We climb down from the battered truck and stare out over Ha Long Bay, its mystic, shrouded lime-rock mountains jutting out of the gray, turbulent sea as though thrust there by giants playing mumblety-peg.

Hai hears it first, the oncoming helicopter, and we take cover, thinking Hanoi has already organized a pursuit, but when I see it round Ile du Brandon and dart toward us only a meter above the tips of the whitecaps, I know Arty is at the controls. Even from this distance I can feel his sure hand. He zips in and lowers only yards from us, grinning out at me like a winning bishop on a chessboard, and waving us to him. He can't accommodate all of us at once. The men insist that I take my son, Thanh Hoa, and Arun for the first extraction, then send the chopper back for them.

I observe that Arty is still sitting on the Norman Vincent Peale book, but that he's wearing a new jumpsuit cross-hatched by so many zippered pockets I doubt that he can ever remember in what pocket he's put what.

"You're two days ahead of schedule," he says.

"So are you," I reply.

"We have our sources," he says. "Well done, my friend. Well done."

He puts Hai up front with him.

"Call me Arty," he says. "I'm in the salt business."

He rounds one sheer outcropping which looms up higher than our present altitude, but Arty wants us to savor the sudden view of the Benetti motor yacht waiting just beyond in Passe Henriette, her bow toward the open sea and the Chinese island of Hainan, where Mao was born, just across the Gulf of Tonkin.

Hai's hand reaches back for mine.

I clasp it.

Thanh Hoa's hand covers both of ours.

Holding to each other, I let myself tumble headlong, willingly and seeking, into whatever tomorrows the three of us may be allotted.

About the Author

Stirling Silliphant was born in Detroit. He began his motion picture work with Walt Disney Studio. His many successful television series with screenplays include *Naked City*, *Route 66*, *Alfred Hitchcock Presents*, *The Poseidon Adventure*, *The Towering Inferno*, *Charly*, the Oscar-winning *In the Heat of the Night*, and, more recently, a thirteen-hour adaptation of James Michener's *Space*, a seven-hour mini-series, *Mussolini*: *The Untold Story*. He lives with his wife and two children in Beverly Hills, California. His novels include MARACAIBO and the first two John Locke books, STEEL TIGER and BRONZE BELL, all published by Ballantine.

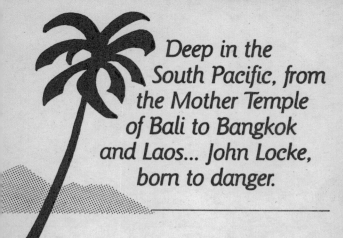

Deep in the South Pacific, from the Mother Temple of Bali to Bangkok and Laos... John Locke, born to danger.

Stirling Silliphant and Ballantine Books

There's an epidemic with 27 million victims. And no visible symptoms.

It's an epidemic of people who can't read.

Believe it or not, 27 million Americans are functionally illiterate, about one adult in five.

The solution to this problem is you... when you join the fight against illiteracy. So call the Coalition for Literacy at toll-free **1-800-228-8813** and volunteer.

Volunteer Against Illiteracy. The only degree you need is a degree of caring.

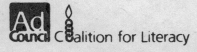

Ad Council Coalition for Literacy

LV-1